Sarah A. Younger

MW01129808

FINALIST
2016
Royal Palm
Literary Award
Competition

Praise for
A Bend in the Straight and Narrow

"The content is heart-stopping. Other than "Gone with the Wind" I never saw the War through a woman's eyes. It is an eye opener."

- Dr. Charles L. Sullivan,
Historian, Professor Emeritus, and
Archivist at Mississippi Gulf Coast College

"The pages are rich in detail and rife in the inner-workings of a complicated family. The prose by novice writer Sarah A. Younger, of Merritt Island, is peppered with apt descriptions of true events that colored the lives of her real family members. This was a pioneer family in the truest sense of the word – not only in how they traversed the land, but also in how they survived the intricacies of the inner workings that often tear families apart."

- *Ocala Star-Banner*

"Sarah Ann 'Sally' Marsh was soft as hand-churned butter on the outside and hard as hand-forged nails on the inside. In Tennessee, in 1859, when she was 15, she would swim in the creek in her undies – which young ladies certainly did not do. It is in the family's convoluted story, which includes a truly devious daughter-in-law, that this book really grabs you."

- *Gainesville Sun*

"Florida author Sarah A. Younger knows how to keep readers interested in her novel, "A Bend in the Straight and Narrow." With her skill of mixing the stories she heard her grandmother tell when she was a young girl growing up in Palmetto with the researched historical fiction, she's written a very good book worth reading."

- Carl Mario Nudi,
Observer News

"Author, Sarah A. Younger has captured the essence of daily life on the Florida frontier in the mid 1800's with her debut novel, A Bend in the Straight and Narrow: A Woman's Journey into the Heart of the Florida Frontier. The story captivates the reader by delving into the value system and what life was like in the post Civil War Era. Younger is a gifted presenter and writer that depicts truth and fiction in her composition."

- Alicia A. Antone,
Library Manager, High Springs Branch,
Alachua County Library District

A Bend in the
Straight and Narrow

Sarah A. Younger

ISBN: 978-1515217831
ISBN-13: 1515217833

DEDICATION

This book is dedicated to Granny O'Steen.

Contents

ACKNOWLEDGMENTS

Thank you to John A. Ware, who made me a better writer. I wish you could have shared in the joy of publication. Thank you to my daughter, Morgan Richie, who pushed this project through as my Project Consultant. Thank you to Elana Whitehead, my friend, who was always so supportive and of course, to my husband, Doug, who put up with all the ups and downs of bringing a dream to fruition. But, mostly, I appreciate my Granny O'Steen for the many, many stories of her grandparents, parents, and family. Although this story follows their life loosely, it is truly historical fiction.

The cover photo is courtesy of the State of Florida Archives. This is not my family, but represents the migration to Florida during and after the Civil War and years beyond.

The cover quilt is constructed of Civil War-era archive reproduction fabrics that I made in 2004. The pattern is the log cabin, my personal favorite.

Part I   1859-1866

Chapter 1 LEBANON, TENNESSEE

I have been contemplating my life and how I came to be such a hard woman. We all start out the same - tiny babies - but life is rough sometimes. Mostly, looking back, it was a good life, but when harmful events take place (especially in wartime), it's like a callous on the bottom of your foot worn by the hard road or bad shoes or a grain of sand. At first you don't notice it but then it gets bigger and becomes the center of your consciousness, always there and always growing. I reckoned I had to start at the beginning, not birth, but the year I was 15 years old. It was truly the beginning, although I thought it was the end.

The year, it was 1859. My name was Sarah Ann Marsh but everyone called me Sally. Sally suited me, as Sarah was much too prim and proper. I wasn't a prim and proper person, but no one knew that, or I would've been punished by my parents for my thoughts and deeds. I loved to run through the wet grass in the early morning in my bare feet, which was unheard of for a young lady in Tennessee in 1859, a young lady of 15 years. I'd even been known to swim in the creek in my underwear as they would dry fast before I dressed again. If I had been caught I would've been in a whole world of trouble, but we lived in a rural area and my folks worked so hard as farmers they couldn't keep track of me all the time. Freedom was the most blissful thing as I did have many chores and limitations.

The worst thing was the shoes. They weren't comfortable when they were new, and then we had to wear them until the family could afford new ones. I had three brothers: Jefferson Lee, Henry Louis, and John David, and an older sister, Beatrice, so we kept our shoes a long time because Pa could only buy one pair at a time. When I took my shoes off and walked through the morning dew, it felt like my spirit had been set free. I knew it was just my feet that had been set

1

free, but it felt more like my whole being.

We owned our own land, five miles north of Lebanon, Tennessee, which was given to my mother by her parents when she married my pa – not as a gift, I'm told, but as a means of support. My mother came from a genteel family, and they were pretty unhappy when she ran off to marry Pa. Even though he was not rich - in fact he was downright poor - my mama loved him enough to defy her own parents. They had met in church, and after they wed, she was really not part of her family anymore, nor later were her children. Being an only child, her parents couldn't forgive her for marrying beneath her station; her mother acted like she hated her for disobeying.

Ma tried to raise us as if we were genteel, though it all seemed unnecessary since we didn't fit in with that class of people anyway. But she sewed our clothes, and we looked nice when we went to church, even though Pa didn't want her to spend the money on cloth. He said it would be better to spend it on victuals. I just would've loved to be able to go barefoot; I wouldn't have cared what anyone thought.

I had only seen my grandparents from a distance, usually as they rode by in their carriage in town. They always seemed very stern. My grandmother wore beautiful clothes as I had never seen the like. Ma said her dresses were made of silk, and that that was a wonderful material, saying silk came from worms, which was a wonder to me.

Ma made me wear a sunbonnet when I was helping Pa in the fields. I would much rather have felt the sun on my skin, but she said a young lady can't have freckles on her face. So, I had to wear long sleeves and gloves, too. In the summertime, it was so blazing hot with all those clothes on. So after the day was done, I usually headed to the creek.

We went to school six months out of the year, so we could help with the farm the other six months. Ma had had a good education, and she made us read and write and do arithmetic during the time at home in the evenings. It made me very sad on our last day of school each year because the teacher was always lending me books to take home to read. During our home-time, we were limited in the books we read as we didn't have that many. Ma said her parents had a full library.

My ma was so beautiful, but she seemed tired a lot. I don't think she was raised to live the life of a farmer's wife. She had had servants when she was growing up and never really learned to cook and clean and work hard. Sometimes I thought she was sorry for the life she had now, but I didn't think there was any way out for her, what with us five children and a husband to take care of. She was trying to prepare my older sister Beatrice and me for something higher, constantly talking to us about finding a man who had means to give us a better life. But I liked our life. I didn't want to go to teas and make conversation with uppity old biddies.

Beatrice, however, thought she was too good for the farm; so much of her work had to be done by my brothers and me. Since she was named for Grandmother Beatrice, I thought Ma did that to get back in her mother's good graces. But my grandmother didn't look like the type to forgive. I was named for my ma, but she was called Sarah.

I could clean and mend and cook, and I didn't mind it a bit, as I liked good-tasting food and a nice house. I suspected Ma was planning a scheme to take Beatrice to see my grandmother so she would help Beatrice find a wealthy husband. Imagining the conversation that might take place between Ma and Grandmother, I thought it probably would peel the paint right off the walls.

Beatrice was very pretty, like Ma, with dark auburn hair and milky white skin, because she had never worked in the fields like me. I knew she was my sister, and I should have loved her, but she was a hard one to love. She didn't seem to like me or the boys, or the life we were born to. The haughty ideas Ma had put into her head made me just want to steer clear of Beatrice.

Pa was a quiet, kindly man who loved his family, but felt like a failure because he couldn't supply my mama with the kind of life to which she had been accustomed. He thought he could make her happy just by loving her, but she wasn't happy. He had such a sweet way about him and always thanked me when I helped him with the work. I loved it when he put his hand on my head and mussed my hair. And I felt protective of him, even though he was bigger and stronger than me.

☼

"Girls, I want you to bathe and wash your hair, and put on your best Sunday dresses," Ma surprised us one day.

"Where are we going?" I asked, so excited to be going on a possible adventure.

"Going to pay a visit to my mother," she said.

We both gasped, and panic filled my throat. I wasn't expecting that *I'd* have to go.

"I don't need to go. I can stay here and fix supper for everyone," I suggested.

"Sarah Ann, Beatrice, do as I say," she said. She always called me 'Sarah Ann' when she was angry.

Beatrice was as happy as a lark, but I was flushed and sweating. I thought I knew why my mama wanted to talk to her mother, and I didn't need to be part of that conversation. Could it be that she wanted to marry me off, too? Couldn't be. I was only 15 years old. Beatrice was of the marrying age of 17. Maybe she just wanted me to meet my grandmother since I never had.

While we were bathing, I couldn't get rid of an uneasy feeling that she might marry me off, too. I couldn't leave my pa and brothers. They needed me. I prayed, "Please, dear God, don't let her do this. Beatrice wants it. I do not."

Our old wagon creaked as I drove it onto the circle drive of that big house, west of Lebanon. The house was really a beautiful sight to behold, with four big white columns on the front, and a balcony up above the veranda. There were large oak trees that shaded the house and flowers blooming all around. The lawn was green and cut close. A black man took the horse and wagon, and we were met at the door by a black maid, probably both slaves. Pa always said a man shouldn't own another man. He meant women too. But that's one reason I loved my pa so much - he had a way of thinking that was unlike other people that we knew.

The maid seated us in the parlor. Ma was very nervous, and she kept twisting her handkerchief in her hands. Because I didn't know what Ma had in store for me, I was scared and nervous, too. Beatrice, though, was grinning like a fool, looking at all the beautiful things in the parlor and touching everything. I felt like a lamb going to the slaughter.

My grandmother walked into the room like a queen. Glancing at

Beatrice and me, she nodded her head, then motioned to my mother to follow her, not saying a word to us. They crossed the hall to the library and I could see the rows and rows of books. As they closed the door behind them, my heart was thumping, not only in fear for Ma, but at the sight of all those books with so much knowledge in them. The voices we heard were subdued but angry, although we couldn't hear the words. Then my ma began to cry and moan and I felt like running from that house and never coming back. Still, I couldn't leave Ma.

After about an hour, Grandmother Beatrice walked out, with Ma following, her head down and great tears falling on her bodice. They sat in wingback chairs, and Grandmother motioned Beatrice to come to her.

"Come here, girl." Beatrice ran to her and curtsied. "Can you cook, clean, sew?"

"Yes ma'am, I can do all those things," Beatrice said.

"Well, your girls are handsome enough," Grandmother said to Ma. "The little one is too lean though. Come here," she crooked her fingers at me. I stood before her with my eyes locked on hers. Her piercing brown eyes made me feel as if I were staring into my own. Her hands were an older version of my slender hands and long fingers. I don't know why that surprised me so; she *was* my grandmother.

"This one is bold. Let's see your teeth," she said. Were we horses? Slaves? I wouldn't show her my teeth for all the tea in China. Beatrice opened her mouth obediently.

"This one will be a problem. She has *too* much spirit." She pointed her bent finger at me. "But I'll see what I can do. I'm not a matchmaker, but I do have a young man who buys cotton from us. He's looking for a good wife. In the meantime, don't come here again in that wagon. It's embarrassing. I'll send the carriage for the girls. And you don't need to come again," she said to my ma, at which time Ma started to cry quietly again. The realization that I was being considered for marriage, also, was seeping into my mind. On the ride home, the only sound besides the creaky wagon was the sound of Ma, who couldn't stop crying.

Finally, I said, "Ma, what are you doing to us? I'm too young to marry. Pa needs me, the boys need me. Please don't send me away."

She looked at me with fire in her eyes and said, "The Scriptures say, 'Children, obey your parents in the Lord: for this is right'."

"But Ma, you didn't obey your parents," I said.

Sitting by me on that wagon bench, she turned and slapped me hard across the face, stunning me. She had never raised her hand against any of us. The tears were welling up in my eyes, but I wouldn't let her know how that blow had hurt my heart.

"You girls have no idea what it's like to live like this, cramped in a two-room cabin, with no extra money. If we had one failing crop, we could starve to death. You must both marry well, so you can help us. We can't feed seven mouths any longer, and I am ordering you to do this for the family." As I glanced at her, I noticed her holding her belly, and I knew there would be another baby: *eight* mouths to feed.

Ma was wrong about one thing; I did know what it was like to live in a two-room cabin and I loved it. And as we drove up to that cabin in the piney woods, I realized that she might be sending me far away from this home and family, that soon I might never see it again. I thought about all the nights Pa would read to us by the oil lamp, with the little boys snuggled next to me, while we listened to stories of adventure. Sometimes when Pa was too tired, I would read to my brothers. The cabin was the most wonderful place on earth. Thinking about my vegetable garden, which was full of marvelous things to eat, and how the deer were plentiful, I knew Ma was wrong: this was heaven on earth.

Our little place was right on the road, even though it was not a well-traveled road. It was such a pretty two-room cabin, and Pa had put such care into building it. He had cut the logs himself, and they were set so close that there was very little chinking in the cracks. There was a loft upstairs where the boys slept. Even though it took him a long time to save up for the big windows, there was glass in them. The lower portion could be raised, so in the summertime we usually had a cool breeze blowing through at night. In the dead of summer, we covered the openings with wet burlap bags to keep the bugs out. Pa had purchased a real cook stove for Ma on their first wedding anniversary and he had made all the furniture.

Water had to be carried from the creek, but Pa said someday he would put in a well. For now, we had to drive the wagon to the creek and fill barrels, bucket by bucket. Beatrice was the only one who didn't have to help with this chore as Ma said she couldn't ruin her hands, because then her future husband would know she was poor. Pa had rigged spigots on the barrels, so it was easy to draw the water once we got it home. There was no barn yet, but that was to be our next project. Pa and I built a lean-to for the milk cow and the horses, but mostly we put them out to pasture. The chicken coop was a thing of beauty, made of planed wood, almost nicer than our house. At least that's what Ma said, and she was angry about that. Our chickens were fat, and our eggs were the best and freshest in the county. And there were so many eggs that we sold them to the General Store in Lebanon.

We didn't have just dirt floors in the cabin either, as some people in the area had. They were nice, wide, pine floors, which did constantly need sweeping because the little boys and Pa tracked in and out all day long. When I watched an old slave lady at the General Store making brooms, I traded her some eggs for a broom. Then I kept those floors spotless.

My only hope was that this cotton buyer would choose Beatrice. She was the pretty one, and her breasts were already developed, even though she had lied about being able to cook. She wanted to escape this life, and I wanted to live here forever. Sleeping came hard the night after we returned from Grandmother's house, but I determined to swim in the creek the next day and wash away some of this worry.

Pa didn't know about this scheme of my mother's; it would have broken him. He loved me the most, I thought, and I knew he didn't want me to leave, especially to go to a man who was much older. What would my life be like? I had never even kissed a boy, much less a man. I knew there was a lot I didn't know about love because I heard my parents at night. And I didn't think they were just kissing. Beatrice and I slept in the parlor area, and we listened to things that we probably shouldn't have, lovemaking, I assumed.

My plan was to protect my pa and, should I be chosen, make him think I wanted to go. It would be hard because I was tortured over this. Still, I didn't think the cotton buyer would pick me, as I was too skinny and too bold and I did have freckles on my face from swimming in the creek under the bright sun. Beatrice was the right choice for him. And that was how I finally slept that night, thinking that she would be his choice, and that would make everyone happy.

Two months later, the carriage arrived to take Beatrice and me to the big mansion, where we would be regarded as animals to be selected and taken away. Beatrice wore a new dress that she and ma had been working on for this event. I tried to get away with wearing my everyday dress, which was faded and worn, but my ma yelled at me to put on my Sunday best. Being so concerned and nervous, I could hardly dress. My breasts were, at last, starting to develop, and they pressed against my dress, which horrified me. Ma said, "Oh no, that will never do," and threw me a shawl to cover myself.

Beatrice did look beautiful. Her auburn hair was shining, and Ma gave her a pair of her amethyst earrings to wear. I thought my ma loved Beatrice more than me, and it hurt me some. My love for Ma was great, but it was hard knowing she didn't feel the same toward me. I could tell she thought the cotton buyer would pick Beatrice too, so I relaxed and actually enjoyed the trip in the carriage. It was springtime; the birds were singing and the dogwoods were blooming. Tennessee is plenty green in the spring and summer months and having a driver freed me to watch for deer and other animals along the way. The sky was blue, with no clouds, and it wasn't hot yet. Life was going to treat me good, I felt. My prayer, however, was "please God, don't let him pick me."

We were seated in the parlor when my grandmother and Mr. Cotton Buyer came through the door, and I was shocked. First off, Grandmother was smiling, which made her look like a different person, almost pretty, and she was holding his arm. Dressed in a gown that was so shiny, I couldn't believe she was the same woman I had seen previously. And this man, he was handsome, with a big moustache and a black suit. Also, he wasn't as old as I thought he would be to be so rich. But he was still a man, about 30 years old, and not a boy. Jacob Henry Winston was his name.

Beatrice flushed beet-red, from her toes to her head. He held her pale, soft hand and kissed it gently. Her eyes were cast down and she only glanced up to bat her eyelashes. Smitten, she was. Then, he was introduced to me, and I looked him straight in the eyes to see what kind of man he really was. When he smiled at me, I felt weak. Then, he took my right hand and kissed it also. I looked at my calloused, red hands and I was embarrassed for the first time in my life and quickly put them behind me.

We sat and had tea and the conversation was light, mostly about the weather. When Mr. Winston asked me what I thought about it, I said the spring weather had been a little soggy for my liking; the corn and beans would rot if it rained too much. Smiling, he tipped his dainty teacup to me. I tipped mine right back at him, with Beatrice glaring at me. The other ladies hung on his every word but I just wanted to know who he was, exactly. Trying to read his face without asking him any questions was like trying to catch a greased pig. But I'm certain I couldn't have asked the kind of questions I wanted anyway, like what was he doing here looking for a young wife.

While studying him to see if there was some honesty in him, I found him very hard to read. When he caught me looking, his blue eyes twinkled. But even though he did have a charming smile, I kept wondering what kind of a man would go looking for a wife in rural Tennessee? Didn't they have women where he came from? Where *did* he come from? I pondered.

Then I just asked, "And where do you live, Mr. Winston?"

"Girl, don't be so bold!" my grandmother snapped.

"It's all right," he said. "I live outside of Atlanta, Georgia. I have a cotton gin there."

"Oh," I whispered. So far away. Please God, let him pick Beatrice.

The carriage took us back home, and Beatrice smiled the whole way. "Handsome, and rich, too," she said over and over. She was off in a fantasy world and heard nothing I said to her. I thought she was packing her bags in her mind.

We arrived at home before Pa got in, which was good because, at this point, he still didn't know of my mother's plan. Gushing over the visit, Beatrice said she was certain the cotton buyer would pick her. I silently agreed with her. "We can only hope," I thought.

My days, in the following months, remained carefree. Aside from the hard work, my life was ideal. And really, I didn't care about the work because it made my pa's life easier.

Chapter 2 A TROUBLESOME TIME

The months passed, and Beatrice was starting to get cranky. We thought Mr. Winston would have asked for her hand by that time. Then, the carriage driver arrived one afternoon with a letter from Grandmother:

"Dear Sarah Ann Marsh,

Mr. Jacob Henry Winston has asked for your hand in marriage. I have given my permission, as your grandmother. He would like to wait until your 16th birthday, as he feels 15 is too young for a wife. He sends his best regards and will return in two months, for the wedding to take place at your church. Then you will make your home near Atlanta.

Sincerely,

Your grandmother."

I collapsed to the floor, Beatrice wailed, and my mother stood there in shock. When Pa came home, he found a totally disheveled house with three hysterical women.

"What on God's green earth has happened here?" he shouted. My mother handed him the letter, and his body crumpled into a chair.

Glancing at me as if to read my mind, he said, "How did this come about?" He stared at Ma and she turned away. "Is this your doing? You would allow a grown man to take our girl away from us to Atlanta? How could you? Sally's a baby. And she's needed here."

Ma had never seen him angry, and he was *very* angry. Unconsciously, she patted her belly then, and it must have been the first time he had realized she was with child again.

He put his face in his hands and sobbed. "Is Sally the sacrificial lamb?" he asked my mother. The devastation was written on his face, and I knew I had to make things better. A lot of secrets had been kept by Ma. It made me wonder where secrets began and deceit ended.

"Pa! I want to do this. I like this man very much. He'll make a good husband, and will help provide for the family. And I'll come back and visit. Please don't worry; it will all be easier now," I said.

"Yes," hissed Beatrice. "Easier for you, while we're stuck here in this God-forsaken land. You stole him away from me, you, with your big brown eyes. Despicable, that's what you are, and I will never forgive you for this." As she ran from the house, Ma was trailing after her, calling, "We'll find you a husband. Just be patient."

I had never felt such heaviness in my spirit. *Everyone* seemed unhappy; even the little boys were out of sorts, and they couldn't understand what was wrong. I left the house, too, and went to the creek, not to swim, but to think. Everything would be different now: no more carefree days, no more happiness in the family. The world seemed upside down. And I had a future before me that was so unknown, with a total stranger for my husband-to-be.

Sometimes, when Pa was alone, and things weren't going quite right, I had heard him cussing up a blue streak. That's just what I felt like doing right then, but instead, I just kicked a clod of dirt and said, "damnation," careful no one heard me. It did make me feel better, kind of cleansed, not like a sin at all, but I knew I'd have to pray for forgiveness.

It seemed the next two months were in total preparation for the wedding. My grandmother did most of the planning and sent lists to my mother of things she needed to do. I think Ma thought this would bring her closer to my grandmother, but it was not to be. Grandmother remained a hardened woman. I wondered what could have so offended her that she couldn't be friends with her own daughter, let alone her grandchildren.

Beatrice, of course, was scarcely seen.

And though two months had now passed since the letter arrived, I was as shaken about it as I was when I received it. To overcome the panic I felt, I often took myself to the woods and made my mind think on other things, like the quiet whoosh of a barn owl's wings as he flew toward his prey late in the day, or the look of a dogwood flower, gently opening. One morning I climbed a tree and saw a red fox on the prowl, not noticing me watching him.

The wedding was scheduled for the second Sunday in August, and my grandmother had sent me a cream-colored, silk wedding gown, to be returned to her after the wedding. I guess she couldn't be embarrassed by a homespun dress on her granddaughter. It was beautiful but it seemed a waste of money for a dress to be worn one time.

Pa was just not the same. He couldn't look me in the eye, and he didn't put his hand on my head anymore and muss my hair. He didn't read to us at night, and we didn't have those conversations about the crops or the livestock or the deer or the vegetable garden. He seemed a broken man, made to feel a failure because he couldn't feed his family without marrying off his daughters. When I would see him walking to the fields, his shoulders were slumped, and his feet dragged in the dirt.

Meanwhile, Ma couldn't believe a man would choose me over Beatrice and I couldn't either, which worried me some. Why *did* he choose me? Even though I turned 16 the day before my wedding, I was starting to feel much older, with the responsibility I felt to help my whole family. I had to do this right, so I would not fail them.

On the day of my wedding, before Pa gave me away, we were standing outside the church and I didn't want him to feel guilty for giving me away to a stranger. "Pa, I love you more than anything in the world. I know you wouldn't do anything to hurt me. I'm happy about this decision. Please be happy for me."

"I would, my girl, if I could believe your words," he said. A tear rolled down his cheek.

As we walked into the church, there he was: Jacob Henry Winston, standing at the altar. I couldn't take my eyes from his, as I was still trying to figure him out. And I just couldn't decipher that face yet. But he was going to be my husband, and I would have lots of time to get to know him. Still, I could not feel good about the events that had transpired in the last few months. The pastor's words were hazy to me, but I did respond with 'I do.'

My grandparents gave a small reception at the church, and many people were there to wish us newlyweds well. My friends from school could only stare at me. I should've been starting school with them soon, and there I was now a wedded woman. What *could* they say?

The gathering was a mixture of people, mostly our neighbors and friends, the food was plentiful, and everyone enjoyed themselves....except me. Of course, Beatrice refused to attend. Mr. Winston was very sociable and had no trouble talking with strangers. I could only think of what was to become of me and I prayed God would help me be strong.

Chapter 3   *GROWTH OF MY HEART*

The trip to Atlanta was long and taxing. And I missed my family so. We traveled in Mr. Winston's coach and even had a driver. He put his arm around my shoulders whenever I wept over the loss of my home and family. But honestly, that only made it worse. I needed my pa to hug me, not a stranger. Kindly, he asked me if he should turn the coach around and take me home. But I said "no," and I realized I had better straighten up and stop bawling: I never liked a whiner, myself.

The first night we stopped at an inn and Mr. Winston ordered a room with two narrow beds. I was so relieved, in spite of the fact that I did have to sleep in the same room with him. But I was in my gown and under the covers before he came to bed from the pub. Even though I was exhausted, I didn't sleep until I heard his deep breathing so I *knew* he was asleep. When I awoke it was light outside, and I sat up in bed. Mr. Winston was pulling on his boots and smiled at me.

"Good morning, Miss Sally Ann." I yanked the covers up to my neck and he came and sat on the edge of my bed. He took my hand and held it with both his hands. His eyes were warm and his smile comforted me somewhat. "I have a fresh-water stream on my property and sometimes I go there to think," he said. "I have liked to go barefoot since I was a boy. There's a deep area that allows for swimming, and when it's hot, that's where I want to be." Smiling down at me, I thought he was trying hard to make me comfortable. And it was actually working.

"I'll take you there when we get home," he said. I smiled back and could only hope I would like my new home and my new husband. As he stood and left the room, I wondered how he knew I liked to swim in the creek and go barefooted as I hadn't revealed those things. After he closed the door behind him, I wiggled my toes that had come loose from the covers at the end of the bed and felt luxurious to still be in bed at this hour of the morning. At home, I would've had the cow milked by now and breakfast started for the whole family. Was it possible I might like this new life I was beginning? Still, I wondered who was doing my chores back at our cabin.

As I unpacked my carpetbag for a fresh change of clothes, a brown envelope slipped out onto the floor. Bending down, I recognized the handwriting as Beatrice's, addressed to *Mrs. Sarah Winston.* Cheerfully I tore the envelope open, anticipating the good wishes Beatrice had finally come to wish me. As I began to read, I realized that would never happen.

Dear Sarah,

I am writing this note to let you know that you are no longer a sister of mine. You, unlike me, are a country bumpkin, married to a sophisticated man, who, as Grandmother Beatrice says, will send you packing within the month. I hope I never see you or hear from you again.

B

I fell back hard against the mantel and gasped at the venom in the note, my heart beating out of my chest. Had there been a fire in the fireplace I would have thrown that envelope and letter into the fire, but instead, I took both with me to the privy, tore them into tiny pieces and dropped all down the hole and then I lifted my skirts and sat down. I was determined that I would never be sent packing by my husband, if only to spite Beatrice and Grandmother.

The conversations got easier as we continued traveling. I told Mr. Winston about our farm and how I helped my pa. I also told him about my ma, the boys, Beatrice, and my grandparents. He talked about the cotton gin and his property. It all made the travel bearable, but I was still a little wary of him, even though he listened intently. It took five days to reach Mr. Winston's home. Each night on the trip we slept in separate beds, but I knew that would not last forever. I wanted to know what to expect, then maybe I could prepare myself.

After we arrived and he showed me to my bedroom, I could see that he was as tired as I was, saying his housekeeper would make my breakfast in the morning. Then he went to his bedroom, which I knew did not seem correct, but I was thankful for the reprieve. By the time I was up and dressed in the morning, he was gone. I slipped down the staircase, taking in his beautiful house and wondering if he had slaves. In the kitchen I found a young girl pouring coffee in a cup for me, and frying bacon and eggs.

"Good morning, Mrs. Winston, did you have a nice trip?" Her smile was so warm and friendly my heart gladdened. I wanted to hug her but felt I shouldn't.

"It was a long one, for certain," I smiled back at her. I was so happy to see she wasn't the old and grumpy woman I had pictured in my head.

"I'm Elizabeth Thomason, Mr. Winston's cook and housekeeper. He asked me to stay until you were up and fed. I'll be back in time to fix supper."

"You're not a slave, are you?" I asked. She was white like me; I had never seen a white servant.

"Mr. Winston, he don't believe in owning people," she grinned. "My pa, Samuel, works for him at the gin."

Well, that thought made me smile inside - a small clue as to who Mr. Winston was. Elizabeth continued talking, but my thoughts had gone to my husband, hoping he was overall a good man. Since I had never had coffee before, I made a face as I sipped. Elizabeth added a lump of sugar and some cream which made the taste so much better.

I felt a good wife should start cleaning, but everything was already so clean. So I took myself to the back yard and started splitting wood for the cook stove. I would have to let Mr. Winston know he wouldn't need Elizabeth now because I could do *all* the work. And it was important that he be happy with me, so he would send my folks some money or cattle or something – and not send me packing.

The inside of the house was decorated beautifully, with very fine furniture, unlike Pa's handmade furniture. The floors were golden-red oak, and they were polished to a glowing shine, with woven rugs that had beautiful bright colors and designs. Someone could slip on those rugs and fall and break a leg. And why would a man need all that finery?

The stairs creaked a little as I climbed them again. As I entered bedrooms I saw they were a little plainer, with bead-board walls, and painted a light cream color. I peeked in the master bedroom, and there was a big, four-poster, canopied bed with a counterpane so soft and fluffy, such as I had never seen before. When I touched it, my hand sank down, as though the cover was made of feathers, with large and downy pillows. I had to admit that the bed looked just plain inviting.

I walked to the big armoire in the corner and opened the doors, feeling as if I were invading Mr. Winston's privacy. There were so many coats and pants hanging there, and shoes and boots on the shelves. How many shoes did a man need? This man was truly a dandy. My clothes would all fit on one nail on the wall. I felt he might be a decadent man, but I would have to wait to see how decadent. With all his money, I was concerned that he might think I had been bought, like a piece of furniture. He didn't seem like that kind of man, but if he turned out to be a wife-beater, or a drunk, or a rounder, I would walk all the way back to Lebanon, if it took me all year.

Opening the top dresser drawer, I could see at least ten white shirts, starched, pressed, and folded. Dear God, my pa owned a work shirt and a Sunday shirt. A heavy feeling came over me, which made me feel I might have to change in order to belong in this house. I didn't want to be a wealthy snob, like my grandmother. My family's simple life style was what I preferred.

Mr. Winston's home was a big two-storied, white, wooden house. The windows had dark green shutters and even had screens on them. That was truly a luxury, much better than burlap bags, to keep out the bugs and let the breezes blow through the house. Walking around the outside, I could tell by the looks of it that there was a big attic over the second floor. The flowers in the front of the house were bright, and it looked like Mr. Winston had a gardener, too. How wasteful! I felt I could do that work also, thinking that my greatest trait was that I was a hard worker. I couldn't think of anything else I could offer up.

There was a big barn in back, painted white with green shutters, like the house, though I thought everyone knew a barn had to be painted red. A row of sheds stood to the side, for all the carriages and wagons he owned, and I realized Mr. Winston was a man who liked to spend money: who needed that many wagons?

Later that evening, in the dining room, Elizabeth had us seated at opposite ends of the large table.

"Elizabeth, please move my wife closer to me," Mr. Winston said.

"I can move myself," I said. I lifted my plate and silver and carried them so that I was sitting next to him.

"Won't Elizabeth be joining us?" I asked.

He laughed and called to Elizabeth, "Come join us, Elizabeth." She declined and said she had eaten already, but she smiled broadly at me as she came into the dining room.

I watched his face as he was talking about his day. Then, suddenly I blurted out, "Why did you choose me, Mr. Winston?"

For God's sake, what had made me say that? What kind of manners would he think I had?

But he just smiled and said, "Sally Ann, I did not choose you. I feel we chose each other. And I like that you are strong, not shy. I know you will stand up to me as well as stand by me. And you are beautiful, though you don't seem to know it."

"But why would you come all the way to Tennessee looking for a wife?" I asked.

He laughed again and said, "I wasn't looking for a wife, until I met you. Your grandmother asked me to meet her granddaughters, and I was just very taken with you. Did you think I was shopping for a wife?"

I flushed head to toe, thinking about when I first met Mr. Winston – so embarrassed to think he thought I was staring at him because I was enamored with him. Hoping he wasn't reading my mind, but feeling he was, he asked, "You were inclined to this marriage, were you not?"

"I was," I lied – my first lie, my first real secret, one he would never know about if I could help it. I was so humiliated that my grandmother had paraded us in front of this man, like prized race horses. My face felt hot, but I did my best to hide my anger.

Then he took my hand and held it, which made me feel so flustered. His touch was gentle, yet commanding. "And," he added, "at some point, I would like you to come to my bed."

Well, there it was, laid out in the open. I knew I was blushing again, but I could not just let the subject drop. "Mr. Winston, you must know I am only sixteen. I know nothing of these matters. I'm afraid you will be very disappointed."

"Mrs. Winston, I know you must have some trepidation, being as young as you are, but I will take good care of you, as my wife. I'll be gentle with you. I won't hurt you, but when you are ready, I really would prefer that you sleep in the master bedroom."

"Yes, I do have a lot of trepidation." I said, even though I didn't know what trepidation was, but I replied, "I will come to you; I know it is required."

But I did not that night. This was a problem that would cause me endless concern. He was an appealing man, but after all he was a man closer to my pa's age than mine. The situation plagued me daily. If I was dusting or building a fire in the cook stove or chopping wood, the thought was just under the surface. Sometimes, I cried out of pure frustration because I didn't know what would happen, until finally, I was ready to have done with it. I found the creek on the property and swam there in the mornings to help me sort through all these feelings.

When he was home, I watched him when he wasn't looking. He was tall with broad shoulders, slim hips, a full head of thick brown hair and a way about him which made me wonder all the more: why did he choose me? There were so many beautiful, fancy ladies in Atlanta, I had heard. It was a mystery to me: I was plain.

One day while he was gone to the gin, I stood in front of my mirror and studied my body without my clothes. My legs were too long, my breasts were still too small, my hair was a plain brown color, even though it was shiny and thick. I had those freckles on my face, and I was awfully thin. But he had said I was beautiful, so I tried to prepare myself to go to him. And I was worn to a frazzle thinking about it. One evening at dinner, a few days later, I asked when he would like me to come to his bed.

Smiling, he asked, "Are you ready?"

I stammered that I thought so, though I felt I would never be ready. He said, "Tonight is good."

I asked, "Tonight? Tonight?"

He said, "If that's convenient for you."

I whispered, "It is."

And so, later that night, I put on my nightgown and crossed the seemingly long distance between his bedroom and mine. My heart was beating so fast, it was like a drum in my ears. My knees were knocking against each other as I tried to walk straight. As he motioned me to the bed, I crawled in beside him, thinking of Beatrice's letter at that moment and wanting so much to please him, yet wanting to run down the stairs and out the front door.

"I'll want you to call me Jacob instead of Mr. Winston since I'm your husband," he said with a smile.

"Jacob?" I said, like I had never heard the word before. But I could barely hear his words with my heart still beating so fast. He took my hand and kissed it, something I was now growing accustomed to, but this time it sent a chill right through me. Then, he kissed my wrist and continued up my arm, and by then, my body was starting to respond, even though I wasn't certain I wanted it to.

"Sally, I can see the whites of your eyes in the dark. Don't be afraid," he said. Only managing a small "Oh," I tried to relax as he continued kissing my arm, my shoulder, my neck, my eyes, my cheeks, my lips, lightly. He kissed my breasts through my nightgown and I gasped at that, but he continued, and then he kissed me long on the lips. I was melting by then in spite of myself, and I kissed him right back, even though I had never kissed a man before. It somehow seemed to come naturally.

When he took my nightgown off over my head, I was shocked, as I was totally naked, and tried to cover my breasts. But he touched me gently, and I became less afraid. Being so unsure as to what I should do, he guided my hands. As he was kissing my fingers, my body started to react to every touch, every kiss, every movement.

I couldn't believe I was actually enjoying lovemaking. Could it be? The culmination was painful though, and I moaned. Afterward, he said he was sorry but that it wouldn't hurt the next time. I felt a gush of blood, and I thought I was really damaged, but he told me it was normal, which made me feel better.

And so, for about a week I slept in my own room, hoping to heal, as I knew the lovemaking would happen again. And I wanted it to happen again. Now, though, I was looking at him differently. Remembering his touch and his kiss, I found myself longing for more.

One evening soon after, at dinner, he smiled at me and asked, "Will you come to me again?

"I will," I said, maybe a little too eagerly.

I found happiness in our nights together. Mr. Winston, Jacob, was a sweet, gentle lover. For the life of me, I couldn't figure out why I had been so afraid. The lovely things he whispered in my ear melted my heart. And I knew a sweet love-child would come from our time together. We now slept together in the master bedroom. And as the days passed, I cared for Jacob a little more each day. When he walked into a room, my knees felt like they would fail me. I hoped he felt that way about me, too.

When Jacob was working, I thought of my family in Lebanon, Tennessee. I missed the little ones. John David, who was three years old, loved to kiss and hug me, and I longed for those little arms and those sweet kisses. Henry Louis was five, and he loved me, too. I had made toys for them both and read them stories, and snuggled them at night. Then, there was Jefferson Lee, who was nine and thought he was so big he didn't need my kisses and hugs, but he did. And Pa, my sweet, strong, loving Pa: I missed him the most, and when I thought of him, tears filled my eyes. Ma should have been about ready to have that little baby. I hoped it was a boy. Girls had a hard time in this life. They couldn't go work at the sawmill or go to sea or work on a ranch out west or fight Indians on the frontier. It was marriage and babies for us, which put me in mind of Beatrice. And so, I wrote a letter for news of my family.

Dear Ma and Pa,   *January 5, 1860*

So much has happened since I left you at home, I wanted to write in hopes you will write to me and tell me what is happening on the home front. I miss you all so much, but I am very happy here with Mr. Winston, Jacob. He's a kind man and we have a very nice home north of Atlanta. I'm with child and hope to deliver in June of this year. I've had the baby sickness for about three months now, and I hope I don't have it the full nine months.

Please write and tell me about the new baby. How are the three little boys? Has Beatrice married? I long to see you all and hope that day will come in the near future. How are the crops and the animals? I am sending all my love.

Your daughter,

Sally Ann Winston.

And so I waited: waited for a letter, waited for my husband to come home, waited for my baby, and waited for this illness to pass. Thank goodness Jacob hadn't let Elizabeth go, as I was too sick to work. She brought me mint tea and hard tack, which helped with the nausea. And she was about my age, loved to talk, and was good company. I liked her a lot, and thought we might become great friends.

I wondered what my husband did all day, as I really knew so little about him. He talked at dinner about things at the mill, but said nothing that gave me information about *him*. And the more I came to love him, the more I wondered if he loved me: he didn't tell me so. Sometimes I allowed myself to wallow in self-pity thinking he only married me to have babies, probably hoping for boys to help with the business. Sometimes, by the time he'd get home, I'd worked myself into such misery, I couldn't even have dinner with him. But then, he'd hold me close at night and whisper such loving things in my ear, and I'd realize how silly I'd been. Still, that nagging thought lay there, waiting to appear again at any moment. And even though I was inexperienced at lovemaking, *he* certainly was not, which caused my imagination to run wild.

Elizabeth said one morning, "Mrs. Winston, you'll probably need a midwife when the time comes. You're young, and you could tear and bleed a lot."

This alarmed me. My knowledge about childbirth was about as much as it was going to my husband's bed. "Do you know one?" I managed to ask.

"Why yes. The same one the former Mrs. Winston used," she said.

"The former Mrs. Winston?" I asked, stunned. "Mr. Winston was married before?"

"Yes ma'am. I thought you knew. She died in childbirth, along with the child."

Being so shocked, I couldn't continue talking about it with Elizabeth. This new information caused me some real confusion. Of course I was angry that Jacob hadn't been straightforward with me, but on the other hand, he had suffered a huge loss. I tried to understand his silence, but the lack of truth is sometimes a lie. Did he love me, or was I a substitute for his dead wife? Had he married me just for children, to replace his lost baby? I wanted to feel sympathy for him, and decided I would have, had he been honest with me.

I sent Elizabeth home and went to bed. When Jacob came home, the house was dark, no dinner was ready, and I was feeling ill.

"Sally Ann?" he called from downstairs. I could hear him coming up the stairs, two at a time. "Sally, what's wrong? Are you sick?"

"Why didn't you tell me about your wife and baby?" I asked, directly.

Stepping back a step, his face paled. "It's not something I talk about readily," he said.

"It's a hurtful thing, I know, but you should have told me. I don't know how to feel about it, or how you feel about me? Am I her replacement?" I asked.

He sat on the bed, eyes down, not touching me. "Sally, I love you as no other."

"I *am* sorry for your loss, Jacob," I whispered. "But I believe it best that we have no secrets between us."

"And I believe you are a wise girl, Sally," he said. I moved closer to him and put my arm around his shoulder. He held me then, and I realized what a man of few words he was in affairs of the heart. But he had expressed what I needed to hear.

"Where the devil is Elizabeth?" he asked. "I'm hungry."

"I sent her home, but Jacob, I can cook." I went downstairs to the kitchen, shored up the fire in the cook stove, mixed a batch of biscuits, and fried the chicken Elizabeth had prepared for cooking. It was the first meal I had made for him.

"I hope you will tell me more about yourself," I said shyly. "There's so little I know."

"All in good time, Sally," he said.

A letter finally came from Tennessee. It was in my pa's handwriting, which concerned me, hoping Ma wasn't sick. I quickly tore the envelope open.

February 10, 1860

"My darling girl,

It seems the decision for you to marry was a good one. I am so happy for you though I miss your smile every day. You were the light of this family. The boys miss you too and ask me to read your letter over and over. I am sad to tell you that your mother lost the baby. She is slowly recovering, but can't seem to be happy at all. I am hoping time will change that. I have planted twenty acres in cotton to sell to Mr. Winston, and I plan to lease another fifty next year. Please give him my best regards. Your grandmother found a husband for Beatrice, Mr. Tom Scruggs, and she has moved into Lebanon, but we hardly ever hear from her. She don't even come to see her mother. She's a different girl from you, but I hear tell she spends time with your grandmother. We love you, and maybe you will visit after your baby comes.

Your loving father,

John Marsh."

Mr. Tom Scruggs. I knew him as a rich, balding, older man, known for his stinginess, which made me smile. Beatrice finally got what she deserved, but I felt sorrier for Mr. Scruggs. My feelings turned sad then for my mama because she had lost her sweet baby and because she felt so hard against life. Ma never counted her blessings; she just looked at what she didn't have. Wondering about who was taking care of Pa and the boys made me think about my own situation. I was young and healthy, but Elizabeth had pure put some fear in me. Thinking about the childbirth that would be on me pretty soon was something I had to put out of my mind. At least I was not sick anymore, but I was growing, and I could feel that boy kick. Somehow I knew it was a boy.

Jacob had started taking Sundays off to spend with me. Our Sunday mornings were what I would declare as decadent; I had mostly never slept past sunup until then. He would bring in coffee and <u>The Macon Telegraph</u>, always more than a week old. Still, it was exciting to read the news. I would read the paper to him as he lay beside me in the bed, one hand on my belly. Some of the bigger words I couldn't pronounce, but Jacob didn't care. He said it was the sound of my voice he wanted to hear, not the bad news. I must say I couldn't have been happier, unless I could have seen my family. Jacob was worried about happenings in Washington DC, saying there was a tempest brewing; it worried me some, too.

The gin was expanding, and Jacob said he wanted to start a canvas mill, which would bring in more revenue. He had yet to take me to the business but said after the baby was born he would give me a tour. I told him I was concerned about Pa growing cotton because he'd only grown food crops previously. But Jacob said he had every confidence in him and cotton was a better cash crop anyhow.

My plan was to put in a vegetable garden in the spring if I was not too big. For now, Elizabeth was buying our food from the farmers, and that was an unneeded expense. I asked her father, Samuel, to build us a chicken coop like my pa's. I wanted to have our own eggs and fresh chicken for frying. When I talked these things over with Jacob, he just smiled that charming grin of his and said, "You're the boss." I knew he was teasing me because he was definitely in charge, with that rare talent of being in control without speaking of it or ever raising his voice. It seemed all right to me because he was such a benevolent man.

That smile was what always won my heart, even though I never knew what he was really thinking. Jacob just seemed such a mystery to me, and I was not. He knew everything about me, and I had just scratched the surface with him. To me, he said, "You amaze me every day. I've never known a girl to be so young and know so much." I told him Pa taught me everything. It seemed we admired each other's traits, even though we were so different.

Chapter 4 *A TEMPEST BREWING*

"Next Sunday, I think we shall go to church and meet my family," Jacob said out of the blue one Sunday morning.

"You have a family? Here? My word! What else don't I know about you?"

He was revealing himself to me in tiny bits and pieces, and it drove me to distraction. My frustration was tempered only by my desire for him and my growing love for him. I was thinking that maybe I should have some mystery about me also. But I was just too plain and simple for that. I felt I needed some secrets, so I would be more appealing to him. Little did I know that he found me extremely appealing just as I was.

It seemed that I had a mother-in-law, Mother Ann, a father-in-law, Jacob Sr., a widowed sister-in-law, Loretta, in Atlanta, and a brother-in-law, David, who lived on the Florida frontier. And I was nervous to meet them, so nervous I hardly slept at night, wondering if he had told them about me. I couldn't think he was ashamed of me because I was going to meet them, even though I was now large with his child. The dress I had worked on I was hoping would hide my belly, but it was useless.

On Sunday morning Jacob ordered a driver to hitch the horses to the coach, telling me the ride was about an hour to the church. I was still worried what they would think of me; they could see right away that I was too young for a man his age. I twisted the fingers of my gloves until they were wrinkled.

"My darling Sally, they'll love you as I do, and they'll love the fact that you are carrying their grandchild, their first," he said, comfortingly.

"But do they even know you're married? Do they know we're coming? Should I be sequestered?" I asked.

"No to the first two questions," he said, and kissed me on the cheek. "And why would I sequester you, when I'm so proud you're with child? It's a silly rule."

When we pulled into the churchyard, there were many parked wagons and coaches with groomsmen or drivers holding the horses. I thought that these must be wealthy people. As we entered the church, people came up to Jacob and greeted him warmly. He introduced me as his wife, and we moved on to a pew toward the front of the church. The three people sitting there could not close their mouths. I could tell they were stunned, as they couldn't speak, and I was feeling a little stunned myself.

"Mother, Father, Loretta, this is my wife, Sally," Jacob said. They still could not speak. And then, his father stood and took my hand and kissed it, and I knew where Jacob's charm came from, smiling that same wicked smile.

"Jacob, I don't know why we're constantly surprised by you, but this is a good one. Your wife is so beautiful, and it looks like the baby will be, too. Really pleased to meet you, Sally," Jacob Sr. said.

His mother jumped up then, grabbed me around the neck, and hugged me like she had known me for a long time. I felt the warmth flow into my body as Loretta smiled and reached for my hand.

"Just like that brother of mine, to keep you from us. You're a scoundrel, Jacob Winston."

"You will come to dinner after church," Jacob's mother insisted. "She's very young, Jacob," she whispered to him.

"Only in years, Mother," he said.

After the services, Loretta and Mother Ann, as she was called, insisted I ride in their carriage to their home. They fussed over me and tucked blankets around me to keep me warm. My own mother had never treated me so well. They had a hundred questions, and we talked all the way to their house. There was no discomfort, even though they seemed wealthy, and I was thrilled.

The Winstons lived right in Atlanta in a big, beautiful home: nothing like my grandparents' mansion, but very nice. It sat back off the street and was made of red brick, with black shutters. There was a large carriage house in the back, also made of brick. After helping me down, Jacob's mother and Loretta each took an arm, as if I were an invalid, and guided me to the front door as the carriages and horses were put away. A fire burned in the parlor fireplace and they insisted I sit and put my feet up. Jacob smiled down at me because he knew I wasn't accustomed to being pampered. He winked at me and I smiled back. I was starting to like this treatment *and* I was also learning that not all rich people were like my grandparents.

After a delicious meal of roasted chicken, corn bread, and green beans, cooked and served by two large black women, Jacob and his father drank brandy and smoked cigars in the library. Later, Jacob whispered to me, "Servants, paid with a wage." I must've had a questioning look on my face at dinner. Loretta and my new mother wanted to know what I needed, was I warm, could they get me anything, would I like a nap, when was the baby due?

"As well as I can tell, in June," I answered. "I have a midwife who will be helping me."

"No, oh no, you'll need a doctor," Jacob's mother said. "I insist that you spend your last month here with us so the doctor will be available at any hour."

"Mother, Sally will be fine. She's young, and the midwife will take care of everything," Jacob said, standing in the doorway. "And now, we must go."

I felt there might be some unspoken words between Jacob and his mother. His eyes flashed angrily for a second when he spoke. Loretta squeezed my hand as we were leaving and smiled at me. I felt we were going to be good friends, not just sisters-in-law. My heart filled with joy. So many of the things I had worried about in my life so far, had been the things that had brought me the most blessings, and I really liked Jacob's family. Saying our goodbyes, we promised to visit again in the next few weeks. I don't know how I could have felt any happier.

The following morning, Jacob announced to me that he would be leaving for three weeks, and that he had new farms to visit in order to buy cotton for the new mill.

"You're leaving me now, when I'm so near to delivering?" I asked, a little agitated. I couldn't believe that he would leave at a time like this. But then, I knew so little about his business; I just had to trust that he would be back in time for the birth. I squeezed my eyes shut so the tears wouldn't fall.

"It's important that I go now while you still have a few months," he said. "I'll have Elizabeth and her pa come and stay in the house with you. If I don't go now, it'll have to be later, and that would be worse. You know I wouldn't take any chances with you or the baby. You're my life."

How could I be upset with this man I loved, who was providing for all of us? He left the next day at sunup. Right then and there, I decided I had been leaning on Jacob too much, and I had to be more self-reliant.

Being in love with an absent man and being with child made me feel the same way – cranky and hungry. Sometimes, I felt I could eat my way through a whole cornfield, just start at one end and work my way to the other end by suppertime. Elizabeth tried to keep me fed; it was a full-time job.

When the weather warmed a few weeks later, Elizabeth and her pa helped me break ground for the garden. I had ordered the seeds through the mail order catalog---- kale, asparagus, beans, peas, and of course, corn. Samuel built the chicken coop and bought Rhode Island Reds from a local farmer, and they were starting to lay eggs. I was so excited about our fresh eggs.

Samuel and Elizabeth moved into our house, in the two other bedrooms upstairs, and I was thankful for the company, although I missed Jacob terribly. I reached for him in the night, but of course he was not there and I held his pillow to me. In the morning when I was dressing, I would touch his shirt and smell it, searching for a lingering hint of him. This was a new pain for me, and worse than anything I'd ever experienced. I missed the soft talking at night as we lay side by side, the tall tales he spun to make me laugh. Once he told me he and Samuel had spun a cotton strand so long that it could wrap around Georgia twice. I missed his breathing as he drifted into sleep and the soft snoring and his arm wrapped around me when I woke in the morning.

As the spring of 1860 arrived, the days grew warmer and the sky was clearer, the ground still damp from the winter rains. It was the perfect time to plant. Samuel had plowed the plot, and he and Elizabeth made the rows. They laughed when I told them I would do the planting, as my belly was very big. But I turned the hoe upside down, made an indentation in the soil, and dropped the seeds, one at a time, hoping they would land where I intended.

The days were long, the nights longer, as I watched the road for Jacob's horse. The three weeks had come and gone with no word from him. My nights were mostly sleepless, and although Elizabeth made Valerian root tea to help me sleep, I wouldn't drink it, thinking it might harm the baby. He kicked more than ever, waiting also. Jacob and I had agreed to name him John Marsh Winston, after my father. What a generous man I was married to, who didn't care if the baby was not named for him. My heart ached for him, the rogue.

Early one morning, I wrapped a shawl around my shoulders and walked out into the backyard toward the barn. My near sleepless nights had caused me to want to walk more, hoping I would tire and then sleep. As I approached the barn, I heard a noise and reached for the hoe as I entered the door. There, in broad daylight, stood my husband, removing his saddle from his horse, a big bay gelding. "You're here," I whispered.

He turned and walked to me, picking me up in his arms, kissing my face and neck. Seeing him made me laugh with joy, relief flooding my body, and I couldn't stop looking at his face, those blue eyes, his smile, his moustache, his tousled hair. When we returned to the house, I felt an exhaustion so complete I could hardly step up the first stair. I went to bed and slept all day and night and awoke the next morning, feeling refreshed for the first time in weeks.

"There's word of secession by the Confederacy," Jacob said at breakfast. "It's all the talk."

"Samuel said there's even talk of war against the federal government. Is it just talk? What does it mean?" I asked.

"It's just talk right now, but I fear it could lead to war. If that happens no one will be safe," he said.

"What of the baby? Should we go to Lebanon?" I asked.

"No! No matter what happens, we won't go north. We'll go south, and if I'm not here, you must remember that! The fighting will be worse in the north." He took me by the shoulders and looked into my eyes, and I knew he meant it.

Chapter 5   MY FIRST

About a month later, I awoke one morning and reached for
Jacob, but he wasn't there. I stood up and when I did, warm water
gushed down my legs. "Oh," I thought, "it must be time." And no
one was in the house!

I yelled down the stairs, "Jacob! Elizabeth!" No one answered
and I felt panic in my throat. I needed the midwife, and I needed
Jacob. Lying on the bed, I tried to calm myself, but I could feel an
excruciating pain moving down my back. As I cried out, my body
tensed with the pain. I knew I couldn't deliver this baby by myself.

"Elizabeth!" I yelled again. The agonizing pang began anew. I
moaned out loud.

"Mrs. Winston! I'm here. What's happening?" Elizabeth called,
coming up the stairs.

"Elizabeth, you must go for the midwife!" I said. And the pain
wracked my body once more.

"Yes ma'am, but it'll take a while," she said. Her eyes were big
as she wiped the sweat from her face with her hand.

"Elizabeth, can you help me deliver this baby?" I asked as
calmly as I could.

"No ma'am. I'll go for the midwife," she said.

"No, Elizabeth. He's coming now. You have to help me; I need
you. Please build a fire in the cook stove and put the kettle on. Then
tear up some sheets and wash your hands," I said, with more
confidence than I felt. I had helped my pa deliver calves, but I
doubted I could do this alone. There was no other choice open to me,
however, except for Elizabeth.

Between pains, I passed out, but when Elizabeth arrived with the
boiling water and sheets, I was groaning and pushing to try to birth
my baby. She looked as if she would turn and run any minute. I

33

knew she hadn't expected to deliver a child.

"Elizabeth," I said, "You *must* help me birth this baby! Can you see the head?"

"Oh yes. What should I do?" She was breathing hard, and I only hoped she wouldn't faint.

"When the head gets out, you must pull him free!" I groaned.

"I can't! I can't!" she whispered.

"Elizabeth! If I can do this, you can. Now, pull this baby!" I had never yelled at her, but I couldn't let her desert me now, as we both might die, mother *and* baby. I never dreamed anything could be that painful and I wondered if all mothers had to withstand that kind of agonizing pain. "Never again," I cried.

She pulled and we wailed loudly together, and the baby boy was born. Then she ran for the midwife. By the time Jacob arrived, the midwife was in control and had cleaned the baby and put him in my arms to hold. She was whispering to Jacob as he stood in the doorway, and I waved him to me. As he knelt by the bed, looking at the baby and then at me, I really was proud. But he was crying and saying everything would be all right, so I knew something was wrong.

"What is it?" I asked. I looked to the midwife and she looked away. "Tell me."

Jacob said, "You're bleeding. She's packed you with the torn sheets. You must rest."

When I awoke, Elizabeth was standing over me, saying, "Mrs. Sally, you have to feed your baby. Wake up so he can nurse."

I tried, but I was so tired and so hot, as if the fever had me. Elizabeth said, "You'll have to have a wet nurse. I believe you have the fever." What in the world was a wet nurse, I wondered as I drifted off to sleep again.

When I next woke up, Jacob was asleep in a chair. Pale, and with a several-day beard growth on his face, his head slumped forward. "Jacob," I whispered. My voice croaked like a frog on a lily pad, which surprised me. His eyes came open and he rushed to the bed. "Oh my God, you're awake. You've been so sick. Thank God! I couldn't bear to live without you."

He looked drained.

"Where's the baby? Is he okay?" I asked, weakly.

"Yes, fine." And he felt my head. "I think your fever's broken." As he held my hand and kissed it, he cried softly. He told me that I had been unconscious for five days. Then, Elizabeth came in with baby John, Loretta, and Mother Ann, all crying at the same time.

My milk had dried up, so I couldn't nurse the baby even though I longed to, but I was on the mend. It was to be a long road, however, and I thanked God every day for Elizabeth. She was a young girl, like me, but she had saved our lives, and had more strength in her than she knew. I was also stronger than I knew, since I survived the ordeal. How did women do it, I wondered. Some families had ten children or more, but I felt we might be a one-child family.

My recovery was lengthy, but I had such gentle care from Jacob and Elizabeth. He had hired a wet nurse, and baby John was very healthy. Jacob's parents and sister visited often and spent many hours with the baby. They were so proud of him, their only grandchild. Loretta loved holding John, watching his every move. My heart was full and I wrote the news to my family.

"Dear Ma, Pa and boys,　　　　　　　　*May 30, 1860*

I have some good news: baby John Marsh Winston was born May 15, 1860. I am so proud of him. He looks like his handsome father. I had some sickness with him, but I am mending now, although it is taking some time. I won't be able to come see you as soon as I thought, but when I'm stronger, and John is older, we will come. How is Mama feeling? How are the cotton crops doing? Please tell John David, Henry Louis and Jefferson Lee hello for me. I miss you all terribly.

Your loving daughter,
Sally Ann Winston."

One morning, I walked in the garden for the first time in months, holding onto Jacob's arm because I was still weak. But the air felt so fresh in my lungs, and I knew I would be strong again. Jacob looked older; he claimed I almost killed him, too. I reckoned he couldn't have borne losing another family. The seeds I planted had sprouted and would give us lots of vegetables for summer. Samuel had been weeding and fertilizing with horse manure and keeping the little plants damp. A fence had been built around the garden to keep the critters out. What would we have done without Samuel? Jacob had released him from the mill, and he now worked for us full-time at the house. He and Elizabeth had become like family – closer than family. Elizabeth said he was happier than he'd been in a long time, since her mother died. What a good man!

Our house was full of people during this time of my recuperation. The wet nurse, Rose, who brought her own baby with her, had a room on the first floor. Elizabeth was still staying in the house in case I needed her while Jacob was at work. Samuel was there all day, although he did go to his cottage at night. Jacob and I had a hard time finding private time for each other, but at night he held me and told me all the things I wanted to hear. How that man did love me.

There continued to be political rumblings in the air; everyone was worried that war might break out anytime. Jacob said there were those foolish enough to think the South could win, and I could only agree with him that the South couldn't win, not because he was my husband, but because we Southerners were mostly farmers, not warriors, which caused more concern about the food supply. His canvas mill was doing well, and he had been approached by some gentlemen who wanted to purchase canvas for the Confederate army, should the war start. Jacob felt the mill would be considered "essential" if that happened, and he wouldn't have to fight. Even so, all this talk gave me such a low spirit.

A letter came from home:

"Dear sweet Sally,   *June 29, 1860*

Thank God for your new baby. I am proud as punch that you named him after me. I bought some cigars and passed them out at the general store. Your mother is changing for the better. She smiles more now. Time is the healer. She sends her love. The three skunks are ornery as ever. Jefferson thinks he's grown. Beatrice is in the family way, but we only hear by gossip. She doesn't write or come around. The cotton is high and beautiful. Give Mr. Winston our best regards.

Love,

Your Pa."

My baby was the most beautiful baby boy I had ever seen, but of course, I might have been prejudiced. Of course I loved this child all the more because he was Jacob's son, with his blue eyes and the shape of his chin, even at that young age. Having this child was another example of a thing I feared being my biggest blessing. He cooed and talked to me, and he smelled so good. I envied Rose, the wet nurse, and her time nursing my boy. My longing to nurse him had to be satisfied with our time playing on the bed, which we did every day.

Chapter 6 BE JOYFUL ANYHOW

In August, 1860, I would celebrate my 17th birthday, and Jacob and I would celebrate our first wedding anniversary. There was talk of a party, but I didn't know if I would be up to it as I was still weak, physically. Jacob said his mother and Loretta would handle everything; all I had to do was arrive.

Everyone convinced me that the first weekend in August would be a wonderful time for a celebration, before the weather turned. It would be all day Saturday, in the beautiful meadow behind our house. My agreement to it continued to come with some reservation, but Loretta and Mother Ann were busily planning a great picnic event, and Jacob seemed excited by the preparations. Samuel was to roast pigs and sides of beef. It seemed it would all happen.

My reservations vanished, however, when the time for the party arrived. If I could have frozen a space in time, it would have been that day of our celebration. I was able to walk by myself, though I still tired easily. A big, soft chair was brought from the house for me to sit in, under the lofty oak tree, with John in a cradle at my feet. There were people everywhere, some I didn't even know. Our neighbors came from miles around, and Jacob's family and friends from Atlanta were there. It was like a Fourth of July festival. Long tables were set up in the shade of the oak trees. Everyone brought food, and I had an appetite for the first time in months.

Most people came in their wagons and would spend the night around the perimeter of the meadow, with picnic blankets spread all over it, like a great patchwork quilt. The children were running and chasing each other. The men had built a dance floor, and there would be dancing starting at dusk.

Despite all the festivities, the talk of war continued: the young men were anxious to go, the older men more hesitant. Young men knew nothing of the ravages of war. I may have been only 17, but I knew that men killing other men was not right, that war was not the answer. And so many of us in the South didn't believe in slavery. But this was our special day, and I wouldn't let the talk of war ruin it.

Loretta grabbed up our baby every time he cried; I hoped he wouldn't be spoiled. Jacob and I walked around the circle greeting people. As I walked back toward my chair, a young boy ran up and smiled at me. My heart fluttered like a hummingbird because he looked just like my brother, John David, and I dropped to my knees and looked him in the face. Suddenly I realized it was John David, and Henry and Jefferson were on his heels. Standing smiling, behind the boys, were Ma and Pa. For a moment, I froze. My mind simply couldn't register what I was seeing, but they were all laughing and coming toward me. My knees felt weak.

"Pa, Ma," I whispered, and I began to laugh and cry at the same time. It had been over a year since I'd seen them and it didn't seem possible they were standing before me. Then we rushed together and were all hugging each other at the same time. "How did you get here?" I asked.

"Jacob sent for us and we came in a railway car," Pa said. The boys were jumping up and down, and everyone was talking at once. I needed to sit down as I was feeling faint. Ma took the baby from Loretta, held him close, kissing and hugging him. I wondered if she was missing her own lost baby.

"Jacob Henry Winston, you are wretched not to have prepared me for this," I smiled at him, and he grinned wickedly at me.

Later, when the fiddlers began to play, I took the baby inside to the wet nurse. Ma and I sat in the parlor and she talked to me like I was her equal: a first. Then in a while she said "Sally, it seems that all has worked out for you. I think we did what was best, don't you?" I simply nodded my head, thinking I heard a slight hint of guilt in her voice.

But I was still hurt that she had taken a gamble on a total stranger treating her younger daughter with respect, that she allowed a man, almost as old as Pa, to take me away. God only knows what could have happened if Jacob had been a different man. As I looked at her though, I realized we would never be able to talk about this subject freely. I felt what she was really thinking about was that the family had benefited from this arrangement. Truly, I remained badly wounded that my ma had had so little love for me. Just because something turns out good, it doesn't mean the path taken to get there was the right one.

The party carried on into the night, but I spent the evening quietly with my family. Pallets were laid on the floor for the boys, and Ma and Pa slept in a bedroom upstairs. They stayed for the next week. Pa told me Ma's cooking was improving. "Her biscuits don't break the floorboards anymore when we drop them," he said. She hit him on the arm. As he had written me, Ma was a happier person than I last knew. I guess having more money, and fewer children, were what did it. I was still working on forgiveness. My pa, however, hugged me and whispered, "I can see that you are truly happy. It is a burden lifted from my heart."

Later that night, Jacob gave me a lavalier, with a little ruby in the center. It was a thing of beauty, for sure, something I had never dreamed of owning. We made love for the first time in months, which I had longed for many nights, but he had wanted me to heal. There was nothing better than loving a man like Jacob; he filled my soul, mind, heart, and body.

When we said goodbye to my family, I cried like a baby. I didn't know when, or if, we would ever see each other again, with the war seeming to be imminent. The future was, once again, so uncertain. Jacob hugged me as we watched the train pull away from the station.

"Jacob, what will happen to my family if the war comes?" I asked him. "They only have cotton planted, no food crops."

"I gave your pa a $200 advance payment for the cotton he'll grow. He's a proud man, however - almost didn't take it," he said.

"Thank you," I whispered to him.

Baby John stood up on Christmas Day, 1860. I had never seen a baby stand so early, and I guessed he'd be walking soon. I determined I would keep him safe even if war came right up to our doorstep. After all, I could fire a rifle. We had learned that the

Southern states planned to secede from the Union right before the new president, Mr. Lincoln, was inaugurated. This was going to tear our country apart, not to mention what it would do to the South alone. All the men in our area were signing up to be in the army, except for Jacob and his workers, as they did get classified 'essential'. And Samuel went back to work at the gin so he too wouldn't have to go to war. At that point, Elizabeth and I had to do all the work, even though there wasn't much to do in the garden until spring. But with my strength returning, I felt great joy in being able to help her.

Elizabeth told me that Samuel was courting Loretta, and I was shocked. It seemed I had not been paying attention to my surroundings. They were not a couple I would've expected to court, because she was so refined, and he was such a simple man. I obviously had to take another look at Samuel! I certainly found him to be pleasant-looking, and he was not as old as I had thought, probably about the same age as Loretta. Although he was quiet and didn't say much, when he did speak, it was usually important. Though he wasn't educated, he surely seemed wise. His skin was brown from the sun, and he had a working man's hands. All in all, he appeared to be most upstanding, and Loretta seemed quite taken with him.

Elizabeth laughed as she said, "Loretta says she loves a rugged man, and that would be my pa." I could tell Loretta wanted a baby also, because of the way she held baby John. Life surely has many turns and twists.

I asked Jacob if he knew about Samuel and Loretta, and he said he had suspected it. "Loretta came and stayed here with my folks when I left once for six months. She's had her eye on Samuel for quite a while," he said.

"Don't you feel they are a little mismatched?" I asked.

"Not for me to say. Samuel is one of the finest men I know, and he is not as uneducated as he may seem. He borrows books from me, so I know he's a reader," he said.

"Still waters run deep," I said. My pa used to say that.

When baby John was eight months old, Rose came to me and said that she had to go home to her husband and that we should start weaning him. That had been a concern of mine for some time, because I wanted John to be clear who his mama was. I knew he nursed not only for sustenance but for comfort, too. It pained me to see him crawl to Rose and touch her breasts with his hands, begging to nurse. Even since we decided to wean him, when he cried, I saw the milk flow to her bodice, and she couldn't resist nursing him. But I released her to go home as she requested.

I had ordered baby bottles, with rubber nipples, from the mail order catalog, and when they came I fed John cow's milk, which satisfied his hunger, if not his need to nurse. When he cried in the night, I went to him and picked him up, and as he nuzzled my breasts, I so ached to feed him. So I took him to our bed and held him close, sometimes rocking him in the rocking chair, until we both slept. It seemed to comfort him and it comforted me, too. Life was giving us too little consolation, with war on the horizon, so I took my comfort where I could get it, and tried to give it as well.

Loretta and Samuel married in a small civil ceremony, since there was a feeling of urgency in the air regarding the war. Only Jacob and I went to the service at the courthouse, because Mother Ann was ill and Elizabeth was taking care of John. After the service, Loretta came to live in Samuel's cottage, for which I was thankful, because she would be close to us, and we could visit and sew and drink tea. She was teaching me the fine art of drinking tea and I found it much more enjoyable than I'd believed it would be and not as snobbish as I'd thought. Loretta said that it wasn't about drinking tea; it was *experiencing* tea. She told me she was 33 years old and wanted a family, and also confided in me that her former husband had been killed in a hunting accident, which she had had a difficult time talking about.

"How old is my husband?" I asked her one day as we were sewing, wondering why I'd never asked Jacob that question myself. "He's 32, but he looks older, I think," she said. "We thought we would lose him when Evelyn and the baby died. He disappeared for six months. We were so desperate for news of him, and then one day he just showed up and took up his life again. My father had to run the gin while he was gone. You, Sally, have changed his life. I've never seen him so happy, and he loves John beyond belief."

There were still mysteries about my husband that I felt needed to be unraveled, even though that was one of the things that enchanted me. He was so intimate with me, and yet, I didn't know who he was, fully. For one thing, I wondered where he went during that six-month period when he had disappeared and what he did. There seemed to be a hurt in him that I couldn't touch or heal. Usually he had a quick smile for everyone but there were times when I could see him looking off into the distance, lost in thought. Thinking that someday he would reveal why he turned sad, I sensed it was because of Evelyn and the baby. I hoped Loretta would tell me, but she was as close-mouthed as Jacob. I was almost half his age and yet, sometimes I felt older. And I always felt protective of him, like I did with Pa.

Chapter 7   *QUILTING SOLACE*

In April of 1861, the Civil War actually began. And though we didn't feel the effects of it in our little Georgia community, we read the newspaper and knew that there was killing taking place. Fathers, sons, husbands, and brothers were being shot down. My prayer was that Jacob and Samuel would never have to go. Jacob began to think of things he had to do to make us all safer in case trouble came to our door. I thought if women ruled the country, there would be no war, but more socials with good food and dancing.

☼

In May, I began to feel the baby sickness again. I wasn't even sure I wanted more children, but if I did, I would rather have waited until the war was over. As long as Jacob and I loved each other in the night, there was, of course, always the chance I would have more. This time I planned to go to a doctor   in Atlanta, so if I developed a fever I would be under   his care, and I wanted desperately to nurse this baby.

I was so happy Elizabeth was still with us. When I'd seen her all dressed up at the celebration back in August, I realized how pretty she was, having always seemed so plain to me, as she pulled her hair straight back and wore ordinary frocks. But she had let her dark hair fall down her back at the party and had on a beautiful pale-blue dress, with a full skirt. I could see too that she had a voluptuous shape, unlike me. It worried me that she might someday leave us, even though I knew it would be the natural way - to marry and move to her husband's home. She was closer than a sister to me, especially what with *my* sister, who had disowned me.

Jacob and Samuel worked long hours into the night, almost every night. The orders from the army for canvas were large, and Jacob hired more workers. Sometimes he was just too tired to eat supper. Happily, Loretta and Elizabeth were staying with me at night to keep me company.

Elizabeth was teaching Loretta and me how to quilt, and we spent many days cutting patterns for our piecing. My ma didn't know how to quilt, and Loretta had never had to learn, so Elizabeth was showing us each step. But it was the hours we spent together that were what we enjoyed most, and in time, we would have a beautiful handiwork too, which was practical as well. My favorite pattern was the log cabin, I thought because it reminded me of my old home in Tennessee.

Elizabeth's mother had had a large quilt frame on which we stretched our backing, the cotton filling from the gin, and our piecing. We had set it up in our dining room and our first quilt was in place on the frame, ready to be quilted one evening, when Loretta began to talk at length - *she* was talking and *we* were listening.

"My first husband was from a wealthy family in Atlanta," she began. Elizabeth and I froze, our needles suspended, looking at each other. Since Loretta had never talked about anything personal, we were entranced.

"He was such a handsome boy, Lawrence. We married young, too young," she said. We leaned in toward Loretta, forgetting the quilting. Elizabeth's eyes were focused on Loretta. I'm sure mine were too. John was playing quietly under the frame.

"He was never taught to work like we were," she continued. Elizabeth and I glanced at each other and Loretta kept her eyes down, her needle moving up and down on the quilt.

"We lived off his family's wealth. I thought at some point he would go to work but he never did. When he got bored with our indolent lifestyle, he began to gamble and other things too," she said.

"What things?" I asked.

"Brothels," she said.

Elizabeth and I gasped. She went on, unfazed by our shock.

"I cried a lot. I wanted children, but he quit coming to my bed. He'd stay out all night long and come in smelling of whiskey, with lip rouge on his face and shirt. I knew he was going to women of the night. My shame was so great; I couldn't tell my family."

By this time, Elizabeth's eyes were large, and she was focused on Loretta entirely. My heart was beating out of my chest. Loretta had just never opened up to us like this before.

"One night he came in at about midnight and made a loud noise in the kitchen. When I went to see what the racket was, he was slumped over the kitchen table with blood all over his white shirt. He had been shot and soon died, right there," she said. We both gasped again.

"You poor thing," Elizabeth said. I went to Loretta and hugged her, though there were no tears in her eyes. But she wasn't finished talking. I sat down again, quickly.

"The police never caught the killer, but Jacob said it was probably someone he owed money, from gambling. I felt bad because I didn't miss him. I was happy to go back to my family and take up my life and name again. The marriage was so miserable, I didn't think I would ever remarry."

She got a soft look on her face and then said, "But I saw Samuel when we came here to live for a time - when Jacob went off traveling - after Evelyn and the baby died. Samuel was so handsome and strong, and he could do anything, build anything. And his quiet ways were very endearing; he was such a gentleman."

Elizabeth was beaming, proud of her father.

"But he didn't seem interested, no matter how I flirted with him. When I came near, he wouldn't talk or look at me. And I just finally gave up. I didn't care that he wasn't rich, but I guess he did," she said. No quilting was being done that night, even Loretta had stopped.

"Then at your party, Sally, he approached me and asked me to dance. I had watched him all day, admiring his easygoing ways and his strong shoulders. When he took me in his arms, I felt weak in the knees, and as he held me close, I knew I was in love with this man. And I somehow knew he loved me too. And that's my story: finally, a happy ending."

"What about Lawrence's hunting accident?" I asked.

"That was Lawrence's family's story. I had to go along with it to protect their family name," she said.

We just sat for a while, quiet, and then, wanting to cheer things, I said, "How about some coffee?"

Elizabeth and Loretta hugged, their bond tightened by this story, and I felt much closer to Loretta for having given us a small glimpse into her life, which I thought had been all roses. I wondered if, someday, Loretta would tell me about Evelyn. So far, I had lacked the courage to ask her about Jacob's first wife and the cause of Jacob's melancholy. Both wanting to hear, and dreading to hear, were the bane of my existence; I was so torn. However, as much as I wanted to hear about Evelyn, I knew Loretta was hungry for information about Samuel's former wife, Elizabeth's mother. Of course, like me, she would never ask.

The next time we sat together, quilting, Elizabeth was not herself. As we said good night, she seemed fidgety and decided to sleep in the downstairs bedroom. Being normally calm and subdued, I asked Loretta about Elizabeth's odd behavior, and she said she thought she was lovesick. Lovesick? Loretta told me that Elizabeth and a neighbor boy, Ernest Watkins, were courting, and that they had spent time together at the August celebration.

The next morning I went down for my coffee, and there was none made and no fire in the cook stove. Elizabeth was not in the bedroom, and the bed hadn't been slept in. I panicked, as I thought perhaps the Yankees had finally arrived and she had been taken. I went through the house, calling her name. Loretta, Samuel and Jacob came to the top of the stairs.

"Elizabeth is missing," I yelled up.

Samuel frowned. "She's not missing. She's run off with that Watkins boy," he said, angrily. After he had dressed and was walking down the stairs, Loretta followed him to the front door, hugging him before he left to find his daughter. John started crying, and Jacob brought him down. While I fired up the cook stove, Loretta held the baby, handing him back to me to go dress.

Chaos seemed to reign without Elizabeth, with the baby crying and clinging to me. I put the coffee on to boil, while balancing him on my hip, and ran to the pump outside to get a pan of water for soft oatmeal. Jacob looked tired and tried to help but he was worthless in the kitchen and John wouldn't go to him. I felt Elizabeth could have left us a note.

"Why didn't she tell us?" I asked Loretta.

"Samuel doesn't approve of the boy. She probably thought you would tell her pa. But Ernest was leaving to join the army, and they wanted to marry immediately. Samuel said no."

Once again, I had not been paying attention. Elizabeth and I had been very close, and I hadn't even known she was in love. No wonder she looked so pretty at the picnic. I thought I could've talked some sense into her had I known. "Where would she be living? Where was she now?" I wondered.

Later that same day, Samuel rode up on his horse with Elizabeth behind him.

"Now, you go in there, and say your apologies, girl!" he said to her. I stood at the front door, both happy to see her and angry at her for deserting us. She ran to me and stood before me, her shoulders down. "I'm sorry. Forgive me. Please take me back."

I gave her a hug. "I've been worried sick, Elizabeth. Of course, I'll take you back. Are you married?"

"Yes'm. But he's gone off to war. We only had a day and night." And she began to weep.

Samuel said "That's a no account man who won't ask for permission to marry my daughter."

Loretta came running with John, both she and the baby crying and hugging Elizabeth. I declare, I had to just stand there and listen to a houseful of folks bawling. So, I joined in. One thing I can say with all certainty: if a woman loves a man, nothing on God's green earth will keep her from him. I can only thank the good Lord that I fell in love with my husband *after* we married; so I didn't run off with some ne'er-do-well. I believe I might have been feeling smug.

Jacob had Samuel build a false room in the back of the third bedroom upstairs, saying it would be a safe haven if we were invaded. And Jacob also built a storage box, that couldn't be seen, into the front of the wagon. Fear filled my body at these precautions. Both being with child and having a baby boy, the thought of having to hide in my own house was frightening. We had no real concept of what the Yankees would do to us – only our imaginations, and they could run rampant. In my mind I pictured them as large, ugly, bearded men, with bad teeth and breath.

"Sally," Jacob whispered in my ear as we lay in bed one night. "I've buried a strongbox of gold coins in the barn under the feed bin. It'll be easy to dig up. But if ever I'm not here, and you must leave, unearth it and store it in the wagon in the storage area I showed you," explaining that he had never had faith in banks or paper money and had exchanged profits from the business for gold. "Paper money is just paper, which can rot or burn, and banks aren't secure either." He continued, "And don't keep the horses in the barn where they can be stolen. Turn them loose in the far pasture. You'll just have to chase them down, if the time comes, and hitch them to the wagon. Then, head for Macon. Once you get to Macon, start south to Florida, to Alachua County. That's where my brother, David, is. I can't tell you his exact address."

"Jacob, I won't leave here without you. I won't. Don't ask me to do that," I said.

"Sally, listen to me. Promise you'll do as I ask. We don't know where this war will go. The South is winning some battles now, but we can't hold out. If we're invaded here, I shudder to think what might happen." He wrapped his arms around me and held me close, and I lay there a long time hoping God would not let this thing happen. How I longed for the nights when life was simpler, when we weren't filled with dread of the coming events.

It was late summer, 1861. Our lives still went on as if nothing were happening outside our community. We milked the cow, harvested the garden, fed the animals, split the firewood, made meals, worked on our quilts, and I continued to get bigger every day. Fall was coming, and I finally begged Jacob to take Sundays off to be with John and me. I missed him so, and usually I was in bed by the time he got home. Because he was continuing to work too hard, I was getting really worried about him, but he promised to take some time off.

I can say plainly, that women sitting around a quilt frame will talk about things they wouldn't dream of revealing any other time. One other such day, Elizabeth began to talk about Ernest Watkins. And this time it was Loretta and me who were all ears.

"Ernest always loved me, since first grade. But I never cared that much for him," she said.

"And do you love him now?" I asked.

"I think so. But he was so desperate at your party because he was going off to war, and I felt I had to console him." She turned to Loretta then, and said, "You must never tell Pa these things. He cannot know."

"Never," whispered Loretta.

"He kissed me in the barn that day and I kissed him back. He begged me to marry him, as he thought he might die fighting for the South. I felt sad for him, and he said that we could be married just by saying the words. We said some words like we'd heard at weddings, and then he took me to the backwoods, and we undressed and made love in the green grass. More than once."

Loretta and I both held our hands to our faces. Elizabeth's face was bright red, and she could not look us in the eye.

"So, you're not legally married?" I asked.

"We are, but I feel he tricked me into making love with him. I'm a little angry about that," she said.

"Dastardly!" shouted Loretta. "Unforgiveable!"

"I got worried about having a baby, so I made him marry me legal-wise, even though I knew it would anger Pa. I couldn't take the chance of being an unwed mother," she said quietly.

Loretta and I went to Elizabeth and hugged her at the same time. Another secret to keep, but these talks were drawing us so much closer. Loretta asked me when I was going to tell some stories about myself, which amused me.

"You know everything there is to know about me," I said. Loretta gave me a smile of disbelief.

"It's true," I insisted, but I wondered how much I could tell them about Jacob and me. I wasn't sure Jacob would want them to know that I had been fifteen when we first met. And I didn't want them to know how I had dreaded coming to this place. Also, I was a little embarrassed about the passion I felt for that man. So, it seemed I finally did have some mystery to me, a few secrets. Smiling to myself, I glanced at Loretta and Elizabeth, who both had knowing looks on their faces as if they could read my thoughts. Maybe someday I would tell them – not today.

Later, that evening, as I was preparing for bed, Loretta knocked at my open door. Her face was flushed and she seemed bothered. She said, quickly, "Jacob was not here when Evelyn and the baby died. I know you want to know that, without asking me. He has felt

50

overwhelming guilt and that's why we were surprised when he married again, but I believe he has found redemption with you, Sally."

I whispered, "Thank you, Loretta. You can't know how much that information means to me." And I knew how hard it was for her to divulge this secret. For me, being secretive was painful; it gave me a headache.

Chapter 8 *LOSS AND GAIN*

Gossip and the week-old newspaper were the only news we had of the battles. Mother Ann had been ill for a long time, and we were greatly worried about her. Loretta and I decided to go to the city to visit her and the doctor: my first visit to a doctor in my whole life. To cheer his grandmother, it was decided John would go with us. Even though he was trying to talk, no one could understand him. Jacob felt it would be best for us not to go, but he hired a driver and asked Elizabeth to travel with us. I was hoping we could learn more about the war once we reached Atlanta.

The idea of the trip was very exciting to us, and we had even planned some shopping for household supplies and maybe some fabric for our quilts. Baby John was excited too: soon we wouldn't be able to call him "Baby" anymore because he was getting so big and ran everywhere.

When we walked in the front door of the Winston home, Mother Ann was sitting in a chair with a blanket over her lap. We hadn't seen her in a while, and I was shocked to see her appearance, so pale and thin. But she seemed in pleasant spirits, so we had a good visit, and she was delighted to see John as he climbed in her lap and hugged her.

She said to me, "Sally, you're as pretty as a robin's egg."

And I said, "About as round, too," which seemed to make everyone laugh. Jacob Sr. came in with a tray and made Mother Ann take her medicine. He was so happy and relieved we had come, throwing John in the air until John was giggling so hard he could hardly breathe.

"The boys are going to the backyard," Grandpa announced.

As we women talked and gossiped, I realized we had some gossip ourselves – about our Elizabeth. Mother Ann was very happy for her, but of course she didn't know the circumstances surrounding Elizabeth's elopement. All the while we were there, my heavy feeling about my mother-in-law kept me from asking the obvious question: was her illness fatal?

While I was getting ready to go to the doctor the next day, Loretta told me she was going with me. When we were waiting to see the doctor, the nurse came out and called out, "Mrs. Loretta Thomason," and Loretta winked at me and followed the nurse through the door. I couldn't believe it! Was it possible Loretta was in the family way? I had to wait patiently until she returned, or impatiently I should say. When she returned she was virtually glowing, and I grabbed her and hugged her to me.

And then I was presented to Dr. Milliken who said, "Mrs. Winston, you must have a doctor deliver this baby, or you and the baby may not make it. I will want you close your last month. I am figuring that to be in January. No more midwives. You can stay with Jacob's family at that time." I agreed with him and felt more comfortable right away under his care.

Later, as we walked down the street, I said to Loretta, "You're a woman of mystery, just like your brother. How could you keep a secret like that from me?"

"I wanted to be certain, Sally. I'm getting beyond the childbearing years, and I wasn't sure. But you're the first to know; Samuel doesn't even know."

I felt like I was seeing Loretta for the first time. Her skin was flushed and her eyes were shining, and she was as beautiful as a woman could be. Her dark hair was shiny and thick and even though she wore it in a bun, she looked very young. I thought, "Samuel is a lucky man."

But on the ride back home Loretta was very quiet, and I saw a tear run down her face.

"It's Mother Ann, isn't it?" I asked.

"The doctor said she only has months. I feel I should go and be with her, but I'm still sick in the mornings," Loretta said. "Maybe you wouldn't mind if I take Elizabeth with me? I know you need her, but it would be a blessing to have her help with Mother." Glancing at Elizabeth, I thought Loretta really should have asked her before me.

"Yes, yes, of course," I said.

Although I was anxious to help, I had grown so dependent on Elizabeth, especially now that my belly was growing. But I had been accustomed to hard work on the farm, and I hoped I wasn't getting too soft. Having to fire the woodstove in the mornings and making the coffee and breakfast with the baby wanting his bottle would be a challenge. Still, it would just all have to be done. It was time John was taken off the bottle anyway, and he hadn't slept with me in months. For that I was thankful as Jacob was getting irritated with the lack of sleep from John's presence. Altogether, I thought this would be a harder time; however, I was determined to do it. But I would be so lonesome for my two best companions.

Mother Ann died right before Thanksgiving, 1861. All of us felt the extreme loss. The skies were gray, and there was no sunshine in any of us. Her funeral was a somber affair, on top of the already sad war-time. Loretta and I wept and held each other, our pregnant bellies touching. There would be no Thanksgiving this year; we were just too sad. Jacob put his arm around his father's shoulder, but Jacob Sr. looked lost. When Jacob asked him to stay with us, he declined.

Chapter 9   *BLOCKADES*

While preparing for her new baby and with her mother now gone, Loretta moved back to Samuel's cottage and I thought he looked relieved. He became a changed man; I saw him smiling, and I had thought there were no smiles left in him. Since Elizabeth was needed by Loretta and me, she went back and forth between the two houses, helping each of us with the chores. By Christmas I couldn't see my feet, and after the holiday, I would prepare to move to Atlanta. I asked Elizabeth to come with me, and Jacob said he would come for the last few days, although I didn't know how he could know when that would be because even the doctor didn't know the exact date.

Even though I was in the waddling stages again, Elizabeth and I canned tomatoes, peaches, apples, and corn for the winter months. And in the back of my mind, I was also beginning to think of our exodus – though I was still somewhat in denial.

One morning Jacob told me he was looking at a grist mill closer to Atlanta and was thinking about buying it, but I was insistent: as it was, he was gone too much. I missed my husband and our carefree Sunday mornings. While I was making coffee, he pulled me to him, hugging my belly, laughing at my remarks about the mill. And I knew he could do anything he wanted. I was putty in his hands.

In January of 1862, there I was again waiting for a baby to come, this time in Atlanta. I wanted to get back to my home and husband, so I was impatient and cranky. After my last appointment with the doctor, he had said he wanted to put me in the hospital because he feared the scar tissue from John's birth might impede the new baby, that I might need to be cut. This was not what I wanted to hear, and I sent a note for Jacob to come. But during the night, the pain started down my back, and I knew the time had come. Jacob's father hitched the horses to the carriage and rushed me to the hospital.

Everything was white and clean in the hospital, but it wasn't like having a baby in my own bed. I dreaded the pain I would have to endure, along with possible surgery, too. The doctor came in, ordered a mask over my face, and that's all I remembered. When I woke up, I had a baby boy in my arms, but I was too weak to hold him.

"Jacob," I called out later, but nobody answered. I cried into the clean, white sheet.

The doctor said it would take me a little longer to recover but I would be fine. To Jacob he said, "No more children," and left the room.

"You heard the doc, no more children. Separate bedrooms for us then," he smiled. We both knew we would not sleep apart.

I was ecstatic that the milk was in my breasts, and smiled every time I put that little mouth on my nipple, even though it was painful. He was hungry and gulped the milk down, and I couldn't have been prouder. God had answered *this* prayer. And Harry Jacob was our second son, born January 13, 1862.

Elizabeth was of great help to me, as always. Sometimes I wondered if she didn't get tired of working for everyone, making their lives easier and not having a life of her own. She must have longed for her husband and a home. But I was happy to be back in my own home, in my own bed, and happy to have her help me, hoping she would never leave us. Bed rest was the order for me for a few weeks. The doctor said I could get up then, but I must take it easy.

It didn't matter that I had bed rest either because I had my sweet baby boy with me, and John came up to see us sometimes. He thought Harry was only there temporarily I'm sure. While Jacob was spending more time at home, I loved seeing his smile, with pride in his family showing on his face. He teased me about having a few more children, but I didn't see the humor.

The blockades of Southern ports had begun a year before, and we weren't able to get a lot of the luxuries we had grown accustomed to. We made our coffee a lot weaker and tried to make it stretch. And we drank it without sugar. Sugar and salt were so necessary, especially salt, for preserving meat. Jacob and Samuel were building a smokehouse in order to have our meat last through the winter. Having money made no difference; there was rationing throughout the area.

Jacob said he didn't think he would be able to gin the cotton much longer as we were dependent on shipping and the railroad also. With no deliveries of cotton, I was afraid he and Samuel would have to go and fight. The idea terrified me, but for now, our world was peaceful. There *was* an undercurrent of fear of things to come, however.

The last two years of my life had been the best and the worst. I had cried more in these years than the whole rest of my life, but I had been the happiest. My husband and two baby boys made me feel at peace with the world. And even though I knew there was trouble coming down the pike, I wanted my life, right then, to be as it was forever. Of course, that was not to be.

Loretta and Samuel left for Atlanta one morning in May, a few weeks before her delivery. We kissed them and hugged them goodbye, hoping they would be safe, but they both smiled and waved as they drove off in the buggy, seemingly without a concern.

Work at the mill had slowed, so Jacob had released some of the workers since the blockades were still preventing raw cotton delivery. My biggest fear was that the mill would have to be closed if there was no cotton. I couldn't go to Atlanta for the birth as I just had too much to do with two small children.

The air in our kitchen was full of wonderful smells as Elizabeth and I were canning fruits and vegetables and smoking venison and hams. We gathered acorns for coffee and flour. She said her mother taught her how to boil the acorns, peel the shells, soak the tannin out, and then roast them to make a hot, coffee-like drink. The flour was made the same way but by fine-grinding the roasted nuts. Elizabeth was so smart and this was a recipe I would use many times over the next few years. It was quite a long process but well worth it in the end. She also showed me how to make corn starch from our own corn, to keep the baby's bottom dry.

Working with Elizabeth made me feel like a child again. We

laughed together as we were cooking. No matter what the chore was, we found something to laugh about. We were, after all, just young, silly girls - young girls with big responsibilities. She was the *best* friend I ever had, or would ever have, I felt.

When I had been at home in Tennessee, my pa and I would go hunting for deer and wild boar. I learned to shoot a rifle then, but I had never even held a hand gun. Jacob took me to the meadow to learn to shoot and I took right to it. But I still felt more comfortable with a shotgun or rifle. He said a handgun was easier to hide; it seemed he was still preparing for the worst, and rightly so. We turned the horses loose in the far pasture where they couldn't be seen from our house. Jacob said it would be harder to catch them, but they would be harder to steal.

For me, I was just hoping the war wouldn't reach us. Hope doesn't always match reality, however. I put the little pistol in my dress pocket and kept it there safely, unless I was with the children. It was the beginning of a life-long habit. Jacob brought yards of canvas home to fit the wagon so that the rain would not soak our belongings if we had to evacuate. He had also laid in canvas for sleeping on the wet ground and for tents.

After three long weeks Samuel and Loretta returned with a new baby girl, Rebecca Ann Thomason. Loretta was proud and Samuel looked like a peacock. He said if he could get hold of cigars, he would pass them out. And I told him if he could get one, I would smoke it, knowing the procurement of cigars was unlikely. Elizabeth had a new sister, eighteen years younger than her. Since Loretta presently needed her more than me, she went to the cottage to help her, as Loretta was not accustomed to hard work. I hoped she wouldn't want Elizabeth to stay too long because I really missed Elizabeth during that period.

In the meantime, I had a very active toddler and a nursing baby who was hungry, and I was worn to a frazzle. Jacob asked me if I would like to hire a housekeeper but I was concerned with the hard times coming that we should save our money. I was doing the washing, cooking, and cleaning and realized my reliance on Elizabeth had made me soft. By the time Jacob came home for dinner, I was exhausted and usually went to bed early with the baby, leaving him to look after John until bedtime. Worn out from the day's work, many nights we simply held each other.

Chapter 10 ENEMY WITHIN

"And I looked, and behold a pale horse: and his name that sat upon him was Death, and Hell followed with him." Revelations 6:8

Rondel Atherton was his name – a fine-sounding name – but he was not a man to match his name. He and his younger brother, Jeremy, a fair-haired boy, rode onto our property one afternoon, as Elizabeth and I were weeding the garden.

"How do, ladies?" he called to us. "Allow me to interduce myself," shouting from atop his horse. Neither man alighted, both wearing poorly-made, grey Confederate jackets.

"I am Rondel Atherton of the Atlanta Home Guard Militia and this here's my brother, Jeremy."

Elizabeth and I stood in the garden, shading our eyes from the sunlight.

"How do you do?" I said. "Will you take refreshment?"

Rondel said, "Yes ma'am, we'd be obliged, but we cain't step down."

Elizabeth ran to the house and brought back two glasses of water, handing them up to first one brother and then the other.

I inquired, "And what does that Home Guard Militia do?"

"Why, we protect all you beautiful women and make certain yore husbands is not on the run."

At that point, Loretta had joined us and with his last statement, I could see she was fired up. She said, "You know very well our husbands are considered essential to the cause. And Elizabeth's husband is off fighting. Why aren't you two off fighting?"

Rondel Atherton leaned low over his saddle horn and grinned threateningly, his teeth tobacco-stained brown. He spat a wad close to Loretta's shoe and said, "Now, I cain't see that's any of yore affair. We was assigned this area and if we hear tell of yore husband's turning yeller, we'll come for you, too."

"Get off my land," I yelled, my hand on my gun.

"Now, Miz Winston," Jeremy said, softly. "We don't mean no harm. We're just doing our job."

"Your job is not to harass women," I said, angrily. "Especially women whose husbands are serving the Confederacy. We do not need your protection. We are armed."

Rondel grinned that evil smile again and said, "I just bet you are."

Handing Elizabeth the empty glasses, Rondel grabbed her hand and wouldn't let go, laughing, his eyes on her breasts. When she pulled loose, they turned their horses and rode away. Once they were gone, I could see we were all three shaken from the encounter. Loretta was red in the face, the vein in her forehead prominent.

I said, "I'd hate to hang for shooting the likes of him. But it may come to that. He is a most unattractive man and I don't mean just in looks."

"He's crippled," Elizabeth said. "That's why he wouldn't step down. A horse kicked him when he was young and broke his leg – never healed right. And Jeremy, he's just a boy, maybe 15. I believe them to be harmless."

"Oh, Rondel is not harmless. They'll be back," I said. "You can bet money on that."

"They're the enemy within," Loretta said.

"Why, Loretta," I said. "You took the bull by the horns."

"I reckon I can if I have to. I've just never had to."

Loretta continued to surprise me. I had a feeling if the dam ever broke loose behind that calm exterior, we would find a powerhouse of a woman.

Our lives were somewhat calm, but we knew things were about to change and the anticipation was exhausting. In October, 1862, Jacob let everyone go at the mill except Samuel. He felt awful about it because those men would now be conscripted and some might die.

But there was just so little raw cotton making it through the blockades, he and Samuel could run the gin and weave the canvas with just the two of them. By stretching out the delivery to the army, he planned to keep the mill open, preventing them from going to war. Even so, the work was more physical than it had been with just the two of them, and they both developed big muscles in their arms and shoulders.

Our Christmas that year, 1862, was a real sparse one as far as gifts went. The weather was very cold, and Samuel and Jacob had to cut down trees on the back end of our property to heat the house and cook stoves. We were sleeping in the downstairs bedroom and had shut down the upstairs to conserve our heat. Since Samuel's cottage was small, they didn't need near the wood we did in our big, old, drafty house and I told Elizabeth to stay there until the spring. But she seemed to want to come home, and I wanted her to come home as she lifted my spirits and I know I lifted hers.

As I was knitting scarves for everyone, I thought how blessed we were that war had not reached our door yet. We were looking forward to seeing Jacob's father Christmas day for dinner. I believe Jacob and Samuel enjoyed their time hunting geese so we could have a stuffed goose for Christmas. And all our canning from last summer had paid off: we would have a plentiful meal, even if the gifts were few.

Jacob's father came a few days before Christmas which surprised us, but he said he would like to go hunting with the men, and seemed cheered by the idea. We opened up the bedroom upstairs and installed a wood stove that had been in the barn. Jacob Sr. moved in downstairs and we moved back upstairs. He was very talkative, seemingly in need of some human interaction, and he was thin and his skin, pale, which made his blue eyes more prominent. I reckoned he'd been eating his own cooking. As we sat around the fireplace at night, the men talked and laughed about their hunting pursuits. They had been returning with two turkeys and a deer, but no geese yet.

Christmas Day was a joy. We women got up early and started with the baking – canned peach and apple pies, biscuits and cornbread. It looked like it would be turkey instead of a goose, but he was a fat one. Our dining room was full of the people we loved, and when we gave thanks it was meaningful. "God, don't break us asunder," I whispered.

Although we asked Jacob's father to stay on, he seemed restless, and left soon after New Year's. The cold continued after the first of the year. 1863: when would news come of the end of the war? There had been snowflakes and the wind was bitter-cold. We stayed bundled near the cook stove or the fireplace. Samuel and Jacob worked very short days, trying to stretch the work out.

The children were glad to see Jacob when he came home, and he played on the kitchen floor with them, since that was the warmest room in the house, even though they were constantly underfoot while I was cooking. These were blissful moments, so I didn't complain. And there were some blessings with less work: we got to spend more time with him, and he was not as tired as he had been. I wanted his time with us to be so happy that he didn't think about the future.

Our nights were as they were right after we were first married, loving each other with such need. It was a powerful thing, this loving. As a young girl, I never dreamed that love with a man could be like that. My ma and pa had such differences that they were at odds a lot, and I thought that was the way it was supposed to be.

One evening Jacob said, "You've become a good lover, Sally. Don't know how long I can stand to be away from you." I smiled inwardly, blushing in the darkness, thinking he had always been a good lover, a thought that made me want him all the more.

"What do you mean by 'become'?" I asked him. He laughed, and said maybe I didn't remember the first night we made love. Smiling, I told him I remembered all right and I thought he had turned into a pretty good lover, too, but he had a long way to go.

He let out a loud, hearty chuckle then, and said, "That's why I love you, girl. You give it right back to me."

With Ma not spending a lot of time doting on me, like she did Beatrice, she didn't give me any notions about what marriage or loving or childbirth would be like. And in the end that was a blessing because it left my heart open and my experiences belonged to me alone.

In March, 1863, the work ran out: finally, no more cotton. When the army or the Home Guard realized it we knew Jacob and Samuel would be sent to fight. And I worried the Atherton brothers would return to harass us and maybe attempt to arrest us all. I was prepared to die protecting my family, especially against that low-down, dirty, stinking skunk.

"Let's run to Florida now, Jacob. We can hide down there with your brother. There's not as much fighting there," I said.

"Sally, the Home Guard would hunt us down and kill Samuel and me. And no telling what they would do to you women," he said softly. "No, we will wait until they conscript us. And pray they don't realize we're not essential anymore. We'll go to work every day until they come for us."

Our agreement to not tell Jacob and Samuel about the Atherton brothers was our way of preventing trouble, even though it may not have been a good decision.

"Home Guard?" I asked, anxiously. "What do you know of the Home Guard?" He explained that they were a militia group, backed by the Confederacy, tasked with bringing in deserters and Union sympathizers. And they were not kind to the wives and families of deserters. Little did he know we would come to know the Home Guard better than we wanted.

When the Athertons knocked on our door, Jacob and Samuel were never home, which made me realize they had already passed by the gin. Many times I went to the door with the rifle under my arm, opening up to see Jeremy standing on my porch.

"What do you want?" I snarled one morning. Rondel always talked but never came off his horse.

"Why, we're just checking on you ladies to see that you're safe. No need for arms, Miz Winston."

"As you can see," I said. "We are fine."

"You are a fine lady, and that's a fact. Yore husband is a lucky man," he said.

"Do not come back here, Mr. Atherton," I said. By that time they had turned and started down the road toward Atlanta, probably to find other "helpless" women to harass.

Chapter 11   THE RIPPING OF MY HEART

On May 18th, 1863, we were celebrating Rebecca Ann's first and John's third birthday when we heard a knock at the door. As we looked at each other anxiously, Jacob rose and answered it.

"Mr. Jacob Henry Winston, Mr. Samuel Thomason, you are hereby ordered to present yourself for service in the Confederate army." The man's voice carried to where we were all sitting in the dining room. He handed Jacob a letter and turned and left. Jacob ripped it open and read it.

Our faces drained of color. Rebecca began to cry, with Loretta trying to comfort her. Both my babies came to me and tried to climb in my lap. Children always seemed to sense when trouble is in the air; parents can seldom hide it. Elizabeth left the table and fled to the kitchen. As Jacob and Samuel looked at each other, Samuel asked, "When?"

"Day after tomorrow, report in Atlanta." Jacob tried to be calm but his voice had a tremor.

Samuel said, "Loretta, get ready to go home. We have much to do. Sally, can Loretta and Elizabeth stay with you?"

"Of course," I answered, stunned. This was the culmination of all our fears. Finally, there would be no more anticipation of the knock on the door.

"It's not just the fact that I'll have to kill men for a cause I don't support, but I'm leaving you all vulnerable," Jacob said. "But we have made proper preparations and if you're careful, Sally, and do as I've said, everything will be fine. You should start for Florida soon."

Being strong was hard for me, but I wanted Jacob to have less to worry about. And, I was learning that pretending to be strong actually made me stronger.

"Don't worry about us. You have made good plans for us and we will be fine. Just come home to me," I said.

"Please don't wait for me before you leave. I don't know when I'll be back." He looked sad and I felt desperate.

"Will you be able to write?" I asked.

"I will when I can, and I'll think of you every day," he said, but was not able to speak further.

The next day was filled with preparations for the ladies and children, and for packing blankets and food in the men's packs. Jacob went over the plans again - if there were blue coats in the house, hide the children and yourselves in the false room. Don't forget the gold coins under the feed bin, and hitch up the four draft horses to the wagon. He spent the morning splitting wood for us. While firing up the smokehouse and hanging meat in it, he whistled a tune, trying to appear happy for the boys and me. I followed him around like a lost puppy and my children followed me around like two lost puppies. I realized I simply had to be courageous for my family so they could not know how truly scared I was. The boys and I went to the parlor and I read to them, and we sang songs. As much as I wanted to cry as I lay in Jacob's arms that night, I would not.

"Jacob, I feel it in my bones - you *will* come back, wherever our home is," I said. He laughed and said, "That's my Sally. I'll find you." I kissed the salty tears on his cheeks and eyes, and I knew God had truly blessed me with this man. No matter what might happen, I had something that many women would never know.

He left before sunrise. He kissed the sleeping children, and I followed him to the barn to saddle his horse. When he finished, he turned to me, touched my hair, and said, "Just the vision of you this morning, in your gown and bare feet, will bring me back." He smiled at me as if he were just going for a short ride. We held each other and I didn't want to let him go, but finally, he mounted his horse and rode away to meet Samuel. I watched his back until I could no longer see his image, the light of day just breaking golden; only the hoof prints remained on the clay road. I pressed my bare feet in the Georgia red soil, tracing the horseshoe print with my toes. I thought I had known what pain was like before, but I hadn't. Prior pain had only been a shadow of this new huge hole in my heart. No sooner was Jacob out of sight when Rondel Atherton rode up behind me, scaring me out of my wits. I crossed my arms over my breasts as he was staring at me.

"You look lovely this morning, Miz Winston. I reckon you won't be so high and mighty with your man gone," he jeered.

"Don't you step foot on my property or I will report you to the authorities," I practically growled.

He laughed bitterly and spurred his horse down the road, following Jacob's trail. That man scalded me but I knew he was as much a threat as any Yankee soldier.

Rondel and his brother rode by our house many times, sometimes pausing on the road, as we looked out the window at them. Once Rondel pointed his finger at me and pretended to shoot. They *were* the enemy but it wasn't like the Yankees. If we shot one of them, we would be hanged and yet, they continued to bedevil us. I felt especially vulnerable now with our men gone.

Elizabeth, Loretta and Rebecca Ann moved into the upstairs bedrooms. Each person had a window to be watchful of, in case there were blue coats or looters roaming around. And always alert, we were never capable of relaxing. It was tiresome.

In July, 1863, the hottest month of the year, when I was rising one morning, I looked down to see someone in my garden. As he was pulling corn and eating it right off the cob, I noticed his gray uniform. I grabbed my rifle that I kept by the bed and rushed down the stairs. The banging of the back screen door caused the soldier to look up right at the barrel of my gun pointed directly at his chest. He stood there with handfuls of corn but no rifle drawn.

"Drop that corn!" I yelled.

Dropping the corn, he backed up a step or two. "Sorry, ma'am. Just hungry. We been walking for days from Tennessee."

"You could've asked, rather than steal from your own people. We've women and children to feed here." I tried to keep my voice calm but it was not.

"Sorry. Don't shoot," he pleaded.

"Take the corn then," I yelled. "Get on out of here and don't come back. You're supposed to be *protecting* women and children, but you're taking food from our mouths."

He grabbed up the shucks and ran toward the front of the house. I knew it would not be the last we would see of this, and I couldn't shoot them all. And this soldier was supposedly fighting for me and my family. I wondered if Jacob would steal to eat or if I would have to.

Elizabeth and I decided we would can as much as possible in the next few days and hide it in the false room, along with the smoked hams. After all, if the enemy found us, what would the food matter? In our minds, we assumed they would kill us all.

☼

In October, 1863, I received a badly crumpled letter from Jacob, delivered by a Confederate soldier, along with one from Samuel for Loretta and Elizabeth:

"Dear sweet Sally,

My thoughts are of you night and day. I can't forget your image the morning I left, standing in the morning dew. It's what keeps me going. I know every day that passes brings us closer to the end of this dreadful war. What a senseless thing is war. I implore you to leave and head to Florida. I know the battles will move southward, and I don't want you and the family in the midst of it. We are fighting in eastern Tennessee at this time, but we are being pushed south daily. Kiss the boys for me and don't forget me.

Jacob, your husband."

Forget him? Could I forget my own left arm? He was that much a part of me. There was no other man like Jacob. There was no address so I couldn't write back to him. But I folded that letter and put it in my bodice, next to my heart, reading his words at least once a day.

As winter started to settled in, we saw more people, mostly Rebel soldiers, going through our garden and smokehouse. As long as they didn't try to enter the house, I decided I wouldn't shoot at them. We had gathered enough food to make it through the winter. I was still nursing my Harry, and Loretta continued to nurse Rebecca. Harry was close to two years old, but my milk seemed to keep him strong. John was very healthy, but was an active youngster so I worried about keeping him quiet should we have to hide.

No mail came for Elizabeth from Ernest Watkins, her husband. Loretta told me she wasn't sure he could write, and we both thought he might be dead. We tried to stay busy during the day so that we could sleep at night. There were always chores to do, and Elizabeth and I had to go farther and farther from the house to gather wood in the wagon. We left the three babies with Loretta, which made me very nervous, so we usually hurried.

"Elizabeth, I want you to know how much you mean to me," I said to her one day as we were pulling the wagon back to the house. "You're closer than a sister. You work as hard as I do and I love you."

She gave me a shy smile. "Mrs. Winston, I can't tell you how that makes me feel."

"Please don't call me Mrs. Winston anymore," I said. "It's Sally. You must know how Jacob and I feel about you. You're like family. Whatever happens, we will take care of each other."

She smiled again, and I could tell she was surprised, but she didn't know I came from parents like hers; only my ma was raised to be a lady. Although I loved Loretta, she was just learning how to laugh, and there was so much she didn't know how to do. She couldn't do hard labor like Elizabeth and me. The time would come when she would have to. For now, she had to watch the children.

Christmas was a sad state of affairs that year, 1863. No husbands, no Jacob Sr., scarce food, and freezing cold weather, but we managed to have a celebration for the children. I was thankful for Loretta and Elizabeth. They made the holiday warm, as we had such love for each other, and we laughed a lot in spite of our plight, enjoying each other's company. And our harmonies were getting better when we sang Christmas hymns.

As we were singing on Christmas Eve, there came a noise at the front door, a light rapping. I ran to the door and opened it, foolishly, hoping it would be Jacob. A horse stood in the front yard, his reins hanging loose to the ground. It was when I was backing up, to slam and lock the door, that I heard a groan and looked down to see Jacob Sr. crumpled on the porch. We dragged his limp body in and put him in the bed downstairs. Being lanky, it took all three of us to get him into bed. His face was red and he was hot with a fever. Elizabeth mixed up a poultice and rubbed it on his chest, and we took turns sitting with him through the night, but his fever continued to blaze the next morning.

"Do you think he's dying?" Loretta asked Elizabeth tearfully.

"He's mighty sick. We've got to get the fever down. I'll make up more herbs," she said.

"How did he ride all that way in the cold, sick as he is?" I asked.

"He's stubborn," Loretta said.

We watched over him for three days, with Elizabeth doctoring him constantly. Finally, on the third day he opened his eyes, bluer than the sky.

"What the gol-durned devil am I doing here?" he asked.

"You've been very sick, Mr. Winston," Elizabeth said.

"Where's my clothes?" he asked.

"They were wet from the rain and we had to take them off," Elizabeth smiled meekly. Blushing, he pulled the covers up to his neck. As he smiled, he said, "Thank you, sweet ladies, for taking care of me, but I'll be needing my clothes. I have to be getting back. There's looting going on in Atlanta and I know you need me here. Feel like a man, drawn and quartered."

"You'll not be leaving until you're well," I said. I turned and left him alone with Elizabeth.

We hid his clothes, and in order that he wouldn't leave, I turned his horse loose in the pasture. If he was as stubborn as everyone said, I figured he'd try to slip off from us.

"Are you holding me prisoner, Miss Sally?" he smiled one morning.

"You surely do not look like a prisoner, with your wait staff and all," I answered.

"It's the truth, and all beautiful," he said. What a charmer.

Jacob Sr. did not run away and he recovered and continued to improve under Elizabeth's care. When he was stronger, he cut firewood and worked around the barn. At that point, I felt he was healthy enough to leave, but he seemed to enjoy our company. He was starting to feel the pull of his responsibilities, however, so he left after being with us for about a month. And we all missed him. He implored us to pack up and go with him so he could help protect us, but I told him we were waiting for Jacob and Samuel to return. Elizabeth told me later that he had told her he was lonely for family at Christmas-time and didn't realize how sick he was. I guessed not, or that there was a *war* going on.

When Elizabeth and I stood in the road watching him ride away, she said, "That is one handsome man." I know my mouth popped open and my eyes widened, but she just smiled that shy smile and walked back toward the house, leaving me standing in the middle of the road, totally dismayed.

Our neighbors were keeping to themselves. Everyone was worried about getting caught out in the open. There were rumors that the Yankees had broken through Southern lines and would be coming our way. The only reason we went out at all was to gather wood, milk the cow, and feed the animals. Loretta kept the children upstairs and watched the windows closely in case she had to hide the babies while Elizabeth and I were out working.

One night in March of 1864, ten months since Jacob and Samuel had left, we were sleeping upstairs. I had my babies in bed with me when I heard a creak on the stairs. The rifle was cold in my hands as I started toward the door. And my heart was racing as I cocked that gun.

"Sally, it's me, Jacob," he whispered.

"Oh my God, Jacob Winston, I almost shot your head off," I gasped. "Oh my goodness, you're home."

I unloaded the rifle, laid it inside the bedroom door frame, and rushed to him. He took my hand and led me down the stairs and into the bedroom, taking his clothes off and kissing me all at the same time. His pa was right: he was a surprising man, showing up in the middle of the war on my doorstep. I couldn't get enough of him, kissing his face and neck. We were starved for each other.

As we lay spent, the sun came up, but we loved more before the house awoke. I didn't ask him any questions until we were up and I had our weak coffee boiling.

Where was Samuel? He didn't know since they'd been separated.

How long could he stay? He had to leave right away.

Where was he going? Atlanta first, to join up with his company.

Was he hurt? Only his heart.

"I have loaded two Spencer repeater rifles in the wagon, along with some ammo. You can fire seven shots in 30 seconds with that rifle. Keep them loaded but away from the children. I took them off the enemy. The enemy," he repeated, sadly.

And then John ran into the room and up in his father's arms with lots of hugs and kisses. When I went upstairs to get Harry, he was sitting in the middle of the bed with his arms held out to me.

"Daddy," he said. I don't know how he knew.

Loretta cried softly from joy at seeing her brother and in sadness with no news of Samuel. We all cried when Jacob left, but I was thankful for one night with that man. "God keep him safe," I whispered, as he rode his horse toward Atlanta. And once again, I watched his back until I could see him no longer. He had said he wanted to check on his father and try to talk him into coming to our house, saying he was such a stubborn man. I said I knew *that*, but I didn't think he would leave his home because he was guarding it against Yankees and looters.

I didn't tell Jacob what a foolish thing his father had done – riding from Atlanta to our home in the middle of a war, with a blazing hot fever. Jacob Sr. could tell that story, which I didn't think he would. Keeping my eye out for Mr. Atherton, I rushed toward the house. Only this time, I carried my pistol.

When I got close to the back door, I was thinking dreamily about Jacob and our lovemaking, when suddenly I realized that a baby could come of our actions. As panic swept over me, I raced to the stream and without taking my clothes off, throwing my pistol and shoes to the ground, I ran into the water. Desperately, I began to wash my private parts, swooshing the water around me. I submerged my whole body, constantly trying to remove any of Jacob's seed. Not that I didn't love him: loved him beyond all reason, but "Never again," echoed in my mind.

Dragging myself and my water-logged dress from the water, I lay in the grass and prayed to God to deliver me from a child. But I knew God had more important prayers to answer, especially with men dying in the War. So, I wearily lugged myself and my heavy clothes back home.

Loretta came running into my bedroom early one morning, a few days after Jacob left, a horrified look on her face. "The Yankees are here," she whispered hoarsely. I gathered my boys up, she ran for Rebecca, and we called Elizabeth as we were running toward the false room. The door closed behind us, and each of us had a baby to hold. I could hear my heart pumping in my ears.

John wasn't happy and wanted to talk, but I held him close to me and whispered into his ear that he must be quiet because we were in trouble. Wiggling some, he then fell asleep because it was so warm in that room with six people. The other children were soon asleep also.

When first Jacob had built this room I thought it was so ingenious, but when we were in it, it seemed so confining. He did think to put a small air vent at the bottom of the wall. The room was about three feet wide and ten feet long, and most of our food was stored toward the area closest to the front of the house. It left very little space for three grown women, sitting cross-legged, each holding a child. The next time I planned to throw some pillows in it for our comfort. At least the door to the false-room was not visible from the bedroom itself as it was made of bead-board and looked just like the other walls in the room.

Suddenly, there was the sound of glass breaking downstairs and then footsteps coming up the stairs. Our beds were unmade so the enemy would know we were close. My chest was so tight I felt it might explode. We were aware of doors opening and things being thrown around. Thank God the children were asleep. The sound of boots coming down the hall and into the bedroom, where the false room was, was so frightening. The boots walked around the room slowly and then left. I imagined he was feeling the bed to see how warm it was.

Waiting until it was finally quiet in the house, we opened the door and breathed fresh air. It was so hot in that room we were all sweating.

As Loretta crawled out on her hands and knees, she whispered, "Meeting up with the Yankees might be preferable to sitting in that hot, cramped cell." We smiled nervously in agreement as we tiptoed around the upstairs, glancing out the windows.

They had gone but when we went downstairs, there was a mess to clean up. Papers from the canvas business were thrown all over the house. What were they looking for? Money, I reckoned. As we began to clean up the house, I imagined we would not sleep well after this. Of course, the cowardly Athertons were nowhere to be found.

We did, however, continue our quilting. Each time we sat down, needles in hand, the routine was like a wellspring of emotions that allowed us to divulge our most inner secrets. For instance, Loretta told us one day she felt wicked when she and Samuel made love, which embarrassed Elizabeth.

I said, "I think it's wonderful, as long as a person is married." I didn't know if Loretta was trying to wrangle some of my secrets out of me, but I was willing to give it by then.

Elizabeth said, "My time with Ernest was short, but I can't forget it."

"I was taught that if you're a lady, you shouldn't enjoy the act, but I do with Samuel. So does that mean I'm not a lady?" Loretta asked. Elizabeth reddened again.

"Well, I'm a lady and I like nothing better than loving Jacob. I live for our nights together," I said, boldly.

Loretta and Elizabeth both blushed. I guess I should have blushed too, but the truth was out and I was glad to say it. This conversation was obviously hard on Elizabeth, whose husband had not been seen since the beginning of the war.

"Sally, as always, I love your honesty, and you make me feel better about my feelings," Loretta said. "After all, look at those sweet babies we have. How else could we have had them?"

I smiled and touched the top of Harry's head as he crawled on the floor. I knew every time we looked at those quilts, we would remember these conversations. Each stitch we took made our love for each other stronger. I felt sorry for women who didn't have companions to talk with, to make their lives easier. Lord knows, in these trying times, we needed each other.

In late April, 1864, a month or so after Jacob's visit, I started feeling the baby sickness again, and I was really feeling low, knowing my bath in the stream didn't do the trick. What kind of war-torn world was I bringing this child into? I didn't want to get up in the mornings I was so nauseated and I cried. My body had betrayed me. Even if I wanted to go to Florida, which I didn't, I couldn't go now. How could I drive a team of four draft horses and a wagon to Florida, feeling this sick? But I also didn't want to leave because Jacob might come back. And so I just thought about our last hours together so that I wouldn't think about the awful predicament we were in.

Thankfully, Loretta began to be able to help out a little more. She would get up early and make mint tea that she and Elizabeth had gathered while they were picking up firewood. I wasn't sure Loretta was up to the task of gathering wood, but Elizabeth said she did well. The mint settled my stomach so that I could get up long enough to dress, if only to make it downstairs, losing the tea over the back porch bannister. Breakfast was unthinkable. So much work to do and I could hardly walk. So I became the keeper of the children, and Loretta and Elizabeth did the hard work. The illness would pass I knew, but I desperately wanted to be up and about.

We had to hide several more times in the next months and by that time, it was extremely hot. I was worried we might die in there if we had to stay too long. Making it even worse, I could not always hold down my food and then the stench was awful. But sometimes the Yankees didn't even come inside. They just took everything that was edible, including the milk cow. Either the Yanks didn't want to expend the time looking for the horses, or they didn't need them. I knew we would have to leave soon. Elizabeth said she was taking oats to the horses in the back pasture; they were looking fat and sassy and would be a little hard for us to catch.

By June, 1864, we were running out of food ourselves. There was no need to plant because everything would be stolen. We had two smoked hams left that we needed for our trip in case Jacob didn't come back. Even though I prayed he would return, my prayers were not always answered. Our canned goods were running low, too. Elizabeth had been wandering in the woods, looking for mushrooms and dandelion greens and other things that grew in the wild. I thought about hunting for a deer, but I didn't want to draw any attention by using the rifle. Our bodies were all a lot thinner, except for Rebecca, who was two years old and still nursing. I was wishing I had continued to nurse Harry because then I wouldn't have been in the family way.

My body was adjusting, and I usually made it to mid-morning before I lost my breakfast. Since I was feeling stronger, one day Elizabeth and I decided to set out some traps for squirrels so that we could have some meat for stews. The children were left with Loretta, and we carried the traps past the back pasture, down to the little stream there. As we were walking in the warm sunshine, Elizabeth began to sing softly.

"I'll twine 'mid the ringlets of my raven black hair
The lilies so pale and the roses so fair,
The myrtles so bright with an emerald dew
And the pale aronatus with eyes of bright blue."

I wanted to shush her, but her voice was so sweet and pure. It was a tune my pa used to hum while he was working back on our farm. Being far enough from the road that I decided I didn't think anyone could hear, I joined in and tried to sing harmony, though I couldn't sing like Elizabeth.

"I will dance I will sing and my laugh will be gay
I will charm every heart in each crowd I survey
When I woke from my dreaming my idols were clay
All portion of love had all blown away"

"He taught me to love him and promised to love
And to cherish me over all others above

How my heart is now wondering no misery can tell
He's left me no warning no words of farewell"

"He taught me to love him and called me his flower
That was blooming to cheer him through life's dreary hour
How I long to see him and regret the dark hour
He's gone and neglected his pale wildwood flower."

"Ain't it so," she said. "Our men are gone." We hugged each other and such a moment of joy passed over me. I knew it was fleeting, so I relished it.

Elizabeth said, "I would love a bath, and I brought a bar of soap. Wouldn't that be glorious?" She reached in her pocket and produced a small piece of tallow soap, her eyes flashing; we were as happy as schoolgirls.

The idea of a bath in a cool stream in the heat of the day sounded like heaven to me. We undressed down to our chemises and pantaloons. When I pulled my pantaloons down, I could see that my belly was starting to grow already. As we moved to the deeper part of the stream, I removed all my clothes, which I'd never done before in broad daylight, but I wanted to wash my clothes, too. Elizabeth pretended to be scandalized but she did the same. We washed each other's hair and backs. She had such a pretty body, with large breasts. My breasts were growing some since I was in the family way. I looked down at my breasts, and then I looked at hers, and we began to laugh. Floating on our backs, we looked up at the sky, so clear of clouds. We splashed water at each other and forgot all our cares. We were so foolish!

"Why hullo, ladies, your melodious voices drifted to me on the wind," a man's voice said. Spinning around, we confronted Rondel Atherton kneeling in the grass at the edge of the pool.

"But I never dreamed I'd come on two naked ladies, just waiting fur me." Covering our breasts with our hands, we backed away from him.

"Come here, you beauty," he said to Elizabeth, and she moved to the far side of the pool. I looked around to see if Jeremy was with him, but he seemed to be alone. Elizabeth looked terrified and I felt the same.

"You are on my property, Mr. Atherton," I said, with as much authority as I could muster, being naked.

He laughed without looking in my direction, and sat down and took off his boots. "Come on now, Elizabeth. This won't take long," he said. She was backed up against a boulder on the far side of the pool, as far as she could go.

"Rondel, please don't. Ernest will kill you," she pleaded.

After he took his boots and shirt off, he then stood up to take his pants off, and he laid his rifle on the ground. When he had stripped down totally nude, he entered the water toward Elizabeth and I could see he meant business, moving easier through the stream than on land. She screamed when he touched her and as he was grabbing at her breasts and kissing her mouth, I stretched to reach for the barrel of his gun. The water slowed my movement, but he was paying no attention to me. The rifle was cold against my bare body, and I was shaking so badly I wasn't sure I could aim the gun.

"Let her go, Rondel," I screeched, my voice sounding like someone else's, as I cocked the rifle.

As he turned to me, he grabbed the gun and tried to pull it from my hands. Quickly though, without thinking, I pulled the trigger and blew him to kingdom come. And in that moment, I was forever changed, the moment I took another's life. Elizabeth and I had blood and brains all over us. While washing ourselves, we submerged our whole bodies, hoping to wash away the horror as well as the blood.

Shuddering as we scrubbed, I could only thank God his rifle was loaded. Elizabeth was on the verge of hysteria. She repeatedly said, "I knew him. I knew Rondel."

"Help me pull his body out of the water and behind this tree over here. Hurry, someone could have heard that shot," I murmured, hoarsely.

As she was shaking all over, her eyes were beginning to glaze. I dug a shallow grave in the soft dirt and leaves with my hands and rolled his body, clothes, and rifle into it. I guided Elizabeth to her dress, watching the blood flow downstream, where I hoped it would dilute and not be seen.

"Be quick! Get dressed," I whispered, but she was going into shock. I had to half-way dress myself and her, too. When I dragged her back to the house, scantily-clad, Loretta greeted us at the back door.

"What in God's name?" Loretta whispered.

"Help me with her, Loretta," I pleaded, my body quivering all over.

If it hadn't been for Elizabeth needing me so much, I might have gone into shock myself. I wasn't yet 20 years old, and I'd never killed another human being. When I thought back on it, it seemed unreal that I had pulled the trigger, but I had, and I knew he hadn't thought I could use that rifle. He might have harmed us both and maybe killed us, thinking we were helpless women. I knew we could never drop our guard again, what with Jeremy being his brother who would come looking for him. And I could hang for this crime!

Since we were dripping wet, Loretta brought towels for us to dry off. I told her, "Don't ask right now." After boiling some Valerian root for Elizabeth and putting her to bed, I told Loretta the whole story. Her first question was: Did he defile her? "I don't believe so," I said.

"Goddamned Atherton! Sally Ann, you are a stalwart woman. Don't you go feeling bad about this because he deserved what he got! You protect us all. I can't believe you shot him." She hugged me, but I didn't feel good about killing a man. However, we were on the battlefront now. I couldn't believe I'd shot him either. God in heaven, what had we become? And, I really had to admit I didn't know Loretta had that kind of language in her.

The scene in that stream would come back to haunt me many times in my life. I would spend countless sleepless nights feeling remorse at having taken a life. The sight of the blood and brains on Elizabeth and me would come to me in dreams, and I would awaken, sweating and shaking. And the fear of being caught and hanged followed me for a long time in my life. I couldn't imagine how Jacob could go to war and kill people, many people.

Elizabeth was slowly recovering but I wasn't sure she remembered exactly what had happened, so we didn't talk about it. I thought it probably would come back to her at some point. In the meantime, I knew my not sleeping well wasn't good for the baby.

We could smell fires burning, and looking south, we could see our neighbor's house burning. I walked down the road aways, but I didn't want to go too far from home. It seemed there were battles going on because we heard gunfire. I could only hope that if Jeremy found Rondel's body, he would think he was killed by the Yankees. But somehow, I doubted it.

In early September, 1864, we were caught off guard again by a group of Yankees riding past our house. An officer dressed in a dark blue uniform rode to the barn where we were working and told us we would have to vacate the premises. He was certainly not the monster I had conjured; in fact, he was clean-shaven and handsome.

"This is my home. I'll not leave it," I said.

"Ma'am, our orders are to burn all the houses and outbuildings. I would recommend your evacuation. I will give you 24 hours," the officer said.

"Burn our houses? What kind of war is this? We have babies," I yelled.

"It's my orders. Please be out," he said, as he turned and rode away.

"Well, at least he didn't burn it around us," I told Loretta. But we knew we had to leave.

I took Elizabeth by the hand and said, "You've got to help me, Elizabeth. We have to bring in the draft horses and put them in the barn." She was still not herself, staring at me with a glassy look and I felt desperate. Knowing I couldn't do it alone, I grabbed her by the shoulders and shook her, yelling, "Elizabeth! You have to help me, or we'll all die."

Suddenly she began to cry and followed me to the barn to get the halters. On the path to the back pasture she said, "I know you saved me, Sally. I'm remembering. I'll help you." I was noticing that Elizabeth sometimes was frozen with fear, both before the shooting and after, causing her to develop a melancholy nature afterward, so unlike her sunny disposition. I had always been curious as to what had happened to her that caused this behavior. Right then, she sat down on a tree stump and told me a story – a hair-raising story - that explained everything. She began, "My mama was half Cherokee Indian, a half-breed." I had to admit, I was surprised. Elizabeth had dark hair and eyes, but she had a sprinkling of freckles across her nose and cheeks.

"You must never tell Loretta because she might not love Pa anymore if she knew," she said.

"You should give her more credit than that, Elizabeth," I remarked.

"My mother's pa was a Scotsman, red-headed and mean as the devil himself. Ma had three brothers who were hooligans. Her pa sent her brothers after her when I was five years old. They said their ma had died and she was needed at home. My pa held a rifle on them outside our cabin, and Ma ran in between them just as they aimed at him. Of course, she took the bullets. Once the brothers realized what they had done, they turned their horses and fled. Pa took Ma inside the cabin and laid her on the bed. And he left me alone with her for two days. When he returned, I was in a bad state. I don't remember it but he has told me the story many times. He has cried and said he was sorry so often, and I forgave him. He *had* to go after her killers. But he never found them, which I'm glad of, because he would be dead also. But I do believe it all affects me sometimes even though I don't remember it."

I put my arm around her shoulder and said I understood, but truly, how could I understand something that awful, not having experienced it? I knew then that Loretta would never hear about Samuel's first wife from me or Elizabeth.

It took us hours to round up those big horses. They had been free too long, but we finally had all four in the barn. Two of them were grey geldings, and I planned that they would be the front two horses as they were older. There was a black mare and a smaller chestnut mare: not very well matched but they were strong, and I knew they were well trained, even though they would have to be disciplined to pulling again. Getting the rigging on would be tough, but Elizabeth convinced me she and I could do it. They were so much bigger than we were. Elizabeth was fast and had the halters on them before they knew what had happened. I couldn't run fast, but I helped get the halters on once she had caught their manes. We were exhausted when we got back to the house. When Loretta saw Elizabeth, she gave me a glance, and I knew she realized Elizabeth was back with us in spirit. Maybe we should have been out chasing horses sooner if that's what it took.

At around midnight, I went to the barn with an oil lamp. Grabbing a shovel, I tried to move that heavy feed bin out of the way. Finally, I used the shovel as a lever to swing the bin around so I could get under it to dig up the strongbox. But the shovel resisted as I stuck it into the ground and began to move the dirt. Although I knew I shouldn't be doing this alone because it might hurt me or the baby, I didn't want Elizabeth or Loretta to know what I was doing. If we were robbed, I didn't want to take the chance that they might give up that information.

When I got on my hands and knees and dug with my fingers, I could feel the box and it felt heavy. Looping a rope through a handle on one end, I pulled it out of the ground with some effort. My body was panting for breath at that point, so I sat for a while on a hay pile. When I recovered, I dragged it to the wagon, carrying the light. Holding on to the ends of the rope, I climbed into the back of the wagon and began hauling the strongbox up over the side. It made a loud noise when it finally landed in the bed of the wagon. Again, I had to sit down for a minute to get my breath.

By the time I got it stowed away in the secret storage box, I was exhausted and felt I had pulled something loose in my belly. As I hurried back to the house, the light from the lantern bounced off the ground, like hundreds of lightning bugs, and when I stepped into the kitchen, Loretta and Elizabeth were standing in the doorway with a candle held high. They gasped at my appearance, and I looked down at my gown and my hands, which were covered in red dirt.

"I was pulling onions," I said. Loretta said, "Well, I see you aren't going to tell us what you were doing, so we won't ask." They turned and headed back up the stairs. I was a nasty mess and washed up the best I could. I knew they weren't buying my story.

Chapter 12 *SMOLDERING ASHES*

By sunup the next morning, we were loaded and had the horses hitched to the wagon, which had been a freight wagon, used to pick up raw cotton and deliver ginned cotton. Made of wood, it was quite heavy, and I hoped we didn't need more horses to pull it. If we didn't have too many hills, maybe the four horses would do the job. There was no other choice anyway. The inside was loaded with bedding, canvas, extra wheels, rifles, cooking pots, utensils and food. Since there was very little room to sit, most everything would have to be unloaded every night if we were to sleep in there. The wagon was slow and cumbersome, but it was what we needed to carry our family to Florida. We took only the bare necessities; all our furniture and possessions were left to be burned.

As I drove down the driveway toward the main road, I looked up at our beautiful house. I was so glad not to stay to see it burned to the ground. I had come to this place a simple farm girl with no secrets at all and now I was leaving feeling full-up with secrets, some I shared with the women in my life and some only I knew.

All along the road, houses were smoldering. Samuel's cottage was gone; only ashes remained. Many of our neighbors' houses were piles of burned wood, unrecognizable. If the Yankees were trying to break our will, they had done it. How could people fight this kind of battle?

The horses were snorting, tossing their heads and pulling hard on the reins, wanting to be free of that loaded wagon, and eventually Elizabeth had to take the reins from me, as driving was straining every inch of my body, especially my neck and shoulders. She was strong and actually was a better driver than I was, even when I wasn't with child. But I didn't think she could handle those horses all the way to Florida. The farther along the road we went though, the more they calmed down, probably tiring, I thought. "It'll get easier," she shouted to me.

Jeremy Atherton rode up alongside, yelling, "Have you seen Rondel? He's been missing for days now, his stallion came home alone." His blonde hair was blowing in the wind as his horse galloped beside us.

"We haven't," I shouted back. It was true – we hadn't seen him since I shot and killed him. Jeremy glared at us and a shiver ran down my spine, knowing he would come after us if ever he found his brother's body.

He pulled his horse back, aware he could go no farther without being captured. But it would not be the last we would see of him. As Elizabeth wrestled with the reins, tears ran down her cheeks.

"He'll come for us," she whispered. I patted her on the back but I knew she was right.

There were countless wagons and people on the road to Atlanta, most headed to Macon and beyond. Everyone figured the Yankees wouldn't head that far south. The rumor was that the capital, Milledgeville, was to be burned down. Surely, that would be the end of the war for Georgia. Bluecoats were everywhere.

It took four hours to get to Jacob Sr.'s house, which was still standing, and we gasped a sigh of relief. Loretta started calling her father's name, and he came around the corner of the house with his rifle aimed at us.

"Lord God," he whispered. It took some talking to get him to leave with us, but we convinced him that we needed his protection; and we surely did. Jacob Sr. wanted everyone to stay in Atlanta at his house, but I told him Jacob wanted us to go to Florida and that's where we were headed.

"Elizabeth is plumb played out, just from the ride here. We need you badly," I said.

He answered, "Hell, I'm acting like a fool to be guarding a property that the Yankees will probably torch anyway." He released the few animals he had left. The servants were long gone. Our procession must have been a sight: three women, one large with child, three small children, and an old man.

Before we left his house, we fed the babies and ourselves. I was already tired, and we had a long way to go, not knowing what lay ahead. It was such a worrisome time, but when hadn't it been a worrisome time lately? It seemed our lives had been in turmoil for so many years, but we just had to keep putting one foot ahead of the other.

Initially as we were traveling, I walked behind the wagon with John so he would burn up some of his energy. The other children mostly stayed in the wagon with Loretta. Jacob Sr. did most of the driving, with Elizabeth helping some. The horses had to keep getting accustomed to pulling again as they hadn't done it in so long. Our traveling was slow with all kinds of people on the road – rich white people, with their slaves in tow, poor white folks dragging their children along, many wailing, adults and youngsters alike. My thoughts were of Sodom and Gomorrah from the Bible.

Word was General Sherman was evacuating Atlanta, so he could burn and level it. There were times when we were stopped completely. The horses pawed the ground, anxious to move forward, but there was nowhere for us to go. I said I thought we might look for some back roads to get away from the traffic. Even though we had brought two big water barrels for the horses, that supply wouldn't last long; a water source would be needed.

John and I rode on the back of the wagon when the throngs of refugees pressed us. With all the excitement, he was talking up a blue streak, his eyes large, watching all the sea of people around us, some crowding a little too close for my liking. And when he looked up at me with those blue eyes, I could see Jacob in him, and my heart ached. I had no idea where Jacob was, or even if he was still alive. But I knew one thing: I would get our children to safety if it was the last thing I did. And sometimes, I believed it would be the last thing I did.

Rifle fire could be heard in the distance, and as we looked back toward Atlanta we could see smoke and flames. Jacob Sr. felt we should find an alternate route also. He thought that with so many people on that road, should the Union army attack, we could all be killed. I said, "You'll have to guide us as I don't know where we're going." Fortunately, having hunted in this area, he knew the lay of the land.

"There's a nice open meadow off this road where we can camp tonight, but it's pretty far off the road," he said. Our journey had taken us only about five miles outside of Atlanta. At this rate, it would take us a year to get to Alachua County. I was exhausted and the children were hungry and tired.

"Lead on," I said, and he did. Several other wagons turned off with us, but they kept going when we stopped for the night. Hungry and bone-tired, we gathered wood for the fire. I knew we would have to sleep close to the fire to keep warm from the damp night air. There was no one else around, for which we were grateful. It was dark by the time we warmed up the ham and canned corn and boiled some coffee.

As we sat around the burning logs, Jacob Sr. said, "Okay, ladies, from now on you can call me Jake. I'm sick of being called Jacob Sr., and I have some things to go over with you. First, this is a perilous journey, especially for three babies and a woman in the family way. Second, we must stay together. I expect there'll be trouble from the Yankees around Macon, 'cause that's where a lot of the supplies come from. I'm proposing we head to the Flint River and follow it as best we can, as far as we can. There should be a stagecoach trail we can follow, and we'll have water for the horses there - and ourselves if we boil it. I can do some hunting if I'm sure there ain't no Yankees close." He smiled at all of us and asked, "Does that meet with your approval, Mrs. Winston?"

"Yessir, Mr. Jake. You're our leader," I said, feeling relieved to share the responsibility. It seemed to me by now I had been taking care of folks my whole life. And Jake did seem to want to take care of us, grinning at the idea. My realization was that this was a big adventure for him, giving him new life. Maybe it was my youth, but it seemed to be an adventure for me, too – part exhilarating and part terrifying - what with me carrying a baby in my belly and two toddlers to worry about and provide for. But I thanked God for my father-in-law.

When we readied ourselves for the night, and had spread the

canvas on the ground, each of the women took a baby to sleep with. I placed Harry closest to the fire, and we pulled quilts on top of us. Jake said he would keep the fire going. I pulled the quilts over our heads and tucked the baby around my belly, and he was asleep instantly. I was not far behind. When I awoke sometime later, there were night sounds. Not since I was a girl on the farm had I slept outside, and it had always been exciting, a little scary. Jake put more wood on the fire, and I fell asleep again.

I awoke to the smell of boiling coffee, from Jake's supplies, and it was the sweetest aroma on earth. My body was surprisingly rested. John was running around the camp, with Loretta and Rebecca still asleep, Elizabeth and Harry just opening their eyes.

"Jake, how far is it to the river?" I asked.

"I believe if we stay on this trail, it will only be a few miles," he said. "The problem is the going is gonna be tough along the river: trails in some places, some not. But it's better to stay away from the main road." We all agreed.

Jake grumbled as we reloaded our supplies, including the extra wheels. He began setting items aside in a little pile, stating, "Ladies, we've got to lighten our load." We all had items he threw away that we thought were necessary. Loretta looked longingly at some of her beautiful dresses. In the end, the pile stood about four feet high. "Less work, less weight," he said.

But we were not happy to leave behind our valuables – and even some pots and pans. When Jake's back was turned, I grabbed up two of the dresses and stuffed them between the wheels, which went back in the wagon. Loretta grinned at me as if we were co-conspirators: we were, in many things.

If we camped by the river that evening, I was hoping to have a bath, even though I was remembering our last bath in a stream. Someone would have to keep watch while we bathed. There was Georgia red clay in my shoes and grit in my teeth. My hair looked like I was a redhead. That thought of a bath kept me going all day. I would take my boys to the river and wash our hair and try to get some of the dust off all of us. If Jacob could only have seen us, I think he would've been proud of his well-laid plans. "Where is he now?" I kept wondering. I did glance back down the trail every now and then, hoping not to see that blonde head of Jeremy Atherton's.

Reaching the river by mid-morning, we brought water up in buckets for the horses to drink, so we wouldn't have to unhitch them. Our plan was to make ten miles a day, but I thought it would get faster once we got the hang of traveling. John was getting tired of walking with me, so I put him in the wagon with Loretta. The trail was wide and good for our excursion, which was actually also worrisome because other folks would be using it, too. It was a desperate time for refugees who were hungry and on the move. I kept the handgun in my dress pocket.

Elizabeth walked with me sometimes when Jake was driving. She and I acted as if we hadn't lost most everything and were not cast out like the Israelites, talking about the new house where we would live in Florida and the parties we would have when Jacob, Samuel, and Ernest came home.

"I don't know how Ernest will find me," she said one morning. "I haven't heard from him since we married, and I can't even remember what he looks like. Maybe I'll remarry if he's dead."

I thought of Jacob's face, and I could see it clear as a bell: those blue eyes, that smile. I didn't say this to Elizabeth, but I did wonder about her wifely devotion.

"At the end of the day I'm taking the boys to the river and scrub them down. Jake will keep watch," I said, changing the subject by design.

She looked horrified. "I don't know," she said. "I can't, I can't."

"You'll have to bathe sometime before the end of the trip," I smiled, but she didn't smile back. Loretta joined us, saying we were having too much fun without her. The children were lulled to sleep by the movement of the wagon and we walked along as if we were going to a picnic, trying to forget the chaos of the past few months. I so loved my friends; they were closer than my own mother or my own sister. Sometimes as we were walking, Elizabeth would begin to sing, and Loretta and I would join in singing harmony. It was hard to believe how much better that made us feel, if only for the moment. Frequently we sang hymns, other times a folk song; it was a joyous time. Later I thought we should have been quieter, not to attract attention, but the wagon made so much noise, it probably drowned out the singing.

Elizabeth said, as we walked, "I guess my mama's quilt frame is just a pile of ashes now."

"Samuel will just have to build us another one. Our quilting-time makes my disposition sunnier, less truculent," Loretta interjected.

Elizabeth and I looked at each other. "What?" I asked.

"Grumpy," Loretta said.

"You've never been truculent," I said.

"Not on the outside. It helps me to talk about things. I've never been able to do that before."

"I like it, too. It makes me know I'm not alone," I added.

"Quilting surely does loosen the tongue," said Elizabeth. We three walked behind that old, squeaking wagon, happy just to be together, and I determined to get some grease for those axles.

As we trudged along, I thought about my family in Tennessee: I didn't know what had happened to them, and I knew there was heavy fighting there. After I reached Florida and settled in, I would write and try to find them. The mail had quit running when the railroad was destroyed; I prayed they were safe.

That evening we stopped before the sun went down so we could cook and get our baths. While Loretta and Elizabeth started dinner, I took Harry and John to the river and told the girls I would clean up the dishes. Jake went with us and stood guard as we found a shallow spot and took off our clothes - except our underwear. With a piece of soap, we lathered up. Laughing and splashing, my boys enjoyed that time in the river. They helped me wash my hair, and I scrubbed their ears and hugged and kissed them in the water. Jake shushed us, but it was hard to keep the children quiet.

The Flint was a beautiful river. We lay back and floated, the trees reaching over the river from both sides. Sometimes the joy of freedom came at the strangest moments, and that was one of them. It reminded me of my childhood times in the creek. Only now I had two precious boys to share my time with. How blessed I felt at the moment.

Jake thought we needed to be more careful in the next few weeks, as there had been talk on the main road of a skirmish near a bridge on the Flint. So far, we hadn't seen anyone on the trail, but we knew sooner or later that would change as there were towns along the river. Always, we could smell smoke, even though we didn't know the source.

As the days passed, I noticed we were all looking stronger, which was strange to me as I thought this trip would wear us down. Jake was looking ten years younger. This traveling had changed him totally, giving him good color in his face. And his face always especially brightened when he talked to John, who liked to ride with his grandpa.

Since Loretta had started walking more also, she was losing the pale color in her skin. We cheered as she cast off her corset, throwing it in a bush on the side of the road. She said she felt as free as a bird; liberation *was* surely sweet for all of us. Elizabeth and I only wore corsets when we went to church so we knew how it felt not to wear one. And even though we wore bonnets, the sun got to us anyway. Elizabeth looked as beautiful as always – I thought she would have no trouble finding a new husband if Ernest were killed. And me, I continued to get bigger with my baby. I was hoping to be settled when I delivered this one.

As we were walking one day, Loretta finally broached the subject of Evelyn – after all this time. "You know, Sally, Evelyn was very pretty and sweet and I loved her dearly." My throat got a lump in it while she continued, "but she had no gumption. She was dainty and I know my brother loved her, but you are a person everyone can rely on. You are brave and strong and full of life. We are so lucky to have you in our family, and Jacob is beside himself with love for you."

"And so am I," Elizabeth chimed in. She put her arm around me and I grabbed Loretta, and we walked down that road together. I just wished Loretta had told me this sooner, but no matter; I was glad to finally hear it. I did notice that Elizabeth looked back down the trail also, usually with a stricken look on her face.

The nights were chilling down. The babies slept well in the wagon with quilts piled on top of them. We felt they should be out of the dew and since the wagon was narrow, we put them together to keep each other warm. I got up constantly to check on them, but they slept well from all the activity during the day. Our hope was that our food would last us until we got to Florida, where Jake said we could live off the land. Sounded like Canaan-land to me.

"When we get to Florida, you can't bathe in the rivers like here," Jake said one evening while we were sitting around the fire. "There are gators and snakes. And mosquitoes big as grasshoppers. So, we'll need to get mosquito nets when we settle."

I said, "Jake, we have mosquitoes in Georgia."

"Not like Florida," he laughed. Loretta shuddered.

"I wish Samuel were with us tonight," Loretta said suddenly.

"Oh, how I wish Jacob were with us tonight," I added. I expected Elizabeth to join in with the same statement about Ernest, but she remained quiet and stared into the fire. Sometimes Elizabeth confounded me. Of course, I was not of an understanding at that point.

The few people we saw on the trail now were heading south, too, many with just a pack tied to a stick, carried on their shoulder. Avoiding people was our goal as we didn't have enough food to share and make it all the way to Florida. We had been on the trail for about two weeks and had heard rifle fire all along the way, but so far, we hadn't seen any enemy soldiers on either side of the river. One day I felt someone was following us, but since I didn't see anything, I thought I was imagining things.

I must say, I had never seen so many cotton fields. Cotton was an amazing plant with beautiful, fluffy balls. It seemed that God had made that plant just so people could wear clothes. There were fields as far as the eye could see. Many times, as we were moving down the trail, there were slaves in the distance, picking the bolls and dragging bags behind them. They looked up at us in wonder and maybe felt as sorry for us as we did for them. We were a pitiful-looking group, but we were free to walk away from our tribulations. They obviously were not, even though President Lincoln had signed the Emancipation Proclamation over a year before. I stopped by the side of the road one day and picked one of those soft bolls. The pod caught my fingers and made them bleed. They looked pretty but were prickly, just like some people, which made me think of Beatrice and that awful letter she had slipped in my bag years ago.

☼

"Once we get close to Montezuma, Georgia, which is a town farther south on the Flint, I think we should head east, which will bring us out below Macon and the throngs of folks," Jake said. "This trail is going to attract even more attention as the battles increase. We might be able to find some wildlife for food in the woods."

"Can the wagon make it through the woods without a trail?" I asked.

"It might be rough, but better than the main road," he said.

Each night it took us about two hours to set up camp. The horses required looking after, being fed, watered, and brushed. The leather rigging needed cleaning, but was oftentimes neglected. The fire had to be started and dinner cooked, the wagon unloaded so the children could sleep out of the dampness. Even though we were always tired from the long day, we couldn't shirk our duties, and although we implored Jake to let us stay more than one day at a site, he wouldn't allow it. Each morning it was the same routine only backwards. We were usually on the road within an hour if we ate a cold breakfast.

At the end of every day we had to wash diapers, rags really, so the children would be clean for the next day. There was a limited amount of diapers, so they were washed and hung to dry daily. However, there were some nights when Jake, instinctively, knew we had to lay low. During that time, there was no fire or hot food and no talking whatsoever. Those were the worst nights of all, but we had to trust him. It was as though he was out hunting and knew there might be a predator out there. I usually sat up with him all night long on those evenings, guns ready. He had no knowledge of the Atherton Brothers at that time.

As we were beginning to pull the wagon onto the trail one morning, Jake set the brake, and we sat, listening to an unfamiliar sound: the sound of marching men. A company of Johnny Rebs passed right in front of us, with eight or nine Yankee soldiers tied together with coarse rope. Each one looked at us, in turn; captor and captive, their expressions were the same: war weariness. And at the end of that string of men was the golden-haired Jeremy Atherton, with a yellow band tied around his sleeve, the sign of a deserter.

"I'll be coming for you," he yelled at me.

A Rebel soldier yanked on the rope and he stumbled forward. Our silence was evident as they passed, and Jake waited awhile after they moved on before releasing the brake and driving onto the trail. We would later realize that we were just a few miles from Andersonville, the Confederate prison, where the captured men were being taken. There wasn't much talk the rest of the morning, each of us lost in a world of sorrow over the misery of War.

Elizabeth cried quietly, while Jake asked, "What the hell was that about?" It was a secret we could not divulge, even to Jake. I was shocked to realize that outside of the Atlanta area, Jeremy would be considered a deserter, no matter his protests.

There were some pleasant things that happened to us, however, while we were on this journey. One evening, Jake pulled the wagon off the road into a dense pine forest, having a lot of trouble maneuvering the horses and wagon into place between the trees. But we slept on beds of pine needles that night, and it was like heaven, the piney aroma surrounding us. I spread a canvas on the needles, with a quilt over the canvas and another quilt to keep us warm. John snuggled on one side and Harry on the other, while I lay on my back and looked up at the night sky with a full moon barely peeking through the pine boughs. The wind in the whispering pines was like a song, sweet and low. I know I was smiling as I fell asleep, and we slept so well we were late getting started the next morning.

Chapter 13 *MONTEZUMA*

It was the middle of September, 1864, according to my recollecting. I had tried to keep track of the days. With the nights getting damper, Loretta and I began taking turns sleeping in the wagon with the children to be sure they were warm. And as we used supplies, the wagon created more space for us to sleep in. Jake had rigged a canvas tent from the side of the wagon to keep the dew off him and Elizabeth. Loretta or I slept at one end with Elizabeth, and Jake slept at the other end, keeping the fire stoked all night, as usual.

As I lay awake in the wagon one morning before sunup, waiting for the smell of coffee, I heard a snuffling noise around the wagon. The horses were stamping their feet and snorting. Since it was my night to sleep with the children, I quietly got up and went toward the end of the wagon where the noise was coming from. By the light of the fire, I could see a big wild boar rooting through our campsite, not far from where Jake was sleeping. Worried that he could charge and kill Jake, Elizabeth or Loretta, I reached for the rifle, which was loaded and stashed in the front of the wagon. As I aimed at that big hog, a blast came out of the tent below, and the boar dropped to the ground with a thud. My heart was beating fast and I hadn't even had the chance to pull the trigger.

"Oh my goodness, Jake, I was just getting ready to shoot," I yelled.

"Look at that, Sally. I haven't lost my touch. Whooee!" he shouted, grinning and poking the hog with his rifle.

"No, you are something, Jake Winston!" I was laughing, too, though my heart was pulsing in my chest.

Elizabeth and Loretta were hugging each other, shivering from fright, and cold too, looking down at Jake's catch. Concerned that someone had heard the shot, I kept my gun loaded. The children were crying, startled from their dreams. I handed Rebecca to Loretta, who took her into the tent.

Jake butchered the hog then and there, by the light of the campfire. We salted it down the best we could and fried some of its meat to eat since we were all awake anyway. Jake was as proud as a man could be, providing for his family and not wasting away in a house in Atlanta. I had never seen a man blossom so in the face of adversity.

My husband wouldn't recognize his father. "Jacob Henry Winston, come home to me," I whispered to the wind.

The next day Jake taught Loretta to drive, and though she was very skeptical about it, it was good to have all of us know as much as we could in order to arrive safely in Florida. Florida: the word seemed so foreign to me, and it seemed so far away, too. I told Jake we needed a day's break from traveling once we reached Montezuma.

"Elizabeth, I think you'll need a bath in the river before we reach civilization," I said, as we walked behind the wagon. She smiled.

"I think we all need a good scrubbing," she answered. Since we had only been washing up in camp with hot water from the campfire, I'm sure we were a sight to behold – red, dusty folks. As Jake stood guard over us, Loretta and I took the three children into the edge of the river, while Elizabeth watched the camp area with a loaded rifle. Any other time, this would have been a joyous occasion, but we were so watchful and skittish that we hurried to wash our hair and bodies. The water was colder than I had expected it would be, so the children were anxious to get out. Rushing back to the campfire, we shivered as we dried our hair and clothes.

Even though Elizabeth appeared fearful of bathing in the river, she made up her mind to do it, what with Jake guarding. As he walked her toward the river, he put his arm around her for reassurance. But while I was dressing the boys, I heard Elizabeth scream. Grabbing up the rifle, I ran toward the river, and a shot rang out before I got there. I panicked: we could not lose Jake or Elizabeth. My mind was running rampant, my ears ringing. But when I got to the edge of the river, Jake was holding a soaking-wet Elizabeth, dressed only in her underwear. She had her wet body pressed into Jake's chest and she was sobbing softly. The intimacy between them stunned me.

"I guess there *are* gators in Georgia," he said to me, smiling weakly. I grabbed her clothes and tried to cover her as well as I could.

"Jake, she's a married woman," I said, icily.

"Sally, I think I know that. Believe me, I know she's a married woman." But his blue eyes were twinkling and he was flushed, as was Elizabeth.

"Well, I guess no more river-bathing for Elizabeth," I said, putting my arm around her shoulder, the three of us walking back to the camp. This was a totally new thought for me: the idea of Elizabeth and Jake courting. He was an old man, my father-in-law!

She kept turning toward him and finally reached for his hand, which he took and kissed, and I knew this was totally out of my control. I wasn't certain what I should have been more shocked at – their relationship or the fact that we bathed with alligators.

This romance was not something I had time to worry about. Jake *was* a very attractive man and was probably only about 55 years old, but Elizabeth was my age. Oh, this was impossible! And she was married!

But I had bigger things to think about: I was seven months with child, and I felt it was my responsibility to get these people to Florida. Loretta would have to handle her father, though I'm not sure she had noticed the relationship developing between him and Elizabeth. She probably thought he was just being fatherly. The whole situation was the last thing I thought about before I finally drifted off to sleep at night – and the fact that I would not swim in another alligator-ridden creek, even if I smelled to high heaven before I reached Florida.

We drove on closer to Montezuma, hid the wagon in the brush, and hobbled the horses away from the wagon. The discussion got very heated when Jake told me I couldn't go into town for supplies because of my condition.

"I'm the best shot and I'm not afraid," I said, even though I was afraid.

"Hell's bells, Sally! How can I protect you if you don't let me? What will I tell Jacob when he finds out I took you into Montezuma, being with child?" Jake asked.

"Hell's bells, yourself, Jake Winston! And what will I tell Jacob when he finds out I let his father go into a strange town alone?" I asked him. " I *will* be going with you."

Laughing as he loaded his rifle, he said, "Yes, ma'am."

I pulled a couple of gold coins out of the strongbox and Jake brought some confederate money which he would try to use. My little pistol hung heavy in my dress pocket; he carried his rifle openly.

Walking cautiously into town, we looked for a general store. The town was built at the bottom of a hill, so Jake had to help me walk. I was more worried about how I would get back up the hill, and wondering why anyone would build a town so low, with the Flint River flowing nearby. There weren't many people on the street, but the ones we saw weren't friendly – we were strangers in a strange land. A small store stood at the end of town, and as we entered, the man behind the counter peered suspiciously at us.

"Where you folks from?" he asked, his hand under the counter.

"Atlanta, heading to Florida. Got any supplies?" Jake asked brusquely.

"Got any money?" he retorted.

"You take confederate?" Jake asked.

The man laughed. "Nope. Quit taking that months ago. Got anything to trade?"

"What kind of supplies you got?" Jake inquired.

"Little cornmeal, sugar, salt, coffee," the man answered.

I reached in my pocket, pulled a gold coin out, and laid it on the counter. "Will this trade?" I asked.

"Sally Ann!" Jake said, alarmed, grabbing my arm.

"I believe we can do business. I can give you a five-pound bag of cornmeal, a cup of sugar, small amount of salt, and a pound of coffee," the man said, smiling for the first time.

"Done, and throw in a can of axle grease," I said. Jake was looking at me like he could hit me. Well, we had to have supplies, I thought, and I couldn't let my children go hungry.

Once we were outside, Jake grabbed my arm again and held

tight. "Woman, now they know we have gold, they'll be after us. Where'd you get that gold?"

"They'll never find it. It's in a strongbox hidden in the wagon. We had to have supplies," I answered.

"Great God, I could have traded a gun or something. This is trouble. We'll pack up and backtrack. I can't protect three women and three babies from a mob looking for gold," Jake said vehemently.

I was right about that hill; Jake practically had to pull me up the incline on the way out of town, and he was almost running, as we clutched our supplies, our breathing ragged. When we got back to the wagon, we quickly packed up, throwing things inside with no order, heading north on the trail we had just traveled. Loretta and Elizabeth exchanged concerned looks when Jake ordered us to load up and move out. Thinking that we had come this far without trouble, I felt concern that maybe I had erred. Jake was sorely vexed with me. I planned to never get crosswise with Jake Winston again; as easygoing as he was, he had a mighty temper on him.

Riding north about two miles, we looked for a trail heading east, even a cow trail. Jake didn't say much and he drove the horses hard, so we all stayed in the wagon. Finally, he turned on a beaten track going east, and at dark we pulled way off the road and didn't build a fire. The horses were hobbled, with feed bags on. Our supper consisted of cold cornbread and salted pork, making us plenty thirsty all evening. We put the children to bed early so there would be no noise.

Jake and I cut branches and covered our tracks on the trail, hoping beyond hope, that trackers couldn't find us. We walked down the road a long way to make sure there were no imprints. By the time we got back, Loretta and Elizabeth were beside themselves. Elizabeth ran to Jake and kissed him full on his mouth, but I wasn't sure Loretta could see them in the dark. Going to bed fully dressed, shoes and all, I knew we would not sleep that night either.

In the night I reached for the Spencer rifle. Horses' hooves vibrated through the ground (maybe three horses), and I could hear hushed voices. They were on the trail, but continued to ride past the place where we were camped. No one made a sound in our camp, not even a sigh, until after they passed us. I turned on my side as my belly was too big for me to turn over. Elizabeth was next to Jake, both with rifles pointed toward the trail, and Loretta was in the wagon with the children, also with a rifle, loaded and ready to protect them. While waiting for the riders to return, I was just hoping it wouldn't be at daylight. After a few hours we heard them coming back, and we waited patiently again. This time they kept going; we had done a good job of hiding. As I breathed a sigh of relief, Elizabeth rolled over and snuggled next to Jake and he pulled the covers up over them. I could hear their lovemaking, and I was so scandalized. War surely does make for strange bedfellows.

During the night the rain began to fall: merciless rain. Cold food, cold bodies, and now, cold rain made us miserable. It ran down the inside of the canvas and dripped on our quilts and blankets. There was no rest to be had that night! I was now becoming truculent.

The next morning I couldn't look Elizabeth or Jake in the eye. Rising early, we got going on the trail with no coffee or breakfast. The wet, red clay made for difficult travel, with the horses' feet making sucking noises in the mud. Walking was next to impossible, so we rode in the wagon. It was five hours of difficult travel before Jake felt it was safe enough to stop for some coffee and food, and he pulled me aside.

"Sally, you can't avoid Elizabeth and me the whole trip. Listen to me - I love her and she loves me. She's given me a reason to live, and she thinks her husband is dead. Please reconsider your judgment," he pleaded.

"Jake, she's married. Does Loretta know? What do you think Jacob would think? I can't condone this," I whispered.

"I told Loretta, and she's happy for us; she approves. She thinks Ernest is dead, too. We want to marry soon." Elizabeth walked up then and took my hand.

"Miss Sally, how many good men do you know? How can I be so fortunate to find someone like Jake here?" His chest swelled as she spoke, and they were both flushed with color, looking at each other. As we stood huddled in the rain, it felt ridiculous for us to be discussing their relationship, when we were all so miserable.

"It's not appropriate for you to sleep together and be unwed. You'll need to marry at the next town," I whispered, knowing I couldn't restrain them. The horse was out of the barn, so to speak.

Loretta smiled at me and said, "Honey, it's not wrong if Ernest is dead. It's wartime now and they do care so much for each other. We could all be dead tomorrow." That statement made me believe there was more to Loretta than met the eye – much more.

Elizabeth and Jake looked at each other and I had to admit, they were blessed to have this love. I wished my Jacob were with me. As I rubbed my belly, I watched them walk away like two youngsters. But as long as they married I deemed it was more appropriate. They did continue sleeping together even though they weren't married yet. Staying in the tent was unbearable for me, but there was no getting around it, as Loretta wanted to sleep in the wagon with the children every other night. The sounds of their lovemaking made me miss my husband. Pulling the covers over my head, I put my hands over my ears and sheer exhaustion took me.

Sometimes when we woke in the mornings, the birds were singing, as if there wasn't a war going on. The cardinals were calling to each other, and the blue jays were fussing at each other, or us, for invading their space. And then when we got up and looked at the sky, it was a normal sky, with no smoke. Sometimes it was blue with wispy clouds. It helped me feel that we would get back to normal one day, and it gave me hope so that I could not give up.

The next day after our discussion, as we were rumbling down the trail, my thoughts did a total turn-around: I was not responsible for the morality of folks on this trip. Wartime caused people to do unusual things, and Jake and Elizabeth were certainly grown-up people. Maybe they felt desperate for each other as we all could face death. We simply had to survive this trip, and I had to get to Florida before this baby decided to appear. I decided that what Jake and Elizabeth did was their concern, and they seemed to feel that way also as they were like two lovebirds. Perhaps I had just been jealous – not having my husband with me.

Each night as we bedded down, we were careful not to have a fire. Though tired of cold food, cold nights, and wet clothes and blankets, we were still trying to put some distance between us and the town of Montezuma. I thought we should be coming to the main road south of Macon soon where there would be more people moving south, and we might feel a little safer. My feet were starting to hurt a lot, and my back too when I walked too much, so John and I rode on the back of the wagon most of the time. He had lots of stories to tell me, especially about his Grandpa Jake. Everyone seemed to sure love Jake, including me.

Sometimes I held baby Harry or Rebecca Ann on my lap. How I loved the smell of a sweet baby. However, more often than not, the children were soggy and smelly. The perfumed corn starch was always handy and many times I used it on myself, too. I'm certain that on occasion a white cloud of corn starch powder could be seen floating out of the back of the wagon.

Chapter 14 THE PROMISED LAND

The main road lay before us at the end of the second day after leaving Montezuma. Blessedly, the rain had stopped, although the ground was still wet. There were many wagons and carriages on the road; some people were walking with their belongings strapped to their back, dragging their children along with them. I longed to take the children into our wagon; their big, sad eyes ripped my heart in two. But of course there were too many of them. Jake yelled to one of the walkers, "Where are all these people coming from?" The man yelled back, "People are fleeing Macon. Sherman is expected there any day."

Later, we would learn that the people of Macon had built a trench around the whole city so that the Yankees couldn't get in. Only one cannonball did any damage and it missed its target: the Confederate Treasurer's mansion. But we were, again, thrust into a sea of people, this time moving toward Valdosta, which would make our journey all the longer. Lord help us all, I thought. In a few miles we saw a clearing where covered wagons, buggies, and carriages were gathered in a tight circle.

A man stepped out in front of our wagon and yelled, "Mrs. Winston!" It was Mr. Brown, our neighbor, who had lived down the road from our home. I waved to him, hoping to hear the latest news.

"Come join us. We can talk at supper," Mr. Brown called to us. Supper: hot food. My mouth began to water. Jake pulled the wagon off the road, and we joined the circle of the other folks who would be moving south. Mrs. Brown came to our camp and gave us our chores for the evening meal. While Elizabeth and Loretta built the fire, Jake got the horses settled, and I began mixing cornbread and cutting slices of salted ham for the frying pan. The coffee was boiling and the smell made me so homesick I almost cried.

Everyone spread their food on makeshift tables, and it was a sight to behold. I was so hungry for hot food, I was hoping I wouldn't lose my manners, even though I felt like shoveling my whole meal into my mouth at once. Mr. and Mrs. Brown came over to eat with us, and their smiling faces were purely welcomed. She was a round woman with a pleasant pink face and white hair. She must've been a good cook because Mr. Brown was plump, too, and they were so very jovial. It would seem at times like this that they wouldn't be smiling, but it must have come naturally; I determined that I'd try to be more like them, which was more like the person that I used to be.

"What's happened in our area, Mr. Brown?" I was almost afraid to ask.

"I hate to tell you, seeing your condition, Mrs. Winston, but there's no going home now. The Yankees burned every house on our road including your beautiful home, and ours. We have to look forward now, not back," he said.

"Goddamned Yankees," I said, under my breath. Loretta heard me and tearfully smiled, knowing that I had learned that phrase from her, but I couldn't hold back the tears, thinking of all the memories in that house. Wiping my face with the back of my hand, I asked, "And Jacob, did you see Jacob before you left?"

"No ma'am, nothing from Samuel or Jacob, but there was a young Watkins boy, asking about Miss Elizabeth here. Don't know where he went off to." Mr. Brown looked from Elizabeth to Jake, and I was hoping he was not reading their faces because they were terror-stricken.

Loretta glanced at me and said, "That boy was always sweet on Elizabeth, but she's too educated for him," trying to throw the Browns off the scent that he was her husband.

"Yes ma'am." Mr. Brown became uneasy and quickly changed the subject, saying, "You folks are welcome to ride along with us. We have family in south Georgia over near the coast, and there's strength in numbers. Where you headin' anyhow?" he asked.

"Florida. My son lives in Alachua County," Jake offered.

If the Browns knew about Elizabeth and Ernest, they didn't let on. They asked no questions, but after the Browns left for the night, our conversation got very active.

"Oh my God, Jake, I can't go back to that boy now that I know you. You're the one I love. What can we do?" Elizabeth asked, as she paced.

Jake said, "This does curdle the cream," looking from Loretta to me to Elizabeth.

"He'll never find us. You can divorce him, Elizabeth," I said, pounding my right fist into my left palm. I had become a part of this conspiracy, but I could see it was the right thing, too. Jake looked so distressed and Elizabeth couldn't be comforted. Then she touched her belly and I knew: God in heaven, what had they done? He walked to her and hugged her and rubbed her back, whispering words in her ear that calmed her. How much he was like his son.

"Tomorrow, we must find a church and get you two hitched. No matter what the cost, we can't have a baby come into this union without you being wed," I said. And that was that. We resolved to never let the Watkins boy find Elizabeth. She smiled at us and looked into Jake's eyes. I had only seen that kind of love in my own marriage. It was a good thing. Sometimes the straight and narrow needs a little bend in the road.

The following morning, after breakfast, we loaded up the wagon and followed the Browns down the dirt road. I could see Jake's and Elizabeth's eyes scouring the countryside, looking for a church. Not far down the way, he pulled the wagon off the trail and up a little hill, where there was a small white church in a grove of big, old, shady, pecan trees that seemed to go on forever. We waited for about half an hour and finally, a skinny man, dressed in a black suit, came around the corner. Startled by our party, he jumped back behind the side of the church.

"Wait!" Jake called, "We just want a wedding."

Walking to Jake, I slid the second gold coin in his coat pocket. As he put his hand in his pocket, he grinned down at me. "Sir, we have money for a wedding," he said. The man then reappeared, grabbed the gold coin up, and opened the church, to perform the ceremony.

When we were done, Jake said, "I would like something in

writing." The man tore out the front page of his Bible, wrote words, and we all signed and dated, and it was truly official. Elizabeth and Jake kissed in that church with such hunger, we all had to look away, especially that skinny preacher.

"God bless you all," he yelled after us, smiling and clutching that coin. And we hurried to catch up with the Browns. It took us till after dark to find them, camped with the other folks from Atlanta, and we were surely glad to see each other. It was surprising how much better we felt about traveling with a group of people we knew.

"What happened to you back there?" Mrs. Brown asked at supper.

"We had a wedding to get to," I said. They both looked at Elizabeth and Jake and no explanation was needed.

"We'll be leaving you at Tifton," Mr. Brown said. "Sorry to break up the group. You're welcome to come with us. But I hear tell Valdosta is free of Yankees, so you won't have any problems there."

"We'll need supplies, Mr. Brown. Have you heard if Valdosta would be a good place to buy them?" Jake asked.

"I hear tell nothing is getting through: no railroad, supply wagons, nothing. We need supplies, too. Reckon we might have to either do without, or do some hunting," he grinned.

Grim as it all sounded - as we were getting farther from our home - I was looking forward to reaching the Florida line. The bluecoats were so busy burning Atlanta and the state capital, I thought maybe they wouldn't be as thick in Florida. Five days later, we waved goodbye to the Browns and rumbled toward Valdosta. Anytime we entered a new town, we all got skittish, and each of us carried a loaded gun. All these Georgia folks had been our countrymen at one point, but then, so had the Yankees.

Several times Elizabeth whispered to me that she could see a blonde-headed man following us. Startled, I watched the trail, but never caught sight of him. "Jeremy Atherton will be hanged," I said. It didn't comfort her.

It was the middle of October, 1864, when we camped outside of Valdosta. Our numbers were down since we were traveling with just two other wagons. But it was better than just our one wagon, and there were more men, although they were all older. The nights continued to be mighty cold, and even the days had gotten chillier. The babies and I stayed in the wagon with quilts tucked around us as we traveled. I tried to mend our clothes so we didn't look like beggars.

I had been considering what the doctor had said after my last birthing, and I hoped I wouldn't die, along with the child. But I had walked many a mile with this baby and felt better than I ever had, even though now I couldn't really keep up, just waddling along. When we rode in the wagon, I tried to keep Rebecca and Harry entertained with songs and reading the few books we had. They couldn't be contained: their energy was bursting out of the wagon, so Loretta would take them, one at a time, and walk behind, with the other child waving from the back of the wagon and calling out hello. John rode between his hero, Jake, and his friend, Elizabeth.

The stopping at the end of each day was the best part of the day for me – no more jostling in the wagon or trying to keep up, trudging behind. We would stretch our bodies and build a cooking fire. Our food was really growing limited now, and the coffee was down to almost nothing. The last night of this leg of the journey, Jake and I discussed the trip into Valdosta the next day.

"I'm going with two other men this time," he said, adamantly.

Raising my hands, palms out, I said, "No argument here."

Grinning, he said, "Big surprise." We thought this a wiser idea what with Elizabeth and I both with child, and Loretta just could not leave Rebecca.

"I brought some old guns whose aims are off, but they might get us some food," Jake said. "We can't trade our good rifles, pistols, or horses. Once we get to Florida it'll be easier to find food. Just a few more miles now to the state line."

When he returned that afternoon, he told us that Valdosta was a dismal little town; the store shelves were all empty. "There's no supplies to be had. Plenty of places to buy things, but no goods," he said. So he returned empty-handed. It seemed that refugees from Atlanta *and* Macon had migrated to Valdosta. My thought was that the storekeepers had saved supplies for their own people. It had been a good time for me to catch up on my rest, knowing Elizabeth and

Loretta were taking care of my children.

The next morning we made acorn coffee and cornbread, and left at daybreak. Our little wagon train consisted of three dusty, ragged wagons heading for the 'Promised Land'. I thought about how we had enjoyed our first few weeks on the road. But the smiles just weren't there anymore, and the children cried a lot: hunger and cold weather had left them weak. I did make it a point to smile at each person every day even though I was so tired and about a month away from delivering and very worried about the lack of food.

One afternoon we camped at what we thought was the Florida state line. There was much joy in reaching this milepost after traveling for what was almost six weeks. The thought of a feather bed in our own home in Florida was something that kept me going.

The three older men in our meager wagon train determined to try their hand at hunting, feeling they were safely away from the fighting. A deer or a turkey or a wild hog would certainly be good in a stew, which would give us the strength to continue. Camped by a river, it was a wonderful place to replenish our water supply, for both the horses and ourselves, always on the lookout for gators. It was also pleasant to be able to wash up without scrimping on water. Hearing rifle fire in the distance, we could only hope to have something good for our dinner. But I cringed at the sound.

After a while Jake burst through the undergrowth, smiling big as you please. "Need a horse to pack those deer out of the woods," he called.

"How many?" we said in unison. "Two," he smiled. "They're dressing 'em while I came for a horse."

"You better wrap that meat in a canvas, or the horse will give you trouble," I said.

"You're right, my sweet Sally Ann," he sang, almost dancing out of camp.

I was so very happy to have sustenance, for myself, my family, and my unborn child. As we sat around the campfire, our spirits were uplifted. Dandelion greens and wild onions were all we could find for our stew, thickened with a little cornmeal, but thank God for His provisions, I thought. Any other time we might've turned up our noses at a stew with so little flavoring, but we could feel the strength filling our bodies. And good, clean water for our coffee grounds. We were filled with food, with joy, with love for one another. I felt I had a bond with these people that could never be broken. Or so I thought.

In my mind, it was hard to remember the man Jake used to be. When he was living by himself in Atlanta I thought he was a dying man, grieving for Mother Ann. Now he was an older version of my husband, but he seemed only to be about 45 years old. He and Elizabeth were constantly together, riding and switching off driving. But he was careful with her as she openly admitted she was with child. Now we were all related! He was my father-in-law, so Elizabeth was my mother-in-law. Loretta was my sister-in-law, Jake was her father and Elizabeth was her step-mother. Their baby would be Loretta's half-sister or brother. Elizabeth was Rebecca's half-sister and the children were all grandchildren to Jake. It was truly mind-boggling.

The only thing that would've made me happier would have been seeing Jacob riding up behind us. I often looked back down the trail for his horse and I knew Loretta did the same. Elizabeth, of course, watched for Jeremy, which made me a little jumpy also. Maybe she was looking for Ernest, too.

It being November, 1864, we were still experiencing really bitter-cold nights, which was no surprise. The further south we traveled, the damper the cold. The dampness seeped into our clothes and quilts, to our bones it seemed. We continued to sleep around the fire to keep warm, with the babies tucked under the covers, the hard wagon seats being far too uncomfortable for sleeping, as compared to the soft, grassy areas. Many nights I awoke with the front of my body roasting and my backside freezing. Jake was up throughout the night tending the fire, as always, and in the morning, was up boiling our acorn-coffee grounds. The coffee was still so weak, we might as well have had hot water.

Jake asked me one morning, "How would you like your coffee today, Madame?"

"Hot," I said, smiling at that wonderful man who could lift anyone's spirits.

We figured to be in Alachua County before Thanksgiving. Our wagon train was down to two wagons now, and our remaining fellow travelers would be leaving us soon to head west to Tallahassee. How lonely and more scared we would be without them. But we looked so wretched and dirt-poor, I didn't think anyone would try to rob us. I was glad Loretta and Elizabeth didn't know about the gold.

"I thought it would be warmer in Florida, somehow," Elizabeth said one evening, as we sat around the fire.

"It is, down in the southern part," Jake said. "Alachua though has winters, according to my son, David."

I don't think any of us really cared about the weather as long as we knew we would be safe soon, in a home with a roaring fire.

Chapter 15   *INDIAN METHOD*

When we camped the last night with our friends, we tried to make a festive meal and enjoy our time together. After we ate, we said our goodbyes since we would be pulling out at daybreak. I took Jake aside to speak with him.

"Jake, I'm ashamed to talk with you about this, but it's getting close to my time; I may not make it to Alachua for the birth, and I may need your help."

"Sally Ann, the girls can help you with the birthing. I'll do what I can, but I can't deliver a baby." He looked dejected, and I did feel mortified to have to speak to him about this subject.

"The doctor told me not to have more children. He had to cut me the last time. If I can't have this baby naturally, I'll want you to cut me and sew me up. I want this baby to be born alive," I said.

"You can't ask me to do that! I can't do that! God in Heaven!" he whispered loudly. We both looked toward the fire, where Elizabeth, Loretta, and the children were sitting, looking at us.

"You're a hunter and know how to use a knife. I may need you. Who else can I turn to? I can't ask Elizabeth, and Loretta is a lady. They can't do it. Please," I pleaded.

He kicked the ground with the toe of his boot. "We'll just have to make it to Alachua County. I can't do it," he whispered. But I knew he would; I just had to prepare him.

Every evening Jake cleaned the horses' hooves. I couldn't help him anymore, and he wouldn't let Elizabeth. One of our lead horses had come up with a stone bruise, the smaller of the geldings. Jake said he would have to revise the rigging so there would be only three horses pulling. The fourth horse would be tied to the back of the wagon. I was surprised we'd come this far without losing a horse.

About five days south of Valdosta, I started feeling pains down my back. I'd been trying to walk more but I could only do so a few hours at a time, and then the wagon had to stop to let me catch up. Once the pains started, I was worried I might get so far behind that I wouldn't be able to wave them down. Luckily, Loretta saw me stop and bend over.

"Jake, we might have to take a few days off pretty soon. I'm starting with the birthing pains," I said when the wagon turned around and picked me up.

As Elizabeth and Loretta jumped down from the wagon to help me up on the back so I could lie down inside, Jake looked distressed. They sat on either side of me, each holding a child.

"Sally Ann, I've read that the Indians have their babies standing up so that gravity will help them," Loretta said.

"It makes sense, but who can do that?" I asked.

"We'll help you, one on either side, until you're ready to drop the baby. Maybe we won't have to pull it this time," Elizabeth said. Of course she was remembering birthing John.

Our wagon turned off the main road onto a path going west and followed it, so that we couldn't be seen from the main road. Then, Jake hobbled the horses, grabbed his rifle and said, "John and I are going hunting." He took John's hand, and they were gone.

"Well, ladies, I guess it's up to us," I said. "We'll have to do this alone."

"He'll be back, Sally, if we need him," Elizabeth said. And I knew he would.

The meadow where we were camped was dry and brown, with most of the trees around it being leaf-barren. The sun was warm; the wind was brisk. We walked from one end of that meadow to the other, as Loretta said I needed to walk. The babies toddled behind us like little ducklings. My pains were coming regularly, and I reckoned the baby would be born this day. I knew it was November, 1864, but I had lost track of the days. Every time a pain grabbed me, Elizabeth and Loretta each took an arm. I felt so fortunate to have friends like these two women. Elizabeth carried a baby blanket over her arm, and she spread it every time we thought the baby was coming. Then, she would pick it up again when we resumed walking.

Finally, I thought the time had come, and I stood over the blanket and pushed as hard as I could, but I was having very little success. My energy was wearing thin even though they held both my arms. There were times when I just wanted to lie down on that blanket and go to sleep, but they wouldn't let me. Harry and Rebecca began to cry from hunger so Loretta took them to the wagon to put them down for a nap. I think they were distressed from my groaning, and I was tired of my groaning, myself.

As we resumed walking, Elizabeth began to talk about Ernest: "I don't know why I married that boy," she said. "I guess I thought I should be married and then, I was worried about babies. He was going off to war, and I felt sorry for him. Now I've wronged him, and I feel awful. But I love Jake, and I can't help that."

When I could talk, between pains, I tried to make her feel better. But truly, she *had* wronged Ernest. My hope was that we never saw him again. I thought she was talking to distract herself, but my thoughts were definitely *not* centered on Ernest.

Finally, when it was just Elizabeth and me, I felt the baby's head move down with the last push. She had to hold me upright, and with me bending my knees, the baby girl splashed into my hands and onto the blanket. Elizabeth laid me down gently on the wet ground and began to clean the baby. She cut the cord, tied it off, and then wrapped the baby in a clean blanket. Laying her on top of me, as light as a feather, Elizabeth went to get Loretta. As they helped me into the wagon, I collapsed on the floor in a bed of quilts. I slept with the baby tucked in my arm and the toddlers on the benches to the side.

When the baby started crying, I pushed my nipple into her mouth, and she began to suckle right away. We both fell asleep again, and when next I woke I could hear Jake talking outside. It seemed he had been successful on his hunt, bringing back three turkeys. The aroma of roasted turkey drifted into the wagon and it was a glorious smell. Peeking over the back of the wooden plank, Jake smiled at me. I motioned him in, and he held his granddaughter,

Mary Elizabeth Winston.

"You did it," he whispered. "You're a grand lady, Sally Ann Winston. There's none like you anywhere, and I intend to tell that rascal son of mine that very thing when I see him. Thank you for not asking me to help."

Chapter 16   HOPE SPRINGS

After three days of camping in the meadow, we resumed our journey. The baby seemed to fare well even though I was worried the trip would be too hard on her, but the rocking of the wagon lulled her to sleep. A week after the birth of Mary Elizabeth I tried walking a little every day. My shoes were worn thin, and I wrapped cloth, torn from my petticoats, around my feet so that I could walk in them, tied with a bow on top, trying to make them look pretty. I did feel my strength returning, though I was exhausted by the time we settled in for the evening. This was my easiest birth, but I was definitely hoping my birthing days were over. And they may well have been if Jacob didn't come home from the war, but I couldn't think like that.

As I was walking slowly behind the wagon one day, I noticed two riders approaching, pulling a packhorse. My hand automatically felt for the pistol in my pocket. Jake put the brake on and ordered us into the wagon. As the riders got closer, Loretta and I pulled the babies next to us. She had her rifle lying flat on the bench, with the children on the floor. I held Mary.

"Pa, it's me, David," one of the riders yelled out, waving.

"Well, I'll be a son of a gun," Jake yelled back.

"We're here to take you home," David called.

Loretta and I looked at each other, tears of joy running down our faces. At last, we were close to the "Promised Land" – Alachua County, Florida. David had the Winston blue eyes, but looked more like Mother Ann. He was of course very surprised that he had a new stepmother and a sibling on the way. Adding to his surprise was how young his father looked. When he was introduced to me, he took my hand and kissed it. So he did have the Winston charm also. He was shorter and stockier than Jake and Jacob, but he was a comely man.

"We are out about five days," David said that night. "The wagon obviously will move slower than a person on horseback."

They had brought us food --- coffee, salt, sugar, flour, ham, vegetables. We hadn't had vegetables in so long. But the coffee was the best, sweetened with some sugar. I held that cup to warm my hands, and the smell and taste were like paradise.

David laughed. "You folks are true pioneers. I'll bet there's some great stories in this old wagon. I can't believe you had a birth, a wedding, and another birth coming."

Of course, I knew we looked the worse for wear. Our clothes were ragged even though I had patched and re-patched. There was red clay all over our shoes, our clothes, and our skin and hair. The children were dirty, too, but our spirits were soaring. We felt safe at last.

"Any word from Jacob?" David asked.

"None. We were hoping you had heard," Jake said.

"Nothing much. A rider came through La Crosse a week or so ago and sent word from Jacob that you were on the way." The conversation got quiet then, and my thoughts were trying to believe Jacob would ride up behind us on the way to Alachua County. But at least I knew he was alive – or was a week ago.

David Winston was apparently a cattleman. He had brought his foreman, Lanier Walton, with him because he was a good shot and a good man. About thirty years old, he looked every inch a cowboy, wearing cowboy boots and spurs and a big cowboy hat. His skin was tanned, and when his hat came off, the top of his forehead was as white as a sheet. It was good he was a quiet man, because David and Jake could out-talk anyone.

"My wife is at home, looking forward to meeting all of you. We've no children, so she is going to love this brood," David said.

As if to read my mind, David began explaining the stand Florida had taken on the War. He said although the governor of Florida was a strong secessionist, he had committed to supplying beef and other goods to the Confederacy in place of manpower. Even though David and Lanier were in the militia, they were not required to fight in the battles outside of the state.

Jake looked so relaxed, and here I thought this trip had been a big burden on him, in spite of his bravado. He sat on a log by the fire, with Elizabeth pulled close to him, her hand on his leg, and they were smiling the whole evening, but then we all were. She stroked her belly, and I could see she was starting to grow. So much had happened in such a short period of time.

"You boys came just at the right time. Taking care of three beautiful women and four ornery children is a big job," Jake laughed.

"And you did a hell of a job, Pa, even married one of them beautiful women. You're a man's man and a ladies' man too, it would seem." We all laughed at that. It was so wonderful to feel safe and secure again and be able to laugh out loud. I looked at each smiling face in our circle around the fire and felt so much relief and peace that I had to thank God for his blessings.

But we still had five more days of travel, and I just hoped the horses and wagon could hold up, as the wagon was creaking more and more each day.

With the help of David and Lanier, Jake removed the two weakest wagon wheels and replaced them with the two we had carried in the wagon for the whole trip. It was a time-consuming, hard job, but it seemed to make the ride smoother. And we had so much more room in the wagon, without the extra wheels, if only for five more days.

We reached the Winston ranch on the evening of the fifth day. They had a big house in an open field, with a porch all around the whole house. It was made of cypress, so it was a dull grey color. Two big barns stood to the back of the house, which were the same grey color, but it was the warmth of the fireplace and the kindness of David's wife, Annie, that filled our spirits.

The bitter wind outside was whistling around the porches as we stood before the fire. Annie took Mary Elizabeth and rocked her for me while I warmed myself by the fireplace. I could see this would be a family to which we could all belong. Elizabeth slept, and Loretta napped with Harry and Rebecca. Our bellies were full, our bodies warm, but my main prayer was for Jacob and Samuel to return safely.

"It's so nice not to hear cannon and rifle fire all the live-long day," I said. "And not to smell smoke coming from burning houses. How peaceful it is here."

"Gainesville has had its share of fighting," Annie said. "But we are too out-of-the-way to have any Yankees near. Rumor has it that the war will be over soon; the South will be surrendering. You must be exhausted. Go sleep for a while and I'll rock your baby."

Annie was a plain-faced woman, but when she smiled, her face became beautiful, her goodness radiating through. She pulled her brown hair back in a severe bun and her clothes were homespun. It was a wonder to me that someone so plain could really be pretty, just because of her warmth and love. I liked her a lot.

There were three large bedrooms in their house, but we were eight extra people, so the rooms were crowded. David said, a little sadly, that when they built the house, they meant to fill it with children – their children. Jake and Elizabeth slept in one bedroom with John. Loretta and I slept in another room, with the little ones on pallets on the floor. What a luxury it was to sleep in a bed, even if we had to share it. God had brought us safely to this place, and Thanksgiving would mean more this year than any other.

"I have a small log house on the property. My men can get it ready, if you want to move there. But you're all welcome here," David said as we sat by the fire one evening. "I don't suppose you have any plans."

"We do," I said. All heads turned toward me, eyes wide.

"What would our plans be?" Jake laughed.

"We'll start a business so that when Jacob and Samuel return, they'll have revenue coming in," I said.

"Sally Ann, did you intend to buy a cotton gin?" David asked.

"I was thinking more on the order of a grist mill," I said. "That's what Jacob wanted to buy before he had to go off fighting,"

"A grist mill? I'll have to do some thinking on that. And who would run it?" David asked.

"Why, I would," I answered.

Everyone looked surprised but Jake, and he said, "If anyone can do it, Sally can. I'm in."

"But money. Do you have any money?" asked David.

"Yes. Gold," I said.

Elizabeth and Loretta looked at me in total puzzlement. "What are you talking about?" Loretta asked. "We went without the whole trip, and you had gold stashed away?"

"That's why those men were chasing us, out of Montezuma," Jake said in my defense. "We couldn't let on we had gold. Besides, there were little or no supplies to be had."

"I don't think there are any grist mills for sale, but gold talks. I'll ask around," David said.

So, I thought we might have a future. I told David I would like to buy a big house where we all could live for the present. After the men came back from the War, we could find separate houses if need be. "I don't think we could stand to live apart at this juncture," I said. "We've come so many miles together." All in all, we had been on the trail almost three months. But really, we had been together much longer than that in our daily lives the last few years.

Chapter 17   MY SOUL LOVETH

"I will seek him whom my soul loveth." The Song of Solomon 3:2

In April of 1865, the South surrendered to the North, and that's when a grist mill became available. The owner, a Mr. Parker, said he was going to Cuba where the Yankees couldn't find him. We bought his business and his house, a large one, with a porch on all four sides, and even his rickety old furniture. And we soon found it necessary to screen that whole porch area: the mosquitoes came out at dusk in droves.

Mr. Parker said he would show us the business before he left. He was thrilled to have gold in his pockets, and we were happy to go to work and become independent. Elizabeth and Loretta decided to stay at home to clean, cook, and take care of the children, and Jake and I went to work. Of course, I had to go home for lunch every day to nurse the baby. We hired two young men to help us, and they were glad for the work as there was little or none to be had.

The mill was built on the Santa Fe River so we had water-power to turn the waterwheel. The waterwheel turned the gears, which turned the stones, which ground the corn. We could later buy corn in the area so local farmers would be pleased to have income also, but what we were using had been stored in by Mr. Parker, as the crops wouldn't come due until summer.

After Mr. Parker left for Cuba and Jake and I started inspecting the grist mill closely, we realized why Mr. Parker was so anxious to sell. Everything had looked good on the surface and it all worked, but there were many problems. The waterwheel was becoming rickety and would have to be rebuilt, and the sluice gate was unreliable and sometimes got stuck in the closed position. The large gear-wheel was becoming worn, along with the smaller gear-wheel. Gear-wheels were things we could only replace, not repair. It was a good thing that the stones were not worn out because I didn't know how we could replace those two huge stones. We continued milling corn and repaired what we could during the day. Repair to the building itself was also necessary; lumber would have to be cut and milled for the building and the wheels. But we were not discouraged. The mill gave us something to occupy our minds so we didn't think as much about Jacob and Samuel - or Ernest Watkins – or Jeremy Atherton. I swear, sometimes I felt like a criminal on the run.

The house and the twenty acres we bought were, happily, a whole other story, built solidly from cypress like David's house, standing high on four-foot pilings. I supposed that was in case the river flooded. Rooms were large and the walls were paneled with cedar, so the house always had a warm, woody smell to it. A tremendous stone fireplace stood in the center of the parlor wall. Three bedrooms flanked the hallway that ran off the parlor. The dining room was directly behind the parlor, and the kitchen was beyond the dining room.

Someone had run copper gutters around the whole house, which ran into a large metal cistern on the back corner of the house. Water was plentiful as it rained a lot in Florida. Even so, we were within walking distance of the river in case of a drought. There was a small barn behind the house, also made of cypress, with four stalls and a loft. Ten acres had been cleared as a fenced pasture; the other ten acres were forest. It was a prized property, that was for sure, in my opinion.

Of course, all this buying of property made me nervous. What if Jacob came home and was angry with me for spending the gold in such a manner? I had never bought anything, much less a property and business. But it was done, and we were putting down roots.

Settling near the small town of La Crosse (pronounced Laycross), the area was remote, and we didn't get news until weeks after things happened. Many of the newspaper offices had shut down since the war ended. David rode up to the house one day and knocked on the door and said, his voice shaking, "The president's been shot and killed by a Southern sympathizer."

With everything we had been through, the murder of our leader made us feel vulnerable again – with no leadership, even though Mr. Lincoln hadn't been the South's leader for some time. Sitting, I put my head in my hands and wondered what else could happen to us. It was a mournful time, and a fearful one, of more reprisals from the federal government. I wondered if we would ever feel normal again and I walked to the mill to tell Jake the sad news.

"Damnation!" I shouted, as I headed down the road, not caring if anyone heard me.

We were in the middle of May, 1865 now, with still no word from Jacob or Samuel. As we were getting ready to celebrate John and Rebecca's fifth and third birthdays, I thought what a glorious day it was for Jacob to come riding down that road. I looked for him that whole live-long day, praying he would come home to me, his two sons, and a baby girl he had never known. But as the sun went down on our celebration, I realized it *wouldn't* be that day.

David had made arrangements for us to sell our cornmeal and grits to the local stores. He was such a big help, so kind, just like Annie. Our grist mill wasn't showing a profit yet, and I thought we would have to broaden our market outside the county. Jake and David had to do all the business agreements, as the businessmen in the area wouldn't deal with a woman, which galled me to no end.

"Sally, you know I was retired from working," Jake said, with a grin, one morning.

I said, "Working agrees with you, and I couldn't do this without you."

"No. *Elizabeth* is what agrees with me. I'm a man who has been given a second chance. You know, I loved Ann more than life, but after she died I thought I would follow her. I was so alone, and then I met Elizabeth. That time, when I was sick at your house, hers was the first face I saw when I opened my eyes - the face of an angel. I fell in love with her that very moment but never dreamed she would love me back. It's not her youth I love; it's her compassion, her zest for life, her willingness to pitch in. I just can't believe she loves me."

Looking down at the floor for a moment, a smile began to emerge on his face.

"Ah, so that's when this all started. Well," I smiled, "she more than loves you, but we all do. And soon you'll be a daddy again."

"Scares me some. I hope I can live long enough to see him grown," he said, which gave me a foreboding feeling.

On the second floor loft of the mill, I had created a little office to do the paperwork for the business – not that there was too much business – indeed, we were slow. One morning the windows were open on either end so I could get a cross-breeze, and as I looked up from my desk, I saw two men on horseback riding across the field. I called for Jake and the boys but got no response. Grabbing the rifle, I headed down the stairs. From the front door I saw one rider was David, and as I lay the rifle by the door and stepped outside, I recognized the second.

A sound came up from my innards that I didn't recognize. I ran toward the two men, and Jacob jumped off his horse, not his beautiful gelding. As he ran toward me, I was screaming and crying and he grabbed me up and swung me round and round. When he set me down, I took his face in my hands and looked into those turquoise eyes.

"Is it really you?" I whispered.

"It's been forever, but I knew I'd come home to you. The thought of you kept me going," he whispered in my ear.

We fell to the ground, and I kissed his face all over. David was forgotten and soon he smiled and said, "See you tomorrow." The field was high in golden grass, and we lay cushioned, looking at each other for the longest time. He had a full beard and his eyes were weary-looking, but he was my same handsome husband. I couldn't take my eyes off him.

He touched my face and ran his hands over my breasts and down my body. I was ready to rip my dress off under the blazing Florida sun and make love to him that very moment, feeling like a wanton woman. But we heard Jake calling my name, and I knew he would be worried. Jumping up, I pulled grass out of my hair and brushed my dress off.

"Come here, Jake. See who's come home: the prodigal son," I yelled.

Jake came running through the tall grass, pulled Jacob off the ground and gave him a big bear hug. We were all crying. "Well, you're a gol-durned sight for sore eyes," Jake said, pounding Jacob on the back. "I could say the same about you, Pa."

"I have lots of questions," Jacob said as we walked toward home.

"We have lots of stories, my boy. Some you won't believe," Jake laughed.

"David would tell me nothing. He said I wouldn't believe him anyway," Jacob smiled.

After a joyful reunion with the family, Jake packed up the women and children and headed to David and Annie's house for the night, knowing Loretta and Elizabeth would take care of my Mary and the boys. God bless him, I thought. "See you in the morning," Jake yelled.

Jacob turned the horse loose in the pasture, turned to me and said, "Woman, I need a bath." He took the tin tub off the wall on the back porch, and I put kettles and pots on to boil. Once the water had cooled some, he stripped off his filthy lieutenant's uniform and settled in the tub. It had a high back, though it was short for his long legs. I washed his hair with lye soap, massaged his scalp and temples, and shaved his beard off, leaving that wonderful moustache.

When he closed his eyes, I thought he was asleep, but as I went for another kettle, he took my hand and asked, "Do we have any brandy? Bring two glasses."

Jake had some brandy stashed in the kitchen, for medicinal purposes he said. I grabbed two water glasses and the bottle. Sitting on the stool I used to bathe the children, I poured our glasses full. It was my first experience with spirits, and it burned going down, making me feel light-headed. As I proceeded to wash the rest of his body, Jacob extended his arm and I kissed the palm of his hand. Water dripped on my bodice, soaking my dress. His hand touched the bun on the back of my neck and he pulled me to him.

"Your smell. I awoke several times at night, thinking I could smell you, that sweet woman-smell," he whispered. And then we kissed a ravenous kiss and I could taste the brandy on his tongue. It was a new sensation for me: I felt so very wicked and I liked it.

There was a new bullet wound in his chest. My finger fit perfectly in the gash, and I touched it gently, my tears falling into the tub. I knew there were stories I would never hear from this man, courageous stories. He did tell me his gelding was shot out from under him, which pained Jacob immensely. In war, he said the loss of a good horse can mean the difference between life and death. So, he stole another horse from a Yankee, which made me smile.

I washed his feet one at a time and massaged his toes, ankles, and calves. He closed his eyes again and leaned back in the tub. As we drank more brandy, I was glad the children were not there to see their mother tipsy. Jacob stood; I poured rinse water over his back, and he turned so I could rinse his chest. He was a magnificent man, his body toned, his muscles pronounced.

I could hardly breathe for looking at him. As I dried him off with a soft towel, he stepped from the tub, and we walked to the bedroom.

Suddenly tired, I sat on the bed. Jacob knelt before me and unbuttoned my soaking-wet dress. He put his head on my chest and held me.

"Sally, you can't know where I've been, but coming home to you is heaven on earth," he whispered. Smelling the soap on his face and the brandy on his breath, my body was on fire.

As we lay facing each other, Jacob said, "My pa looks more like my brother than my pa. He's so fit and tanned. What happened to him?"

"As you can see, he and Elizabeth fell in love and they wanted to get married. I told Jake she was already married. But she said she couldn't go back to that boy, now that she had a real man."

Jacob thought that was funny, laughing out loud, and I had to tell him the walls were paper thin. He said, "Well then, thank the Lord no one is here to hear us." And he rolled on top of me and we made love with such passion that I thought it would last all through the night. God had answered my prayer: my man had come home safely. I hoped He would also answer my prayer of no more babies.

The next day Annie prepared a huge meal for all of us. I

introduced Jacob to Mary Elizabeth and reintroduced him to John and Harry. Loretta looked like she would bust wide open to ask about Samuel, but I think she was afraid of the answer. As Jacob hugged her, I heard him say he'd heard nothing of Samuel since they were separated.

"I can tell you, I sometimes wondered if I would ever sit around a dinner table like this again, eating fried chicken, collards, and biscuits with the people I love most. This war was an evil thing and I thank God to be here with you," Jacob said.

"That was good enough grace for me. How about you, Annie?" David asked.

"Heartfelt," Annie said.

Later that night, when we were back at home, Mary cried out. I picked her up and put her in bed to nurse, and Jacob held us both in his arms. I reached back and grabbed a handful of his hair as if to hold him and not let him drift away from me.

"So, is Elizabeth a bigamist?" Jacob asked me in the early dawn.

"It seems she is. But we are determined Ernest Watkins will never find her," I whispered. "He may be dead." I felt awful wishing it so.

"And you, how did you fare with the birthing?"

"It was long but the easiest I've had yet. Mary was a tiny baby and I think that helped, but I pray it to be the last."

"Well then, separate beds for us," he grinned.

"Never. You'll never leave me again. Promise."

"I promise." And he kissed me so very sweetly. By that time the sun was up, and I could smell coffee. I guessed the whole house had heard our lovemaking, and we didn't look anyone in the eye when we reached for our coffee cups.

"Lord have mercy. We may have to move to the log cabin," Jake whispered to Jacob.

Jacob could only smile. I didn't want him out of my sight and had to keep touching him on the arm as we sat at the table. If I walked behind him, I touched his hair or his face. I guess I felt if I kept one hand on him, I could keep him with me. He held my hands and looked at my broken fingernails and red fingers, kissing them in front of everyone, and I didn't care.

After breakfast we walked to the mill and talked about the

business. I had some new ideas that I had wanted to tell him about. He listened to me run on about cornmeal sacks, made out of flowered material, that women could use for quilting or sewing clothes.

"Would you rather stay home with the children and let me handle the business?" he asked.

I was shocked and hurt and it must have showed on my face because he immediately back-tracked and said, "I only meant that you've worked so hard, I thought you might want some time with the children. You've done such a good job, Sally. I couldn't have done better myself."

Chapter 18   *UNTIL I RETURN*

John and Harry were shy with Jacob. It seemed as if John wanted Jake to be his pa and I knew this hurt Jacob, but I told him that time would change this. John just hung on Jake and wouldn't even hug Jacob, a stranger to his own children, but Harry was younger and hadn't spent as much time with Jake so he was a little more affectionate with his pa. Mary Elizabeth loved her daddy, and he spent evenings holding her and talking to her. Having missed out on so much of his children's lives was painful for him. He was trying to catch up, but in spite of what I'd said I doubted that John's bond with Jake would be easily broken. After six months, John was still sleeping with Jake and Elizabeth, though I knew that would have to end.

Jacob wouldn't talk about the war; he said he had to put it out of his mind, that talking about it would only bring it to the forefront. So we talked of menial things and the business. The waterwheel had to be rebuilt, and he had to let one of the workers go since he was back. He said he would have to let the other one go when Samuel returned though the hope that Samuel would return was dwindling in my mind.

But when we walked home from the mill for lunch one day, Loretta came screaming out of the house, waving a letter in the air. "He's alive! He's alive! He's in a hospital in North Carolina. His leg's been shot."

As we gathered around her, she read Samuel's letter. Jacob said he would take a wagon and go for him, even though everything was chaos in Georgia and the Carolinas. My heart sank.

"Loretta, write back and find out when the hospital will release him. Tell him I'm coming," he said.

As soon as the letter came from the hospital, Jacob left. We hugged him goodbye, but I couldn't speak and left early for the mill. As Loretta would say, I was truculent. Later that day, Jake came charging into the office. "It's Elizabeth. You've got to come," he yelled. Elizabeth was in labor with her first child, and her eyes looked purely terrified.

"Sally, I need you here with me. You know what to do. Please, I'm paining," she cried.

Truth be known, I had never delivered a baby and though I had prepared myself mentally for this day, I was worried about my abilities as a midwife. Elizabeth had of course delivered my babies so I wanted to do the best I could. Jake took John and they headed to the woods, as was their habit in these circumstances. Loretta guided the three babies to the yard to read under the big oak tree. It was Elizabeth and me again, and as I washed my hands and put two kettles on to boil, the wait began.

"Do you want to try the Indian method?" I asked, but she said no; she wasn't strong enough for that. I thought she *was* strong enough, physically, but maybe lacked the will. To relieve the pain, I massaged her belly and her back. At last, when the sun was setting, she pushed out a beautiful baby boy, and just as she had done for me, I cleaned him up, cut the cord, and laid him on her chest. She was eight hours birthing, and the strain had taken her strength but she wasn't bleeding.

While Elizabeth slept, I took the baby boy and sat in the rocker and sang a lullaby to him. He felt like my own, and I loved him as my own. When Jake came back in with John, he knelt down on the floor and hugged me and the baby. I'm sure a year ago he never thought he would be having babies again.

When Mary Elizabeth cried for me, I handed the baby to Jake, went to my bed, and fell asleep nursing her. Exhaustion overpowered me, and I slept the whole night through, without any supper.

The baby would be called Jacob Samuel Winston, born June 14, 1865: not another Jacob, I thought, but Elizabeth insisted on the name. When I counted back the months, I realized this union between Elizabeth and Jake had started long before I knew it. Adultery going on in the camp, and I didn't even know it! My mother would have been scandalized, Mother Ann would have been scandalized, but everyone else seemed fine with it. I guess we all had our own worries and couldn't be concerned with our neighbors'.

Jacob had taken a light buggy from David because it was faster, along with two fresh horses as we felt ours couldn't make that long trip again. It was two months' time before Jacob and Samuel returned. Samuel was on a crutch, had a bad limp, and was thin and pale, but we were so glad to see him. And I again welcomed my husband back home. Samuel was tired from the trip, which had been harrowing since so many roads were closed, causing them to backtrack many times. Jacob seemed tired, too, even though he was also relieved. Loretta couldn't stop crying.

"I believe we will take David up on that log cabin," Jake said to Jacob the next day as we walked to the mill. "It's getting mighty cramped in our house. And John needs to know who his daddy is."

My heart was sad, but really, I knew it was the right thing to do. Jacob told Jake there was more gold, and that part of it belonged to him since he had been a partner at the cotton gin. Jake thanked him, shaking his hand.

"I'd like to continue on at the mill if you'll have me," Jake said.

"We outright need you," I said. "Jake, we would've never made it on the trail without you. Just want you to know how much I appreciate you," I said.

"Thanks. That means a lot coming from a woman like you." He looked at Jake and said, "She's a helluva woman, Jacob." To me, he said, "We've come a long way, girlie."

Chapter 19   A QUESTION OF GUILT

Having written my family in Tennessee several times without receiving an answer, I worried that they might have been killed. The fighting had been terrible in that part of the South, and my pa was not a warring man. I looked for a letter every week but none came.

I had also written away for a mail order catalog. When it came I planned to order the new Dr. Edward Foote's "womb veil," which would keep me from having babies. It was six dollars and I knew that was a lot of money, but I didn't think I could live through another birthing. My three children would need me to raise them. I hadn't told Jacob about this as I believed, strongly, that this was a woman's secret. I hadn't even told Loretta or Elizabeth.

John cried for Jake at night. I felt I should have never let him sleep with Jake and Elizabeth, and Jacob was losing patience with him. I began to go sleep with him until morning, and Jacob was not happy about that either. But I couldn't have Samuel and Loretta awake all night because John was missing Jake. I had to nurse the baby, too, so my nights were not restful. Sometimes I thought it would've been better to send John to live with Jake. But it just wouldn't have been right.

I *had* to figure a way for John to sleep with Harry and be happy about it. I thought maybe when he started to school, things would change, but for now, he still longed for Jake and hunting with him. I knew these worries were trivial compared to what we had faced on the trail, but they were still daily trials. And I surely still thanked God for my three healthy children, my safe husband, and my extended family.

Loretta and Samuel were talking about building a house at the edge of our property. Even though we would be able to see their house, each family would have their privacy. With my night hours, I was no longer going to the mill. Samuel worked part time, even with a very bad limp, and Jake and Jacob worked full time; we had let all the laborers go.

The men cut the trees for Samuel and Loretta's house. The logs were then sent to the sawmill to be cut into lumber and seasoned. Heart pine was the wood of choice in Florida, along with cypress. It was supposed to be a hard wood and termite-resistant also. In Tennessee, and Georgia, oak was the wood we had mostly used for building. But we were being advised by David, and he seemed to know what he was talking about.

Amazingly, their house went up in a week's time after the lumber came back, with all the help from our neighbors. I made curtains for the windows and a tablecloth for the table Jacob was making for them. It was a small house, but Loretta said they were done having children, so they didn't need any more room. I wondered how she could be so sure of that.

When my "womb veil" arrived, I read the instructions and tried it out, smiling to myself at how ridiculous it seemed. It was to be used before the "act" so I kept it in a safe place. But if it really would prevent another child, I certainly wanted to try it. Elizabeth and Loretta would have laughed if they had known. But they only had one child each so it wouldn't have been as important to them.

Jacob bought me the prettiest little red velvet rocking chair, called a nursing rocker because it had no arms and sat low to the ground. Most days, around noon, Mary Elizabeth and I sat in that chair in the parlor and closed our eyes while she nursed. One hot August day when I was feeling tired, Mary and I took our places on the little rocker, when I heard Jacob's horse ride up out front. I kept my eyes closed and drifted off, knowing the boys were safely playing under the old oak tree.

"Why, Mrs. Winston, ain't you just a sight!" My eyes popped open and there, standing before me, looking lecherous, was Ernest Watkins. His dark eyes were flashing and anger showed in his red face. Dirty and dusty from traveling, he was almost unrecognizable.

"Ernest, what're you doing here?" I tried to hide my breast, but I only had my hand to cover it. I pulled Mary away and began buttoning my chemise. As she started to cry, I set her on the floor and rose to put myself between her and Ernest. He stood with his rifle pointed to the floor but it was still menacing. It was the one time of the day when I didn't have my little peashooter – when I was nursing.

"I'm here to take back my wife and baby," he growled.

"Elizabeth doesn't work for me anymore. You need to get on out of here. Go on home."

"I know she married that old man and she has my baby. I aim to find her, with or without your help. Either she goes home with me, or I'll expose her to the whole community. I know all about you church-goers."

Out of the corner of my eye I saw Jacob come through the screen door, quiet as a shadow, his rifle lifted, pointed at Ernest's head. Ernest's back was turned to him.

"And if I don't find her, I'll come back for you." He pointed his finger at me, threateningly.

I glanced at Jacob, and Ernest turned to look down the barrel of that rifle.

"Go on back to Atlanta, Ernest. There's nothing for you here," Jacob said.

Ernest brushed past Jacob and said, between gritted teeth, "You better keep your children close." Then, slamming the screen door behind him, he mounted his horse and rode away.

Trembling, I grabbed up Mary, and Jacob caught me around the shoulders.

"Bring the boys in and stay inside. Keep your pistol close. I've got to warn Pa," he said, and rode out.

My heart was pounding out of my chest. We had become far too relaxed, thinking we were safe in Florida. My doors were always unlocked. I determined to have keys made and keep the doors locked. Jacob didn't return for several hours. Jake and Elizabeth lived on the Winston Ranch, which was about five miles west of our place. Their cabin was off the main road so it wouldn't be easy for Ernest to find.

"Pa is fixing the roof, and he said he's not worried about Ernest," Jacob said, when he returned. But I could tell he *was* worried and Elizabeth seemed very concerned also. We'll have to wait and see what happens. I told them to come here for a time, but he is bull-headed."

I knew Ernest would find them, given enough time, as we had become ingrained in the local community and people would talk to him. In a couple of days, I decided to take the buggy over to speak with Elizabeth and Jake. Jacob wouldn't have approved, so I didn't tell him. I dropped the children off with Loretta, who was happy to have someone for Rebecca to play with. As I explained the situation to her, she became frightened. I must admit, I looked over my shoulder the whole way. Ernest was mad enough to hurt somebody, and it could be me. When I got to Jake's house, he was up on the roof replacing shake shingles.

"Howdy, Jake. Come on down off there. I need to talk with you and Elizabeth," I called to him.

"Good God, woman, can't you see I'm working? But, okay, I do need a break," he grinned.

When I sat with Jake and Elizabeth, I said, "I'm not sure you know how serious this business is with Ernest. He's mad, and he thinks the baby is his."

"What? Baby Jacob is Jake's son. You know that, Sally. I hadn't seen him in months, and we only had a few nights together before he went to war." She looked shyly at Jake.

"I'm sorry, Jake. It had to be said," Elizabeth whispered.

At that very moment, we heard, "Elizabeth, get out here!" It was Ernest. "I done followed Mrs. Winston. I knew she'd lead me to you," he laughed harshly.

Elizabeth put the baby in the back bedroom and grabbed up a rifle, loading as she headed toward the door.

"Wait a minute, Elizabeth. You aren't going out there," Jake snapped.

"This is not your battle, Jake. It's mine." She brushed by him and was out the front door with him on her coattails. This situation was not faring well. Grabbing my pistol out of my pocket, I followed them out the door.

"You lying bitch, I want my son!" Ernest yelled, eyes wild.

"He's not your son, Ernest. He's Jake's son," she said.

"That old man. He didn't father that baby!"

"Watch your mouth, Ernest," Jake said. "Go on home. Elizabeth thought you were dead. We *are* married, legal and all, and that *is* my son."

Ernest still wore his confederate uniform. I thought that was a strange thing at the time as the war was over. He had his wool coat on, and it was a hot day. Later I would realize he was in battle mode.

Raging, he yelled, "I could take you off with me right now, you and my boy."

"He's not your boy. I don't love you, Ernest," Elizabeth said.

Ernest lifted his rifle, one-handed, and shot Jake before any of us could make a move. With wild eyes, Elizabeth raised her rifle and shot Ernest in the chest. The blood flowed onto that grey wool jacket like a red morning glory opening to the summer sun. My pistol never fired a shot. Ernest fell from his horse, dead, I reckoned.

"Jake! Jake!" Elizabeth screamed and fell to the ground. Samuel and Jacob came riding up then and jumped off their horses, with David not far behind.

"Get him in the house!" Jacob ordered, looking at me in anger, and I knew I had done a stupid thing by leading Ernest there; I was devastated.

David rode for the doctor. We put Jake on the kitchen table, got his shirt off, and I could see the bullet-wound in his chest, but couldn't tell how serious it was. He was bleeding a lot, and we packed the wound with cloth and held it to keep him from bleeding to death. He was unconscious, and Elizabeth began to sob.

"It's my fault. I should've never married Jake." She looked up at us in desperation. "Sally, *you* can help me save him."

I felt so helpless as we waited for the doctor. He arrived just at sunset. "Help me turn him, boys," he ordered.

"Looks like the bullet went clean through. Now all we have to do is keep him from bleeding to death or getting a fever. Can you stay through the night?" he asked all of us.

Then he pulled a bottle of whiskey out of his pocket and poured it in the bullet-wound. Jake was no longer unconscious; he howled in pain.

As we nodded to the doc that we could stay through the night, Jacob said, "Sally, you need to go get those children and take them home."

"Jacob, I can be of help here," I said. He grabbed me by the arm and dragged me outside.

"Sally, I'm trying not to blame you for this, but so help me, God, you are trying my patience. You should've told me you were coming here. You're too damned stubborn. That Watkins boy was just waiting for you to lead him here," he yelled at me.

"I wasn't lying to you, Jacob, but I didn't think Jake and Elizabeth were taking this seriously," I pleaded.

"You have too many secrets, Sally. What else don't I know? What is that thing in the dresser drawer? Are you limiting the number of children we will have without asking me?" he yelled.

My mind was stunned. Deep, dark, heavy guilt overpowered me for not being forthcoming with him. And now Jake might die because of me. The guilt was more than I could bear. I walked to the wagon, climbed up and drove away, sobbing as I left Jacob in the dust. My heart was broken as I felt I hadn't met my responsibilities. Jacob and I had not had cross words like that in our whole marriage. Then, though, my righteous indignation rose, as I had brought our family safely out of Georgia to Florida while carrying a baby in my body. Was I not capable of making decisions? I was angry and sad and heavy-hearted, all at the same time.

By the time I arrived at Loretta's, she was frantic, so I had to tell her the whole gruesome story, sobbing as I spoke. When John heard that his Jake had been shot, he got hysterical. I knew I had to get my children home and calmed down.

Sleep would not come that night. I was at wit's end that our dear Jake might die because of my stubbornness. When John cried out in the night, I went to him and held him for a while. As I was climbing back in bed, I heard Jacob coming in the front door. He dropped his clothes and slid into bed beside me and buried his face in my neck. "I'm sorry. I'm sorry," he whispered.

"I'm sorry, too, Jacob. I would never harm Jake. I love that man," I whispered back.

"He's going to make it, the doc said. Samuel is with Elizabeth now. Tell me you forgive me, Sally."

"I do." And tears fell down my face onto his face, and we held each other until sleep took us.

Jake was alive, but he would be bedridden for a long time, the doctor said. Ernest's body and horse were turned over to the sheriff, who said it was self-defense so there would be no inquiry.

"What makes a man turn into a monster like Ernest?" I asked Jacob. "Surely he wasn't always like that, or Elizabeth wouldn't have married him."

"War makes us all crazy. Ernest was a jilted man; nothing worse than a soldier coming home to his woman, and she's gone with another man. And look at the things you've had to do. You should've been living a life of luxury. Instead, you were walking over 300 miles in the cold, with very little food. And me, having to kill other folks who I don't hate. Look at us now, struggling to scratch out a living with an old, broken-down grist mill."

"It just needs some work, some boards replaced, the wheel repaired again. We're better off than most folks. And you are home with your family. That's my biggest blessing," I said.

We'd been taking dinner to Jake and Elizabeth most nights. The children loved to see their grandfather, especially of course, John. Elizabeth looked haggard when I hugged her as we went into the cabin one evening; she felt limp.

"Are you sleeping, Elizabeth?" I asked her.

"Can't sleep. Between the baby and Jake and worrying about someone coming after us. And feeling shame over killing Ernest. I did him wrong, Sally. I'm a bad woman, sleeping with Jake when I was married to Ernest. I can't seem to feel good about anything. Ernest wasn't a bad man; I drove him to try to kill Jake. And then there's Jeremy....when will he come for us?'"

"Elizabeth, you *are* a good woman, a strong woman. You couldn't know Ernest was alive. You couldn't know he would do such a terrible thing. He was damaged from the war," I said, trying to believe my own words. "And Jeremy's dead, I'm certain."

"I knew Ernest was alive when Mr. Brown told us, and still I married Jake. I put all of us in jeopardy. I'm no good. I can't even be a good mother to my baby when I've done such horrible things. You think I'm strong, Sally, because you're so strong. You don't know who I am," she said.

That was a conversation which caused me no end of worry. I had heard of women going a little crazy right after having a baby, but Elizabeth seemed far beyond that. I began to visit more often, to help with Jake and see how Elizabeth was. But our conversations always turned to the weather and Jake's condition; nothing about her condition. Jake was starting to sit up in a chair, and he smiled when the children came in one evening.

"Elizabeth needs some cheering," Jake said. "I want you to take her to Gainesville for a few days, and buy yourselves some new frocks. I'm worried about her."

"We'd love that," I replied. He touched my arm then and said, "Tell me about Jeremy Atherton." I nodded my head back and forth and said, "I can't. We made a pact."

But that trip never happened. David found Elizabeth, face-down in the lake behind their cabin within days of our conversation. I was there when he pulled her lifeless body from the water, and I wish I hadn't seen her. Dressed in her beautiful blue Sunday dress, she had her shoes on and her hair was in a lovely bun at the back of her neck. Leaning against a cypress tree, Jake could not be consoled. I held him and tried my best to calm him, but he collapsed to the ground, sobbing into his hands. Of course, he blamed himself.

Elizabeth had known I was bringing Sunday dinner for her family. I wondered if she hoped I would be the one to find her, but quickly realized she was devoid of all hope. With her fear of water, and the bad things that had happened to her in water, I questioned how she could she have walked into that lake. My anger toward these events was so great I could hardly speak. Of course it stemmed from overwhelming sadness that we would never see each other again in this life. I guess sleeplessness, coupled with guilt and her extreme fear, caused her mind to stop working.

The baby, Jacob, was six months old and still needed his mother. I took him to my house so that I could nurse him. Because Jake was an invalid, he went to David and Annie's home, but David said his father was going downhill fast. Elizabeth had to have been in the depths of despair to leave her love, Jake, and her new precious baby. My grief for my sister-friend, Elizabeth, and my father-in-law, loves of my life, was like a hot poker in the center of my soul, allowing me no happiness, not even when Jacob hugged me and kissed my face and tried to make me smile. I just had no smiles in me – on my face or in my heart. I was finding that sometimes the aftermath of war could be more devastating than the war itself.

Chapter 20   LOOK FORWARD

The question that would plague me for the rest of my life was: why wasn't I faster to shoot Ernest, before he shot Jake? But I've also wondered if we didn't all feel guilty for wronging him while he was away fighting a war for us. I will never know the answers, but I did realize I had the strength and will to kill Rondel Atherton, so I had the ability and yet, I let Ernest shoot Jake. It was a heavy burden I would bear until the day I died.

Jacob voiced this concern also. "I had the chance to pull the trigger that day in our home," he said more than once. Maybe he could not kill a fellow soldier. I felt if I had killed him in place of Elizabeth, she might have stayed with us.

Jake passed away two months after Elizabeth, leaving us with sweet baby Jacob to raise. Sadness just seemed to be the normal way those days. I was a wet nurse to their baby, and I would have to be his mother, too.

I went to see Jake before he died and held his hand. I kissed it and begged him not to leave us, but his spirit and body were so sorely wounded I knew he could not recover. He said, "We cannot all be like you, Sally. I wish I were stronger. Please take care of my baby boy." I was so perplexed that people thought I was strong. I didn't feel strong, especially at that point. But there was no choice for me but to continue.

Annie and David visited our house on the Sunday after Jake's funeral. Annie held baby Jacob, but he cried for me. At that moment, I had the finest idea. Annie was hungry for a baby and although I loved baby Jacob, I needed time to raise my own three children.

"Annie, I'll have a few more months feeding baby Jacob, but would you like to adopt him then?" I asked.

Tears filled her eyes, and I could see that this thought had already occurred to her. Just then David walked in with Jacob and she ran to him.

"Sally has offered baby Jacob to us, David," she cried.

I'm sure my husband was beside himself over me because once again I hadn't consulted him on a large matter. But he saw the joy on David and Annie's face and he smiled at me.

In a few months I started weaning baby Jacob so he could go and live with Annie and David. They had a milk cow and could start him on a bottle at that time. I knew I would miss that little body; a woman can't feed a baby and not form a bond with him. Annie was as happy as a woman could be, but when she and David came to take him home, I had such bittersweet emotions. His fat little hand reached toward me as they pulled away, and I could hear him crying all the way down the road. He had lost two mothers in as many months. But I knew Annie would be a good mother and that we had done the right thing.

My poor, poor Elizabeth, whose life began in tragedy and ended in tragedy. I could've written a book about her. She was my friend, my sister, my mother-in-law, in the end. We were more alike than anyone I'd ever known, true kindred spirits. Our modest beginnings and need to nurture other people had often bonded us together. She had the purest heart of anyone I knew, being quiet and beautiful, inside and out. I didn't know how I could stand to see the sun shine and know she would never stand in it again, that we could never bathe in a river again or laugh at nothing. Sometimes, in my mind, I could hear her sweet voice singing. My heart hurt, and I knew my life would never be the same without her.

And Jake. If ever there was a man I could love as much as my own husband, it was Jake - so good-natured and brave. I only knew him to be agitated with me one time and that was on the trail, about the gold coin. But I made it up to him when he got married and I dropped the other coin in his pocket. Those sparkling blue eyes and charming smile - I just had to look at John and I saw Jake all over again. And John missed Jake more than anyone, being too young to understand death. He was angry about it, and, really, so was I. I wanted Jake back in our lives so much, though it was not to be. Goodbye, my wonderful friend, my travel companion, and one of the best men I ever knew.

Work became my salvation: taking care of the children, housework, gardening, helping at the mill. I worked until I fell into bed at night and prayed for sleep so I didn't have to relive the events of the past few months. Sometimes I fell asleep with Mary so I didn't have to get up with her in the night. Jacob would reach for me in the night but I was too tired. It didn't seem right to make love when I was so sad. Loving was meant for happy times. But Jacob didn't understand.

"Sally, don't leave me. Talk to me," he pleaded one morning. "We have each other."

Words couldn't explain my feelings. "Leave me be. I have to work it out myself," I said.

He walked away and didn't come home for supper that night.

When he came to bed, I could smell liquor on his breath and it was disgusting to me. He kissed me on my neck and face, and I couldn't stand the thought of making love with him. When I tried to leave the bed, he grabbed me by my arm. As he pulled me on top of him, he began to caress my body.

"I can't, Jacob," I whispered.

"Sally, I need you and I love you. Don't you realize that that was my father and that I loved Elizabeth too? I need you now." But I couldn't be with him then. I had to find my way first, and the smell of liquor only made things worse. As I broke away and went to sleep with Mary, I heard him leave.

I felt like I was going down the same road as Elizabeth. Things were spinning out of my control, and I was becoming lost in a world of sadness. The realization that I could lose my husband was paramount in my mind, and yet I couldn't change my actions. There was no joy in my life as before, even in the care of my children's needs. Jacob was a virile man, and I knew I had to welcome him back into my bed.

Loretta walked from her house with Rebecca one morning. By the look on her face, I knew she wanted to talk about her brother.

"Jacob is beside himself, Sally. He is drowning in sorrow and doesn't find consolation with you. I'm worried about him," she said.

"You can't reject him now when he needs you so."

"I can't, Loretta. And he's drinking."

"He's drinking because he thinks you don't love him, and he misses Pa and Elizabeth. He said he could stand anything but your not loving him," she said tearfully.

"You know I love him, but I'm confused right now. I just need time."

"You don't have time. He's wasting, and you must help him. We're all suffering; Samuel lost a daughter, I lost my father," she pleaded.

Jacob came home late that night. I was sitting in the little rocker with an oil lamp on the table. He was surprised to see me still up as I was usually in bed by sundown. Motioning for him to come and sit in the chair beside me, he hesitantly sat down, with no smell of whiskey about him. His hands were in his lap, and he looked down at them, sighing.

"Jacob, I'm sorry. I've only been thinking about myself," I began. "Please forgive me. He was your pa, and I know how you loved him."

Big tears rolled down his cheeks, onto his hands. He didn't try to hide them from me.

"I can bear anything, Sally, if you stand by me. You're my strength; I feel I'm nothing without you. I can't bear this grief alone." His voice was ragged, and his words broke my heart. Kneeling before him, I kissed his tear-stained hands. He held my head and touched my hair until it fell down my back.

"I have been so selfish, such a fool," I said, and kissed his face and his salty tears and his eyes and neck and chest. Standing, I pulled him to me and to the bedroom. We melted together as only we could. I *had* been a damned fool. But it did occur to me how different men and women were, especially where emotions were concerned.

☼

As we entered the year of 1866, I felt older than my twenty two years. As I looked at Jacob, who would be thirty seven that year, I noticed his hair had started to gray already, the lines around his eyes very pronounced. He was still so handsome he stopped my heart, but the light had gone out in his eyes. I was hoping time would heal these deep wounds that we both shared.

John would be six years old in May. The schoolhouse was ten miles away, so Loretta offered to school John, Harry and Rebecca during the day. I found that to be an answer to prayers as John had been unruly lately, and his mind needed to be channeled. The school was too far for us to travel daily. I even thought perhaps our neighbors might want Loretta to teach their children also.

I still had no answers to the three letters I'd written to my parents. It left my heart heavy, but we had experienced so much during this war, I didn't know that my heart could take any more. Loretta kept telling me that life was for the living, and I was trying to overcome this low feeling. If anyone could help me it was Mary Elizabeth, who was such a lively, happy baby. She touched my face when she was babbling to me, and I looked into those bright eyes, so full of promise. It was a tough old world out there, but she didn't know that yet.

I ordered white leather shoes for her baby feet to protect them from sand spurs and brambles. I would make sure her life would be easier than mine. I wanted her to always have food on the table, and warm clothes for the winter, and never to be subjected to war. My dream for her was a good man of means, who would love and respect her, as Jacob had me. And her face wouldn't be freckled from the sun as mine was. The dreams I had for her I never had for myself. Sometimes it made me sad that she couldn't have the childhood I had, but the world had changed. She made me smile enough that my heart of stone started to soften somewhat. Strangely enough, when I started to melt, Jacob's eyes started to get the twinkle back. I never really knew how strongly I affected him.

Loretta and I spent a lot of time together, sewing and quilting. She was a wonderful person, even if she was not Elizabeth. She seemed so much more prim than I was, and was not really happy about hard work. But we had a lot of hard work to do. We had put in a vegetable garden, which we shared; she was not prone to pulling weeds, though.

The chicken coops needed to be raked out at times, and she always offered to watch the children while I raked. I loved her, I did.

But I missed my work-mate, who could work as hard as I did, and laugh while doing it. Loretta had always had a servant to do her cleaning, so much of her housework went by the wayside. Since she was teaching my children, I helped her clean her house at times. And I must say she was great as a teacher, having so much more knowledge than I did. My book-learning had definitely gone lacking, even though I loved reading, but books had come at a premium since the war ended. My words were so ordinary, and Loretta had a very flowery way of speaking. The children benefited greatly from her teaching.

Slowly, my feelings for my husband were coming back stronger than ever. It had taken time not to just go through the motions in order to keep him happy. I now looked forward to his coming home for supper and always had a hot meal ready, and he was so appreciative. As we sat around the table as a family, he would touch my hand ever so gently. I knew I would love him till I died, no matter what hardships we had to overcome.

He was trying to build a relationship with John and had decided to take him hunting one Saturday, which John was very excited about. John's little heart was still broken with the death of Jake, and I thought only his father could help mend it.

Finally, a letter came from home: it was in Ma's handwriting.

"Dear Sally Ann,

I just received your last letter. We didn't know where you had gone when you left Georgia. I have some sad news to tell you: your pa and Jefferson were killed during the war. Jefferson was too young to go off fighting, but he ran away one night, and your pa went after him. We had awful fighting in Tennessee, and they were killed by cannon fire. I have John David and Henry Louis with me. We live in a shack on your grandparents' plantation. Your grandparents were killed when the main house was set afire. Beatrice and her husband and children have moved into the big house and are making repairs.

She has been very generous with us. I clean the big house in return for our cabin.

Hoping this letter finds you well,

Your loving mother."

When Jacob came home for lunch, he found me in my little rocker with the letter in my hand. I somehow could not cry over my poor pa and little Jefferson. Maybe it was because they had been killed two years earlier. Whatever the reason, I couldn't explain my lack of tears. And my ma, living as a servant to my sister. The world certainly was upside-down. Nothing made sense anymore.

He took the letter and read it and said, "Send for them. They can live here."

"You're a generous man, Jacob, knowing how close our money is," I said. "But my ma would never leave Tennessee. I'll send money when we can spare it." I thought about my sweet pa, and how he had shaped my life. He was in heaven, I was certain of that.

There was one thing I *was* happy about, however, and that was that the womb veil had worked, and I was fixing to order another one. My worry was that it would wear out and fail me. That had been the best six dollars I ever spent. Jacob always laughed at me at night when I reached for the dresser drawer. I never failed to use it.

I guess everyone's life has a mile marker that indicates a turn in it, just like in the history books. Ours were the deaths of Elizabeth and Jake. We were all changed forever, especially we travelers who made the exodus from Atlanta. I could never go back to being that young carefree girl in Tennessee who ran barefoot through the dew or swam in the creek and drank in the warm sunshine. My daughter would not be that kind of girl, either, because I would keep her close to me, and though she wore shoes to church, I couldn't bear the thought of her wearing them at home. She once stumbled and lost her balance, so I took them off. I was determined she would find a man of means, a good man. There would be little freedom in her life so that I could protect her.

Had I become my mother or worse, my grandmother? Maybe they knew something I did not, at that young age. But I did know what was best for my daughter and it was not to run off with the first young man she thought she loved. Did I blame Elizabeth for the trauma to our family? No. Given the same choices, I would have chosen Jake also, but Jacob and I and our children had been profoundly affected by her choices. Her loving Jake was not the problem: it was loving Jake when she was married to another man. And Jake, he had no option but to love Elizabeth and in the end, he could not go on without her. But there was no sense looking back down the road we'd come; we couldn't change it. As Mr. Brown had said on the trail, "We have to look forward now, not back."

Part II   1866-1881

Chapter 1 *RECONSTRUCTION*

Reconstruction had begun in our part of the world. We were the conquered. The South was being punished for participating in the war, and I didn't know why they called it reconstruction; it was more like destruction. Acreage had been taken away from many Southerners by the Freeman's Bureau and given to former slaves: over 160,000 acres in Florida and 350,000 acres in Georgia. There were carpetbaggers everywhere, even in our part of Florida, especially in the Gainesville area. These were Northerners who came to the South to take advantage of our impoverished plight. They bought up properties and businesses that we could no longer afford.

We tried to steer clear of the larger cities as that's where the opportunists congregated, but there were times when we had to buy supplies that we couldn't get locally. It was a changed world, not safe for a family or women alone. If it hadn't been for General Robert E. Lee's negotiations, the whole South would have lost the right to vote. Of course, women couldn't vote at all anywhere, and I couldn't rightly understand that.

A fancy buggy pulled up to our front driveway one morning as I was getting the children ready to walk to Loretta's house. Two men got down and knocked on my door. Feeling safe that Jacob could see the house from the mill, I opened the door and kept my hand on my little pistol in my apron pocket. The screen door latch was on.

"Good morning, ma'am," the taller man said, dressed in a suit and shiny vest, with a gold watch hanging from his pocket. His dark hair matched his sinister eyes. The other man, who was breathing hard, as if he had run a long way, was short and pudgy, with a bright red face. He, likewise, was dressed in very fancy clothes; their accents were definitely not Southern.

"Good morning, gentlemen. Do you need directions?" I asked.

"No ma'am, looking for a Mr. Jacob Henry Winston," the short man said.

"I'm Jacob Winston," Jacob said from behind them.

They both spun around, surprised, as Jacob could be as quiet as an Indian when he wanted, which came from hunting with his pa.

"Mr. Winston, wondered if we could have a word in private with you?" the tall man said.

"Speak in front of my wife. We're partners," Jacob said.

"Partners?" They both smirked.

I bristled and stepped out on the porch, with my hand on the trigger of my pistol, hidden in my pocket. Both men stepped back away from me.

"Well, here's the thing of it. Talk around town is that you folks are in a bit of trouble and could use some revenue. We're here as a generous gesture, to offer you a goodly sum for your property and mill," the short man stammered, looking frightened, though the tall man did not.

I looked at Jacob, and he was eyeing the tall man, as we both figured he was the protection for the short, fat man. Jacob picked up the rifle he had leaned by the front door and calmly said, "No, we are not in need of assistance. I thank you for your interest, however. Now, I must get back to work. Good day to you."

No one moved. I could hear the children playing inside, and I felt very vulnerable. But I knew I could shoot the tall man before he shot Jacob, if he decided to.

"Here's my card if you ever consider selling," he said, and they backed off the steps.

Once they were gone, I collapsed in the rocking chair on the porch. Jacob knelt beside me and said, "Times are different now and we have to be more diligent. The children must not walk to Loretta's alone, as close as it is, and you *must* keep your pistol loaded. And do *not* open the door to anyone."

There would be no going back to days when people were safe, when children could walk down a road alone, even though we were at a dead-end road with no traffic to speak of. These two men would return several more times, and finally Jacob asked them not to come back. It's hard to say why we felt so threatened by them, but in the end, they did us no harm. For myself, I thought maybe the Freeman's Bureau was coming to take our land from us, and I suspected these two men might have been a little afraid of us also.

☼

Loretta had started carrying a little pistol in her apron pocket, too, which was humorous to me as she was so feminine I wasn't sure she could shoot anyone if she tried. But early one morning, before the children went to her house for schooling, we heard loud gunshots ring out in the direction of Samuel and Loretta's cabin. Grabbing my pistol, I followed Jacob out the back door on our way to their house. Jacob was loading the rifle as we were running. When we got closer, Loretta stood at her back door, with a broom in her hand, beating a small black bear on his backside. She raised her pistol and shot it in the air several times more, with the bear running away from her as fast as he could. I knew we shouldn't have laughed, but it was a sight I would never forget, and one we didn't think we would ever see. Loretta *was* getting tougher. Samuel came running from the mill and joined us in laughter, but Loretta did not find the situation, or our laughter, entertaining.

It seemed the bear had gotten into her pantry before she was out of bed, and the noise woke her and Rebecca. Immediately, she fired at the bear and of course, missed him, but it scared him into running out the back door, with her on his tail. She was in her nightgown when we arrived and huffed her way back into the cabin. The three of us, Jacob, Samuel, and me, cleaned up the pantry, and we didn't see Loretta again that morning. We were truly pistol-packing women.

Samuel said, "Loretta is vicious when it comes to protecting Rebecca. She *is* a mama bear."

☼

The Southern cotton farmers had fallen onto hard times. Even if they managed to hang on to their farms, there were very few young men left to work the fields. Some slaves stayed on the farms as they didn't know what else to do. Many nights, at suppertime, a black family would show up at my back door with their children in tow, looking tattered and hungry, their big searching eyes hoping for a handout. Jacob said I was looking for trouble, but I just couldn't let children starve. Sometimes, a single black man would show up, and I would wrap some biscuits up for him and send him on his way. Oftentimes we had chickens and eggs missing the next morning, but we couldn't guard the henhouse all night long. Jacob bought a guard dog, which warned us of intruders – Charlie was his name.

My thought was that we could put the men to work but Jacob wouldn't have it. He said that if I must feed them, I should then send them on their way. I felt my house had been marked as an easy touch. How could I know that this would affect us later in our lives?

☼

He was a man I couldn't recognize right off, something about him so familiar to me, however. His grey wool jacket a sign of his Confederate service, a red bandana tied around his neck, he was a ghost of a person.

Not many old soldiers showed up on my back doorstep, mostly former slaves, but he was hungry-looking and pitiful, except for the six-gun stuffed in the waist of his ragged pants. I wrapped up some fresh-baked biscuits in a cloth and unlatched the screen door, when Mary came toddling out on the porch and hid in the folds of my skirt, whimpering.

"That your girl?" he croaked. Picking her up, I offered him the food, which he grabbed, tears running down his face. And that was when I recognized Jeremy Atherton. As I backed away from him, latching the screen, he said, "I'm not here to hurt you," his voice but a whisper.

"Why are you here?" I asked, my voice shaking.

"I want to know what happened," he said. "I found Rondel's body. I need to know the story. I know now he wasn't a good sort."

Jeremy looked to be fifty years old, but I knew he was not yet in his twenties. His hair was matted and grey, his front teeth missing, thin as a rail. He removed the bandana and showed an angry red scar on his neck.

"They tried to kill me, but I lived, and yet, I'm a dead man, dying slowly. I need to know about him," he said.

Pushing Mary into the kitchen, I shut the wood door while she wailed for me.

"I can't talk about it," I said. "I've made a promise."

Just then, Loretta rounded the cistern with her handgun pointed at him, emboldened from her recent bear experience. She said, "I'll tell you the story. It's a bad one, about your heathen brother who attacked two innocent women and tried to rape and kill them."

"Loretta, don't," I said.

"He did have the evil in him, I know it," he whispered. "Who shot him?"

We both said, in unison, "I did."

"Where's sweet Miss Elizabeth?" he asked.

"Dead!" Loretta said. "Half scared to death you were coming after her most days."

"I'm truly sorry for my part in it," he said, wiping his eyes with the filthy bandana. "I was angry at first, but I've made my peace. Thank you for the biscuits – and the knowledge."

Loretta kept her gun on his back as he trudged down the driveway, as I felt for the pistol in my apron. He was a sad sight, for sure, but I hoped he kept on walking. We would later learn he shot himself not five miles from our house. As afraid of him as I was, I couldn't help but feel compassion for him, but not the wrong road he had chosen.

Chapter 2   *WICKEDNESS*

Our social life centered around the church in La Crosse. The congregation consisted of respectable folks who met there on Sundays to hear the good pastor, Joshua Lathem, speak. Once a month, on Sunday, we had "dinner on the ground," which was where everyone brought a covered dish and we spread the food out on long tables. The reason it was called "dinner on the ground" was because people laid their blankets and quilts on the ground like a picnic. This was where I had met so many talented women, and we were forming a quilt guild. Even the very young girls were quilters in this part of the country. Loretta, Annie and I were very excited about the prospect of socializing while quilting, though Loretta warned me that we would have to keep a close watch on our tongues at the quilting bees. I had to laugh as I knew she was thinking about our times in Georgia as we sat around our quilting frame. How that made me miss our Elizabeth. I told her I didn't think we would slip up.

Before we ate, we sang hymns and the sound was so beautiful that I cried nearly every time, thinking of Elizabeth and our singing as we walked to Florida. It had been a year since we lost Elizabeth and Jake. The pain was still as strong, but I didn't feel it quite as often - mainly at times like this. Baby Jacob was walking and he was happy and healthy. Annie was a doting mother and didn't let him out of her sight. At times I had seen Samuel watch Baby Jacob, and once in a while, he picked him up and held him close. I wondered if the baby knew Samuel was his grandfather, or if Annie would someday tell him about his real parents, Jake and Elizabeth. Samuel, Loretta and Rebecca were such a close-knit family, very protective of each other.

All the children played together in the meadow beside the church, and I loved watching them chase each other, laughing. It was truly the one time of the week I felt totally secure. The men usually stood around and talked and smoked cigars after dinner, and although this was frowned on by the pastor, old habits died hard. I noticed the daughter of one of the men standing with Mr. Lander, the general storekeeper. She was a young girl of about 18 years, with hair like corn silk, falling to her waist. She had flashing green eyes and I saw that she looked at Jacob a lot, smiling and engaging him in conversation. Well, I had never felt jealousy before, but I can tell you it was not a pleasant thing. My body got hot and my face was flushed, I know; it felt like I had a fever. Since I was holding Mary Elizabeth, I couldn't stand at that moment, but I watched Jacob and it seemed he was talking with that young girl.

Loretta asked, "Sally, what's wrong? You look distraught."

"Loretta, does it look like Jacob and that young woman are trifling with each other?"

"My brother is not a flirt. You are the only woman in his life," she said, and then she turned her head in their direction, and I could certainly see by her expression she thought he might be flirting, too.

"Who is that girl?" I asked.

"That's Mr. Philip Lander's daughter, who's been away at school. Wonder what they're teaching her in that school." she said.

I looked down at my plain dress made of calico and my worn shoes. My hands were red from doing the washing. My hair was tied up in a tight bun, with no style to it at all. I felt like a plain-Jane compared to Lily Lander, who had on a pink satin dress with a parasol to match and shoes of a pale creamy silk fabric. Just then Jacob leaned away from Lily and smiled uncomfortably, and I could see his eyes were searching for me. I was devastated.

The ride home was endless. I was so angry with Jacob for flirting, and myself for letting myself go. He tried to engage me in conversation, but I could not form the words.

"Sally, what's wrong with you? Are you sick?" he asked.

Samuel and Loretta were in the back of the buggy, so I chose not to say anything. Loretta asked if the children could stay and play at their house, and I knew she wanted us to have some time to talk. Jacob looked surprised, but he grasped something was amiss. Once we were home, he asked me again what was wrong.

"I guess I have become unattractive to you since I don't have fancy clothes and schooling," I said.

"Sally, I don't care about that." He asked, "Are you referring to Lily Lander?"

"So you are aware of the flirtation that was going on between you two. I guess I'm not enough for you, not pretty enough or educated enough."

"I wasn't flirting. I was simply talking to the girl, who's young enough to be my daughter," he said.

"And just how old do you think I am? I guess I'm not interesting anymore. You weren't just talking, you were smiling and laughing with her."

"I'm sorry. I didn't realize…." He reached for me but I pulled away.

I really had never felt ugly since I'd met Jacob, but that day, I felt homely and old. The mirror on the wall confirmed my suspicions. My hair was awful, pulled tight from my face, in an old-fashioned manner. My clothes were all handmade and plain, in drab colors, and I didn't have one pretty pair of shoes, much less a parasol. No wonder he was attracted to another woman.

As he stood behind me, looking at me in the mirror, the tears were running down my face. His hands gripped my shoulders and he turned me around. He took my hair down and held my face: I felt broken.

"You are the only woman for me. You are more than beautiful, outside and in. That girl means nothing to me. You're all I've ever wanted," he whispered hoarsely.

At that moment I believed his words, and he kissed me gently, but a small chink had developed in my trust for him. He held me and stroked my back and whispered loving things in my ear.

"There's no one like you. You make my heart sink at the sight of you. I'll love you forever," he said.

He unbuttoned my dress, which dropped to the floor, picked me up, and carried me to the bed. I cried as he undressed, as I felt I had no power over my love for him.

We made love differently that day. It was a desperate feeling for me, a feeling of loss and a need for change on my part. For him, it was a need to reassure me. His loving was sweet and gentle but the damage was done. Perhaps this was damage that could not be repaired.

Chapter 3   *LYDIA E. PINKHAM*

To describe myself as low in spirits would be an understatement. My faith in Jacob was shaken and 'betrayed' was the word of choice to name my feelings. Work kept me busy, but I felt resentment about washing clothes in hot water and ruining my hands. In my mind, I could see Lily Lander's pretty, creamy hands holding her parasol, with no sun permitted to reach her skin. Even when Loretta or Annie came to visit, I just couldn't force a smile. Jacob apologized over and over, but the more he made of it, the more I was suspect. Loretta said I must let this thing go or it would destroy me. I believed her, but I couldn't seem to change my thoughts and feelings. Jacob had always made me feel pretty, but now I didn't feel pretty even though he continued telling me I was.

"This isn't like you, Sally," Loretta said one Saturday morning as we drank coffee together. "You're tenacious. It was you who brought us here to this place. Can't you see how much my brother loves you? That girl was the culprit."

"Loretta, you were there. You saw the dalliance. How can I trust him now?"

"I saw that vixen trying to get his attention," she said. "You need some perspective. We need a shopping trip to Gainesville."

"No! I don't want a trip to Gainesville. Our money is too tight. How can I take an extravagant trip like that? And Jacob would never allow it."

"Great day, Sally, don't you know a thing about your husband? He suggested it because he wants you to be happy."

"No! I won't go, even to help him alleviate some of his guilt."

After she walked home, I cried again, searching for a way to make this right, to renew my trust in my husband whom I loved so, but I was still galled at him. I had listened to Loretta's words,

156

however, and wondered if Jacob could've been innocent. Every day I looked in that mirror, and tried to figure how I could change my looks and attitude so I could feel that Jacob would love me again. But what really made me most unhappy was that I was relying on Jacob for my opinion of myself. That had to change.

Finally, I gave in to Loretta's coaxing and agreed to travel with her to Gainesville. She said it would be fun for her also as she rarely left home. Annie asked to keep the children for us and Jacob hired a driver and carriage to take us into town. Another expense, I thought. And then Loretta said she had booked a room for us at the Laurel Leaf Inn on the outskirts of the city. I wanted to back out, what with all those expenses, but Loretta was so excited and I had to admit the feeling was becoming contagious. I began to look forward to the trip. Jacob gave me some gold coins, out of guilt, I was certain. I told him the driver was unnecessary, as I was as good a driver as anyone and I always carried my little pistol. Maybe that was part of my problem: I was not feminine enough.

Loretta talked of nothing but new dresses and shoes and hair salons, where women curled your hair and made you pretty. The only new dresses I had ever had were the ones I sewed myself. She said that there were dresses that were ready-made, and you didn't have to wait for them. I found that hard to believe but the more she talked, the more my spirits lifted. Maybe I could be pretty again, though I was still somewhat vexed at myself and at Jacob. Lily Lander was only a few years younger than me, but I looked and felt much older.

It would be a long trip for us, but the weather was pleasant, and Loretta's mood continued making me happier.

"I don't think you need worry about Jacob, Sally. I know how much he cares for you," she said quietly.

"I'm to blame also for letting myself go. I am a fool, once again."

"Well, the time has come for a change," she smiled.

The Laurel Leaf Inn was a red brick house that had been altered after the war, the owners needing revenue since selling off most of their property. There were only three bedrooms, so we were grateful that we had such a nice place to stay, with all the meals included. Blooming roses cascaded over trellises and the gardens were a bright green from the spring rains.

Our driver asked if we wanted him to take us into town the next day, and pick us up at 5:00 p.m. at the railroad station, after we finished shopping. Of course, we said yes. We settled in for the night, after our supper, to a modest room with two small beds.

When we drove into Gainesville the next day, I couldn't believe all the activity. The railroad station was loaded with cotton bales, and there were carriages and wagons everywhere, with no driving rules: it was utter chaos! I don't think I could have driven in that traffic. There was construction going on in every direction; the sound of pounding hammers filled the air.

Gainesville was a transformed place since the end of the war. There were so many different types of people on the streets, so many well-dressed people. The first thing I noticed was the beautiful women, in their stylish dresses and shoes and jewelry. Most had their hair piled on top of their head, with lovely little ringlets falling around their neck and face. I wanted that type of hair.

"Loretta, how can my straight hair be made to look like that?" I whispered.

"Just you wait," she said.

The first dress shop we entered had ready-made dresses, hanging on wooden forms: beautiful dresses in silk, peau de soie, satin, brocade - in every color. They took my breath away. Loretta pulled out a pale peach silk dress, with lace at the neckline and sleeves. I touched it gently and sighed. How could I wear a dress like that? It was too prideful.

"I couldn't," I whispered.

"Try it on, Sally," she said. Maybe it wouldn't hurt to just try it on, I thought.

The owner took me to a small room, with three dresses to try on. Trembling as I undressed, I tried on the peach silk first. I couldn't believe it fit so well, needing no alterations. As I walked out to look in the full-length mirror, I was stunned. Loretta smiled and said, "It's a beauty, on a beauty."

The dress was cut very low, and the tops of my breasts were

showing. Loretta took the pins out of my hair, which fell down around my shoulders. She whispered in my ear, "I think you've finally developed." I blushed and I had to admit I didn't recognize that beautiful girl in the mirror. Then I tried on silk slippers to match. The price was expensive and I had a hard time deciding. On the one hand, I loved how I looked. But to spend that kind of money on a dress I could only wear for my husband seemed so extravagant.

"No. No. I can't. I need a dress that's plainer, made of cotton," I said. "I can't wear this."

"Just think Lily Lander," she said and handed me the silk shoes to match, along with the matching parasol. Those were the words I needed to hear, and I bought the whole outfit, plus two more cotton dresses and a dark blue satin dress, which I changed into as I could not wear my old dress another minute. Loretta also bought two dresses because she had lost most of her beautiful clothes in Georgia. Her eyes were sparkling as we headed out the door to the hair salon.

Of all things, they were curling hair with hot irons. I had heard about these things, but I had never actually seen one. When the lady got through with me, my hair looked so pretty I knew Jacob would never look at Lily again. She brushed some rouge on my cheeks and lips, and I was really impressed with my looks, and Loretta's, too. We bought curling irons and a pot of rouge to take home with us. I felt like I had just come out of a drought and into an oasis of loveliness. And being in a buying mood, we also bought a bottle of Lydia E. Pinkham's Vegetable Compound for female complaints.

While walking out the door, every man on the street took his hat off to us. The attention was a little worrisome, but Loretta was accustomed to it. She told me to hold my head up and walk tall. I had to admit that I liked being noticed, though I was ashamed of my feelings.

"I want to buy candy for the children," I said, and we set out to find the general store. By the time we had finished shopping it was close to five o'clock, and we hurried to the railroad station for our ride, carrying our many shopping bags. It had been a busy day, and our shopping hadn't allowed us time to eat. My body was weak.

The Inn was preparing for supper when we got back, and as we sat around the table with four other travelers, I began to feel light-headed. I tried to make pleasant conversation and follow Loretta's lead, but my mind was fuzzy. Feeling faint, I excused myself, went to the room and lay across my bed, becoming nauseated. As exhaustion overcame me, I fell asleep, and when I woke up, I was violently ill. Loretta found me on the floor, retching into a water pitcher.

"Oh no," she whispered. "You're not….." She grimaced and wiped my face with a damp cloth.

"No, it can't be," I murmured. And then I thought back to the Sunday when Jacob and I had made love, and I had been so distraught that I forgot my womb veil.

"Oh my, Loretta," I cried. And then I sobbed. How could I go through another birthing, which might kill me? Loretta tried to comfort me but there was nothing, and no one, who could make it better. I wondered if Lydia E. Pinkham's Vegetable Compound could help with this complaint.

She said, "Don't you know about Dr. Foote's womb veil?" I admit, I had to laugh as I thought I was the only one using it.

My sleep was fitful that night. I had been so foolish in so many ways: becoming jealous when I knew how Jacob loved me; not using my womb veil; spending so much money on myself, on clothes that were too fancy for me; and being in the family way, which could take my life.

By morning my senses had returned to me, and I realized Jacob's view of me had never changed: it was my own view of myself that had diminished. My mistakes were monumental, but I determined to search the mail-order catalog for a product that would help me lose the baby. What a sin that would be, but dying was worse than sinning.

I was physically sick all the way home, hanging my head over the side of the carriage, and so low in spirits. The driver stopped now and then and asked if I needed a doctor, but I just motioned him on. I'm sure he cringed when he thought of cleaning his beautiful carriage. My joyous trip had been ruined, but I was bound to keep this secret hidden from Jacob.

When Jacob came home in the evening, I was resting, and he came in to see the things I'd bought.

"Oh Jacob, I'm sorry. I spent money we don't have on frivolous things," I said.

"Sally, I *want* you to have these things. You've never spent money on yourself. Now, get up and try them on for me."

I, of course, put on the peach-colored dress first, with the shoes and parasol. I walked out into the parlor, and I knew the price of the dress was worth it all when I saw the look on his face. He made me proud to be a woman when he looked at me that way, his skin flushed, his eyes twinkling. It was as if he had never seen me before.

"Well, you'll be wearing that dress for me alone," he said. He walked to me and kissed me passionately. I felt I had solved one problem, but another lingered in the air.

"Sally, I don't need you to dress like Lily Lander. I love you, not your clothes," he said after we made love. And I knew he meant what he said, but sometimes the wrapping on a package makes the gift a little more special. I don't think he really knew how much that dress - or me in it - attracted him. But I did notice that he steered clear of Lily Lander from then on out, or any other woman who tried to get his attention.

My main concern, at that point, was how to keep myself alive.

Chapter 4 OLD AUNT LOU

My boys were growing up strong, like their pa. They rode and herded cattle and worked hard, just like Jacob, even at their young age. I was proud of the way they were turning out. And my Mary, she was so pretty and sweet. Loving my children was reason enough to find a way to have no more. Jacob noticed my sickness and asked me about it. How had I thought I could hide that from him? I wondered.

"I can't have another, Jacob, as I could die," I said.

"What else can you do? You can't lose the baby on purpose. That would be a sin," he said.

"Would it be a greater sin to do nothing and die?"

He looked down at the floor and would not meet my eyes. "What?" I asked.

"I've heard of an old lady who lives outside of La Crosse. She mixes potions for things like that. But I'd be afraid it might kill you."

"Tell me where she lives, and I'll go and speak with her," I said.

"No. I'll take you there. We'll determine together if it's safe."

My hands were shaking as Jacob knocked on the door of that weathered old house. The door creaked open, and an ancient, white-haired, black woman opened the door. Bent over and walking with a cane, she said, "Yes?"

"Like to talk with you, Aunt Lou, about your potions," Jacob said.

"Come in and sit," she croaked. She sat opposite us at the kitchen table, smoking a corn cob pipe and blowing the smoke in my direction, I thought to see if I was with child. At that moment, I wasn't sure I could sit there talking potions when I felt so ill. That smoke entered my lungs, and I was certain I would lose my breakfast. Her eyes were very penetrating, and I found myself unable to look at her.

"Baby?" she asked.

"Yes," Jacob answered.

"Cost be high," she said.

"Will it work?" I asked.

"You listen to Aunt Lou. I brew it tonight and it be ready tomorry. Mista Winston, stay away from this woman for a month after. "

"I'll be back tomorrow," Jacob said.

On the way home, I became concerned. "She could be a witch, Jacob. This could be poison."

"Other people have used her, wealthy white women, who wanted no more babies," he said.

"How do you know these things?" I asked.

"Men gossip, just like women." I reckoned I knew that, but had never heard it from a man's mouth.

Jacob stayed true to his word and picked up the potion the next morning. It was a vile-looking mixture: black and thick. The specific instructions were to take one-half cup every night, outside by the light of the moon, for five nights. Frightened as I was about this, I was more frightened of childbirth. The first night was the worst, the taste bitter and strong, and I gagged drinking a whole half-cup. The children were asleep and Jacob helped me. Standing outside by the light of the moon, we felt like fools.

"Tastes good," I jested. He replied, "I see that it does by the look on your face."

Strange dreams came to me that night, smelling smoke and hearing gunshots. Thinking I saw Elizabeth come through the bedroom door, I stood, so happy to see her, and fell to the floor. Jacob picked me up and laid me gently in bed. "I hope this wasn't a mistake," he whispered.

The next night I had dreams again but they were sweet dreams, in which Jacob and I were walking in a field of flowers - beautiful, long-stemmed, pink daisy-like flowers. He picked three of the prettiest ones and gave them to me. But when I picked one for him, he refused it. I began to cry and I awoke crying, with Jacob holding me and comforting me. "Maybe we should stop the potion," he said.

But I continued until the mixture was gone, and on the last night I knew I would lose the baby. My stomach cramped, and I became nauseated. By morning I was no longer in the family way. I would not look to see if it was a boy or girl, and Jacob wrapped it in a baby blanket and buried it somewhere on the property, making me sad that it would not be in a cemetery. After that, I was not well and had to rest for a few weeks. Annie came, with baby Jacob, to take care of me and the children. It was a difficult time for my family and a hard time for me, feeling guilt for the lost child. The sound of a whippoorwill in the night, the sound of a departing soul, made me more heartsick.

If I hadn't loved that man so much, I believe I could've gone without lovemaking. But that wasn't possible. I simply had to be diligent to use my womb veil. My husband couldn't resist me and I couldn't resist him either.

Chapter 5 *SHADOWING*

1870: The mill had started showing a profit at last, and with the revenue it brought in and a small amount of gold left over from Georgia, Jacob started to buy other properties surrounding ours. I didn't know why we needed so much land, but as people became desperate to sell, Jacob bought. And people were desperate to keep their land out of Yankee hands. The ranch was now up to around a hundred acres, and once that was fenced, he would buy some cattle from David. I thought Jacob was a good businessman, and we lacked for nothing at that time. He had stashed gold in an undisclosed location, which even I didn't know about, but he said he would tell me where it was before he died.

Even though the boys were young, they wanted to help with the cattle drive. It worried me some as Harry was only eight and John was ten, but they were tough little cowboys. David and Lanier had taught them to rope, herd with a whip, and brand. Loretta and I, and the little girls, took them dinner and supper every day, which was a large job. We hadn't cooked big meals like that for a while and Loretta was not the best cook. And sometimes it was hard to get to them if they were camped in a pasture way off the road, but it was an adventure for us. Usually we could locate them by the loud cracking sound of the bullwhips they used to move the cattle – a sound so loud, it carried through the air. And I loved seeing their faces light up when they saw us coming because they were so hungry.

We really were primarily cattle ranchers by that time and had to hire someone to help Samuel at the mill. Jacob had hired two ex-slaves to help with the cattle, one being a man I had fed in the early days. Watching me closely when I took them dinner, he acted as though he wanted to say something. But I did not encourage him as I didn't know his intentions.

"Missy Winston?" he called to me one afternoon when we were packing up the wagon. He was holding his hat in his hand, head bowed.

"I wants to thank you for saving my life in them early days. You fed me when no one else would," he said.

"Glad to do it, Lester," I said. "Happy you can work for us."

"I, I, ma'am, I stole some chickens and eggs from you, and I want to repay you. I am powerful sorry," he said, his eyes on the ground.

"Well, take your money then and buy me three Rhode Island Reds and we'll call it even."

"I, ma'am, I took more than three hens, more like five hens."

"All right, five it is then, and you're forgiven," I smiled.

"Thank you, Missy Winston."

I had wondered how this situation would ever be resolved and wanted to trust him, but I wasn't sure we ever could. However, the thieving stopped when we got our watch dog, Charlie. With him, no one could get near the horses, cows, chickens, or our family. But I did feel better about Lester and he was true to his word. He rode up one day with five, fat, squawking Rhode Island Red hens, tied upside down to his saddle horn, bought, he said, from the chicken farmer down the road from us. I do know that even an honest man will steal when he's hungry.

Jacob continued to buy land adjacent to ours. The large cotton growers were the ones making profits, mostly people from the outside who took advantage of the area after the war. But the little farmer had to sell to feed his family. Jacob kept fencing more and more property and buying more cattle. I believe our ranch, at that time, was bigger than David's, and beef prices were good. With the railroad repaired, we were able to ship cattle up north at an ample price. I never thought we would be prosperous again after losing everything in Georgia, but the Winston men were good at landing on their feet. When Jacob went to Gainesville on business, he always came home with gifts for Mary and me. He doted on Mary and her whole face lit up when he came through the door. Even though he was hard on the boys, he spoiled Mary something fierce. And once he brought me jewelry: emerald earrings. What a thing of beauty they were.

"We must talk about the boys," Jacob said one morning. "They're wanting to quit school and work full time on the ranch, and I could use them."

At that time, 1875, John was 15 and Harry was 13. I knew they were no longer interested in school because Loretta had told me they were ready to move on to the big school, meaning they weren't paying attention in class. But they knew not to misbehave or there would be hell to pay from me and their pa.

John looked more like Jacob, tall and handsome, with those Winston eyes, but he had a somber personality. Maybe it was because he lost Jake at such a young age, or maybe that was just his nature, somewhat moody, rarely smiling. Harry looked like me, with big brown eyes, lashes so long and dark he always looked sleepy, and though he was tall, he was not as tall as John, but he had his father's lighthearted attitude. Laughing readily, he was so easy to be around. I tried not to favor any of my children, but Harry was my heart.

"Well, they can read and write and do arithmetic. I guess they're ready to start to work with you," I said. "Loretta will only have Rebecca and Mary to teach, so she may want them to go to the new school in La Crosse."

We had been very protective of Mary and Rebecca, and I was worried about them going to school with children I didn't know. In the end, we decided to send them to La Crosse, and I would take the girls to school. Annie agreed to pick them up for me until I could collect them, after feeding the men. It would make for a long day.

I was hoping to talk to Jacob about hiring a cook and building a separate kitchen when he built the new bunkhouse. It would give Loretta and me more time for our quilt guild. But Jacob was already ahead of me and had hired Lester's wife, Abigail, to cook.

"You are too pretty to be bending over a hot stove all day," he said. We determined that Lester would deliver the noon meal, and the men would take their supper at the ranch in the evening. Of course I continued making our family's meals at home.

☼

Many times I had sat in on Loretta's teaching while I was cleaning her house, and I felt much smarter by doing so. I learned so much listening to her classroom lectures until I felt I was as well-educated as Lily Lander. She remained the standard by which I judged everything, and I did feel I could compete with her now, even though she had left the area many years ago. She had changed my life, and she'd left town! I never let my guard down when it came to my looks. My husband never saw me in a bedraggled state again. When his supper was served, my hair was curled and I had a nice clean dress on, not a silk one, but a pretty frock, and he appreciated it too. He always told me how beautiful I was. And I believed him.

My vocabulary increased tremendously from listening to Loretta teach my children. Some of the words felt so good on my tongue and had such a nice sound to them. For instance, I loved to say the word "enlightenment," and I loved its meaning also. It's a wonder how much I thought I knew, until I learned more, and then I realized how little I knew. But Loretta lent me books, and I was reading almost every day. I knew there was a lot of knowledge to be found in books, but a person had to have the books to read in the first place and they had been scarce in our lives. I finally understood Loretta's level of sophistication and hoped I could be more like her in that way.

Chapter 6   *BLINK OF AN EYE*

Jacob was 48 in the year, 1875, and I was 32. Our age difference didn't seem so great at that stage of our lives. Mary was 11 years old and Rebecca was 13. They were as close as sisters, and even looked like sisters. I saw that Rebecca was developing early and had an interest in boys, which I was hoping would not rub off on Mary. But Mary was not a leader; she was a follower, and I knew she was very influenced by Rebecca. She had always been obedient with me, but I noticed that Rebecca had sassed her mother a few times. Mary knew not to sass me, but she did have her father wrapped around her little finger.

Baby Jacob was ten years old and looked just like his pa, Jake. He was tall and lanky, and so charming that he was greatly loved by everyone. David and Annie were proud of him and he loved them dearly. He went to school in La Crosse also and seemed to be as smart as a whip. I loved him as my own and watched him sometimes when he couldn't see me and wondered how things would have turned out if Jake and Elizabeth had lived. I could already tell the women would love him with those eyes. Sometimes I wondered if he remembered me holding him and giving him nourishment and the love I had for him. He was a boy who would have no trouble in life as everything seemed to come easy for him.

Samuel had aged the most of anyone, and I thought his leg still pained him, even though he continued to work the mill. Loretta was near 50 and was still as pretty as she could be, but her hair had turned grey, and the lines around her eyes had deepened. They were happy, and I loved Loretta. She had become my best and dearest friend. Thinking she would never be a mother, her greatest joy was her beautiful Rebecca.

Our lives were so joyous, but I held my breath as I had seen happiness yanked away in the blink of an eye. I took nothing for granted, and I thanked God every day for my blessings. Never in my wildest dreams, as a youngster, did I think I would be living in Florida with a prosperous older husband and three children, with beautiful clothes hanging in my closet and emerald earrings in my ears. And never did I think I would love a man as much as I loved Jacob.

One morning early, before Mary was awake, I walked out on the front porch with a cup of sweet, strong coffee in my hand. I was surprised to see Jacob standing by our big oak tree with his right hand on the trunk, his back to me. He was usually at the barn at that time of the morning.

"Jacob?" I called.

He didn't answer me, and I could see from his back he was bending over some. My coffee splashed to the floor as I ran out the screen door and around to face him. His face was full of pain and he held his left hand over his heart.

"Dear God, what's wrong?" I asked.

He couldn't speak and I grabbed him to keep him from falling. His knees gave way and he slowly crumpled to the ground. My heart was beating in my chest and panic overcame me.

"Jacob? Jacob? What is it?" I cried.

Just then John rounded the corner of the house and knelt beside us.

"Send Harry for the doctor!" I said desperately. "Then help me get him to the bed."

I felt the breeze blow by me as Harry's horse raced by us and down the road toward La Crosse. John helped me get Jacob to the bed, and by that time, Jacob was coming around.

"Sally, it's nothing," he whispered.

"Ma," John said, quietly, "He's been having these spells for the last few months."

"And no one told me? John, shame on you."

"He made me promise."

My anger was white hot. I looked at Jacob and wanted to kill him myself. And John too.

"Jacob Henry, do you want to die and leave us alone? How could you not tell me?" I asked him.

He smiled that smile and I knew my anger had no power over him. Too weak to get up, he tried to laugh but he was exhausted.

Once the doctor came in, he ordered me out of the room, but there was no way I was leaving so that secrets could be kept again. He listened to Jacob's heart and then announced that Jacob had a heart problem, that he would need bed rest and quiet. Well, I could've told him that. How would I ever keep this man down? How could I keep him alive?

Trying to lighten the mood, even in his condition, Jacob said, "Doc, I don't think there'll be any rest for me, not with Sally here," he grinned weakly.

"Hush, Jacob. I'll take care of you," I said. "Is there no medicine for him?" I asked the doc.

"There is something we can try," he frowned. "Let's do it, then," I said, wondering what he was waiting for.

When we were alone, I laid my head on Jacob's chest and sobbed. He put his arms around me and held me.

"I'll be all right," he said. "Just need some time. Don't cry, my girl; I won't leave you."

"No, you won't. I won't let you, for it would surely kill me, too."

Because of Jacob's physical limitations, we had to hire more workers, since the cattle had to constantly be moved: from pasture to pasture, to the railroad to be shipped to the north, and to the butchers for the market in Gainesville. Jacob wasn't happy resting, but until the doctor released him, he had to stay at home. John was in charge and he really was as knowledgeable as his father. I put Jacob to work on the paperwork so that he had some distractions. And he walked to the grist mill every day to see what was happening there.

When the doctor visited next, he told Jacob he was going to have to take it easy for good. Jacob acquiesced, but I knew in my heart he never would do that. The doc's diagnosis caused me no end of worry; the thought of my life without Jacob was unimaginable, though it was something I couldn't dwell upon. I felt we should go to a heart doctor in Gainesville but Jacob resisted that idea.

Chapter 7 *HOLDING BACK TIME*

On Rebecca's 18th birthday, May 18th, 1880, Samuel and Loretta announced that Rebecca was marrying a young boy she had gone to school with, Nathaniel Lawson. He wasn't rich; in fact, his father was a tenant farmer on the other side of La Crosse. But he was a nice young man, handsome and polite. I wondered if he knew how spoiled Rebecca was, their story reminding me of my mother and father.

Mary was inconsolable. She and Rebecca had been inseparable, and now Rebecca was going to live with her in-laws, about ten miles away. Mary's eyes were swollen and red most of the day. Even though she was 16, she was still small in stature, like a little sparrow. Her lips had always been full and easy to pout but now they turned down at the edges, and I couldn't coax a smile from her. Her pa couldn't get her to laugh either, but they sat together in the evenings, not talking much, while I was preparing supper. He would put his arm around her, while she rested her head on his chest. Being a shy girl, and so reliant on Rebecca, I didn't know if she would be able to make new friends. Caught up in her wedding and her husband-to-be, Rebecca didn't even notice that Mary was devastated. Mary wanted to quit school to help on the ranch, but she was not really needed as she couldn't ride like the boys and we didn't need a cook anymore – not that she could cook. This would be a dilemma.

Jacob continued buying land and I believe that was how he stayed busy without being physically active. We had to hire more hands as he was also procuring more cattle. The Herefords were his favorites and our pastures were full of them. Now, he said he was buying land to grow hay for the winter feeding, but truly the pasture was good year round. I didn't interfere, as it was Jacob's area of expertise, and he had brought us this prosperity. Even David and Annie were amazed at his financial abilities. Jacob gave Samuel the grist mill - lock, stock and barrel.

Rebecca's wedding was planned for September, and she asked Mary to be her maid of honor. This cheered Mary a little, but when she was at home she remained sad. I promised to take her to Gainesville to shop for a new dress, and we were looking forward to the trip. I hoped to see her smile again.

Meanwhile, Jacob hired two young brothers from Georgia to work on the ranch, Thomas and James Mullins. I watched them, and they worked those cattle like nobody else, even my own boys. They broke the new horses with such ease that Jacob put them in charge of the job. Mary and I watched them working in the corral, and she seemed to have taken an interest in the manner in which they worked. To my relief, she stopped crying and developed a desire to learn all about ranch work. I warned her to stay out of the sun and cover her hands and arms at all times.

She also sometimes assisted Abigail in the kitchen and seemed to find joy in helping to serve the food. This was not what I had planned for my lovely daughter either, but I was gratified that she was no longer feeling despair. My hope was that I could keep her in school for one more year, and then Jacob and I would begin searching for a suitable husband for her.

Jacob wanted her to live on the ranch forever, but that would never do because she was too pretty to be an old maid. "I want a man like you for her," I told him. He was flattered but retorted, "There are no more men like me." He grinned, but I wondered if he might be right.

Rebecca's wedding was a lovely affair, taking place on a dry, cool Saturday at our church in La Crosse. Samuel and Loretta had asked us if they could have the reception on our property, under the shade of our oak grove. We were happy to offer it, and our workers and cooks helped with the joyous occasion. I was reminded of the celebration on my 17th birthday, which now seemed so long ago.

Rebecca was beautiful in her white brocade gown, and her

husband was so adoring. There were about a hundred people attending, and the food flowed from Loretta's kitchen and from Abigail's. Lester was roasting a side of beef over an open fire, and I had never seen so much food in one place: a sight I dreamed about on our trek to Florida. There was music and dancing; Jacob and I danced for the first time in our lives. He was so graceful, and as the sun went down, we danced on in the candlelight. "I'm getting a little jealous," he whispered. "Lanier seems to be very taken with you." Surprised, I glanced at Lanier Walton, leaning against a tree. I said, "You're being foolish. There's no one for me but you." And then he kissed me right on the dance floor.

Our ranch hands got plates of food and stood back toward the barn so they would not look like they were part of the party. An uneasy feeling crept into me when I watched Mary take a piece of wedding cake to one of the Mullins brothers, the youngest, Thomas. She was so small and yet, when she saw him, she looked like a woman. My heart sank. He glanced down at her and the smile on his face said it all. They gazed into each other's eyes, and I sensed we were in trouble. I knew I'd have to nip this in the bud, and Jacob would need to help me – the next day. This night I just wanted to dance with my husband. I wore a new green silk dress, with some added lace at the neckline, and he held me in his arms, dancing until the musicians packed up their instruments.

Chapter 8 *BETRAYAL*

In mid-October the painted buntings arrived. It was an event I looked forward to every fall as it heralded cooler weather. When we first came to this land and I saw those beautiful, little, colorful birds, I took it as a sign from God that this was the place we were supposed to be. From that point on, I never dreamed again of going back to Georgia or Tennessee. Jacob built me a feeder and I hung it in the oak tree in front of our house, and every October the buntings returned to bring us joy. They stayed until May and then they were gone again. Sitting on my front porch in my rocking chair, watching those beautiful creatures, was one of my greatest delights.

One thing I did miss about Tennessee and Georgia was being able to look out from the hilltops and see great distances, watching a rider approach. In Florida, the vegetation was so thick and the land so flat, that a rider was on a person before you knew it. I think this made people a little more suspicious and watchful.

As we sat on the porch one morning, I spoke to Jacob about what I saw at the wedding, but he did not want to hear about it or talk about it.

"Jacob, we must send her to Annie and David's for a few weeks," I insisted.

"You misjudged the scene. Our Lizzie's too young for that nonsense, and that boy is too smart to jeopardize his job," he said, irritated.

It was an argument I couldn't win at this time. Only when he saw for his own eyes would he believe. And I began to question my own credibility as I had drunk some wine. The matter was dropped for now, but I knew I would keep a watchful eye.

Mary went to school every day, but when she came home, she changed her clothes, and was in the kitchen working with Abigail.

At least she was learning to cook, which she had never had an interest in previously. Fifteen people were now employed on our ranch, including our boys and Abigail. The dining hall was built next to the kitchen, and Mary helped serve the meals and took her supper with the hands also. Usually, she didn't return to our house until dark, and always had a big smile on her face.

After a few weeks of this troubling behavior, I decided to walk to the dining hall one evening to witness this change in our daughter. She and Thomas sat at one end of a table, very close to each other. No one saw me standing in the doorway to the kitchen as they were all too busy eating. As he put his arm around her waist and pulled her closer, she smiled up at him, and I knew my fears were confirmed. I slipped silently out the dining door and through the kitchen. How could I convince my husband that I was right?

"Jacob, I saw it with my own eyes. Maybe you should join them for supper one night, but go unannounced," I said. "She's too young to be courting any man, rich or poor.

"I'll do that, but you're making a mountain out of a mole hill," he insisted.

A few days later, when he returned from dining with the hands, he too was convinced. "I hate to let that boy go," he said. "He's too valuable."

"Send Mary away then," I suggested again.

"I don't know if I can do that."

"Only for a few weeks, till we can sort this thing out."

On Saturday morning, Mary rose early, dressed in her work clothes. Her father and I sat at the dining table and motioned for her to sit.

"I must hurry to help Abigail with breakfast. I'm in charge of cooking the grits," she said.

"We've made arrangements for you to go and stay with David and Annie for a few weeks," I began.

"Why? Ma, I'm happy here. I love the ranch work, and Abigail needs me," she pleaded.

"Your mother and I feel you may be getting too close to Thomas," Jacob said, quietly.

Her tears began to flow as she looked to her pa for reassurance, though she would not look me in the eye.

"Please don't send me away. We're just friends. Pa, please don't make me go," she begged.

I could tell Jacob was folding, and I didn't want this to strain his heart. "The decision has been made by your pa and me, and we've talked with Annie and it is done," I said.

"I won't go! I won't go!" she repeated.

Here was an obedient girl who had minded me all her life, had never sassed, and was the epitome of meekness. I was speechless and could say nothing more as she ran from the house, out to the work-kitchen. Jacob followed after her, leaving me dumbfounded, as I realized fully that she loved that boy. But I would not allow her to ruin her life and live as my mother had, in misery. As much as I loved my pa, I knew he could never have made my ma happy while he was alive. And then he had left her in poverty when he died. Now Ma was dead, and her life had been miserable. Before my brothers left for Colorado they had written a letter telling me of her broken heart, followed by her death.

Jacob came back to the house and said that Mary had agreed to go to Annie's for two weeks. I hoped that would be enough time. But before the two weeks were up, Thomas and James had resigned, collected their money, and ridden away from the ranch. Relieved, I had the buggy brought to the front of the house and told Jacob I would pick Mary up after school that day. He smiled for the first time since she had left.

Annie and I visited and quilted a little, waiting for young Jake and Mary to arrive from school. She asked me why Mary cried so much.

"She liked a ranch hand, and we didn't want it to get serious," I said.

Young Jake rode up on his horse then, with his books tied to his saddle horn. Annie and I rushed to him, questioning where Mary was.

"She walked the last mile this morning and never showed up for school," he said. "I did think it strange."

My heart was pounding in my chest. No wonder the boys had

resigned. Now they had taken my baby girl, probably to Georgia. I felt I should've handled this situation more carefully. By the time I reached the ranch, it was nearly dark and I couldn't find Jacob or the boys. I ran to the kitchen and asked Abigail if she had seen them. She said they were at the hay fields, looking at the new growth.

"It be Miss Mary?" she asked.

"You knew about this, Abigail, and you didn't tell us?"

"Everybody knows, Missy Winston. Those two in love and planning a wedding," she said. "I reckoned you knew."

"A wedding? Oh my God, she's only 16." And I realized how ridiculous that sounded, since I had wed at 16, and to a stranger. But it was a different world now. The buggy stood where I left it, with the horses waiting patiently. I raised the whip to get them to Jacob in a hurry, even though they were tired from the ride to the ranch. The gates in the fields were all closed, so at each one I had to climb down and open it, wasting precious time. Jacob and the boys met me on their way back to the ranch for supper, with the sun almost totally down.

Jacob and Harry saddled new horses at the barn, and Abigail packed food for them. I implored them to wait until light, but Jacob was very distraught. "Can't you send John?" I asked, worried about his heart.

"John will take care of the ranch and you. Harry and I will take care of Thomas and James," he said. Shoving his rifle into the scabbard, he kissed me, and they mounted their horses and rode away. Dust from the horses caught in my throat, and the tears on my face were stained with it. With Mary gone, and now Harry and my sick husband, John, my only son left at home, put his arm around my shoulders and walked me back to the house.

"Don't worry, Ma. They'll bring her back," he said, but his voice wasn't convincing. "But you know, she went willingly."

The floor boards creaked a rhythm as I paced at night, sleepless. Even eating made me sick, as I was so worried about my family. My head ached, throbbing another rhythm. I could lose almost my whole family in this craziness. The next day David and Lanier rode into the yard and called out to me.

"Which way did they go?" David asked.

"Toward Georgia," I answered.

"My God, that's a long way from home," David said, and they turned their horses and galloped off.

As I walked the next night, I hoped for sleep or the sound of horses on the road and Mary running to me and throwing her arms around my neck. But it was five days before they rode back, with Harry and Lanier holding Jacob up in the saddle. I began to cry and thought he was dead. It seemed he was having one of his spells and so they put him to bed, and John went for the doctor.

"We lost the trail," David said softly. "We'll try again when Jacob is sounder."

"Thank you, David, Lanier. I'm afraid we've lost Mary to love. I won't risk Jacob's life again for a frivolous girl." If I sounded angry, I was.

Chapter 9   *MY CALLOUSED HEART*

Doc came right away, but he could only shake his head. He left a bottle of Trinitrin pills for Jacob, for when he woke up. "Nitroglycerin," the doc said, "but not the explosive type." I lay beside my husband and slept soundly for a few hours, holding him close, thinking, as always, that I could keep him from slipping away by my touch. When he did wake up, he cried for the loss of his girl.

"I failed you, Sally. I should have listened when you talked about Thomas and Mary," he said.

"Now you hear me, Jacob Henry. This is nobody's fault but Mary and Thomas. You've got to get well. Abigail says they're going to marry."

Of course, this did not make him calmer. I made him take the pills and he slept through the night, but he was very weak the next day. As he slept, I looked at his tired face, a face I loved more than my own life. Holding his hand, I kissed his palm and prayed to God to save my man again. Chicken broth was cooking when he awoke and I fed it to him, looking at his handsome face. He smiled weakly, but it was not the smile I wanted.

After a few days, he was able to walk around the house with a cane, one he'd whittled for his father. I knew he would be stronger again, but I didn't know how many of these episodes he could endure. My anger was aimed at Mary and Thomas for threatening her father's life. If she truly loved him, I felt she wouldn't have done this.

A month later, we received a letter from Mary, postmarked Georgia, although I couldn't make out the town. She was now Mrs. Thomas Mullins and was very happy, even though she missed the family sorely. Thomas had taken another job on a ranch in Georgia, and they were going to live there. I threw the letter on the table and walked to the ranch kitchen to help Abigail, as I needed to throw some pots around myself. Mary had had no concern about her pa and me and could stay in Georgia for all I cared. She was *not* my daughter, and I would *not* answer her letter.

I determined to make my husband stronger, if by sheer will. His recovery was slower than the last time, but I made him good meals - lots of broths for strength. He came into the kitchen one afternoon as I was shoring up the cook stove, and he wrapped his arms around me from behind. He said, "Sally, I loved you from the first day I laid eyes on you. Your big brown eyes blazed a hole clean through my heart. I could think of nothing but you for the next few weeks. I didn't think I should marry a girl so young, but I wanted you for my wife. And your grandmother was sure anxious to marry you off," he grinned.

"Well, I must say, she did me a big favor. I love you so much, too, Jacob, and that's why I want you to be healthy." All these years later and he was just telling me these important words – that he loved me from the first day. It was an amazing revelation.

He kissed me and held me, and I had never felt safer, thinking, foolishly, that *I* could keep him from sickness or death. How I did love that man.

In a few more weeks, Mary wrote again:

"Dear Ma and Pa, I'm so sorry to have left you like I did, but I didn't think you would understand. Thomas and I love each other, and we wanted to be wed like Rebecca and Nathan. I know you wanted me to marry well and I believe I have. Please write to me and tell me about everyone. I'm so homesick.

Love,

Mary."

I would not write to her. If Jacob wanted to write, he could, but I was angry with her. My feelings were so conflicted: I did miss my girl but I could not condone her actions. When Jacob sat to write her, his tears flowed so steadily that the ink got all smudged. He wadded up the paper and threw it on the floor.

"She's thrown her life away," he said.

"Times are changing for women," I said. "There are many things they can do that I couldn't do. But she did *not* marry well. They'll always be poor."

"She could do worse," Jacob said. "He's a good, honest boy, but they're too young. And they were like thieves in the night. I don't hold with sneakiness."

The ranch continued to grow and Jacob continued to get stronger. John and Harry were the backbone of the business. John was good with the operations, and Harry and his pa were great at negotiations. I didn't even know how much land we owned or how many cattle grazed on our land. I did know we were doing well financially, and I thought Jacob sent Mary money every now and then. Even though I felt he was rewarding her for disobeying us, I didn't voice my opinions as I didn't want her to do without either. But still, I did not write.

Chapter 10 GRUDGING

Loretta and Samuel came for dinner one Sunday after church and told us that Rebecca would have a child in the summer. They were ecstatic with joy, and we were happy for them. But I wondered how long Rebecca and Nathan would live with his family in that cramped little cabin, with no privacy. I couldn't imagine that Rebecca was happy having to do manual labor. Having grown up much like Loretta, not learning how to work hard, I wondered if she could care for a baby. And even though Samuel and Loretta were not rich, they had given her anything she asked for.

"We were wondering, Jacob, if you had a place for Nathan on the ranch?" Samuel asked. "He's been a farmer, but I believe he'd learn fast about ranching. I would like to build them a cabin not far from ours, if you wouldn't mind," Samuel said.

"Let me talk to the boys and see how we're fixed for hands," Jacob answered. "Of course, you can build a house for them, and we'll help you."

I smiled at Jacob and said, "You'll not lift a hammer, but you *can* help draw up the plans."

He patted my hand, patronizing me. "Yes ma'am. Not many plans needed for a log cabin."

A few weeks later, we received another letter from Mary telling us that *she* was in the family way. Laugh or cry, I didn't know which way to feel. She was too young to be a mother, but that would make me a grandmother. I figured I should be happy and forgive her. But though she begged me to write to her, forgiveness continued to be difficult for me. Holding a grudge was an easy way for me to deal with hard feelings. There were things I didn't like about myself, and this was one of them.

As we were having supper one night, Jacob told me he wanted to tell me where the gold was buried.

"No! Do *not* tell me!" I said. "That'll mean you think you'll die. Don't tell me at all. I don't want to know."

"Sally, you need to know," he said, in that calm manner he had, which irritated me to no end.

"No!" I wagged my finger at him and left the room.

Chuckling, he called after me, "You are some kind of woman. I'll write you a letter and tell you its location. How does that sound?" He left the house, headed for the barn, laughing as he went.

Sometimes, when I watched Jacob walk back to the house from the corrals, at the end of the day, it was like looking at a peach pie and tasting it before it was in my mouth. He had a swagger that I loved, so much confidence. By the time he reached the back porch, I had his bath water drawn and towels ready for him, and I knew our time together would be precious. I was aware I would lose him some day, but every day was sweet because of that knowledge. One evening he decided he would bathe me, but I wouldn't allow it as we didn't have the privacy we used to have. Hanging a blanket on the drying line, for *some* privacy, he stripped me down to my underwear and set me down in the tub of water, amidst my protests. Then he massaged my toes and feet and threw water in my face. I knew our hired hands could hear us, but we laughed out loud anyway. I was a fortunate woman.

Chapter 11 BORROWING JOY

The building had started on Rebecca and Nathan's new cabin.
And of course, my husband was in the middle of the fray. So happy
to be working with Samuel, John, and Harry, he teased his sons
about when they would be building for their wives. John blushed
beet-red and said he would never marry, at which we all laughed.
Harry was another matter as he had too many girls chasing after him.
I didn't think he would settle down anytime soon either. Nathan
helped, but, mostly, he was not a competent builder so he ran
errands... a lot. I had a feeling he might not be a good rancher either.

Rebecca stood and held her big belly while telling the men what
to do, and they would agree but then do things their own way.
Loretta gently guided Rebecca to her house so she would be out of
danger from the construction and so she wouldn't be bossing the
men. Abigail and I cooked a big dinner and rang the dinner bell for
the men to come to the dining hall, Loretta and Rebecca following
behind. I remembered how it was to walk when I was that large with
child, waddling really. It made me sad to see these two women, so
close and so happy, to be welcoming Rebecca's baby into the family,
and my girl so far away and so estranged from me. I was hoping to
absorb some of Loretta's joy into my life when her grandchild
arrived.

Once the cabin was finished, they were going to build a newer,
bigger barn on our property. And Harry wanted to build himself a
cabin in the woods behind the ranch, near the lake, so he could fish
in the evening. So life stayed busy at the ranch, although I was not as
busy as I once was. We hired Abigail's sister to do the washing, and
that was a big job as she washed all the worker clothes also. But I
did quilt a lot; Rebecca and Loretta and I were making baby quilts
for the two new babies we were expecting. We enjoyed our time

together, and Rebecca always placed an extra chair for the day Mary Elizabeth would return. My hope just couldn't reach that far. I still hadn't written to her, and I knew I should, but yet I just could not bring myself to do it. I reckoned that Jacob's health had been more important than Mary's happiness. Reconciling that fact was causing the delay to write.

A letter arrived one day for Jacob from Mary, and I laid it on the table and then walked around the table several times, wanting to open it, but feeling it bore bad news. It seemed to glow as it sat there, and finally I had to put a book on top of it. I left the house until Jacob came home to read it. At noontime, I called to him, and as he came in, I handed the envelope to him.

"Sally, you could've read the letter. I wouldn't care," he said, opening it and reading.

"Dear Pa,

I am writing with sad news about Thomas. He was gored by a bull last week, and we buried him on Saturday. I am so sad I don't know what to do. James has said he will take care of us, but I really want to come home. I've been homesick since I came to this place, but I know Mama is still mad at me since she won't write, but I miss you all so. Please say you'll help me come home. I can ride in a railway car, even though I am with child. James will escort me there if you can help me with the fare.

Love,
Lizzie."

Jacob and I both cried and held each other. Our girl was coming back to us and bringing our grandchild with her. He said he would send Harry to get her and would give him enough money for their fares and food. We were very happy, but I knew I had to deal with my dark feelings about Mary before she came home. And I had to grieve for the father of my grandchild, about whom I knew so little.

Thomas had been a fine young man, but I could not reconcile my feelings about the way they left, knowing how it would hurt us. Still, I simply had to put these thoughts behind me and move on to love this new child. My Grandmother Beatrice came to mind, and I knew I did not want to be like her. So many times, Jacob had said to me, "My darling girl, you don't have it in you to be like your grandmother, although I think that's your biggest fear."

Chapter 12 *MY SOFTENING*

The train pulled into Gainesville late in the day, with Jacob and me waiting anxiously. My hands were sore from wringing them, and I had paced until my legs hurt. Even though Jacob was uneasy, too, he got very quiet. I wondered if Mary had changed, if she had forgiven me for not writing, if she was so sad that she might lose this baby. I was glad Harry had brought her home as I knew he would take good care of her.

The station was extremely busy, and we watched crowds of people get off the train, our eyes searching for Harry and little Mary. As soon as I saw her, I forgave her, with tears rolling down both our cheeks. We held each other for a long time, and she kept whispering, "Mommy, Mommy." Harry was grinning from ear to ear, and Jacob grabbed Mary up and hugged her to him.

"Be careful with her, Jacob. Can't you see she's showing?" I exclaimed. Paying me no mind, he swung her round and round. It was obvious he had a favorite, too.

We piled quilts all around Mary for the ride home in the carriage; it was still cold on April nights. Harry and Jacob drove and we didn't arrive home until after midnight. As I held Mary close to me, she slept most of the way. It's funny how sometimes I struggled to forgive, with no good results, and then it would just happen, with no effort on my part. But no matter, I was happy just to have my family reunited - a growing family at that.

Our reunion was plenty joyous, but when Rebecca and Mary were reunited, it was like July 4th fireworks. It reminded me of Loretta and me hugging, with our big bellies touching, long years ago. They went to Rebecca's house, and I didn't see Mary the rest of the day. Life was good again on our ranch. Mary seemed a little sad every now and then, but it was to be expected. I knew she was glad to be home. Figuring the months on our fingers, we supposed Rebecca would deliver in June and Mary in July or August, the hottest time of the year. I insisted that the doc deliver these two babies. That was a job I didn't relish ever doing again.

Jacob seemed to be getting stronger every day, even though he still wasn't working the cattle. His color was good, and when he came home in the evening, he looked for Mary first, and they spent time together as I was making supper. I watched them from the kitchen and felt nothing but contentment, trying to hold onto these precious moments. Sometimes the boys came for supper, but mostly, they ate in the dining hall with the hands. We all had great love for each other. I could not've asked for more.

Loretta sent Samuel for the doctor early in the morning, on June 12th, 1881. I didn't know Samuel could ride that fast. By the time I reached their cabin, Rebecca was screaming, with Nathan holding her hand and Loretta boiling water. "Mommy, help me!" she cried to Loretta.

I walked into the bedroom and sent Nathan to work with John. Rebecca was sweating and her bedclothes were soaked. Loretta, being no help at all, was beginning to panic. When I took a look at Rebecca, I could see the baby's head.

"Everything's normal, Rebecca. You'll be fine. It just takes a while," I said.

"I'm in pain, Aunt Sally. Do something!" she demanded. "Honey, it's painful to have babies. Just push as hard as you can. The doctor will be here soon."

"No! I can't wait. *You* help me! *You* can do it!" she cried.

Turning Rebecca on her side, I massaged her back until she slept. When she awoke, I massaged her belly. Loretta stood in the doorway, useless, eyes big. Rebecca screamed suddenly, and I could see the baby's head peaking, the doctor nowhere to be seen.

"Loretta, bring the water and towels. You'll have to help me. Just push, Rebecca," I said, trying to calm her. She pushed hard and the baby rushed out, and Loretta fainted, while I cut the cord and cleaned him and his mother. Lord, sometimes I wondered how

Loretta had made it this far in the world. But we had a strapping young boy with strong lungs and a happy, if tired, mama. The doctor arrived just in time to say, "Good job, Mrs. Winston."

I yelled to Nathan on my way home, "It's a boy, Nathan." Now, there was a happy man, yippeeing with the other workers. When I got home, I woke Mary up and told her the good news. She giggled joyously and said, "I'll get dressed and go and see that precious child."

She motioned me to sit on her bed and said, "Mama, I don't want a doctor to deliver my baby. I want you."

"It drains me so, Mary. I just don't want to deliver another child. We might need a doctor," I said, thinking she could have a hard time.

"I want you to know about Thomas, too, Ma. He was such a good man, so much like Pa, gentle yet strong, and we planned to have a place of our own, just like you and Pa. He wasn't lazy a bit, and he loved me like Pa loves you." She began to cry and I hugged her to me and felt awful for the anger I had felt toward her and Thomas. I whispered, "I wish I could've known him. I'm sorry I was so bull-headed, and I *will* try to deliver your baby." But I had my doubts because she was so small, and this baby appeared to be large. I would make sure the doctor was at least close by when the time came.

Chapter 13   THE LONESOMEST SOUND

When Jacob started riding with the boys again, I was furious with him. But he just grabbed me and kissed me, and I knew he was much happier than doing paperwork and idle chores. There was a choice: should he be careful and miserable or reckless and happy? I would have chosen miserable for him because I wanted him to live, but I wasn't going to add to his pressures.

Every day Mary and I walked to Rebecca's to see baby Samuel, and we spent time holding him when Loretta wasn't holding him. Mary could hardly walk, but I forced her to, as I remembered when she was born how much easier the birth was because I had walked so many miles. She was within days of delivering and I was jittery. The last time Doc was out to check on her, I told him of my concern, and he said he would be near-at-hand.

The heat was miserable in August of 1881, the mosquitoes so bad that we could not be out of an evening. Sleeping was near impossible as I would wake up drenched with perspiration. Many nights I dragged a pallet to the front porch, hoping for a breath of fresh air, listening to the mournful cry of the whippoorwill in the distance, the lonesomest sound on earth. I tied a knot in the bed sheet even though I didn't really believe in that superstition, but I would take no chances that another baby-soul would depart this earth too early. And just for good measure, I tied a second knot in another corner of the sheet. Mary did suffer and her feet swelled until she couldn't wear shoes, and we carried hand-fans wherever we went. Even the ranch hands were complaining about the heat and mosquitoes.

One night in late August, as I lay on my porch-bed, I heard Mary cry out. I jumped up and ran to her bedroom and she was writhing in pain. Lighting the oil lamp, I looked down at her in her wet nightgown and sheets. "It's time," she cried. I called to Jacob to send for the doctor and to wake Abigail and have her come to the house to help me. Pulling on his pants and boots, he left the house, shirtless. When he returned, Abigail was with him, and I could hear a horse ride down the driveway, heading for La Crosse.

Mary's eyes were wide and frightened when I went to her, but she did not scream like Rebecca, even though I could see she was in pain. I rubbed her back from her shoulders to her backside, hoping to ease the birthing pangs. When she turned on her back and tried to push as I instructed her, I rubbed her belly gently to push the baby down. It would be a lengthy birth I was certain. Three hours later, the doctor arrived, and Mary was still struggling and beginning to wear out. Remembering my first baby and how close I came to dying, I was gripped with fear for my daughter.

"I will have to cut her as she is so small," he said to Jacob and me. I cried and prayed she wouldn't bleed to death. He said he would need Abigail, but it was better if we weren't in the room.

Jacob and I passed each other several times as we paced the length of our house, and finally he left for the barn. Prayer was my only consolation, begging God for forgiveness for all my sins, especially for not being supportive of Mary when she ran away. I promised that if God would spare her, I would change my ways and not hold another grudge against anyone or have hard feelings for anyone, a big task on my part.

And God did spare her, but barely. The doc stitched her up and she was bed-ridden for over a month, with no strength at all. Abigail was a huge blessing to me at that time because I had to take care of both Mary and her new baby girl. But my joy was overwhelming in holding that baby and loving her with an immeasurable love, rocking her in the little red rocker for hours.

Mary couldn't nurse, and so Annie brought in a wet nurse who helped Abigail in the kitchen when she wasn't nursing. This was history repeating itself. Mary named the baby Sarah, after me. How proud I was. Again, history repeating, but I would be a better grandmother than Grandmother Beatrice. This baby would know immense love from her grandparents. Jacob was so sweet with her, too, and held her while I made dinner. I thought she might be a spoiled child as she was held every blessed minute of the day.

Once Mary was on her feet, I planned a large Sunday celebration. It was a cool day in October, and the hands set out tables under the oak trees. All the family was there: David, Annie and Jake, Samuel and Loretta, Rebecca, Nathan and baby Samuel, Jacob, myself, John, Harry, Mary and baby Sarah. All our hands and workers were invited, too, and Abigail and Lester cooked a big meal. We introduced baby Sarah to the family and everyone applauded. Mary was so proud. What a joyous time, but as usual, I could never feel completely comfortable in my happiness as I knew it couldn't last forever. I struggled, yet again, against this negative trait of mine.

Chapter 14   *CAN THE SUN SHINE?*

I walked down the trail behind the barn to Harry's beautiful little cabin on the lake one Saturday afternoon, not expecting to find anyone there, with all the ranch hands out in the pastures. As I stood on the dock by the lake, a cheeky, cottonmouth moccasin swam by below my feet. Head lifted, with no fear, he looked me dead in the eye and dared me to approach him. My body shuddered as I stared back, while keeping my distance. After he swam on, I realized that there were many dangers in this land, and that a person had to be on her toes all the time. We definitely could not swim or bathe in these waters. And I had known a few people who reminded me of that snake.

Looking out toward the lake, I saw Harry and a girl in a rowboat, a girl I didn't recognize. As I called to them, Harry rowed to the shore. After tying off the boat, he helped the beautiful girl out of the boat and onto the dock. She had on a lovely dress, not appropriate for a rowboat, but I could tell she was refined by the way she carried herself. I couldn't understand why she was not chaperoned. Harry blushed and introduced me to Susan Marley, an auburn-haired beauty, tall and slender. Harry blushing? That was a first, as he had girls following him wherever he went.

"Are you alone here?" I asked.

"Why yes, Mother," he said. He had never called me 'Mother' before. "Susan is from the North and they don't need chaperoning. It's a thing of the past."

"I see," I said, feeling old-fashioned. "I'm sorry I intruded."

"Mother, I've just asked Susan to marry me and she has said yes," he smiled.

Well, of course, I was happy for them, but we didn't know this girl. I was flabbergasted. However, I said, "How lovely. Welcome to the family."

194

As I walked the trail back to the house, I just couldn't believe how things had changed in the last few years. I didn't even have a hint that Harry had a sweetheart and wondered if Jacob knew.

"I had heard a rumor, but I haven't met her," Jacob said when I returned.

"She's a city girl, Jacob. She'll never be happy here."

"I don't think I'll interfere in this one, Sally, nor should you. We should've learned our lessons by now." And he was right. I would let Harry make his own decisions.

John came running into the house early one morning as I was rising, shouting for me to come to the barn. I ran after him in my nightgown, barefooted, my hair uncombed and flying everywhere. There, inside the barn door lay my husband, Jacob, on a bed of fresh straw. He was breathing raggedly and I fell on my knees, hoping this was not the day I had dreaded.

"Jacob," I whispered.

"My girl," he said.

"You're not leaving me?" I felt my heart clench.

"I feel I am, but we've had a good run. I know you'll take care of everything. You always have. I will love you forever, Sally."

"Please, Jacob, please don't go. I can't live without you. I *can* make you better. Don't quit on me," I begged.

"John, go for Harry and Mary," I cried, and John, tears running down his cheeks, ran out the back door.

"Sally, the gold is under the feed bin," he whispered.

I had to laugh. "What? Couldn't you think of a better place?"

He smiled weakly. I bent over him on my knees, my ear by his mouth so I could hear his words.

"The boys will run the ranch. You'll never lack for anything," he said.

"I *will* lack for you. You can't know how I love you and have always loved you."

"Not always," he smiled.

My tears were dropping onto his face. "Don't be sad, my girl," he said. Harry and John ran into the barn just then and knelt on each side of their father, Harry next to me.

"I'm proud of you boys. Take care of your mother and Mary and the ranch. You are good men. I couldn't ask for better sons." They began to cry. I hadn't seen them cry since they were small boys. And then Mary came to the door of the barn and fell at her father's feet, sobbing. He smiled at her, but the life was draining out of him, and I knew it *was* the day I had dreaded. I wanted one more day, one more hour, one more minute, but it was not to be. And the light went out of my life that day. It would never be the same after Jacob's death; that incomplete joy I had always experienced was just the knowing that one day it would come to this.

After Jacob's funeral, my family and friends gathered around me, hoping to ease the pain. But they just could not; absolutely nothing could. Actually, I wanted to be alone; their presence made me more aware that Jacob wasn't there. Never again would he hold me and love me at night. He wouldn't smile at me, and I couldn't touch his hair, his face, or wrap my arms around him. Why was the damned sun shining when I was in so much darkness? And the nights were the worst, of course. I buttoned his shirt around a pillow just so I could sleep. But when I woke in the morning, I became aware of the knowledge that he was gone.

In the days that followed, I would disappear for hours, walking alone in the woods, trying to overcome my loss. And of course, everyone else was dealing with their own grief, and I couldn't help them. I couldn't be the strong one; the pain was just too overwhelming. Thank God for Abigail and Lester, as they kept us fed; at least we had physical nourishment though our souls were depleted, and they were grieving also. I truly wasn't certain I could go on, and many days sat by the lake, understanding, finally, Elizabeth's decision to end her life.

David found me by the lake one afternoon and sat down on a rock beside me. I wanted him to leave but couldn't bring myself to tell him that.

"You know, Sally, Jacob wants you to be happy. He doesn't

want you to mourn."

"Then he shouldn't have left," I said sadly.

"Do you think that's what he wanted? He would've given anything for a few more years with you. He loved his children, Sally, but he more than loved you. I don't think love is a strong enough word for how he felt about you. You were his source of energy and life. He told me so many times. He said that if it hadn't been for you, after the war, he couldn't have gone on with all he'd seen," he said.

"I know he loved me."

"No, Sally, he worshipped you. You don't understand. He would've given his life for you."

"Thank you, David. I appreciate your kind words, but I've always had a hard time with death; it just takes me some time."

"Just remember, Jacob doesn't want you to be sad." And having said that, he stood and walked away.

I knew Jacob wouldn't want me to be sad, but I *was*, and I had to work through it my own way. When I came out of the woods that day, I have to say, my heart felt a smidgen lighter, and I realized that I had totally neglected my children and my precious granddaughter, whom I hadn't even held in three weeks. John and Harry glanced at me hesitantly as I walked by, and I managed a smile. They looked relieved.

And there, at my back door, stood Loretta: my oldest, dearest friend, whose brother, my husband, had just died. I hadn't yet comforted her, even though she had tried to alleviate my grief. We rushed together and hugged, crying on each other's shoulders. How could I have neglected my sweet sister who had traveled that long road with me? I knew it would take forever to feel better, and maybe never again would I feel joy. But if I loved Jacob that much, at least I wanted him to be content that I would make it through this.

There were many times when I thought this would be the end of my life, but it was really the end of my life with Jacob, the most important part of it, but still the beginning of another life. Mary began courting one of our ranch hands after her father died. I realized she would never marry a man I wanted for her so I gave up on that course of action. She would probably eventually marry the ranch hand and have more grandchildren, grandchildren Jacob would never meet.

My greatest joy would be Mary's daughter, Sarah, who happened to love me fiercely. She was a lot like her grandfather with her easygoing nature, and seemed to enchant everyone around her. I saw Jacob in my children and grandchildren, each one with a little touch of him, which always made me more aware of the fact that he was not here. When I dreamed about him, that was when I felt he was the closest. But of course he was never within reach, always just beyond my touch.

Daily, there were people around me, family, friends, our workers, but never the one person I wanted to be there. Sometimes, just being alone was still more comforting than being in a crowd of people that I loved. As usual, I absorbed myself in hard work, helping Abigail with three meals a day and cleaning the kitchen afterward. I assisted with the washing and barn work, and I looked after the children when I was needed. I would do any job that wouldn't let my mind wander to my loss. By night time, I was too physically tired to think of Jacob. And that was my life for the first year after Jacob's death.

When Mary married her ranch hand, they moved away from us. Mary's husband was not kind to Sarah which galled me to no end. Sarah begged to stay on the ranch with me, which was her home, after all, and finally, Mary gave in, after many months of being separated. And that was when I realized that I would raise this child so that Jacob would be proud of Sarah and me. It was the beginning of my new life. She would be my salvation, and I felt it was okay to relax and enjoy myself, at least somewhat, as much as I could without Jacob. I taught her to work hard and how to quilt and cook, and I told her about her grandfather, with endless stories about Jacob. She begged to hear the stories of when we first met, and she was amazed to hear I was only fifteen when I met him. I told her of my life and family in Tennessee, our life in Georgia, the perilous trip from Georgia to Florida, of Jake and Elizabeth, and the new beginnings in Alachua County. And I spoke of how her grandfather had built our ranch from modest beginnings after coming home from the War Between the States. When she was old enough to write, she began taking down all these stories, and I knew she would keep Jacob's memory alive long after I was gone. And that brought me peace and happiness, to know that a man like Jacob would not be forgotten, and I thought she would remember me also.

Part III   1881-1888

Chapter 1   LACK OF TRUTH

"Show me a liar and I will show thee a thief." George Edward Herbert

I never could abide a liar. It's a quality I always looked out for, when first I met a person, trying to read their face, but if they were a practiced liar, it was hard to decipher the truth. That truth just came from a feeling I got, deep down in my heart. People need to trust that feeling because, otherwise, they are at a total loss and will believe any charlatan.

I have known certain persons to look me dead in the eye and tell me any story they think I want to hear or that they want me to believe. Others simply omit the truth, which I have done myself, and consider it to be no less a sin. But it's the low-down, dirty rascals that tell a deliberate lie, which can hurt many people, that I cannot stand. Such was the case with my beautiful daughter-in-law, whom most folks thought was an angel. But I felt she was a liar and a thief, from the first day I had conversation with her. This made me feel like a hard woman, to believe such a thing about a relative, but I will tell a story that could curl hair: a story of avarice, jealousy, deceit, and damage to a family that could never be repaired.

The year, 1881, was the most important year of my life, the year I lost my beloved husband, and it was also the birth-year of my granddaughter, Sarah, my little blessing, my namesake, though no one ever called me Sarah. Our ranch was up to about a thousand acres in central Florida, managed by John and Harry. For the most part, we lived in harmony on the ranch. My two sons were as close as twins, working together, fishing and hunting together. I hardly ever saw one without the other. Their younger sister, Mary, adored her brothers. She thought they hung the moon. And so did I. They found so much pleasure in each other's company. But when Harry decided to marry Susan Marley, it changed the dynamic between the two boys. For as long as I could remember, John and Harry always laughed together. It reminded me of my good friend, Elizabeth, who died the first year we lived in Alachua County.

Always the person to make us laugh, Harry had such a lighthearted manner. Everyone was surprised when he decided to marry because he had his choice of girls, having broken many a heart. Susan Marley was a very sophisticated girl, a few years older than Harry, claiming to come from the Boston area, which was strange for us, as Harry was as Southern as fried chicken - a true Southern boy. But Susan Marley was a beauty; she won his heart and took his soul.

During those days, after Jacob died, I did not have the presence of mind to notice that Susan was overtaking my family. I knew John was missing his brother because all they were doing was working together.

"John, it's normal for your brother to spend his free time with Susan," I said. "She'll be his wife."

"Ma, he's changed. That's *all* he wants to do is be with her. She's staying in his cabin, you know," John said. "He's sleeping in the bunkhouse for appearance's sake." The hurt showed on his face.

Well, I hadn't known that, but I hated to hear it from John. It felt like he was tattling, a trait I couldn't abide, but I determined to have a talk with the girl. Harry and Susan had decided to wait a period of time before marrying, because of Jacob's death, which I appreciated. My state of mind was not clear enough then to help with a wedding. And tradition, of course, demanded that the girl's family plan and pay for the wedding in their hometown.

"Susan?" I called, as I knocked on the door of the little cabin on the lake. No one answered, so I pushed the unlocked door open. It was just a one-room cabin, but Harry had built it himself, finishing it inside with beautiful, planed-oak paneling. A brass bed stood in the center of the wall under a window. It was unmade, sheets disheveled, pillows on the floor, scattered with clothes, beautiful silk dresses, women's underwear, lovely shoes. On the dresser were several pieces of expensive-looking jewelry. I couldn't believe the total disarray of the once-impeccable room. There was a small wooden table and two chairs, plus a wood stove to warm the cabin in the winter. Both of the boys ate at the dining hall with the other ranch hands, fed by Abigail and Lester, our cooks for many a year.

The door hinge squeaked behind me, and I turned to see Susan silhouetted in the bright light.

"What're you doing here? she asked, haughtily

"I was looking for you, and well, this *is* my property," I said. Something about that girl rankled me. Because she was Harry's fiancée, I tried to hold my tongue but it was difficult.

"I'm sorry. You just surprised me. I was intending to clean up today," she said.

"I thought we might have a sit-down talk," I said. My feeling about this girl was not a good one. It wasn't that she was messy, as I figured she probably had had servants in Boston to clean up after her as Loretta had always had. It was something more, an uneasy intuition that I had about a person I didn't feel was quite truthful.

I sat at the table, looking over the mound of her clothes. She grabbed them up and threw them on the bed. Motioning for her to sit, she hesitantly pulled out the other chair and sat down.

"We have not talked about the wedding. Will it be in Boston?" I asked.

"My parents are elderly and they're not well. I don't think we can count on them," she said. "I was hoping we could have it here, at the ranch."

"And will your parents be paying for the wedding?"

"Harry doesn't want them to pay for it. He wants to take care of everything," she smiled.

"And will they be attending?" I asked.

"They're too ill to travel."

I could hear Harry's boots on the decking outside, and soon he stuck his head inside the door.

"Mother? What are you doing here?" he asked.

"Came to survey my kingdom," I smiled. "Susan and I were just talking." He seemed uncomfortable, I assumed because I rarely paid a visit to his place. But I hadn't paid attention to a lot of things in the past few months, and I thought it was time I did.

"Have you set a date?" I asked.

"June, sometime in June," Susan offered.

"I see. I guess we'd better start planning then," I said. "And are you living here, Susan?" Harry hurriedly said, "It's only temporary, Mother."

Both Harry and Susan seemed self-conscious in my presence so I decided to go, but I left the cabin feeling discomfited. My judgment was usually right on target, and Susan just continued to give me an uneasy feeling. It was very inappropriate for a young couple to be alone in a house with no chaperone.

When Harry said he would pay for the wedding, he meant *I* would pay for the wedding. And I wasn't certain this girl would settle for an ordinary country wedding.

As I headed to Loretta's house, I thought of the long journey she and I had made together, the arduous trip from Atlanta to Florida during the war, and I realized that this little problem was minor. Loretta and I sat at her kitchen table, relishing the sweet joy of strong coffee. We never took coffee for granted again after doing without on our trip.

"That's a wonderful girl your Harry's going to marry," she said. "Rebecca and Mary love her. She gives them beauty tips and styles their hair."

"I don't know, Loretta. She appears to be hiding something," I said.

"In my opinion, she's an open book. She talks about her family all the time. And she's the most beautiful girl I've ever seen."

"Well, it's Harry's life. I'll try not to interfere, but there's something not quite right," I said. Mary and Rebecca came in the back door with their babies, and I forgot all about Susan Marley. Playing with Sarah and Samuel was my favorite pastime.

Chapter 2   *YOUR BROTHER'S INTENDED*

Our ranch was truly a compound. Loretta and Samuel had added a porch to their house on the edge of our cleared ten acres. The grist mill now belonged to Samuel, which was located on the Santa Fe River, also on our property. He and Nathan, their son-in-law, ran the mill and made a good living for their two families. Nathan had tried working for the ranch, but he never seemed to do well; he was a bit clumsy; not a good characteristic when working with cattle. Our concern was that he might have gotten injured. Next door to Samuel and Loretta was where their daughter, Rebecca, lived with Nathan, and their son, little Samuel, born the same year as my granddaughter, Sarah.

Before Jacob died, we had built a bunkhouse, dining hall, and kitchen. Abigail and Lester had managed all the meals for everyone for many years. Ranch hands came and went, but Abigail and Lester were always there, more like old friends than workers. They had built a cabin in the woods on our original 20 acres, where they raised their two daughters.

Harry had constructed a cabin on the lake because he liked to fish every evening. It became a joyful place we all liked to go to since he had built a deck off the cabin facing the lake and a long dock where a boat could be launched. There was only one door and it faced the deck and lake. John stayed in the bunkhouse, but I think he envied the cabin. I never understood why he didn't build himself one on the lake or elsewhere. Overall, the ranch was always a busy place. Our hands numbered anywhere between eight and twelve, depending on the time of year and the amount of work.

In the early days, Elizabeth was my dearest friend, and Loretta was more just my sister-in-law/friend. But through the years I had come to greatly respect Loretta and to realize that she was as solid as a rock. I used to feel that she was lazy, but more than anything, I later felt she just didn't know *how* to do things; never had had to learn them. But she was always there for me – through all our trials and deaths in the family. She repeatedly said that I was the strong one, but, truly, I believed she was the formidable one.

Having lost my way after my husband died, Loretta stayed the course. She never faltered, even though Jacob was her brother and she grieved, too. Many times she said to me, "Life is for the living." During those times, my grief was so heavy I couldn't think straight. The memories of those days became more cloudy to me later, probably a protection for my heart.

Loretta was older than me, older than Jacob had been, even. In 1882, I was 38 years old. Loretta was 54, but looked younger than her years as she had hardly ever been in the Florida sun. I never knew exactly how old Samuel was but I believed him to be about her same age. Samuel's leg injury from the War caused him to still walk with a bad limp, which seemed to worsen as he aged. I had never heard him complain however, working as hard as a man with two strong legs.

A package arrived on a Friday one week: my riding breeches. So that I could help with the roundups, John insisted that I learn to ride a horse. As I looked back on it, it was a mystery that I had never learned to ride, growing up on a farm and living on a ranch. I could drive a wagon or carriage as well as any man, so John insisted I would be a natural. While everyone was out on the range, I slipped my breeches, shirt, and boots on, and met John at the round pen. He laughed when he saw me coming, as it was not seemly for a woman to wear breeches, but riding side-saddle was not for me.

"How did your talk go with Susan?" he asked as I saddled the horse he had picked for me.

"I feel there's something amiss, John, but I can't pinpoint it and I can't interfere."

"Harry's work is falling by the wayside. He goes back to his cabin for lunch every day, which is a lot of time wasted. He still doesn't want to go fishing or hunting with me. It's so unlike him that it worries me," he said as he hoisted me into the saddle. I don't know why John's talk of Harry irritated me so. It's the only way I could learn these facts. And yet, I felt he was betraying Harry's confidence somehow.

The lunge-line was hooked to the bridle, and John stood in the middle of the ring, giving me instructions. He was a good instructor, and taught me to post and to keep my heels down; I took right to it. "You just need more practice, but you'll be a good rider," he said. That made me happy as I was still trying to occupy my mind, to keep from thinking of Jacob every minute. Eventually, I would be able to ride with the men during roundup, and at other times, also.

Susan rounded the corner of the barn and had a shocked look on her face when she saw me in breeches and boots. Standing at the fence of the round pen, she watched as I rode round and round, with John's face turning red as she watched him carefully. Waiting until we were finished, she asked John if he would teach her to ride.

"I believe your husband-to-be can do that," he said, brusquely.

Opening the gate, I walked toward the barn, leading my horse, a chestnut gelding. I could see that John was trying to avoid Susan, but she was following him. "I have asked Harry to teach me, but he said it wasn't necessary for me to learn, and you have such a way of teaching," she said, smiling up at him with a flirtatious smile. John was stammering and his face was blushing.

"Susan, I believe you were on your way somewhere," I called to her.

Glaring at me, she said, "I was," and she turned and whirled away toward Rebecca's house. I thought that this girl would be the death of me. John helped me take the saddle off and brush the horse down.

"That girl is trouble," I said.

"Yes ma'am," he said, quietly.

Susan Marley was a girl who *would* have her way, no matter the consequences. John began giving her riding lessons in *her* breeches and boots. I noticed they did not do this if Harry was around, and I asked John about it.

He said, "It's not on purpose. It just happens like that. She names the time and I meet her."

"John, that is your brother's intended. Do not let that girl manipulate you. You and Harry are closer than most brothers," I said.

"I'm starting to see why Harry loves her. She's so beautiful, and sweet. I've never met a girl like her before," he said softly.

My heart sank. What was this girl doing to us? I was furious.

"John, do *not* fall in love with her. That would be a disaster! You must stop the riding lessons, now!" I said.

"I think you're right," he said.

Susan showed up on my backdoor step the next morning, dressed in her riding habit. She called to me and I asked her to come in and sit.

"Why did you tell John to quit teaching me to ride?" she asked, angrily. "I was hoping to surprise Harry with my new skills." She slapped her crop on the table, startling me.

"Susan, you can't have both my sons. You can have one of them to marry, and that would be Harry. Leave John alone."

"I don't want John. Harry is my betrothed. I wanted to give him a present for our wedding, and I thought this would be perfect," she said.

"Your flirtation with John is evident."

"It's called being friendly. If John sees it otherwise, that's his problem," she hissed.

"You may manipulate the men of this family, but you will not manipulate me," I said.

Jumping to her feet, she knocked the chair over, and flounced from the room and out the back door, slamming the screen door loudly.

I determined that this girl would not be the center of my life, with a daughter and granddaughter to think about, plus my good friend, Loretta, and her family. Perhaps this conversation would take care of the problem, though it seemed doubtful.

A few days later, Harry came knocking at my back door. I motioned him in and he sat, as Susan had, at the dining table.

"Mother, what have you done to Susan? She won't tell me what's wrong, but insists you don't like her. She wants me to build her a house in Gainesville," he said.

"Gainesville? And just how would that work, exactly?" I asked. "Your livelihood is here."

"She says I can come home on the weekend. What happened between you two? I know this can be worked out. I love you both."

Well, this was a total dilemma for me. I couldn't tell him that his brother was giving his wife-to-be riding lessons and that she was flirting with him. Nor could I tell him that John was smitten with her.

"We had a slight disagreement, just minor. I will try to hold my tongue from now on. I'm sorry, Harry. It was probably my fault," I said.

"Mama, I know you. You're the best person I've ever known. If she has done something that I should know about, please tell me."

My sweet Harry. How could I break his heart? I couldn't tell him what I suspected about this girl.

"Harry, it will all work out. Just please don't move to Gainesville. We need you here," I pleaded.

"Ma, what on earth would I do in Gainesville? I'm a rancher." And that ended that conversation.

My daughter, Mary, and my granddaughter, Sarah, were still living with me in our three-bedroom house on the ranch. At that time, April of 1882, Sarah was still a baby, eight months old. Our world was rocked with the death of my husband, who was greatly loved by the community and our family. I was still reeling from Jacob's death, and felt that maybe my perspective was not normal because of that; perhaps Susan *was* just being friendly with John, and maybe she did want to surprise Harry with a wedding gift. A truce was needed, but I didn't want her to think she had the upper hand.

Mary asked me the next day, "Mama, what did you do to poor Susan? She's distraught. Were you unkind to her?"

"My word, is that girl running to everyone?" I asked.

"Mama, I'm shocked at you! Susan is the prettiest, sweetest, kindest person. She's even been to college in Boston. Harry is lucky to marry someone like that!"

I just stared at her, dumbstruck. "No, Mary, Susan is the lucky one." I took Sarah and we went to the front porch to rock in the rocker and watch the painted buntings, which would be leaving any day. My mind needed distraction from the chaos Susan Marley was causing in my family. Clearly, I was looking like the villain, but not to my sweet Sarah. This was a child who I loved with all my being, and she loved me in return. She sat in my lap and looked up at me with those clear blue eyes, babbling her baby talk, and smiling at me, much like her mama had done years ago.

Harry and Susan's wedding was scheduled for the second Saturday in June. Over two hundred people had been invited, and I resolved to make it the social event of the year because Harry deserved it. Susan and I avoided each other during the planning months, but I couldn't avoid the bills. Hundreds of dollars were spent on flowers, bridesmaid dresses (four), her own gown, and she hired a chef to oversee the food. I asked Harry where all these people would be seated, and he informed me that the wedding and the reception would be held in the fanciest hotel in Gainesville.

"What do you mean, in Gainesville? I thought the wedding would be here, like Rebecca's." I was furious. We were frugal people. We didn't spend money like that.

"I'm sorry, Ma. I've tried to rein her in, but she insists that this is *her* day," he said, miserably.

"She'll break us, Harry. You must put a stop to this! We're just ranchers, not wealthy people. And no help from her parents? I won't continue to pay these bills, and you can tell her that! Or better still, I will tell her that."

"Mother, please! I told her I would pay for everything."

"But you don't have this kind of money, Harry."

"I didn't realize she would go all-out. Just help me through this," he begged.

"Are you sure Susan Marley is the girl for you?" I asked. "She sure doesn't seem to be a country girl."

At that moment, I felt so dishonest. But I couldn't involve his brother, as he would feel betrayed by both Susan and John. Even though I didn't think anything had happened between Susan and John, I felt she was not above becoming involved with John, as well as Harry. I hoped this would all be resolved as soon as the wedding was over. My Harry had always been the most easy-going boy. Nothing phased him; he made light of everything. And now, he looked worried and tired.

"Life was sure a lot easier before Susan, but what can I do? I love her. She is the most exciting girl I have ever met," he said.

Harry was certainly of an age to be marrying, at 20 years. But he was not worldly, as I felt Susan Marley was. I believed her to be around 24. His life had centered around the ranch since he was very small – he'd never even left the state of Florida since we arrived here.

He had always been special to me, not only because he looked like me, but he had his pa's personality. Tall and lean, he had the same walk as his father. His sleepy-look was due to his long, thick eyelashes, and his eyes were as dark as the Suwannee River. My love for him was so great, it broke my heart to see what this girl was doing to him.

"I noticed you aren't wearing a hat these days. Do you need a new one?" I asked.

"Susan wants me to get rid of my white forehead," he said, quietly.

"God in heaven, is she aware you're a rancher?" I asked angrily.

"It's just for the wedding, Ma. Don't be mad."

Everything this girl did galled me. She was letting me know she was in control. I would be putting a stop to this after the wedding; she *would* be reined in. My thoughts were constantly on this problem; she *was* becoming the center of my life. I hugged Harry and sent him on his way, watching him walk, slump-shouldered, to the barn. What kind of hold did she have on him?

Chapter 3   LOSING THE BATTLE

Loretta knocked on my door later in the week, and came in for coffee. As we sat, I saw that she was flushed and seemed bothered by something. Since she had always been a person who had a hard time speaking her mind, I asked her what was wrong.

"Sally, you embarrass Samuel by offering to pay for our rooms at the hotel," she said.

"Loretta, what are you talking about? What hotel? I don't understand."

"Susan told Mary and Rebecca you were paying for all our rooms at the hotel, for the wedding," she said. Samuel is very upset over it. We can afford to pay our own way."

"This girl will be the death of me. She is spending money right and left. I will have to put an end to this!" I was so angry I could not see straight.

Loretta's eyes were big as I stomped out of the house. Heading for the cabin on the lake, my vision was blurred with rage. I walked fast and hard, rushed on to the deck, and threw the cabin door wide. My horror at the scene before me was evident as I gasped for air, and took a step backward. There, on the brass bed, amidst pillows and rumpled sheets, were two naked people, Harry and Susan, making love. Horrified, he stood, covering his body with a sheet. She, on the other hand, did not cover her body at all.

"Harry, you are supposed to be helping with the cattle. Get dressed! John needs you!" I said angrily. Harry rushed out the front door, dragging his pants on, as he went.

Susan stood and walked to her clothes, and began to pull on her chemise, leisurely, her glossy auburn hair falling around her shoulders, a vision of loveliness – on the outside. At that point, I knew how she had controlled my son. Her body was perfect, with large, firm breasts, and she turned to me, full on, so that I could see her. Slowly, she pulled her chemise over her head. I was horrified and enraged. Then, she sat on the bed and pulled her pantaloons up one leg and then the other, deliberately. Her legs were long and her stomach was perfectly flat. All the time she was dressing she was looking me dead in the eye. I thought of the water moccasin I had seen on the lake the first day I met her. There was no shame in her. I couldn't get my breath, but I knew Harry was making a big mistake marrying this hussy. She smiled at me, wickedly, and said, "You wanted to see me?"

"I will put a stop to this wedding. No more bills will be paid. You are a trollop, and my son will not be marrying you," I said, barely able to contain myself.

"*This* is why your son loves me. We've been doing this since we first met. The country girls here can't do the things I can do for him. He hungers for me, comes to me at lunchtime, and at night. He can't get enough of me. Do you really think you can stop that? And John wants me, too. All I would have to do is crook my little finger and John would follow me anywhere."

A shudder passed through my whole body. She lay back on the bed, only dressed in her underwear, and lit up a little cigar. My face felt hot and I could not form words.

"We shall see. Be sure you are gone by this evening or I will call on the sheriff and have you evicted," I said and turned and left the cabin. I was shaken to my core, wondering if she could have been a prostitute, never having met such a brazen girl. She *was* the devil incarnate.

Loretta was still sitting at my dining room table when I returned. The tears on my face were evidence that things had not gone well. As I told her all that had transpired in the last few days, she was genuinely shocked. It was hard for her to believe that an angel like Susan Marley, as she viewed her, was not what she appeared to be.

"What will you do?" she asked.

"I will put an end to this wedding. Harry will not make this mistake."

Later that day, Harry hitched two horses to the carriage, loaded Susan's bags, and drove her into Gainesville, where he rented a house for them. My heart was broken. I felt I was losing my son to a woman of the night, a cigar-smoking woman at that. He didn't return for several days. When he did return, I caught up with him in the barn and he wouldn't look me in the eye.

"Harry?" I called to him.

"Ma, I'm sorry, but she's going to be my wife. I wish you hadn't barged in on us like that. She was a virgin when I met her, so this is my fault, too," he said.

I laughed, bitterly. "That girl was no virgin when you met her. She has you fooled, Harry. She will ruin your life. Please, let her go," I pleaded.

"I'll be leaving the ranch, and moving to Gainesville, hoping to find a ranching job close to town. Susan has requested that you not attend the wedding," he said sadly.

Collapsing on a bale of hay, I tried to fathom the things he had just said to me. I could not. These things wouldn't be happening if Jacob were here. My life was coming apart and I knew this girl had won the battle.

I had known sadness in my life, but the loss of a child, especially under these conditions, was unbearable. Loretta said her family would not attend a wedding that I had been barred from. David and Annie and young Jake wouldn't be attending either. When they heard the news, they came to our house and sat in the parlor with me. As young Jake came in, I couldn't help but smile. He hugged me, and I held his face in my hands to see the handsome man he had become, so sweet and good-natured.

David said, "What in the hell has been happening here?"

The tears came without my knowing it, running down my cheeks and onto my dress. Annie hugged me and cried with me.

"I have been barred from Harry's wedding, but I wouldn't go anyway, to see him marry a girl who'll ruin his life," I said tearfully.

"This doesn't sound like our Harry. He's one of the finest boys I've ever known. And I know he loves his mama," David said.

"This girl has bewitched him. She's a worldly thing and even smokes cigars," I said.

Annie gasped and said, "I knew there was something not right about that girl, being a Yankee and all."

I laughed and said, "That's not the problem. She isn't who she says she is, and when she finds out Harry has no money of his own, she'll be gone. I can't even begin to repeat some of the things she has said to me." I couldn't tell them about John and his infatuation with Susan. John intended to be at the wedding, which hurt me, too. But I didn't get to see David and his family that often, as they lived ten miles away, and I didn't want all our conversation centered around Susan. So, we talked about the ranching business, and David laughed when I told him I would be riding in the roundup.

"We'll be over to help with the branding next month. You probably can use some help with things in an uproar," he said.

"I believe John is doing okay, but we could use the help, and we'll be over to help you when the time comes also," I said, knowing that, once again, I would lose myself in work. We spoke no more about Susan Marley, as if she never existed. And how I wished that were true. It was a good thing that I had stopped carrying my little pistol.

John continued to give me riding lessons, but we didn't discuss the events that pivoted around Harry's wedding. When I asked him if he would attend, he said, "Yes, I want to support Harry, and Susan wants me there." My mouth was open in dismay, and then he quietly said, "I believe you are in the wrong this time, Ma."

My children were looking on me as a villain. Time would have to prove me right, but any discussion of the matter was so upsetting to me that I could not talk about it anymore. Mary thought I was wrong also and she planned to attend the wedding, and truly, I did want Harry to have their support. He would need it later on; I was certain of that. Loretta put her foot down with Rebecca, maybe the first time she had ever done that. She told her, "I know your Aunt Sally better than you do, and I will not allow my family to attend a wedding to which she was not invited."

So, there was turmoil around the ranch in the days that led up to the wedding. Most of the ranch hands hadn't been invited, men that

Harry had worked, eaten, and drank with. I could tell by the looks on their faces that they were disappointed. If the wedding had been at the ranch, they would definitely have been invited.

Chapter 4 BILL

On the day of the wedding, Mary and John left early in the morning, dressed in finery. John broke my heart, looking down at me from the carriage, with his father's blue eyes. His new suit was dark blue and he looked so much like Jacob the first time I saw him that I had to look away. Needing distraction, I decided I was an accomplished enough rider to take a ride around our property. I headed to the barn to saddle my horse as they drove down the road.

Lem was my horse's name, and he was as sweet and gentle as a horse could be. We headed to our largest pasture, where I could ride for long distances. Once the gate was opened and reclosed, I mounted my horse, and we rode over the rolling hills that were part of our land. I talked to Jacob as if he were riding a horse beside me since there was no one for miles around.

"I miss you, Jacob, not just at night, but in the managing of the ranch and our family. You seemed to handle things effortlessly. I'm sure you know about Susan and the awful things she's done. I've had to spend $500 on this wedding, a wedding I couldn't even attend. I can think of a lot of other things that that money could have gone toward. A little guidance would help, if you could see some way to help me. You know I love my children, but they aren't standing by me on this one. And Susan Marley *Winston* is an evil woman; the things she has done are wicked. And Harry is so in love with her. She uses her body to have her way with him, and he's moved into Gainesville and quit our ranch."

Lem looked back at me and snorted. I guess he thought I was talking to him. As we rode on into a stand of live oaks, I could hear a low grunting noise. Under one of the trees, I saw a heifer stretched out on the grass. Her head was on the ground, so I could tell she was having a hard time and was worn out. Dropping the reins, I stepped

216

off my horse and approached the cow. I could see little hooves, trying to be born, sticking out of her backside. The mama couldn't even lift her head to look at me. Stooping down low to try to assess the situation, I wrapped my gloved hands around those small legs. Pulling with all my might was not budging that little fellow. So I sat on the ground, placed my boots on the cow's haunches, and pulled hard. A slight budge. Taking a breath, I shortened my hold and pulled again. About an inch. Again, I shortened my hand-hold, and readjusted my boots on her butt, careful that she wouldn't kick me. The legs came all the way out. I pulled again, straining as hard as I could, and the head popped out. I let out a yelp, thinking I had saved calf and mother. When I pulled the last time, his whole body rushed out, with a whoosh of liquid and blood, all over my new riding breeches, but I was ecstatic I had helped birth him.

Just then, as I was standing, I noticed a rider coming toward me, Lanier Walton. I waved to him and he waved back. When he got closer, he called, "Thought you might need some help, but it doesn't look like it."

"You can help me clean him up, and get the mother up, Lanier," I said.

"Only my enemies call me Lanier. It's Lani," he grinned.

We worked on the baby and had him standing shortly, but the mother was finished. The strain had been too much for her and she closed her eyes and died. Lani took his bandana from around his neck and tried to wipe off my breeches.

"Never saw a woman in pants before," he said. His voice was very deep, and he stood looking down at me, his eyes twinkling. I was so embarrassed as I knew a woman shouldn't be wearing pants, but I wasn't expecting company either. He smiled again.

"Better get that baby to the barn. I'll throw him over my horse and ride back with you," he said. We rode back to the barn and rigged a bottle to feed him cow's milk. He was a little guy but he was surely comely. I named him Bill, Bill the bull.

"What were you doing out there?" I asked.

"David said you might need some help, and he can spare me right now. I brought my bedroll."

"Nonsense, Lanier, Lani. Stay in Harry's cabin. He's moved to Gainesville. I'll just have to clean it for you," I said.

We put the calf in a stall, and walked to the cabin. When I opened the door, the memory of that day with Susan came flooding back to me. The cabin was a mess, and I stripped the linens, and began to sweep the floor. He put his hand on mine, on the broom, and said, "Don't bother. I'll only sleep here, and I'll sleep in my bedroll." His touch electrified me. It was a gentle touch, but I hadn't been touched by a man since Jacob died. I pulled back from him; he looked hurt.

"Sorry," he said, and walked out the door.

☼

I was in the barn feeding the baby calf when John and Mary returned the next day. They weren't talking about the wedding to me, although I believe Mary was filling Rebecca's and Loretta's ears with all the good times. John was quiet and didn't look me in the eye. I was too proud to ask how the day went. He smiled at the new calf, and said, "I think I'll move into Harry's cabin."

"You'll have to wait until Lanier moves out. He's here to help us for a spell," I said.

"Lanier? Why'd you do that? We don't need his help."

"Your Uncle David sent him over. We do need help, with Harry gone and branding starting soon. I thought you'd be pleased," I said.

John turned on his heel and left the barn. He may have looked like his pa, but he didn't have Jacob's good nature, seeming to be getting moodier all the time. I thought it was just the events that had taken place lately. They had made me kind of moody, too.

"Do you want to hear about the wedding or not?" Loretta asked me later that day.

"Yes and no," I said.

"One or the other," she said.

"Okay, tell me about the wedding."

"Mary said it was a grand affair. The hotel was decorated with potted palms and strung lights. She said she had never seen anyone as beautiful as Susan. Her dress was a pale pink silk and it was cut very low, so that her bosom was showing. Her hair was pinned up in the latest style. The flowers were magnificent: the bouquet was yellow roses and she had four bridesmaids that no one knew, all beauties. They had on yellow silk dresses to match her bouquet and carried forget-me-nots. Sounds wonderful, doesn't it?" she asked, breathlessly.

"It should. It cost enough," I said.

"There's more. During the reception, Harry went to the bar and started drinking with the men. When he didn't come back and the band started to play, Susan and John started dancing together. Well, you know John has never danced, but she taught him and they were dancing close when Harry came back into the ballroom. He pulled John away from Susan and threw back his fist to hit him, when John turned and bolted out the door."

"Oh my! I am so glad she has moved to Gainesville. I tell you, Loretta, she is the epitome of evil. I'm hoping things will get back to normal soon. I'll miss Harry, but I will not miss that witch. By the way, Lanier Walton is helping us on the ranch now. David sent him over. He helped me with a calf yesterday," I said.

"He's sweet on you, Sally. He's always looked at you with love in his eyes," she laughed.

"Well, he can look at me all he wants. He's not Jacob Henry Winston, and never will be. I could never love another man," I said.

"You could get mighty lonesome, Sally, and he is a handsome man," she laughed again.

"Is he? Well, he doesn't look like Jacob, so he's not handsome to me."

Life on the ranch was getting back to normal and I was so happy not to have to deal with Susan Marley Winston. My riding was getting better, and I was learning to rope and brand. David and a few of his men were coming to the ranch for roundup, and we were all excited to be doing ranch work. Packing up my bedroll one evening, I planned to spend the night with the men out in the pastures, when John came to the house.

"I'd like to see Harry back at the ranch. He was one of our best workers," he said.

"I heard what happened at the wedding. Do you really think he would come back here when he thinks you want his wife?" I asked.

He blushed. "I don't want his wife. How can you say that? I love Harry," he said.

"You can ask him to come back, but I don't think he will," I said.

"Will you be riding the range with us, Ma?" he grinned.

"I'm going to do my best."

"When will Lanier be leaving? I don't think we'll need him after the branding," he said.

"Don't worry about Lanier. No one is a better worker than he is. As long as David will lend him to us, he can stay," I said.

"I'd like to move into the cabin. I *am* the foreman, you know," he said.

"We'll work it out." But I wondered why he was so anxious to move out of the bunkhouse. I had thought he preferred it there. My trust in John was waning.

Chapter 5   *RIDING THE WAVE*

I had never realized what hard work the roundup was. Riding in the saddle all day, throwing a rope around strays, was exhausting. At suppertime, Abigail and Lester laid out a spread for us that we hungrily lapped up. John insisted that I sleep in a tent, since I was the only woman on the trail, except for Abigail, who slept in the chuck wagon with Lester. At the end of the day, I crawled into my tent before the sun had even set. I could hear the men, sitting around the campfire, laughing and talking. Lani started playing his guitar when I drifted off to sleep.

Early the next morning I could smell coffee boiling and bacon frying. When I rolled over, every bone and muscle in my body hurt. I groaned. The men grinned at me when I joined them around the fire, but I could tell they respected me for the work I was doing. Women didn't usually work the cattle. But I didn't think about Harry and Susan, or the loss of Jacob, while I was working the roundup. I could tell that John was missing his brother, however, because he looked back down the trail the whole day. I determined to send Lani back to David's ranch after the branding, even though I thought we could use his help. John needed some 'alone' time and the cabin would be just what would help him to get over these worries.

At the end of the range work, I held a party on the ranch for all the workers and our family. It was a feast, indeed. Being still stiff, I walked as if I were crippled. Loretta laughed at me as I settled in at the long table set up under the oak trees.

"Ma, you did great!" John said, sitting down beside me.

"Thank you, John. Hard work!" I said, as I accepted a bowl of mashed potatoes and even that hurt.

"I'm going to take your advice and send Lanier home," I said quietly. Smiling, he said, "Thank you."

Of course, telling Lanier that we didn't need him would be hard, but I'm sure David would be glad. I found Lanier in the barn after the party, grooming his horse.

"Hi, Lani. Got a minute?" I asked.

"Always for you, Miss Sally," he said. We sat on the wooden bench and he was careful not to touch me. He had worked faithfully for me these last few weeks and I appreciated it, but I felt John's wishes were more important to me.

"Thank you, Lani, for all your hard work," I began. He looked at me with his hazel eyes, that I had never noticed before.

"Are you dismissing me?" he asked.

"Not dismissing, but I can't ask David to give up his foreman anymore," I said.

"I see," he said. "I'll be gone by morning."

I didn't quite understand him. He seemed hurt that I was letting him go, when he worked for my brother-in-law. I talked with David later in the evening and he said, "I believe Lani has been in love with you since he first laid eyes on you, when we came to meet you on the trail."

Loretta had teased me about it, but to have it confirmed by David made it too real.

"You know I'll never love another man, David."

"I know, Sally, but Lani can't help his feelings," he said.

"Then it's better if he leaves. I have no feelings for him," I said.

"He's a good man, Sally, the best I've ever known. You may get lonely one day and you're a beautiful woman."

I laughed, thinking I would never be lonely with so many people living on the ranch, but I think David was thinking of something else.

As I lay awake, early the next morning, I heard Lani's horse ride by the window. A lonesome feeling did pass through my body as I listened to the sound get farther away. When I first lay down at night, I always missed Jacob. I had slept with his shirt wrapped around a pillow every night since he died. Missing him was part of my life now; I expected it, but I didn't expect to think of Lani in that manner. It's another thing I would have to forget, as I didn't want another man.

☼

Abigail and I cleaned the cabin on the lake while John was out working the next day. How I loved that little cabin and how I missed my boy, Harry, wondering where he was working and if he was happy. I longed to see him and hug him and laugh with him. Abigail saw my tears and touched my arm gently.

There was a letter on my dining table, when I returned from the cabin. It was addressed to 'Mr. John Winston', written in a woman's handwriting with no return address. I picked it up and smelled it and it was perfumed. My heart sank and immediately I knew it was from Susan Marley. Would this situation never end? I thought with the wedding being over and her settling in Gainesville with her husband that peace would come to the ranch again.

At the end of the day, I called John to the house. As he came in, I handed him the letter, and he turned a bright shade of red, looking away from me.

"John, you must put an end to this. This is your brother's wife," I said.

"Ma, you don't understand. I love Susan with all my heart."

I felt as though I would faint. Was it possible to despise this woman more? She really didn't care who she hurt, and she was succeeding in destroying my family.

"And how about your brother? Do you love him, too?"

"I do. But Susan isn't in love with him. She loves *me*. She told me so at the wedding."

"God in heaven! Then why did she marry him?" I asked.

"She said she couldn't back out at the last minute," he said.

"John, I am advising you to end this! Have you had relations with her?"

He sat down on the sofa in the parlor and put his hands over his face. He said, "I have, but I can't end it. I want her too much. She's all I can think of, day and night."

"Don't you see how wrong this is, John? She's destroying both you and Harry. She's evil," I said.

"You don't know her. She's the most intelligent, most desirable woman I've ever met. She makes me feel I could do anything. She thinks I'm the strongest, most handsome man in the world."

He began to cry. I sat beside him and held him, feeling his pain, but hating the source of it and at a loss as to what to do. Two brothers loving one woman, and a depraved one at that, could not end well. I felt awful that Harry did not know about Susan and John, but the one thing I did not want was for my sons to hate each other.

☼

During the next few months, I began to feel ill. The destruction that was happening to my family had taken a toll on me. I knew that shortly John would go to Gainesville on business. My first thought was that he was going to visit Susan while Harry was away at work. As I confronted him, I knew John would always be honest with me.

"Are you visiting your brother's wife?" I asked him.

"How will this end?" I asked him. He could only shrug. "If you're going to shirk your work, I will give the foreman's job to Lanier," I said.

The shock on his face registered. He said, "Don't worry, I won't shirk my work."

There were times when I felt I was riding on a wave on the ocean in a big storm, and not always at its crest.

Chapter 6 MISDEEDS

On a cool October Sunday, everyone had gone to church, except me. My stomach had been upset for days; nerves, I thought. There was no one on the ranch but a couple of hands, and they were out in the pastures. I usually started the mornings off checking on our little bull, Bill, that I had delivered a few months past. As I walked into the barn, I heard a noise in the loft, an owl I figured. Owls can do some damage in a barn, so I decided to climb the wooden ladder, careful not to startle him, so that he wouldn't fly out at me. Keeping very quiet, I peeked up over the straw in the loft and almost lost my grip on the ladder rung from what I saw. Susan was lying in the straw with no clothes on, and John was on top of her, totally naked. I gasped, and they both looked at me, John in horror, Susan, with a slight smile on her face. "Lord have mercy," I whispered.

I could hear someone calling my name, through the roaring in my ears. Harry! I climbed carefully off the ladder and could see Harry standing in the sunshine, outside the barn. My heart was in my throat as I walked toward him, not hearing anything much he was saying. He rushed to me and hugged me, saying, "I have missed you so much, Ma."

Numbness was all I felt as I hurried him to the house, so that he would not know of the betrayal taking place. He smiled and seemed so happy to be home, as it had been months.

"Ma, you look pale. Are you sick?" he asked.

"Just a little stomach problem. I'll be fine." But I was not fine, overcome with mixed emotions: sorrow and joy at seeing my Harry and anger at that vixen, and John.

"I was looking for John," Harry said. I was hoping to come back to work here. My salary is not enough to support us, and Susan has a lot of needs. Since you don't get along with her, I thought I would go home on the weekends. I sure have missed you and John and the rest of the family. We're better ranchers than most people I've learned. And we treat our people better."

"I, I guess that would be okay. We've missed you, too," I stammered.

But truly, how would that work? John and Susan were in the barn loft at that very moment, fornicating, as I tried to make conversation with my son. My head was hurting, throbbing. Harry looked out the window then and said, "There's John now. I hope he'll forgive me for getting drunk at my wedding and throwing a punch at him. I'm going to talk to him."

Before I could stop him, he was out the door and running toward his brother, throwing his arms around John and giving him a bear hug, laughing. My heart was breaking. But Susan at least had the good sense to stay put. Women like her have caused men to kill each other, even brothers.

John hired Harry back on, and I wondered if he didn't think this would be better for his trysts with Susan, knowing where Harry would be while he went to Gainesville. I knew John wouldn't give her up at that point. The guilt I felt in knowing these things, and not revealing them to Harry, was dominant in my thinking. I had become a liar also – the trait I hated most. And meanwhile, again, I had other people in my life that I was neglecting. This situation had to be put out of my mind or it would make me crazy.

1883: A year had gone by with everything happening the same way: Harry was staying in the bunkhouse and would go home on the weekends. Sometimes, he only went home on Sunday if the workload was heavy. John went to Gainesville on business every other week and stayed overnight, sinning with his brother's wife. I knew he felt guilt but he simply wouldn't stop. And I had stopped talking with him about it. He tried to explain the loft day, but I had held my hand up, to signal I wouldn't talk about it.

"When you end this thing, I'll talk about it. Until then, don't bring it up. Are you foolish enough to think she isn't sleeping with her own husband also?" I asked.

"She says she isn't," he said.

"And she was a virgin when Harry first took her," I laughed harshly, shaking my head.

"That's what she says," he said. How did I raise such naïve boys? They were just too pure at heart, though John was surely losing his purity and I knew his betrayal was weighing heavy on him. I dreaded the day Harry learned of the treachery, but I knew it would come, and he would know of my duplicity also. That thought haunted me. I was sorry to say that, at that point, I did not like my oldest son.

I was still trying to pay attention to the rest of the family. Mary had been a little cool toward me after the wedding, but she was starting to warm up. She was courting one of our ranch hands and things were getting serious I thought. His name was Joshua Courtland, a hard worker and knowledgeable, a man without many smiles, however, and I wondered what the attraction was. He wasn't bad-looking but I thought Mary could have done better. She said he was looking for a foreman's job and I told her as long as John and Harry worked the ranch, we wouldn't need a foreman.

"He's asked me to marry him, but he wants to wait until he has a better job so he can support us," she said.

My determination was not to interfere further with my grown children's lives. I felt I had made a mess of it so far. Even the Susan Marley debacle weighed heavy on me, not being certain what part I played in her vindictiveness. She was *definitely* out to destroy my family.

I asked Mary, "Will Joshua be a good father to Sarah? That's all I ask."

"Of course he will," she said. But I never saw him hold Sarah, or talk with her, or show love to her. I had my doubts. He just always seemed to be quite cross.

And right when I thought our status quo would remain peaceful, in spite of the dastardly deeds happening, Harry came to me and said, "Susan and I would like to move back to the cabin. She says she thinks she can forgive you now. We're apart so much, she's lonely."

That girl constantly surprised me; her misdeeds were phenomenal. There's no way I could let her disrupt our lives any more than she already had. And forgive *me*?

"No, Harry. John is in the cabin now and he deserves it. Susan will not be allowed back on this ranch as long as I have breath," I said.

"You're holding a long grudge, Ma. We want to have children and raise them here. She's sorry for the disagreement and I want to come home. Pa would want me to come home," he said angrily.

"Don't you speak for your pa. He would not want that woman on this land," I said, vehemently. "You can't control your wife, Harry, and she is a vicious woman. No! No!"

He turned and left, seething. His walk was angry as he headed to the barn. John came in later and sat. He said, sadly, "If you don't let them come back, Harry is going to suspect something."

"I will not have that woman near decent people. You are either going to have to quit her or tell Harry. I cannot condone this conspiracy, of which I am a part," I said. This situation had been going on for over two years and I was worn to a frazzle.

"Ma, don't you understand? I love the woman. She's in my system."

I simply couldn't talk about this subject any longer. Maybe I was the one who needed to leave. The exasperation was more than I could stand. And who could I talk to? – no one. How could I tell Loretta the things that were going on with my boys, how awful it was that John was in love with Harry's wife? I had raised my sons better than that.

Harry would not speak to me or look at me. This was the child that I loved more than life itself; that smiling, bright-eyed boy that had brought me so much happiness. There had never been a time when he wouldn't come to me and hug and kiss me, even when he was grown, telling me he loved me every day since he could talk, saying "I luf you," when he was three. But our peace was once again interrupted.

John avoided Harry like the plague. If Harry came down to the cabin to fish in the evening, John would leave, claiming he had barn work to do. Their relationship was being ravaged by a woman who I felt cared little for either of them. What did she want? Revenge on me? What was she after – money?

Chapter 7 *DISPERSING*

John began his weekly trips to Gainesville again, having slowed up a bit when Harry came to work at the ranch, only going to see Susan every other week. Every time I saw him ride down the road, I felt like dying. And I knew he didn't feel good about it either. But she had a hold on him and he couldn't control it. I wondered how all this would end; not well, I knew.

After one of his "business" trips, John asked to speak with me privately. Mary took Sarah and went to Rebecca's. As I sat, waiting for him to speak, he was nervous, pacing back and forth in the parlor.

"I need money," he said.

"How much, and what for?" I asked.

"I would like to sell my part of the ranch," he said.

"You don't have a part of the ranch until I'm gone," I said.

"Then, I would like to borrow a thousand dollars until I can get on my feet."

"Are you leaving us, John?" I knew he wouldn't lie to me.

"Ma, I...," he whispered. The tears were falling down his face.

Knowing before he told me what he was going to say, I waited.

"I have to go. Susan loves me and we want to make a life for ourselves, in Boston."

"Boston? What will you do in Boston? Have you taken leave of your senses?"

"Susan doesn't want to be with Harry anymore," he said. "She wants us to go away and start a new life."

I had no strength left to fight this woman. She had won yet another battle; she was the victor, and my boys were the spoils.

"You know that she will leave you also when the money runs out. And I don't think there's much ranching in Boston. Will you tell Harry?" I asked.

"How can I tell him? He'll kill me. Will you tell him for me, Ma?"

On top of everything else, he was cowardly, with more than just one character flaw. But I knew Harry *would* kill John, because he was as much in love with Susan as John was. How could I give John money to spend on that woman? And yet, I knew he would go, money or not. So, I gave him a thousand dollars and had him sign a promissory note. He was gone by early morning the next day. I cried all day long, holed up in the house. Mary asked me repeatedly what was wrong, but the words wouldn't come. She went for Loretta.

When Loretta came in, I was lying on the bed, crying.

"My darling girl, what's wrong?" she asked.

Turning my face to the wall, I sobbed. She made tea for me and sat in a chair by my bed as I told her the whole tale. Her eyes dilated and she was sighing loudly by the end of the story.

"It is truly unbelievable! What will you do? Does Harry know?" she asked.

Harry came through the door at that very moment and saw my distress. He hadn't entered my house in weeks.

"What's going on?" he asked.

"Your mother has had a setback, Harry. Now's not a good time," Loretta said.

"Mary said you were sick," he said. "Where's John today?"

"Thank you, Loretta, but now's as good a time as any. Sit down, Harry," I said.

Harry's innocent face went from hurt to embarrassment to rage. At first, he couldn't fathom what I was saying, looking bewildered. Then, it dawned on him that his older brother had been carrying on with his wife since before they were married. Standing, he paced the room, growing angrier and angrier and I was feeling fear for myself.

"How long have you known?" he asked, his face red.

"From the beginning."

"And you didn't tell me?"

"I tried to warn you, if you remember. But I thought once you were married and moved to Gainesville, it would end," I said, apologetically. But he was furious, and I was the only one left to take it out on.

"So, not only am I betrayed by my wife and brother, but by my mother also," he yelled.

"Harry, I tried to get him to tell you. I tried to get him to stop, but that woman wouldn't leave him be. She's a harlot!" I cried.

Loretta had gone in the next room and I was glad because I had never seen Harry that angry. He ran from the house, sobbing. I had fear for anyone who crossed his path.

He didn't return for a week after he left the ranch, and I was more worried for him than I was for John. His life had been turned upside down, his faith in me shattered. John and I were the two people he trusted most in the world and we had not just let him down, we had formed a conspiracy. It was not a thing I was proud of, tortured by the fact that I had not told him about the affair between his brother and his wife, which by then had gone on for over two years.

☼

Harry knocked on my backdoor, one early morning. I was still in my gown and robe when he came in, looking disheveled and bleary-eyed. I hugged him to me and cried on his shoulder. How I loved this boy still, above all my children.

"Ma, I want you to know I don't blame you. If I had known, I would have shot John. You did right. What I'm trying to understand is Susan: she talked about a family, and living here on the ranch. We loved each other in the night every night we were together. There was no clue that she didn't love me. But how could I not see it? All the time, she was loving my brother, too. I've been such a fool. Maybe all our workers knew, too. How can I be a boss to them when I look like a cuckold? Their respect is something I wouldn't have. My plan is to go to Colorado," he said.

"Oh no! Harry, you wouldn't leave us. Who will run the ranch? I don't think I'm capable," I said.

"I'm sorry, Ma, but I don't feel capable either right now. I've got some thinking to do. Do you know where your brothers' ranch is in Colorado?"

"They are east of Ft. Collins, but that's a long way from Florida. Please don't go. I'm not sure anyone knows about John," I begged.

"They know. Abigail said everyone knew and hated John for laying with my wife," he said.

"Oh," was all I could say, feeling foolish that I had thought this was a secret.

In the end, I gave Harry a thousand dollars and bought him and his horse a train ticket to Colorado. I wrote my brothers, John David and Henry Louis Winston, and told them what a good worker Harry was. And I hoped he could find a place on their ranch; if not, on another one in the area.

Chapter 8 STRICTLY BUSINESS

After I saw Harry off at the railroad station, I drove straight to David and Annie's. I spent the night with them, and asked David for help with my ranch.

"I can spare Lani again, until you can find a foreman," David said.

Annie cried when I told her the events that had taken place in the last few years, and I cried along with her.

"Soon all my children will be gone," I said. "Mary intends to marry Joshua Courtland and move away."

"Let's walk to the barn. I believe Lani is there," David said.

Lani was cleaning tack in the barn when David and I walked through the door. Glancing up, his smile was wide. "Howdy," he said. He was such a strong-looking man with pronounced muscles in his arms, tall and taut, with the big moustache that I loved. I confess that I felt a chill pass through my body at the sight of him and wondered what was wrong with me. Ashamed of my feelings, I knew I was still mourning the loss of Jacob.

"I think Miss Sally will be needing your assistance again, Lani," David said.

"Glad to give it to a beautiful woman," he said.

"Thank you, Lani. I'm in your debt," I said.

"Don't tell him that," David laughed.

Once again, Lani had saved me and I was so appreciative that David would allow him to come to my ranch, which would mean more work for him at his place.

As I drove the wagon home that day, with no one around, I felt the need to talk with Jacob.

"Things are a mess here, my love. I know if you were here, everything would be better. Help me through this time. Both the boys are gone, Mary is getting ready to leave, and I am so lonely for you. I want you here with me to hold me and tell me everything's going to be okay." I cried because nothing would be okay with Jacob gone, and soon all my children, too.

Mary greeted me as I drove the wagon into the barnyard. She had a smile on her face, the first smile she had given me in a while.

"You were right about Susan, Ma. I'm sorry I couldn't see it. We've all been shocked at the news," she said as I stepped down from the wagon. Lester took the reins from me and began to unhitch the horses as I walked with Mary to the house.

"Does this mean you'll be hiring a new foreman?" she asked, as I put coffee on to boil.

"Lani Walton will be filling in while the boys are gone," I said.

"Lani Walton? Why would you hire him when you could hire Joshua, so we could get married.

"I've known Lani for years. I know he can handle the job."

"Ma, don't you care about me at all? It's always been the boys that you loved. You never cared about me," she said, tears running down her face.

"Mary, how can you say that? I've loved you all equally," I said, shocked at her words.

"You've always loved Harry the most. John and I both knew it. And now, you give a job to Lani Walton, and not my Joshua?" She ran from the house, and I declare, I just wanted some peace and quiet. My life was in total chaos, and no one was helping except Lani.

After the conversation with Mary, Joshua went to Lani and resigned. Now, if he had been a man, he would have talked to me as owner of the ranch. I just didn't like Joshua, hard as I tried. Mary was so upset with me when he left, she stayed at Rebecca's house for days. Loretta said Sarah cried for me every day.

Lani had made a list of everything that needed to be done. With the money I had spent on Harry's wedding and what I had given to the boys, I was running short on cash. I didn't give Mary any money, and I felt awful about that.

We sat at the dining table and he went over the projects that needed work: wood replaced in the barn and outbuildings, fencing replaced, new tack and tools bought, new roofing on all the buildings, stalls rebuilt. The list went on and on.

"I'm afraid my boys have been distracted the last few years," I said.

"Yes ma'am. I understand how a woman can be a distraction," he said softly.

I felt my face burning. I was not wanting to think of his interest in me.

"I'm afraid we'll have to sell some of the two-year-olds to improve my cash flow," I said.

"Let me help. I have money, never spent too much. I've saved all these years."

"Thank you, Lani, but this is my problem. You've done far too much already."

"Sally, I'm nigh onto fifty years old, and I feel I have some things to say to you," he said. "You probably don't remember the first time we met on the trail."

"Of course I remember," I said.

"When I saw you holding baby Mary, I thought you had to be the most beautiful thing I'd ever seen. Your hair was shining and long, your skin so pretty with your freckles. I was dumbstruck. Couldn't talk. I have loved you mightily over the years. The night that you danced with Jacob in that green dress, I could hardly stand to watch the love you had for him. Don't get me wrong, I had the highest regard for your husband, but it didn't keep me from wanting you. I've watched you over the years at family parties and church, and I've yearned to be a part of your life. I would just like to help you, and I can if you'll let me. I've had women," he blushed. "But you're the only one I've ever wanted."

He put his big hand over mine and I felt a surge, but this was creating another problem that I didn't want to think about. I wanted peace in my life, not more turmoil. And I couldn't forget about Jacob; I didn't think he would want me to love someone else.

"Lani, I'm sorry. I'm still mourning Jacob. Just be my foreman and that will be enough for now."

"We'll begin cutting trees tomorrow for the barn repairs," he said quickly and stood to leave.

At the back door, he turned and looked down at me. Then he bent and kissed me full on the lips, and the taste was sweet. I hadn't meant to, but I kissed him back. How good it felt to be held by a man again, a strong man like that. But I realized what was happening, and I pulled away quickly.

"We have to have a business relationship," I said. "We've had too much scandal on this ranch."

"There's no scandal in loving someone," he said softly. "And I do."

Well, I was shaken to my very core. Although I didn't want any more turmoil, that kiss had set me on fire. My thoughts were distracted as I thought of Lani's tender touch and the notion that a man would actually love me all these years and never tell me. Before I went to sleep at night, I thought of that kiss, and dreamed of it when I slept.

Lani said no more to me about the subject and I avoided looking at him, except when we were discussing business. Even then, I could feel a flush on my face, and I reckoned he could see it. He was working hard, making the ranch look new again. We did sell off some of the stock so that we could afford to make the changes he thought necessary. The cabin was his home again, and Abigail stripped the linens and cleaned it every week. David did not ask for Lani to come home, and for the next year he worked our place tirelessly. John had let the record books become a mess, and Lani also worked on them every night at the cabin. I felt drawn to see him, but I knew that was dangerous business for me, not wanting to break his heart or have mine broken either. So I stayed my distance.

Mary's man, Joshua, had secured a foreman position at a ranch in Newberry, about 20 miles away. They planned a short civil marriage ceremony, and I was not included in the plans. The following day, Joshua came for Mary and Sarah and their things. Joshua was not respectful to me, and was surly as he was taking items out of the house. This reinforced my feelings of dislike for him, but he was Mary's choice, not mine. I just prayed he would be good to them, especially my baby, Sarah. As they drove down the driveway, Sarah screamed at the top of her lungs for me, reaching her hand out, and I followed them down the road aways, crying as loud as Sarah.

When I walked back to the yard, there was my good friend, Loretta, and standing by her was Lani, with sorrowful looks on their faces. They both hugged me, but I was not to be consoled. I thought I knew loneliness when Jacob died, but I had my children. Now, I didn't even have Sarah, my honey-girl. Loretta asked me to come to dinner that night, but I wanted to be more cheerful when I went to her house. I no longer prepared large meals, as I was now the only one living in my house, and I missed my family something fierce. But at least, there was no more discord, which I was thankful for.

My ranch looked better than it ever had. Not only were the buildings looking better, but the pastures were greener due to the rains, and the cattle were fatter. I thought our profits would be larger than they ever had been, and I could only thank Lani for that. Riding together across the fields, we would inspect the hay fields and pastures, and he was good company, talking about the cattle and ranch. I still helped with the roundup and the branding and herding of cattle to the railway line. Many times I threw a long skirt on over my breeches, so that I would not cause any more discredit to our family than we already had.

As we returned to the barn one evening after our rounds, I asked Lani if he would like to have dinner with me. His eyes lit up and he said, "I'll bring my guitar."

While I was fixing dinner, he sat in the parlor and played cowboy songs, so sad and sweet. He was comfortable in my home, and it felt right, but I still had that nagging feeling of being unfaithful to Jacob, which I was trying to overcome.

As he said grace, he held my hand in his. His voice was deep, and I couldn't help but watch him while he prayed. There was a little gray at his temples, but mostly his hair was dark. He had laugh lines around his eyes, and I realized I was greatly attracted to him.

"It's a rare trait for a woman to be such a good cook and be so beautiful, too," he said.

"Lani, you're too kind. I don't really think I'm beautiful," I said.

"Yes ma'am. You are. Just ask any of the ranch hands here. They'll tell you how pretty you are, and good to them also. They appreciate you. Yes ma'am," he repeated.

After dinner, we sat on the sofa and he sang and played his guitar, and I was taken aback at how I wanted to repeat that kiss. Closing my eyes, I leaned back on the sofa, and he kissed me softly. I was hungry for him, for a man's touch, and for the love of a good man.

"I would marry you tomorrow, if you would have me," he whispered. Laying his guitar down, he kissed me again and I knew I could not control my desire for him. But I also didn't want anyone to know about it, feeling the hypocrite.

"How about some brandy?" I said, as I jumped up.

"Okay," he smiled.

Pouring two small glasses of brandy, I sat down again, farther away from him. As he tasted the drink, he grinned. Remembering drinking brandy with Jacob when he came back from the war made me sad. I just couldn't love this man, and would only hurt him. I thought my need for him stemmed from my need for my husband. And I *was* so lonely.

My body relaxed completely as I drank the brandy slowly. Maybe I had needed a drink for a long time. As I glanced at Lani, I realized how masculine he was, how handsome in a rugged way. He reached for me again and I snuggled against him and he kissed me passionately. I tasted the brandy on his tongue, and I gave in to his kisses. When he stood to take me to the bedroom, I resisted, however. I couldn't make love with him in Jacob's bed.

"I'm sorry. I can't," I whispered.

He said, "I understand." And he was gone, without another word.

☼

A letter arrived from John. He had been gone a year. He said Susan had a lawyer who was drawing up the papers for the divorce from Harry. Once that happened, they would marry. Money was what he needed from me again so that they could pay the lawyer, saying I was right about Boston: there was no work for him there. Five hundred dollars was what he was asking for. I sent it to him, along with Harry's address in Colorado, writing that it was the last I would send. In my heart, I knew she would never marry John; he was not rich enough. But this was a relief for me because I didn't want her trying to take the ranch.

I had heard from my brothers, my little brothers, who I hadn't seen in so long, writing that Harry had arrived safely and that both their families were in love with him. He was a hard worker and charming, too, they said. How happy that made me. I so hoped that Harry would find happiness on the frontier, and that he would find a sweet girl, too, and have a family of his own. I also hoped he would write to me, but no letter came.

Chapter 9   *THE TOUCH*

It was during the roundup of 1885 that I decided I had mourned for Jacob long enough. I rode with the men, ate with them, slept out under the stars with them and I had watched Lani long enough to know I had fallen in love with him. When he would walk by at the end of the day, I longed to touch him, and I so wanted to be held again. As we sat together after supper, around the fire, he played his guitar gently, and I sang harmony with him, something I hadn't done in years. After the men were snoring in their bedrolls, he would reach over and kiss me lightly on the lips, and then crawl into his own bedroll, while I went to my tent. My yearning to sleep next to him was so strong I could hardly contain myself. It was not just the loving I missed; it was the closeness also.

On the evening we returned to the ranch, when roundup was over, I walked down to the cabin on the lake. It was so quiet and peaceful, I wondered if Lani had gone to town with the boys. The sun was going down, and I stood and watched the color change on the water, the fish jumping for mosquitoes, herons and egrets flying toward their nightly roosts. I knocked on the door, and he opened it, standing shirtless in the opening. Motioning me in, he grabbed his shirt and put it on. Looking at him made me breathless. As we sat down, I began to lose my courage. What if he didn't want me after all these years?

"You look lovely this evening," he said simply.

"I just wondered if you still wanted to marry me. If you'll have me, I'll marry you," I said quickly, before I lost my courage.

"You're not just feeling pity for me, are you?" he grinned.

"I'm just tired of watching you walk by, and not being able to put my hand in yours," I said.

I stood and walked to him where he sat, and leaned down and kissed him softly at first, and then fervently. He put his head on my chest, held me, and sighed.

"I've waited a long time to make you my wife," he whispered.

As he stood, I knew I wouldn't be able to resist the temptation of loving him that night; we would have to marry soon.

And so we did marry, a simple wedding, on the ranch. The new pastor from the La Crosse church came for the afternoon, the Reverend Cook, a young man. There were only a few people attending: David, Annie, Jake, Loretta, Samuel, Rebecca, Nathan, baby Samuel, our workers, and Lester and Abigail. The meal under the oaks was simple, but delicious. The mood was as it had been years before, before Susan Marley had entered our lives. I felt we were finally getting back to the happiness that had been stolen from us. And Lani was handsome in his new black suit.

He had disappeared for a few days after we got engaged, and I was worried that he had gotten scared, run off, and taken my wagon to boot. But he returned with a new bed-frame and mattress, which made me laugh. He had bought himself the new suit, a new green dress for me, and a small diamond ring. I was thinking I had wasted a lot of years, pining for Jacob, years I could have been loving Lani. It occurred to me that every time I talked to Jacob and asked for his help, Lani appeared. I took that to mean Jacob approved of Lani for me.

When we toasted with wine, at sunset, David said, "It's about damned time." Our laughter bounced off the oak trees and made my heart feel light. I was a young girl again, embarking on a new marriage with a strong, handsome husband. When Lani smiled down at me, I noticed he had a marvelous smile, and bright white teeth. How did I get so lucky? And I thought it *was* about damned time.

Loving Lani in the night also made me realize how I had missed being loved. We made up for our lost years, however. I believe we made love every single night of our lives. If we missed a night, it was because we were parted, and that was not too often. Life was good again on the ranch, and every time I passed that man I touched him, just to feel he was mine. He always smiled.

One night, he whispered that he had dreamed of loving me so long, he would wake up in the morning, thinking he had dreamed it again. "Then, I saw you sleeping beside me, your beautiful hair flowing over the pillow, and I knew it was real."

Lani was truthful about his money; he had plenty. We put the ranch in his name and mine, and we began buying more land around ours. He had taken us from the brink of disaster to a very prosperous, working ranch. When we made our will, John was left out of it, in case he married Susan. She would not inherit anything from me. If he ever broke away from her, I would put him back in the will. I just couldn't take the chance that she might inherit the harvest of our labor.

Mary wrote me a letter from Newberry, saying she was in the family way with Joshua's child, and that Joshua was never kind to Sarah; he felt I had spoiled her, since she cried for me daily. And she asked me if I would consider taking Sarah, for Sarah's sake. When I showed Lani the letter, he hitched up the carriage that very day and we left for Newberry.

It was a long trip, but it seemed short because Lani and I enjoyed each other's company so much, talking about anything and everything. When we reached the ranch where Mary and Joshua lived, it was close to sundown. Mary had supper ready for us, and we sat down with her and Sarah, but Joshua never appeared. She made excuses for him, but I knew he was a coward. All during supper Mary wiped the tears from her face with the back of her hand, trying to smile all the while, as if giving her child away were a normal occurrence. It was not and we all knew it. I had been happy to see my little Mary and overjoyed at seeing my Sarah, who had run to us when we pulled into the yard of their small home. Mary grabbed my arm as we were walking toward the wagon to leave and said, "I can't leave him, Mama, now that I'm with child. I would only be a burden to you. Please forgive me." I smiled down at her and hugged her goodbye, but I had a hard time figuring how a mother could give up her child. However, it was as she said, for Sarah's benefit. Somehow, I felt it was my fault that Mary was so submissive.

Perhaps I had been too protective of her. Sarah waved to her mother when we left, but didn't cry for her. As she snuggled next to me, we searched for an inn, in order to spend the night, on our way back home.

Chapter 10 *BROKEN*

"Ye who are weary come home." 1880 Hymn

Lani was good with Sarah, reading to her and telling her cowboy stories, and teaching her to sing while he played the guitar. When we went horseback riding in the pastures, she rode in the saddle with him, her smile big. At times, he would walk his horse with Sarah sitting in the saddle, holding onto the horn. Her balance was good at her young age; I knew she would be a natural, like her grandma.

When Bill the Bull was a calf, he followed me around like a dog. Once he started growing, we had to put him in the pastures and he would stand by the gate and bellow until I found him and scratched his head and petted him. While riding in the fields, Lani, Sarah, and I would watch as Bill would come running to us, charging like a buffalo – a frightening sight, unless a person knew him. Sarah would scream with joy, watching him barreling toward us. He was huge, our biggest bull, but he was useless as a breeder. Sweet as a new puppy, we turned him out with the rest of the herd once his horns were polled. However, I gave the order that he was never to be butchered; he would have to die of old age as far as I was concerned. After I had dismounted and scratched his head, he would ride along with us. I reckoned he still thought I was his mama – and I was.

"I feel like I've finally come home," Lani said one night as we lay in bed. "This is what I've been searching for my whole life. I wondered if it would ever happen."

Contentment was mine, too, finally. My joy was, at last, complete. Laughing with Lani felt so normal, and I thought I had certainly come home, also. Sarah was the baby we would never have naturally, and how the three of us enjoyed each other's company. On Sundays, we joined the families at our La Crosse church for dinner on the ground and other get-togethers. Loretta said she was so happy to see my smile again; it had been absent too long. I agreed.

David said he felt like cupid, and we laughed heartily. I said, "It sure took you long enough." He said, "My subjects were obstinate."

He had made young Jake his foreman after Lani came to work with me, and their ranch was prospering also. Young Jake was a born rancher and he was smart, too. His ideas were very innovative for the times, and Lani listened to him, putting some of his ideas to work for us also. He was just considered 'Jake' at that point; he was a grown-up man.

As we were saddling our horses for a ride one morning, I glanced up to see a man walking up our driveway. When I got closer, it was like an apparition coming toward me. My heart sank because he looked like Jacob, the same walk, the same smile, the same blue eyes, but suddenly I knew it was John. Running toward him, I started crying. My legs were too slow to get me to him fast enough, and I grabbed him and hugged him tight. Hugging me back, his body shook with sobs. Talk about a prodigal son.

"Ma! Ma!" he whispered.

John was very thin and had a full beard. He looked like Jacob when he returned from the War, only John's war had been with himself. And he was filthy dirty. The first order of business was a bath and a shave, so I put the kettles on to boil. But I couldn't stop looking at his sweet face, ravaged by the many mistakes he had made. Shame and guilt were reflected on his countenance, but he knew that I would always welcome him with open arms. And maybe I could quit worrying about him now.

The tales he told were unfathomable. After the money ran out, Susan left him for an older, rich man. He had spent the last six months trying to get home, walking part of the way.

"I would have sent you money to come home," I said. "Did you marry?"

"She wouldn't marry me without money, called me a down-and-out cowpoke. Told me to get on home," he said tearfully. "You were right, Ma. She wanted the money."

"No matter. You're home. When you're rested, you can go back to work for us." I said.

"I've got to clean things up with my brother. I've ruined our relationship and it's got to be mended," he said sadly.

"I don't think that's a good idea, John. Harry was very hurt when he left for Colorado."

"You mean he's not here? Gone to Colorado for good?" he said incredulously.

"He's working for my brothers and doing well now. He's had a rough time of it, but you may need to give it some more time," I said. He cried again.

"But the cabin's yours if you want. I am married now…to Lani, and things are good here on the ranch. You can make a life for yourself."

He smiled Jacob's smile, and my contentment enlarged. Lani came in then, carrying Sarah, and they both hugged John and welcomed him back into the fold.

When Harry had first started writing to me, his letters were tentative: brief, halted, fact-filled, about menial things. But the more I wrote him, the more he began to open up to me. He loved Colorado and his Uncle John and Uncle Henry, and their wives and children. Colorado was the most beautiful place he had ever seen, and the ranching was different from Florida – less water and quality pasture. I figured he would never come home again because his experiences here had been too painful. The papers had been signed for the divorce, and it was finalized. Having begun to court a pretty little girl on a neighboring ranch at that time, he was thinking about buying a place and settling down with her. My happiness for him was overwhelming, and I didn't want John to open old wounds. This was a situation that would have to be handled gently. My hope was that Harry could forgive John; though I had my doubts.

"I'm ashamed to say it, but I have always loved Harry the most. And he was the one most damaged by Susan Marley," I said to Lani, shuddering at the sound of her name.

Lani said, "Harry has moved on and is finding happiness. It's John who's broken. He's been climbing fool's hill these last few years, and I believe he won't find happiness until he can forgive himself. Maybe when that happens, Harry will be able to forgive him. Nothing worse than an evil woman."

"And how do you know about evil women?" I smiled.

"I figured you would be the death of me. Wasn't sure how much longer I could wait for you. Thought I might have to head to Colorado myself," he said.

"Are you calling me evil?" I asked.

"Only at night when you wrap your legs around me like a vine," he laughed. "You own me, body and soul."

I hit him on the chest, laughing at the same time. Lani had some secrets in him, and I loved him like I thought I would never love again.

Chapter 11   NO FORGIVENESS

John moved into the cabin and began working as a ranch hand, given no special privileges, his pay the same as any new worker. I believe he was just happy to have a job and family. Abigail's cooking put some weight on him and he became the muscular boy I had always known, but he had deep lines around his eyes and a tinge of gray to his hair at his young age of 26. I thought he had learned a valuable life lesson. A mother could only hope.

Lani was not Sarah's blood-kin, but he certainly was her father. I was her grandmother, but she thought of me as her mother. We were a true family unit, always together, and by the time she was five years old, she could ride as well as I could. When one of our mares gave birth to a pretty little paint filly, Lani started training her for Sarah. These were times of golden joy. My three children were in a place where I didn't have to worry about them, and I loved a man as much as I possibly could.

I spent many hours with John, helping him settle in and letting him know how much I loved him. On Saturday mornings I would sometimes fish off the dock with him, just so we could have that rapport. We didn't have to talk too much, but I knew my presence was a comfort to him. Gradually he began to smile more, but his relationship with his brother still hung heavily around his neck like a weight. He told me one day he wanted to go to Colorado to make things right with Harry, but I convinced him to give it more time.

Letters from Colorado, from Harry and his new wife, were full of happiness, and I had a new granddaughter. I did let Harry know that John was back on the ranch and had left Susan, but said no more. My hope was that one day there would be a reconciliation, even though I knew it would never be like it was before Susan Marley.

Mary wrote letters on occasion, telling me of her growing family – two more children. I wrote back and asked her if she was happy and if Joshua was good to her, and she said she was happy but that she missed the family. She said Joshua was very good to her; he was just a solemn man, so unlike her daddy.

Chapter 12   EPIDEMIC

In 1886, the influenza epidemic hit our area hard. Whole families were laid to rest in the cemeteries, and we tried to quarantine ourselves from the outside world. Nonetheless, two of our ranch hands died, and we buried them in the La Crosse church cemetery. Nathan, Rebecca's husband, caught the disease and barely pulled through, even though we thought he wouldn't make it. When I helped Rebecca with him, Lani made me wear his bandana over my nose and mouth and had me wash it and my hands before I came home, being so worried about Sarah and me. Many of our friends did die, but we stayed home from the funerals, fearing the disease's spread. Local doctors sent out letters to everyone advising them to stay home and avoid crowds. It was such a lonesome time. We had not seen David and Annie and Jake for six months, but I wrote to them every week and they seemed to weather the storm. How I missed our church socials and quilting bees. I had to be content to quilt with Rebecca and Loretta, which was fun, as always, but I missed our other quilting friends. That was the time that I began to teach Sarah how to quilt.

Gradually our lives got back to normal, but it had been like the plague from the Bible, with people struck down in the prime of their life. Our cemeteries were full at that point and new ones had to be opened. The population was dwindling in our area.

John was growing restless and talking with him grew difficult. He felt he was getting older and wanted to be more than a ranch hand. On his salary, he couldn't afford a wife and family. And he simply could not seem to move forward until he saw his brother face to face. Writing that letter to Harry was one of the hardest things I've ever had to do.

Dear Harry,

I am writing to you to tell you that your brother needs your forgiveness. He cannot move on with his life until he has it. Do you think you can find it in your heart to do that? He would like to come to Colorado and meet with you. But if you think that is out of the question, please tell me. He has been greatly damaged by this situation.

I love you,

Your mother.

The weeks passed and John questioned me every day. Had a letter come? No, was always the answer. Then, finally, one day, it came.

Dear Ma,

I've had to do some hard thinking on your letter. You know I loved my brother more than life, and I would have never betrayed him like he did to me. But I have been working on forgiveness the past few years, and I am doing better. And I think the time will come when I can meet him face to face, but it is not now. I do love him, but the wounds are still raw. Hope you understand. I miss you the most.

Love,

Harry.

How could I tell John that his brother didn't want to see him yet? At least there was hope, and that's how I had to present it. His head hung low as I read the letter to him.

"It's true," he said. "He wouldn't have done the things I did.

Looking back on it, I was crazy with lust, lust for an impossible woman. I *still* think about her."

Chapter 13 **MIRACLES**

And then, a miracle walked into our world one day. She was a young girl, around twenty, with bright red hair and freckles, wearing boots and breeches underneath her skirt. Her hair was braided in two pigtails, and she had her saddle on her shoulder. Lani called to me from the back door. As I walked out to the corral, she stood with one foot up on the lower rung of the fence. Pretty was not a word I would use for her, but she definitely was striking.

"Howdy ma'am, sir," she called to us. We shook hands with her and she began to talk.

"Looking for ranch work of any kind. Heard you folks were down with the epidemic and all. I can do anything: I'm strong as a man, and I can ride better'n most men. My horse died on me last week. I can brand and rope and break horses. I can shoe horses, nail a nail, cook a meal..." she would have continued, but Lani interrupted her.

"Whoa, girl, what's your name?" he asked.

"Suzanna Baldwin. I come from over on the coast, around Brooksville-way. Been looking for a job for a week. No one will hire a woman. My pa's farm failed and he had to sell, but I can pull weeds, harvest a garden, wash a load of clothes, chop a tree down in nothing flat, make horseshoes, do smithing......"

"Hold on, Suzanna, I'm Lani Walton and this here's my wife, Sally. If you can do all the things you say, we'll try you out for a month or so. See how you do. I'm trying to think where we'll bunk you," he said.

"We'll move John to the house and put her in the cabin," I suggested, although I knew John wouldn't like that. But I believed he had spent too much time alone with his thoughts and guilt.

As we walked toward the cabin, Suzanna continued, "I can play a guitar, sing a fair harmony, say a good grace, help with the children, catch a fish, fry it to tender perfection..."

"Suzanna," I said, "You're hired."

"Yes ma'am. I just want to stay on after the month is done," she said. She smiled wide and showed a gap between her two front teeth.

"She might be our next foreman," Lani whispered to me, grinning.

This was my kind of girl; I liked her a whole lot right off. She wouldn't be a whiner and would get things done. Pampering was something she wasn't familiar with.

She said, "My pa taught me everything." I heard that familiar voice from my past and felt she might be a kindred spirit.

Lani packed up John's things and moved them to the extra bedroom in our house. We helped Suzanna get settled, and then Lani said he and Suzanna would ride out and talk to John before he came home and found her in his cabin. As moody as John had been lately, I wasn't sure he would be happy about these changes, but I saw no other solution. As Lani and Suzanna rode down the driveway, I could hear her voice telling Lani all the other things she could do. She had a kind of hoarse voice that carried on the air, making me laugh.

But John was not laughing when he came to the house, picking up his things from the bedroom, without a word to me, and leaving for the bunkhouse. He was doing penance.

"That is one helluva handsome man, that son of yours. Sorry about cussin', Miss Sally. I been working with men too long," she said.

John was not taken with Suzanna, however. If she was in one place, he was not, taking his meals with us at the house, rather than be where she was.

"She hurts my ears," he said. "She never stops talking. Where on God's green earth did you find her?"

"She walked in off the main road, carrying her saddle after her horse broke his leg - said she had to shoot him," Lani said. "She's a worker though, works harder than a man."

"If you can stand to be around her," John said.

We had hired Suzanna in the summer of 1887, and by November, she was still with us. Our fall had been a warm one, and we planned to have Thanksgiving outside. She came to my house one afternoon a few weeks before our celebration. It was the first time she had looked shy.

"Miss Sally, you're so pretty and feminine, and yet, you work like me. How do you do it?" she asked, blushing. Taken aback, not thinking of myself as pretty and feminine, I remembered years ago, when Loretta had taken me to Gainesville, and we had bought pretty clothes and had our hair styled. I made sure that Lani never saw me shabby-looking, even when I was riding on the range.

"I like that boy of yours, but he don't like me. I want to get his attention," she said.

Knowing the kind of woman John liked - Susan, I didn't think he would ever be attracted to a girl like Suzanna. She was what he needed, however, in my opinion.

When we washed and hot-ironed her hair, it was beautiful, shiny and curly. She was about my size, so I let her try on some of my dresses. When she walked out of the bedroom, with one of my silk dresses on and her hair down, she looked downright pretty. Of course, nothing could be done about the gap in her teeth, but I had heard that some men liked that. The tears ran down her freckled cheeks when she looked in the full-length mirror.

"I don't know quite what to say. My ma died when I was five, and I never had anyone help me. My pa remarried and his wife never liked me, even though my pa loved me a lot. Now, look at me. I could've been looking like this all along. But John will make fun of me. I can't go out like this," she cried. She rushed into the bedroom and changed her clothes and braided her hair quickly.

"Sorry I wasted your time, Miss Sally." And she was gone, but I thought she'd be back. Later, I gave her a couple of my fancy dresses and suggested she wear one to our Thanksgiving dinner. She handed them back to me, and said, "I couldn't. I would look the fool."

But as the day drew near, she grew quieter, and I could tell she was considering what I had said.

"Okay," she said to me one day. "I'll do it." And she took the dresses.

It was a glorious Thanksgiving, sunny and warm, clear skies. David and Annie came with Jake and his new wife, who was large with child. The food was spread on the tables and when we sat down to eat, I wondered where Suzanna was. As Lani was beginning to say grace, he squeezed my hand and nodded his head toward the corner of the barn. There stood Suzanna, as beautiful as a woman could be, her hair radiating around her face, her green eyes sparkling, wearing a dark maroon dress I had given her, which fit like a glove. My eyes went to John, and I could see he was surprised. Standing, he offered her a chair next to him, and she sat down and was actually shy with him. My heart gladdened.

Trying not to watch them as they talked shyly together, I knew the time had come for a change in John's life, and probably in Suzanna's life also. Perhaps Suzanna would be the catalyst that would save my family.

John and Suzanna began spending not only working hours together, but on weekends went fishing on the lake, packed picnic lunches, and rode horses all day long. She was a changed woman; love had softened her hard edges. But my greatest joy came in the change I saw in my formerly-broken son, as he laughed readily and smiled constantly. They were obviously in love. And Suzanna was a woman who would stand by John, not run off with the first rich man that came through town.

"Ma" John said one day. "I want to marry that girl."

I laughed. "I love her, John. She would be a good wife and daughter."

The wedding was planned for June, 1888. My hope was that John's brother would come and bring his growing family, two daughters and a son. I wrote to Harry and offered to pay their train fare if they could make the trip. Patiently, I waited for a letter.

As Suzanna and I were cleaning tack one morning, she looked at me nervously.

"Miss Sally, I need to talk with you about John," she said quietly, looking around to be certain no one was listening.

"What's wrong?" I asked, hoping she wasn't getting cold feet.

"He's got a dark secret that I can't work out of him. Sometimes he cries about it," she said, her face turned to the ground.

"Yes, he does have a dark secret, but he will have to talk to you about it. I can't. It wouldn't be right," I said.

"How can I marry him, not knowing everything about him? It's about his brother; I know that much. My pa always said a husband and wife can't have secrets, or the secrets will fester and break open in a bad way," she said.

"I'll talk to John. Give him some time, Suzanna; he'll tell you eventually."

"He'll have to, or I won't marry him, even though, God knows, I love him more than my horse," she laughed.

Our laughter must have been heard by John, as he appeared in the doorway of the barn, smiling. His smile drained away when I asked him to follow me to the house, knowing a lecture was coming. He followed me into the kitchen, holding his hat in his hands, looking like a scolded school boy. His eyes were cast down, and my heart hurt for this grown man, who had been broken and cast out like an old tea cup. Would he ever recover?

"I was just talking with Suzanna," I began.

"I love how you two get on. She's crazy about you, Ma," he said.

"I can't even begin to tell you how happy I am that she walked into our lives. She'll be a good wife for you, but you're going to have to tell her about Harry and Susan. She won't marry you with secrets between you," I said softly.

"How can I tell her, Ma? She'll leave me for sure. There'll be no trust in our love: no trust in our marriage. How can I tell her the awful things I did to my brother? I love her too much for her to know what a low-down cuss I've been. And if she left me, I couldn't make it," he said. "I'm just starting to get over what I did, and the awful consequences."

"She's a better person than that, John. And if you don't tell her, she'll go."

"Will you help me tell her?" he asked.

258

"I will," I said, hoping Suzanna would be understanding. I thought she would.

He left to get her and when they walked back in, his eyes had a worried look. They sat on the sofa, and I sat opposite them in my little red rocker.

"What could be this bad?" she asked.

"I did a terrible thing, Suzanna." The tears flowed out of his blue eyes, tears of fear and remorse. And I felt tears rolling down my cheeks, too; I just couldn't hold them back, suffering for my son.

"I took my brother's wife to lay with, even before they were married. I carried on with her for over two years. I hungered and lusted after her and followed her to Boston, leaving him here alone. He had no knowledge of all this. It was an evil, evil deed," he sobbed. "And now he can't forgive me, and I can't forgive myself, either. You see why I couldn't tell you? You can see what a wicked wretch I've been."

I held my breath while the silence enveloped us. My voice wouldn't come, and what could I say anyway? – he had wronged his brother and wouldn't give up that woman for love nor money. It was a long time before Suzanna spoke.

"Whoa, that is truly a bad tale, I must admit," she began. "Certainly not the words I thought that would be coming from those lips. What would it take for you to forgive yourself? 'Cause I don't think you'll be a fit husband until you can do that."

My heart sank. I saw the fear in John's face. He truly loved this girl and by telling her his dismal secret, he could lose her.

"I need my brother to forgive me before I can forgive myself," he said.

"No. You need to forgive yourself before your brother will forgive you," she said.

"I've been trying to do that and can't seem to."

"I'll help you then, 'cause God knows I want you for my husband," she smiled.

She put her arms around his neck and they cried together. I slipped out the back door, but I knew now for sure that Suzanna was an angel, sent from God, to answer my prayers for John. I believed this was the beginning of his redemption, and I was gratified to know that repair was being made to what I thought was a flawed character.

Chapter 14 *POISON IVY*

It had been six years since John had started the affair with Susan Marley. And it had taken him three years before he could start forgiving himself. The letter arrived from Harry a few days after the conversation with Suzanna.

Dear Ma,

I can't begin to tell you how I have missed your sweet face. You know I love you so much. I have talked it over with Belinda, my wife, and we will be coming to stay for a few weeks, to see that skunk married. Suzanna must be something for John to be marrying her. My happiness is so great, that I find I must have forgiven John and not even known it. Belinda says John did me a big favor by taking that woman off my hands. She's right; there's nobody like Belinda. She loves me with such a powerful love, I can't help but be thankful to God for sending her to me. And you should see your three grandchildren – they are tow-headed beauties. Two of them are already in the saddle. Our ranch has prospered, and we lease 500 acres, in addition to the 500 we own. You won't need to send us money for the fares. We are doing well. Can't wait to see everybody, especially you.

Love,

Your son,

Harry.

It was a Saturday when the letter arrived, and I had to wait until John and Suzanna rode back in from the pastures before showing them the letter. My heart was beating out of my chest, and my happiness was written all over my face when I handed John the letter in the barn.

"Is he coming?" he asked.

"Read the letter. You too, Suzanna. You're a wise girl," I said, and hugged her to me. "You've saved my family." They were reading the letter when I went looking for my husband - speaking of happiness. I wanted to kiss him that very minute and I would, when I found him.

I found him mending a fence down by the lake, and I went to him and hugged him from behind. He laid his hammer down and turned around. His kiss was so loving and I felt so much joy.

"What's happened?" he asked when I could finally stop kissing him.

"Harry's coming home," I whispered. I saw a tear run down his face.

"We better get on home," he said. "There's poison ivy here, and I don't relish it on my backside."

Laughter. What a grand thing is laughter. And Lani was just the one to make me laugh, hurrying home to make love before Sarah came home from David and Annie's. The sun was going down when Lani lifted me into the brass bed he had bought before our wedding. He whispered in my ear, "You were worth the wait."

"I love you, Lani Walton. I'm just sorry I waited so long."

It was April, 1888, two months before the wedding, and the ranch was alive with work. The houses and barns were being spruced up, the trees were being trimmed, the fences mended. John was making an arbor for the ceremony. There was excitement in the air.

Suzanna and I planned a trip to Gainesville to find a wedding gown for her. Since she had become a quieter girl those days, she didn't need to brag about herself anymore. It was John who couldn't be quiet about her. More than once, I heard him telling someone, "She can outride, out-brand, outcook, outclean, outrope....." I knew more than ever how smitten he was with that red-haired beauty. How could I know what would follow in the next few days?

We booked a room at a nice hotel in Gainesville, planning to spend two days shopping and having a good time. As Suzanna drove the carriage into town, I thought how much like me she was in her 'take charge' ways, counting my blessings to have her for a daughter.

The room we settled into had two beds, and the covers were very fancy, with soft pillows; there was a writing desk and sofa and chair. Suzanna touched everything and looked at the pictures on the wall.

"I declare, I never knew hotels looked like this on the inside. It's like a mansion," she said.

It was getting dark when we decided to go to the dining room for supper. The candles were lit on the tables, the white tablecloths starched and shining, the waiters dressed in uniforms. Suzanna's eyes were big, and I could see she was nervous.

"Just follow my lead, honey. It's no different than eating at my table," I whispered.

The menu was extensive, but Suzanna said she just wanted some fried chicken and collards. So, that's what we ordered. Out of the corner of my eye, I saw someone approaching our table, and looked up to see Susan Marley standing in front of me. My heart started pounding and I could hardly breathe.

She leaned over, exposing her cleavage, and whispered to me, "Hello, Mrs. Walton."

"Susan Marley, what brings you back to our neighborhood?" I breathed, my ears ringing.

"Why, I came back for John," she hissed. "I'm certain he'll tell you all about it."

Suzanna's fiery eyes were locked on Susan, as she said, "Is this the whore John speaks of? She looks like the trollop she is."

"Must be John's betrothed. Doesn't look his type. I will tell you, honey, you will never satisfy that man. When you lie with him, he's thinking of me and what I can do for him, that is if you lie with him at all. He can't resist me, and I know how to make him happy. When he learns I'm back, you'll be cancelling your wedding."

"Susan Marley, leave us or I will call the manager. If I hear tell of you coming near John or the ranch, I will have you arrested," I whispered loudly.

"John is a good roll in the hay, honey. Ask your mother-in-law-to-be to tell you what she saw in the hay loft," she laughed harshly.

I yelled, "Manager!" and she was gone.

Shaken to our core, Suzanna and I ordered our food brought to our hotel room. Suzanna stood looking out the window for a long period of time, crying softly.

"She doesn't look like a whore," she sobbed. "She's the most beautiful woman I've ever seen. She's sophisticated-looking…and her clothes and jewelry are so glamorous. I don't think I can compete with her."

"You don't have to. She only looks good on the outside; she's evil to the core. I've never met anyone as crass or coarse as she is. John is done with her," I said, hoping my words were true.

"I believe we should go home tomorrow. John must know about this, and I have to see where he stands with her," she said.

"But what about your dress?" I asked.

"I may not need a dress. John will have to make that decision."

"John loves you, Suzanna," I said.

"We haven't laid together yet. I wanted to wait until after we're married, and, and…..I'm a virgin," she cried into her handkerchief.

The horses were hitched to the carriage, and we drove away from the hotel just as the sun was coming up the next morning. I had slept fitfully and Suzanna had paced all night. There was no conversation between us; she was seething, I could tell. Driving the horses hard, we arrived at the ranch before noontime. After she unhitched the carriage, she headed to the cabin, with not a word to me. I hoped to Heaven she wouldn't leave us.

Along about suppertime, John came running in the back door, calling my name.

"Suzanna is packing her bags," he said frantically. "She said you saw Susan Marley, and that she is coming for me. I guess nobody has any faith in me anymore. Ma, you got to talk to Suzanna."

Hurrying to the cabin, I realized I hadn't known the extreme severity of the impact that meeting with Susan had had on Suzanna. I threw open the door and rushed into the cabin, to see Suzanna stuffing her clothes into a carpet bag.

"You're leaving? You'll be leaving not only John, but me and Lani and Sarah and everybody who loves you here," I said.

"I've been fooling myself all this time – trying to be a lady. I'm no lady; I'm not even pretty, with this red hair and freckles and gap in my teeth. Who would take me over Susan Marley? John would leave me eventually; if not today, later. I was a fool to think someone as handsome as John would want me. I'll leave before my heart gets broken further," she cried.

"Well, I reckon you might as well hand him over to Susan Marley if you leave. If you break his heart, he'll probably go running off with her, maybe back to Boston. If that's what you want, go ahead. And I'll give you a gift of a horse – so you don't have to drag your saddle down the road again. And I'll write you a good recommendation, too, so's you can get a good ranching job, and spend the rest of your days punching cattle, until you're so old, you'll be good for nothing but the graveyard. Write when you find work," I said, as I slammed the door behind me, smiling as I walked back to my own house.

A few minutes later, I saw Suzanna and John standing at the round pen, talking loudly to each other. I was certain everyone on the ranch heard it, too. And then, I saw him bend down and kiss her gently. She took his hand and led him down the trail to the cabin, and I thought we had better get them married quick, before a new baby arrived. Seemed to me we were always getting folks married quick around here. Maybe Susan Marley caused Suzanna to realize there was more to love than holding hands. After that evening I didn't think we would need to worry about Susan Marley.

Making love was supposed to happen only after two people were married in our part of the world. But I also knew the importance of intimacy between two people, and I figured if they couldn't wait two months to lie together, it wouldn't matter that much. Passion was a thing that sometimes wouldn't wait. I knew about that first-hand.

John received several perfumed letters from Susan Marley in the next few months, throwing each one into the fire, which made me proud of him. Eventually, we made it back to Gainesville to buy Suzanna's dress, but we never stayed in that hotel again. And I warned the sheriff about a trespassing woman. He smiled and said he'd keep an eye out. I prayed never to see that woman again, though I felt certain that wouldn't happen.

Chapter 15   SWEET REDEMPTION

"I will think on thee no more." Unknown

Harry and his family were to arrive the week before the wedding and stay for a week after. I was so excited to see them I could hardly sleep at night. Harry had taken adversity and turned it into a blessing; that's one reason I loved him so much. And John was as nervous as a long-tail cat in a room full of rocking chairs. Work was where he found his release, and talking with Suzanna, who had a calming effect on him.

Wanting his first meeting with Harry to be private, with just the three of us, John asked only me to be there with them at the cabin. On the day they were to arrive, Lani and I hitched the team to the carriage, with John's nervous fingers trying to help. I told him, "Go ride your horse. It'll help." Suzanna waved goodbye to us as we started toward Gainesville.

Their train was to arrive around 3:00 in the afternoon, but did not pull into the station until around 6:00 in the evening. Actually, that was considered 'on time' for these parts. But it made for a long trip home in the dark. Waiting for it, I paced the wooden platform at the station, until Lani said, "You're wearing a path in the oak flooring." Sitting down beside him, he put his arm around my shoulder and pulled me close to him.

"Did you know I love you?" he whispered. I turned to him and smiled. He always caught me off guard, but it calmed me, and I snuggled closer to him, smiling inwardly.

When the train finally arrived, Harry was one of the first people off, as excited to see me as I was to see him. As he was helping his beautiful wife and children off the train, I ran to him, and when he turned, I couldn't move. Harry had definitely changed; he was so handsome and tall, looking younger than his 26 years. We stood staring at each other, as if no one else were there, and then he grabbed me and wept, hugging me tight against him. I cried right along with him. His children were clambering around our legs, and finally he broke away and introduced me to his wife, a small, curly-haired, blond beauty. And my grandchildren: Claire was four years old, Elizabeth three, and John two.

"You named him John?" I asked, in awe.

"Yep, after the person I love most, after you and my wife and children, of course," he said, grinning.

They *were* beauties, each one with soft, golden curls around their angelic faces. I picked John up and looked him in the eye; he looked right back at me. He would be a character, I was sure.

"Where's my brother?" Harry asked.

"Waiting at the ranch," I said. And then, Lani walked up and grabbed Harry around the shoulders. "Lanier," Harry said, laughing.

"Only my enemies call me Lanier; it's Lani," he said in that deep drawl of his.

I had brought a picnic for the ride home as I knew they would be hungry. And so tired. All five of them slept on the way back.

It was late when we arrived at the ranch, and Harry said he would see John the next day. I was relieved because this had been a hard enough journey for Lani and me.

The sound of children's laughter was what woke me the next morning. What a joyous sound. Lani was already up and gone. As I went to the kitchen in my gown and robe, to put the coffee to boil, Suzanna came in the backdoor.

"Lord, that man didn't sleep a wink last night and he kept me awake, too," she said. And then she became embarrassed, as their sleeping arrangement was supposed to be a secret. We both blushed. The children rushed into the kitchen, and I introduced them to Suzanna, whom they seemed to love, with her friendly smile and red hair. Who couldn't love that girl? Harry and Belinda came out of their room, looking both tired and sleepy, and Suzanna hugged them both. They smiled when they met her. I'm certain they couldn't have expected John's wife-to-be to look like her, but they liked her instantly.

"John is waiting for you both," she said to Harry and me.

After I dressed, Harry and I grabbed a cup of coffee and started down the trail to the cabin, both too groggy to say much. As we turned the corner of the cabin, John was sitting on the deck, looking out over the lake, with a cup in his hand. He looked at his brother and then looked away from us, and I could see his hands were shaking.

"John," Harry said.

"My God, you're a sight," John breathed.

Harry walked to his brother, who stood, and they embraced. I could see all the tension drain away from John, and they were back to being children again. We all cried together.

John was 28: only two years older than Harry, but he looked ten years older. Still, Harry's forgiveness would set John free. And they started talking as if they had not been separated for four years. I slipped away, to start breakfast.

A big family was seated around my dining table again, and I couldn't have been happier. Everyone was talking at once; Suzanna held little John on her lap. She might have been the happiest person at that table, knowing John would be a better husband now that his redemption was assured.

Then, Loretta and her family came in, and I started cooking all over again. What a joyous reunion! And of all things, Rebecca announced she was in the family way again. Loretta and Samuel were excited, to say the least. At last, we could put the Susan Marley events behind us.

Abigail's two grown daughters would be helping her with the food preparation for the wedding reception. Abigail, like me, was starting to lose steam. The whole day would be a large social gathering, with friends coming from the La Crosse area, too. Reverend Cook would marry John and Suzanna in the arbor created by John that he wrapped in jasmine at the last minute. Two o'clock was the time for the ceremony to begin, and at eleven I watched a black carriage drive up the driveway. I thought it was just our guests arriving early, so I paid no attention.

Suzanna spent the day at Loretta's so the groom would not see his bride-to-be until the ceremony. As I was thinking of what to do next, it dawned on me that the person in that carriage might be none other than Susan Marley. My heart sank and I ran from the house and quietly walked to the cabin, my heart beating out of my chest. John stood, shirtless, in the doorway as I rounded the corner. Susan stood on the deck.

"What do you want, Susan?" he asked, tiredly.

"I want you," she said, touching him.

"Did you know that today is my wedding day? Do you know that I love this girl?"

"I can tell, John, you want me right now," she said.

He backed up to the wall, his arms limp at his sides, his eyes closed. I thought this would be the time to be strong, John. I had to let him handle this or else she would continue to haunt him. Watching them, I felt ashamed, like a voyeur, but they both knew I was there.

"I've missed you, John. That old man can't satisfy me like you can. I long for you in the night. Come away with me. I have money now," she said, and turned to look at me.

"I can't. I can't," he said. I could see his resolve melting and I hung my head. I wanted to run from that place, but my legs were frozen to the spot where I was standing.

"Please, just this once. No one but your ma will know, and she won't talk."

He looked at me in anguish, and said, "Ma, please."

I said, "John," and turned, and as I was leaving, he took her inside, and I walked to my house, crying as I went. What a damned fool he was, but there was nothing I could do about him.

An hour later, I watched Susan step into the carriage and it drove down the driveway and was gone. Everything I had worked toward the last three years was gone where John was concerned. Once Suzanna found out about John and Susan, she would be leaving, and this time, I would not keep his damned secret. I waited for John to come and tell me the wedding was off.

As he entered the backdoor, I felt sick to my stomach. He came in and took my hand.

"You're a fool, John," I said.

"I *am* a fool, Ma, a fool for Suzanna," he smiled.

"You mean you resisted temptation? You looked like you wouldn't," I stammered.

"Would it be called temptation if I didn't want it? I wanted her, always have, but I want Suzanna and the life we'll lead more. And I want your respect again, and Harry's respect. But I had to sit down with Susan and tell her I didn't want her, that I didn't love her anymore. I don't want her coming back into my life again and again because I might weaken at some point and give in. She thought if she kissed me, I would fold, but I didn't. I held her at arm's length and told her she should try prostitution. I don't think she'll be back."

"John!" I said, shocked, but then I started laughing and I knew for sure, Susan Marley was out of my life and John's for good.

When Harry and his family came in with Lani and Sarah, I was rejoicing. They all smiled at me as if I were crazy. "What is it, Mama?" Sarah asked.

"Joy, honey, pure joy!" I cried, and I picked her up and hugged her.

"I reckon this is what weddings do to women," Lani said.

John said, "Especially this wedding. We need a grand celebration, don't we, Ma?"

☼

How Lani got grass to grow on that lawn was a wonder to me. We had never been able to grow grass there. But the arbor was placed at the end of the lawn, and everyone would sit for the ceremony, people bringing their own chairs, and many people planned to stay the night as the dancing would go on well into the evening. Lord knows we had enough room: our ranch was up to around fifteen hundred acres at that time.

Lani said to me, "I hope you're wearing your dark green silk dress because I'm dancing with my wife tonight." I knew he was remembering watching me dance with Jacob years ago, yearning to dance with me, as he had said.

"I am, and I'll be wearing my emerald earrings to match," I said, and remembered the day Jacob gave them to me. It made me sad that Jacob wouldn't be here with the whole family, sharing our victories and love. But, I thought, maybe he will be, because he had been with me, through all my trials. I whispered, "Thank you, Jacob. I still love you mightily. And thank you, God."

Lani was wearing his wedding suit, with cowboy boots, and I had to laugh. Well, what else? I was married to a cowboy, and a fine one at that. He asked me why I was smiling, and I said, "You. You just make me smile, Lani Walton."

Chapter 16   SECRETS REVEALED

"This is the Lord's doing: it is marvellous in our eyes" Psalms 118:23

We had not seen Suzanna all day and when she walked down the aisle in her beautiful dress, I didn't know her, except for that shocking red hair. When she smiled at me, she was our Suzanna; I would know that smile anywhere. It wasn't the dress, or the rouge on her cheeks and lips, or her hair style that had changed her; it was the glow about her. John's eyes were sparkling as she came toward him. I had seen Jacob look that same way at me many times, and it hurt my heart to see him looking like his pa. The tears came, and Lani wiped them with his handkerchief. Jacob was in this place I knew for sure.

It *was* a grand celebration. Mary and Joshua came from Newberry with their two babies that I had not yet seen. Sarah was shy with her mother, but she was not shy with Harry's children. They ran and played all over our new lawn.

I tried to spend as much time with Harry's family as possible as I knew they would be gone in a week, back to Colorado. Harry talked about my brothers, whom I had not seen in 28 years. "They love you, Ma," Harry said. "They remember you fondly. My uncles want you and Lani to come for a visit. And I'd like to show you my spread."

"I'm so proud of you and Belinda," I said, as we sat off to the side." You have shown great strength of character. There was a lot for you to overcome, leaving here with nothing but shame."

"It was all because of you, Ma. You made me strong, like you. And I knew you would always love me no matter where I was, or what I did. That was my strength."

John walked up then, holding his namesake, baby John. They

were both smiling, and it was obvious that they were very taken with each other.

"So, where will the honeymoon be?" Harry asked John, grinning.

"St. Augustine, but not until you leave. Suzanna has never seen the Atlantic Ocean."

Harry laughed, "Neither have you."

"It's true, but she doesn't know that. She thinks I'm going to show her the world."

"She's a good one, John. Treat her good," Harry said.

"I'm the lucky one, salvaged from the jaws of death," he smiled. But the truth was in that statement.

When Suzanna joined our circle, I hugged her tight. "You are beautiful. I believe I could handle some red-headed grandchildren," I said.

"We might have to expand the cabin," she whispered to me.

"We'll build a new two-story house on the lake. We've got the trees and the workers. Lani and I might use the little cabin every now and then," I said.

It was a full-moon night, and as the fiddlers began to play, Lani took my hand and led me to the wooden dance floor. He whispered in my ear, "Another thing I have had to wait for, but I know it will be worth the wait. You're more beautiful than you've ever been."

I hadn't danced in years, and I was very surprised at what a good dancer Lani was. He told me he had been taking lessons from Loretta for the last two months. How I laughed at that statement. This was true love; a cowboy, born to the saddle, usually had two left feet. Loretta had had her work cut out for her.

In the week that followed, Harry and I spent the days together, riding out in the pastures. I treasured each moment with my favorite child. I've said it before: a mother shouldn't have a favorite but I did, and I knew I would miss him terribly when he was gone. We didn't have to talk; our silence was comfortable. But when we did talk, it was easy. He was my same Harry, sweet and funny, making me laugh like a schoolgirl. How I loved him.

He spent time with John, too. I don't know what they talked about, but they smiled and laughed together like old times. I'm sure there were still some reservations on both their parts, but it didn't show.

The day we took Harry's family to the train station was a weepy day for me. "Do you think you'll ever come back home?" I asked Harry.

"Not for good, Ma, but we'll come back for a visit every five years," he laughed.

"I reckon Lani and I will have to go west for a visit before we get too old."

"You did right, marrying Lani. He's a good man and a good rancher."

"I do love him. That doesn't mean I don't miss your pa. I miss him every day, a lot. But he's gone and I can't bring him back."

"I still miss him, especially when I'm doing things he taught me to do. Sometimes, I feel he's near. Don't know how he found his way to Colorado, but I'm glad he did," he smiled.

And then, they were gone. Hard to believe they were with us for two weeks, and in a second they were gone. Though I was sorry to see them go, I was so glad my Harry had found happiness. That's all you can ask for, for your children: happiness. And that's what we hope for, for ourselves. It's not a full-time thing – happiness, but overall, it helps to have fullness in your heart.

Before John and Suzanna left on their grand trip to St. Augustine, John caught me in the barn on a hot afternoon.

"After I say this one thing, Ma, I won't want to discuss the subject further. But I don't want you to hold hatred in your heart for Susan. She grew up an orphan, in a Boston orphanage, treated badly all her childhood. She was abused by men at an early age, and the matrons beat all the children. No one would ever adopt her because she was too pretty and people mostly adopted boys to work on their farms. She learned how to act like a lady by watching the rich Boston ladies. Schooling was provided so she had an education, and she was very smart. When she learned how she could have her way, she began to manipulate the men in her life. She thought she would get rich by marrying Harry, but she had no idea she would run up against you. She said she won some battles, but you won the war."

I was aghast. There *were* secrets she was keeping; I felt that. But that she was an orphan and told that tale about her elderly, ill parents? I had to feel compassion for her, but I was glad it would be at a distance.

He added, "I thank God for parents like you and Pa; your love and support have brought me through this time. Thank you."

John and Suzanna left in the carriage, with a tent and two bedrolls, and a week's worth of food. They were going to camp on the ocean and swim in the salty brine, according to Suzanna. She was beside herself, and John couldn't stop smiling. How far they had come and what a blessing they had found each other. They were both floundering when first she walked up our driveway. Jacob must have guided her down that road, to help a son that he could only help through other people. I was sure he was our guardian angel.

Years later, I received a letter from Susan Marley, who was dying of consumption. She asked my forgiveness for the damage she had done to my family, especially John. She said she wished she had had a mother like me, who would have stood up for her and loved her like I loved my children. "I wouldn't have needed a father, if only I had had a strong, loving mother. But I had neither. I am sorry now for how I've lived my life: always taking, never giving."

Of course, I forgave her, and I wrote her a letter letting her know that. What good is forgiveness, if you don't release the other person? And a dying person at that. However, I knew that if things had turned out differently, if she had won, I could not've been so generous.

Chapter 17 WIDE OPEN SPACES

As Lani was sitting on the sofa one evening with his guitar, he called to me in the kitchen. "I've written a song for you and I want to sing it," he said, shyly. He strummed the guitar and sang, his voice deep and resonant.

"From a distance, I have loved you for so long,
Not expecting even a glance,
What could a cowboy offer a girl like you?
Only love and romance.
It couldn't be riches,
I didn't even own a place,
But, if given a chance,
I'd like to make my case."

He stopped and said, "Now, this is the chorus, but remember the mountains are in Colorado, where we'll be going someday."

"I own the wide open spaces, the mountains in the spring,
The rivers running swiftly, I own most everything.
The blue skies above us, the pine trees standing tall,
The green grass on the hillside, you know I own them all."

Well, I tried to sing along, but I couldn't believe a man would write a song about me. My tears were flowing, but he wasn't finished. I wiped my eyes and sat up straighter.

"You weren't impressed by riches,
Although I didn't know it,
Your clothes were new and fancy,

The horse you rode was showy,
It's true you didn't notice me,
Until you heard my song,
About the life I longed to lead,
A life with you alone."

"Now here's the chorus again," he said. "Try to sing with me."

"We own the wide open spaces, the mountains in the spring, The
rivers running swiftly, we own most everything.
The blue skies above us, the pine trees standing tall,
The green grass on the hillside, we really own them all."

When Lani finished, he was grinning ear to ear and I could hardly speak. He pulled me to him and kissed me like it was our very first kiss. How could a woman be this blessed in a lifetime – to have two wonderful men love her? My cup was overflowing, so to speak. As hard as my life had been, at this moment, it was perfect. My children were all settled, I had a cowboy who wrote and sang songs for me, and we had a beautiful granddaughter to raise. It was something I wished for every woman, but I knew there weren't many men like Jacob and Lani. I felt Jacob was happy for me even though I never dreamed of him again in that way, always reaching for him. But I thought about him every day of my life. And Lani, he was with me every day of my life, from then on, and filled it with such joy and happiness. How contented I was. It's too bad we aren't born with wisdom, instead of making so many mistakes, and only gaining wisdom when we're older. Still, I was certain I was bound to make many more mistakes before I died. I knew at this point in my life, I could handle anything thrown at me, and welcomed the challenge.

The End.

About the Author

Sarah A. Younger is a native Floridian whose ancestors settled Florida in the post-Civil War period, with some branches on the family tree traced to the 1820's. The stories Sarah has passed on in the novel, "A Bend in the Straight and Narrow," were told to her by her grandmother, Granny O'Steen. Since the stories were a mere skeleton, she filled in the gaps with historical fiction. Not only did the inspiration come from family narratives, but after studying the picture of the real Sarah, the author thought that as a young girl, she could not have looked that stern. From that reflection flowed the story like water over a broken dam. Much of the research done for this project was accomplished by visiting graveyards in the Bradford and Alachua County areas. The search for Jacob Henry's and Sarah's graves is ongoing. Many of the markers revealed things not known previously in family history, such as an epidemic that killed three people in the family, including her grandfather's mother, one week after he was born. The last names in the book have been changed, but many of the given names remain the same. Sarah has a BA degree from Baylor University and an Education degree from the University of Southern Colorado. She has an avid interest in history and quilting. She lives in Merritt Island, FL with her husband.

Made in the USA
Middletown, DE
02 October 2022

11407909R00179